Size 12 is not Fat

A Heather Wells Mystery

Meg Cabot has lived in Indiana and California, USA, and in France. In addition to her adult novels, *The Guy Next Door*, *Boy Meets Girl* and *Every Boy's Got One*, she is the author of the highly successful series of children's books, *The Princess Diaries*. Meg and her husband divide their time between New York City and Key West.

Be sure to check out Meg's websites:

www.megcabot.com

www.megcabotbookclub.com

Also by Meg Cabot

The Guy Next Door
Boy Meets Girl
Every Boy's Got One

and published by Macmillan Children's Books

All American Girl
Nicola and the Viscount
Victoria and the Rogue
All American Girl: Ready or Not
Avalon High
Teen Idol
The Mediator: Love You to Death
The Mediator: High Stakes
The Mediator: Mean Spirits
The Mediator: Young Blood
The Mediator: Grave Doubts
The Mediator: Heaven Sent

The Princess Diaries Guide to Life
The Princess Diaries
The Princess Diaries: Take Two
The Princess Diaries: Third Time Lucky
The Princess Diaries: Mia Goes Fourth
The Princess Diaries: Give Me Five
The Princess Diaries: Sixsational

Meg Cabot

Size 12 is not Fat

PAN BOOKS

First published 2006 by Avon Books,
an imprint of HarperCollins Publishers, USA

First published in Great Britain in paperback 2006 by Pan Books
an imprint of Pan Macmillan Ltd
Pan Macmillan, 20 New Wharf Road, London N1 9RR
Basingstoke and Oxford
Associated companies throughout the world
www.panmacmillan.com

ISBN-13: 978-0-330-44393-7
ISBN-10: 0-330-44393-3

3 5 7 9 8 6 4

A CIP catalogue record for this book is available from
the British Library.

Printed and bound in Great Britain by
Mackays of Chatham plc, Chatham, Kent

For Benjamin

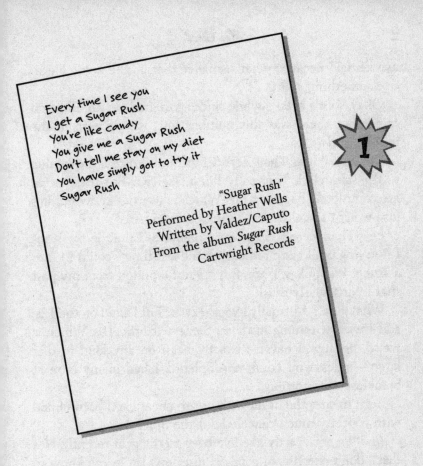

Every time I see you
I get a Sugar Rush
You're like candy
You give me a Sugar Rush
Don't tell me stay on my diet
You have simply got to try it
Sugar Rush

"Sugar Rush"
Performed by Heather Wells
Written by Valdez/Caputo
From the album *Sugar Rush*
Cartwright Records

1

"Um, hello. Is anyone out there?" The girl in the dressing room next to mine has a voice like a chipmunk. "Hello?"

Exactly like a chipmunk.

I hear a sales clerk come over, his key chain clinking musically. "Yes, ma'am? Can I help you?"

"Yeah." The girl's disembodied—but still chipmunklike—voice floats over the partition between our cubicles. "Do you guys have these jeans in anything smaller than a size zero?"

I pause, one leg in and one leg out of the jeans I am squeezing myself into. Whoa. Is it just me, or was that really existential? Because what's smaller than a size zero? Negative something, right?

Okay, so it's been a while since sixth grade math. But I do remember there was this number line, with a zero in the middle, and—

"Because," Less Than Zero/Chipmunk Voice is explaining to the sales clerk, "normally I'm a size two. But these zeros are completely baggy on me. Which is weird. I know I didn't lose weight since the last time I came in here."

Less Than Zero has a point, I realize as I pull up the jeans I'm trying on. I can't remember the last time I could fit into a size 8. Well, okay, I *can*. But it's not a period from my past that I particularly relish.

What gives? Normally I wear 12s . . . but I tried on the 12s, and I was swimming in them. Same with the 10s. Which is weird, because I haven't exactly been on any kind of diet lately—unless you count the Splenda I had in my latte at breakfast this morning.

But I'm sure the bagel with cream cheese and bacon I had with it pretty much canceled out the Splenda.

And it's not exactly like I've been to the gym recently. Not that I don't exercise, of course. I just don't do it, you know, in the gym. Because you can burn just as many calories walking as you can running. So why run? I figured out a long time ago that a walk to Murray's Cheese Shop on Bleecker to see what kind of sandwich they have on special for lunch takes ten minutes.

And a walk from Murray's over to Betsey Johnson on Wooster to see what's on sale (love her stretch velvet!): another ten minutes.

And a walk from Betsey's over to Dean & Deluca on Broadway for an after-lunch cappuccino and to see if they have those chocolate-covered orange peels I like so much: another ten minutes.

And so on, until before you know it, you've done a full sixty minutes of exercise. Who says it's hard to comply with the government's new fitness recommendations? If *I* can do it, anyone can.

But could all of that walking have caused me to drop *two whole* sizes since the last time I shopped for jeans? I know I've been cutting my daily fat intake by about half since I replaced the Hershey's Kisses in the candy jar on my desk with free condoms from the student health center. But still.

"Well, ma'am," the sales clerk is saying to Less Than Zero. "These jeans are *stretch* fit. That means that you've got to try two sizes lower than your true size."

"What?" Less Than Zero sounds confused.

I don't blame her. I feel the same way. It's like number lines all over again.

"What I mean is," the sales clerk says, patiently, "if you normally wear a size four, in stretch jeans, you would wear a size zero."

"Why don't you just put the real sizes on them, then?" Less Than Zero—quite sensibly, I think—asks. "Like if a zero is a really a four, why don't you just label it a four?"

"It's called vanity sizing," the sales clerk says, dropping his voice.

"*What* sizing?" Less Than Zero asks, dropping her voice, too. At least, as much as a chipmunk *can* drop her voice.

"You know." The sales clerk is whispering to Less Than Zero. But I can still hear him. "The *larger* customers like it when they can fit into an eight. But they're really a twelve, of course. See?"

Wait. *What?*

I fling open the door to my dressing room before I stop to think.

"I'm a size twelve," I hear myself saying to the sales clerk.

Who looks startled. Understandably, I guess. But still. "What's wrong with being a size twelve?"

"Nothing!" cries the sales clerk, looking panicky. "Nothing at all. I just meant—"

"Are you saying size twelve is *fat*?" I ask him.

"No," the sales clerk insists. "You misunderstood me. I meant—"

"Because size twelve is the size of the average American woman," I point out to him. I know this because I just read it in *People* magazine. "Are you saying that instead of being average, we're all fat?"

"No," the sales clerk says. "No, that's not what I meant at all. I—"

The door to the dressing room next to mine opens, and I see the owner of the chipmunk voice for the first time. She's the same age as the kids I work with. She doesn't just *sound* like a chipmunk, I realize. She kind of looks like one, too. You know. Cute. Perky. Small enough to fit in a normal-sized girl's pocket.

"And what's up with not even *making* her size?" I ask the sales clerk, jerking a thumb at Less Than Zero. "I mean, I'd rather be average than not even *exist*."

Less Than Zero looks kind of taken aback. But then she goes, "Um. Yeah!" to the sales clerk.

The sales clerk swallows nervously. And audibly. You can tell he's having a bad day. After work, he'll probably go to some bar and be all "And then these women were just ON me about the vanity sizing . . . . It was awful!"

To us, he just says, "I, um, think I'll just go, um, check and see if we have those jeans you were interested in the, um, back."

Then he scurries away.

I look at Less Than Zero. She looks at me. She is maybe twenty-two, and very blond. I too am blond—with a little help from Lady Clairol—but I left my early twenties several years ago.

Still, it is clear that, age and size differences aside, Less Than Zero and I share a common bond that can never be broken:

We've both been dicked over by vanity sizing.

"Are you going to get those?" Less Than Zero asks, nodding at the jeans I have on.

"I guess," I say. "I mean, I need a new pair. My last pair got barfed on at work."

"God," Less Than Zero says, wrinkling her chipmunk nose. "Where do you work?"

"Oh," I say. "A dorm. I mean, residence hall. I'm the assistant director."

"Rilly?" Less Than Zero looks interested. "At New York College?" When I nod, she cries, "I thought I knew you from somewhere! I graduated from New York College last year. Which dorm?"

"Um," I say, awkwardly. "I just started there this summer."

"Rilly?" Less Than Zero looks confused. "That's weird. 'Cause you look so familiar . . ."

Before I have a chance to explain to her why she thinks she knows me, my cell phone lets out the first few notes of the chorus of the Go-Go's "Vacation" (chosen as a painful reminder that I don't get any—vacation days, that is—until I've passed my six months' probationary period at work, and that's still another three months off). I see from the caller ID that it is my boss. Calling me on a Saturday.

Which means it has to be important. Right?

Except that it probably isn't. I mean, I love my new job and all—working with college students is super fun because they're so enthusiastic about stuff a lot of people don't even think about, like freeing Tibet and getting paid maternity leave for sweatshop workers and all of that.

But a definite drawback about working at Fischer Hall is that I live right around the corner from it. Which makes me just a little more accessible to everyone there than I'm necessarily comfortable with. I mean, it is one thing to get calls at home from work because you are a doctor and one of your patients needs you.

But it is quite another thing to get calls at home from work because the soda machine ate someone's change and no one can find the refund request forms and they want you to come over to help look for them.

Although I do realize to some people, that might sound like a dream come true. You know, living close enough to where you work to be able to drop by if there's a small-change crisis. Especially in New York. Because my commute is two minutes long, and I do it on foot (four more minutes to add to my daily exercise quota).

But people should realize that, as far as dreams coming true, this one's not the greatest, because I only get paid $23,500 a year (about $12,000 after city and state taxes), and in New York City, $12,000 buys you dinner, and maybe a pair of jeans like the ones I'm about to splurge on, vanity sized or not. I wouldn't be able to live in Manhattan on that kind of salary if it weren't for my second job, which pays my rent. I don't get to "live in" because at New York College, only residence hall directors, not assistant directors, get the "benefit" of living in the dorm—I mean, residence hall—they work in.

Still, I live close enough to Fischer Hall that my boss feels like she can call me all the time, and ask me to "pop in" whenever she needs me.

Like on a bright sunny Saturday afternoon in September, when I am shopping for jeans, because the day before, a freshman who'd had a few too many hard lemonades at the

Stoned Crow chose to roll over and barf them on me while I was crouching beside him, feeling for his pulse.

I'm weighing the pros and cons of answering my cell—pro: maybe Rachel's calling to offer me a raise (unlikely); con: maybe Rachel's calling to ask me to take some semicomatose drunk twenty-year-old to the hospital (likely)—when Less Than Zero suddenly shrieks, "Oh my God! I know why you look so familiar! Has anyone ever told you that you look *exactly* like Heather Wells? You know, that singer?"

I decide, under the circumstances, to let my boss go to voice mail. I mean, things are going badly enough, considering the size 12 stuff, and now this. I totally should have just stayed home and bought new jeans online.

"You really think so?" I ask Less Than Zero, not very enthusiastically. Only she doesn't notice my lack of enthusiasm.

"Oh my God!" Less Than Zero shrieks again. "You even *sound* like her. That is so *random*. But," she adds, with a laugh, "what would Heather Wells be doing, working in a dorm, right?"

"Residence hall," I correct her automatically. Because that's what we're supposed to call them, since calling it a residence hall allegedly fosters a feeling of warmth and unity among the residents, who might otherwise find living in something called a dorm too cold and institutional-like.

As if the fact that their refrigerators are bolted to the floor isn't a dead giveaway.

"Oh, hey," Less Than Zero says, sobering suddenly. "Not that there's anything wrong with it. Being assistant director of a dorm. And you're not, like, offended I said that you look like Heather Wells, are you? I mean, I totally had all her albums. And a big poster of her on my wall. When I was eleven."

"I am not," I say, "the least bit offended."

Less Than Zero looks relieved. "Good," she says. "Well, I guess I better go and find a store that actually carries my size."

"Yeah," I say, wanting to suggest Gap Kids, but restraining myself. Because it isn't her fault she's tiny. Any more than it is my fault that I am the size of the average American woman.

It isn't until I'm standing at the register that I check my voice mail to see what my boss, Rachel, wanted. I hear her voice, always so carefully controlled, saying in tones of barely repressed hysteria, "Heather, I'm calling to let you know that there has been a death in the building. When you get this message, please contact me as soon as possible."

I leave the size 8 jeans on the counter and use up another fifteen minutes of my recommended daily exercise by running— yes, *running*—from the store, and toward Fischer Hall.

I saw you two
Kissin' and huggin'
You told me
She's just your cousin
You Wish
You Wish
You Wish
If you want me
You gotta be true
So what does that mean
About me and you?
You Wish
You Wish
You Wish

"You Wish"
Performed by Heather Wells
Written by Valdez/Caputo
From the album *Sugar Rush*
Cartwright Records

2

The first thing I see when I turn the corner onto Washington Square West is a fire engine pulled up on the sidewalk. The fire engine is on the sidewalk instead of in the street because there's this booth selling tiger-print thongs for five dollars each—a bargain, actually, except that when you look closer, you can see that the thongs are trimmed with this black lace that looks as if it might be itchy if it gets, well, you-know-where—blocking the street.

The city hardly ever closes down Washington Square West, the street where Fischer Hall is located. But this particular Saturday, the neighborhood association must have called in a favor with a city councilman or something, since they managed to get that whole side of the park shut down in order to throw a street fair. You know the kind I mean: with the incense guys and the sock man and the cartoon portrait artists and the circus-clown wire-sculpture people?

The first time I went to a Manhattan street fair, I'd been around the same age as the kids I work with. Back then I'd been all "Ooooh, street fair! How fun!" I didn't know then that you can get socks at Macy's for even less than the sock man charges.

But the truth is, it turns out if you've been to one Manhattan street fair, you really have been to them all.

Nothing could have looked more out of place than a booth selling thongs in front of Fischer Hall. It just isn't a thong kind of building. Towering majestically over Washington Square Park, it had been built of red bricks around 1850. I'd learned from some files I'd found in my desk on my first day at my new job that every five years, the city makes the college hire a company to come and drill out all the old mortar and replace it with new, so that Fischer Hall's bricks don't fall out and conk people on the head.

Which is a good idea, I guess. Except that in spite of the city's efforts, things are always falling out of Fischer Hall and conking people on the head anyway. And I'm not talking about bricks. I've had reports of falling bottles, cans, clothing, books, CDs, vegetables, Good & Plentys, and once even a whole roasted chicken.

I'm telling you, when I walk by Fischer Hall, I always look up, just to be on the safe side.

Not today, however. Today my gaze is glued to the front door of the building. I'm trying to figure out how I'm going to get through it, considering the huge crowd—and New

York City cop—in front of it. It looks as if, along with dozens of tourists who are milling around the street fair, about half the student population of the building is standing outside, waiting to be let back into the building. They have no idea what's going on. I can tell from the questions they keep shouting to one another in an attempt to be heard over the pan flute music coming from another booth in front of the building, this one selling, um, cassettes of pan flute music:

"What's going on?"

"I dunno. Is there a fire?"

"Someone prolly let their potpourri boil over again."

"Naw, it was Jeff. He dropped his bhang again."

"Jeff, you suck!"

"It wasn't me this time, I swear!"

They couldn't know there'd been a death in the building. If they'd known, they wouldn't be joking about bhangs. I think.

Okay, I hope.

Then I spy a face I recognize, belonging to someone who DEFINITELY knows what's going on. I can tell by her expression. She isn't merely upset because the fire department won't let her back in the building. She's upset because she KNOWS.

"Heather!" Magda, seeing me in the crowd, flings a heavily manicured hand toward me. "Oh, Heather! Is terrible!"

Magda is standing there in her pink cafeteria smock and leopard-print leggings, shaking her frosted curls and taking long, nervous drags on the Virginia Slim she's got tucked between her two-inch-long nails. Each nail bears a mini replica of the American flag. Because even though Magda goes back to her native Dominican Republic every chance she gets, she is still very patriotic about her adopted country, and expresses her affection for it through nail art.

That's how I met her, actually. Almost four months ago, at the manicurist. That's also how I heard about the job in the dorm (I mean, residence hall) in the first place. The last assistant director before me—Justine—had just gotten fired for embezzling seven thousand dollars from the building's petty cash, a fact which had enraged Magda, the dorm—I mean, residence hall—cafeteria's cashier.

"Can you believe it?" Magda had been complaining to anyone who would listen, as I was having my toes done in Hot Tamale Red—because, you know, even if the rest of your life is going down the toilet, like mine was back then, at least your toes can still look pretty.

Magda, a few tables away, had been having mini Statues of Liberty air-brushed onto her thumbnails, in honor of Memorial Day, and was waxing eloquent about Justine, my predecessor.

"She order twenty-seven ceramic heaters from Office Supply and give them to her friends as wedding presents!"

I still have no idea what a ceramic heater is, or why anyone would want one as a wedding gift. But when I'd heard someone had been fired from Magda's place of work, where one of the job benefits—besides twenty vacation days a year and full health and dental—is free tuition, I'd jumped on the information.

I owe Magda a lot, actually. And not just because she helped me with the job thing, either (or because she lets me eat free in the caf anytime I want—which might be part of the reason why I'm no longer a size 8, except in vanity sizing), but because Magda's become one of my best friends.

"Mag," I say, sidling up to her. "Who is it? Who died?"

Because I can't help worrying it's someone I know, like one of the maintenance workers who are always so sweet about cleaning up spilled bodily fluids, even though it's not in their job description. Or one of the student workers I'm supposed to supervise—*supposed to* being the operative words, since in the three months I've worked at Fischer Hall, only a handful of my student employees have ever actually done what I've told them to (a lot of them remain loyal to the sticky-fingered Justine).

And when any of them actually do what I ask, it's only because it involves something like checking every single room after the previous residents have moved out and cleaning out whatever they've left behind, generally half-full bottles of Jägermeister.

So then when I get to work the next day, I can't get a single one of them to come downstairs and sort the mail, because they're all too hung over.

But there are a couple kids I've genuinely come to love, scholarship students who didn't come to school equipped with a Visa that Mom and Dad are only too happy to pay off every month, and who actually need to work in order to pay for books and fees, and so will take the 4 P.M.–midnight shift at the reception desk on a Saturday night with a minimum of begging on my part.

"Oh, Heather," Magda whispers. Only she pronounces it Haythar. She is whispering because she doesn't want the kids to know what's really going on. Whatever it is. "One of my little movie stars!"

"A student?" I can see people in the crowd eyeing Magda curiously. Not because she's weird-looking—well, she IS kind of weird-looking, since she wears enough makeup to make Christina Aguilera look as if she's going au naturel, and she's got those really long nails and all.

But since it's the Village, Magda's outfits could actually be considered kind of tame.

It's the "movie star" thing people don't get. Every time a student enters the Fischer Hall cafeteria, Magda takes his or her dining card, runs it through the scanner, and sings, "Look at all the byootiful movie stars who come to eat here. We are so lucky to have so many byootiful movie stars in Fischer Hall!"

At first I just thought Magda was trying to flatter the many drama students—and there are tons, way more than pre-med or business majors—that go to New York College.

Then one Fix Your Own Sundae day, Magda dropped the bomb that Fischer Hall is actually quite famous. Not for the reasons you'd think, like because it's on historic Washington Square, where Henry James once lived, or because it's across the street from the famous Hanging Tree, where they used to execute people in the eighteenth century. Not even because the park was once a cemetery for the indigent, so basically all those benches and hot dog stands? Yeah, they're sitting on dead people.

No. According to Magda, Fischer Hall is famous because they shot a scene from the movie *Teenage Mutant Ninja Turtles* there. Donatello or Raphael or one of the turtles—I can't actually remember which one—swung from the Fischer Hall penthouse to the building next door, and the kids in the building all acted as extras, looking up and pointing amazedly at the stunt turtle's feat.

Seriously. Fischer Hall has quite an exciting history.

Except that the kids who acted in the movie as extras have long since graduated and moved from Fischer Hall.

So I guess people think it's weird that Magda is still bringing it up, all these years later.

But really, you can see how the fact that a scene from a major motion picture was shot at her place of work would be, to someone like Magda, just another of the many things that make America great.

But you can also see how, to someone who doesn't know

the story behind it, the whole "my little movie star" thing might seem a little . . . well, wacko.

Which probably explained why so many people were looking curiously our way, having overheard her outburst.

Not wanting the kids to catch on that something was seriously wrong, I take Magda by the arm and steer her toward one of the potted pines that sits outside the building—and which the students unfortunately tend to use as their own personal ashtray—so we can have a little privacy.

"What happened?" I ask her, in a low voice. "Rachel left a message that there'd been a death in the building, but that's all she said. Do you know who? And how?"

"I don't know," Magda whispers, shaking her head. "I am sitting at my register, and I hear screaming, and someone says that a girl is lying at the bottom of the elevator shaft, and that she's dead."

"Oh my God!" I'm shocked. I'd been expecting to hear about a death from a drug overdose or violent crime—there are security guards on duty twenty-four hours a day in the building, but that doesn't mean the occasional unsavory character doesn't manage to slip inside anyway. It *is* New York City, after all.

But death by *elevator*?

Magda, moist-eyed, but trying valiantly not to cry—since that would tip off the students, who are prone to dramatics anyway, that something is REALLY wrong (it also wouldn't do anything much for Magda's many layers of mascara)—adds, "They say she was—what do you call it? Riding on top of the elevator?"

"Surfing?" I am even more shocked now. "Elevator surfing?"

"Yes." Magda carefully inserts the tip of a finely crafted nail at the corner of her eye, and dashes away a tear. "That is why they are not letting anyone inside. The little movie stars need the elevator to get up to their dressing rooms, but they have to move the—"

Magda breaks off with a sob. I put my arm around her and quickly turn her toward me, as much to comfort her as to smother the sound of her crying. Students are glancing curiously our way. I don't want them to catch on that anything is seriously wrong. They'll find out, soon enough.

Only they probably won't have as hard a time believing it as I was.

The thing is, I shouldn't have been so surprised. Elevator surfing is a problem campus-wide—and not just at New York College, but at universities and colleges all over the country. Teenagers with nothing better to do than get high and dare each other to jump onto the roofs of elevator cabs as they glide up and down the dark, dangerous shafts. There'd been account after account of kids getting themselves decapitated in drunken dares.

I guess it was bound to happen at Fischer Hall sometime. Except.

Except that Magda kept saying "she." That a *girl* had died.

Which is weird, because I've never once heard of a *girl* elevator surfing. At least not in Fischer Hall.

Then Magda lifts her head from my shoulder and says, "Uh-oh."

I turn to see what she's talking about and suck in my breath real fast. Because Mrs. Allington, the wife of Phillip Allington—who last spring was inaugurated as the college's sixteenth president—is coming down the sidewalk toward us.

I know a lot about the Allingtons because another thing I found in Justine's files—right before I threw them all away— was an article clipped from the *New York Times*, making this big deal out of the fact that the newly appointed president had chosen to live in a residence hall rather than in one of the luxury buildings owned by the school.

"Phillip Allington," the article said, "is an academician who does not wish to lose touch with the student population. When he comes home from his office, he rides the same elevator as the undergraduates next to whom he resides—"

What the *Times* totally neglected to mention is that the president and his family live in Fischer Hall's penthouse, which takes up the entire twentieth floor, and that they complained so much about the elevators stopping on every floor on their way up to let the students out that Justine finally issued them override keys.

Aside from complaining about the elevators, President Allington's wife, Eleanor, seems to have very little to do. Whenever I see her, she's always just returning from, or heading off to, Saks Fifth Avenue. She is uncannily committed to shopping—like an Olympic track athlete is dedicated to her training.

Only Mrs. Allington's sport of choice—besides shopping—seems to be consuming vast amounts of vodka. When she and Dr. Allington return from late-night dinners with the trustees, Mrs. Allington inevitably kicks up a ruckus in the lobby, usually concerning her pet cockatoos—or so I've heard from Pete, my favorite university security officer.

"The birds," she'd once told him. "The birds hate your guts, fatty."

Which is kind of mean-spirited, if you think about it. Also inaccurate, since Pete isn't a bit fat. He's just, you know. Average.

Mrs. Allington's drunken verbal assaults are a source of much amusement at the hall's reception desk, which is staffed round the clock by student employees—the ones I'm supposed to supervise. Late at night, if Dr. Allington isn't home, Mrs. Allington sometimes calls down to the desk to report all sorts of startling facts: that someone has eaten all her stuffed artichokes; that there are coyotes on her terrace; that tiny invisible dwarfs are hammering on her headboard.

According to Pete, the students were at first confused by these reports, and would beep the resident assistants, the upperclassmen who, in exchange for free room and board, are expected to act as sort of house mothers, one per floor. The RAs in turn would notify the building director, who would board the elevator for the twentieth floor to investigate.

But when Mrs. Allington answered her door, bleary-eyed and robed in velour—I know! Velour! Almost as good as stretch velvet—she'd just say, "I don't know what you're talking about, fatty."

While behind her (according to various RAs who've repeated this story), the cockatoos whistled maniacally.

Spooky stuff.

But apparently not as spooky to Mrs. Allington as it is to the rest of us, probably because she never seems to remember any of it the next day, and heads off to Saks as if she were a queen—the Queen of Fischer Hall.

Like now, for instance. Loaded down with shopping bags, Mrs. Allington is looking scathingly at the cop who is blocking Fischer Hall's front door, and going, "Excuse me. I live here."

"Sorry, lady," the cop says. "Emergency personnel only. No residents allowed back in the building yet."

"I am not a resident. " Mrs. Allington seems to swell amid her bags. "I'm . . . I'm . . ." Mrs. Allington can't seem to quite figure out what she is. But it's not like the cop cares.

"Sorry, lady," he says. "Go enjoy the street fair for a while, why dontcha? Or there're some nice benches over in the park there. Whyn't you go relax on one till we get the all-clear to start lettin' people in again, okay?"

Mrs. Allington is looking a bit peaked as I come hurrying up to her. I've abandoned Magda because Mrs. Allington looks as if she needs me more. She's just standing there in a pair of too-tight designer jeans, a silk top, and tons of gold jewelry, the shopping bags drooping in her hands, her mouth opening and closing in confusion. She is definitely a little green around the gills.

"Did you hear me, ma'am?" the cop is saying. "No one's allowed in. See all these kids here? They're waiting, too. So either wait with them or move along."

Only Mrs. Allington seems to have lost the ability to move along. She doesn't look too steady on her feet, if you ask me. I step over and take her arm. She doesn't even acknowledge my presence. I doubt she even knows who I am. Though she nods to me every single weekday when she gets off the elevator across from my office door on her way out to her latest binge—I mean, shopping expedition—and says, "Good morning, Justine" (despite my frequently correcting her), I suppose seeing me on a weekend, and out of doors, has thrown her.

"Her husband's the president of the college, Officer," I say, nodding toward Mrs. Allington, who appears to be staring very hard at a nearby student with purple hair and an eyebrow ring. "Phillip Allington? He lives in the penthouse. I don't think she's feeling too well. Can I . . . can I just help her get inside?"

The cop gives me the eye.

"I know you from somewhere?" the cop asks. It's not a come-on. With me, this line never is.

"Probably from the neighborhood," I say, with excessive cheer. "I work in this building." I flash him my college staff

ID card, the one with the photo where I look drunk, even though I wasn't. Until after I saw the photo. "See? I'm the assistant residence hall director."

He doesn't look impressed by the title, but he says, with a shrug, "Whatever. Get 'er inside, if you want. But I don't know how you're gonna get 'er upstairs. Elevators are shut down."

I don't know how I'm going to get Mrs. Allington upstairs, either, considering she's so unsteady on her feet, I'm practically going to have to carry her. I fling a glance over my shoulder at Magda, who, seeing my predicament, rolls her eyes. But she stamps out her cigarette and heads gamely toward us, ready to offer whatever aid she can.

Before she quite gets to us, though, two young women—garbed in what I consider standard New York College attire, low rider jeans with belly rings—come bursting out of the building, breathing hard.

"Oh my God, Jeff," one of them calls to the bhang dropper. "What is up with the elevators? We just had to walk down seventeen flights of stairs."

"I'm going to die," the other girl announces.

"Seriously," the first girl pants, loudly. "For what we're paying in tuition and housing fees, you'd think the PRESIDENT would be able to invest in elevators that don't break down all the time."

I don't miss her hostile glance at Mrs. Allington, who made the mistake of letting her photo be published in the school paper, thus making her a recognizable target around the dorm. I mean, residence hall.

"C'mon, Mrs. Allington," I say quickly, giving her arm a little tug. "Let's go inside."

"About time," Mrs. Allington says, stumbling a little, as Magda moves to take hold of her other arm. The two of us steer her through the front door to cries—from the students—of "Hey! Why do *they* get to go in, but we don't? We live here, too!" and "No fair!" and, "Fascists!"

From the careful way she's putting one kitten heel in front of the other, I'm pretty sure Mrs. Allington is already a little tipsy, even though it's not quite noon. My suspicions are confirmed when the three of us pass into the building and Mrs. Allington suddenly leans over and heaves her breakfast into one of the planters in the front lobby.

It definitely looks as if Mrs. A. had a few Bloody Marys to go with her eggs this morning.

"Santa Maria," Magda says, horrified. And who can blame her?

I don't know about anyone else, but when I throw up (and, I'm sorry to say, it's something I do regularly every single New Year's Eve), I like a little sympathy, even if the whole thing's my own fault.

So I pat Mrs. Allington on her padded shoulder and say, "There. Don't you feel better now?"

Mrs. Allington squints at me as if she's noticing me for the first time.

"Who the hell are you?" she asks.

"Um," I say. "I'm the assistant building director. Heather Wells. Remember? We met a couple of months ago?"

Mrs. Allington looks confused. "What happened to Justine?"

"Justine found another job," I explain, which is a lie, since Justine was fired. But the truth is, I don't know Justine's side of the story. I mean, maybe she really needed the money. Maybe she has relatives who live in Bosnia or somewhere really cold, and they don't have any heat, and those ceramic heaters kept them alive all winter. You never know.

Mrs. Allington just squints some more.

"Heather Wells?" She blinks a few more times. "But aren't

you . . . aren't you that girl? The one who used to sing in all those malls?"

That's when I realize that Mrs. Allington has finally recognized me, all right . . .

. . . but not as the assistant director of the building she lives in.

Wow. I never suspected Mrs. Allington of being a fan of teen pop. She seems more the Barry Manilow type—much older teen pop.

"I was," I say to her, kindly, because I still feel sorry for her, on account of the barf, and all. "But I don't perform anymore."

"Why?" Mrs. Allington wants to know.

Magda and I exchange glances. Magda seems to be getting her sense of humor back, since there is a distinct upward slant to corners of her lip-linered mouth.

"Um," I say. "It's kind of a long story. Basically I lost my recording contract—"

"Because you got fat?" Mrs. Allington asks.

Which is, I have to admit, when I sort of stopped feeling sorry for her.

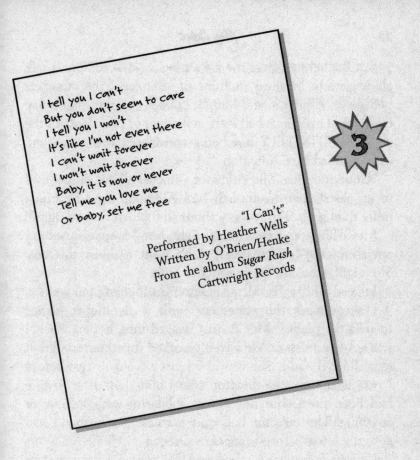

I tell you I can't
But you don't seem to care
I tell you I won't
It's like I'm not even there
I can't wait forever
I won't wait forever
Baby, it is now or never
Tell me you love me
Or baby, set me free

"I Can't"

Performed by Heather Wells
Written by O'Brien/Henke
From the album *Sugar Rush*
Cartwright Records

Fortunately I'm spared from having to make any sort of reply to Mrs. Allington's remark about my weight by the fact that my boss, Rachel Walcott, comes hurrying up to us just then, her patent leather slides clacking on the marble floor of the lobby.

"Heather," Rachel says, when she sees me. "Thank you so much for coming." She actually does look sort of relieved that I'm there, which makes me feel good. You know, that I really am needed, if only $23,500-a-year worth.

"Sure," I say. "I'm so sorry. Was it—I mean, is it—someone we know?"

But Rachel just gives me a warning look—like "Don't talk about family business in front of strangers," the strangers being Mrs. Allington and Magda, cafeteria workers not being considered residence hall staff, and wives of presidents of the college DEFINITELY not being considered that way—and turns toward Mrs. Allington.

"Good morning, Mrs. Allington," Rachel all but shouts, as if to an elderly person, though Mrs. Allington can't be much more than sixty. "I'm so sorry about all this. Are you all right?"

Mrs. Allington is far from all right, but—even as upset as I am about the fat remark—I don't want to blurt this out. She's still, after all, the president's wife.

Instead all I say is "Mrs. Allington isn't feeling too well."

I accompany the statement with a significant glance toward the planter Mrs. A. just heaved into, hoping Rachel will get the message. We haven't worked together for all that long, Rachel and I. She was hired just a week or two before I was, to replace the director who'd quit right after Justine had been fired—but not out of solidarity with Justine, or anything. The director had quit because her husband had gotten a job as a forest ranger in Oregon.

I know. Forest ranger husband. Hmmm. I'd have quit to follow him, too.

But while Rachel is new to the live-in position of director of Fischer Hall, she's not new to the field of higher education (which is what they call it when you're involved in the counseling, but not the teaching, part of college life, or at least so I read in one of Justine's files). The last dorm—I mean, residence hall—Rachel, a Yale grad, ran had been at Earlcrest College in Richmond, Indiana.

Rachel told me that it had been a bit of a culture shock, coming to New York City from a place like Richmond, where people don't even have to lock their doors at night. But as far as I can tell, Rachel hasn't exactly suffered any long-term hardships from her stint in the Hoosier heartland. She has a wardrobe any New York career gal would be happy to call her own, heavy on the Armani and the Manolos, which—considering her salary (not much more than mine, since directors get a free apartment in the building thrown in as part of their pay package)—is quite an accomplishment. Faithful weekly attendance of designer sample sales helps keep Rachel on the cutting edge of fashion. And her strict adherence to the Zone and two-hour daily workouts ensure that she stays a size 2, enabling her to fit into all those models' castoffs.

Rachel says that if I stop eating so many carbs and spend a half hour on the StairMaster every day, I could easily get back down to a real size 8. And that this shouldn't be a hardship for me, because you get free membership at the college's gym as part of your benefits package.

Except that I've been to the college gym, and it's scary. There are all these really skinny girls there, flinging their sticklike arms around in aerobics classes and yoga and stuff. Seriously, one of these days, one of them is going to put someone's eye out.

Anyway, if I lose enough weight, Rachel says, I'll definitely get a hot boyfriend, the way she's planning to, just as soon as she finds a guy in the Village who isn't gay, has a full set of hair, and makes at least a hundred thousand a year.

But how on earth could anyone ever give up cold sesame noodles? Even for a guy who makes a hundred thousand dollars a year?

Plus, um, as I frequently remind Rachel, size 12 is not fat. It is the size of the average American woman. Hello. And there are plenty of us (size 12s) who have boyfriends, thank you very much.

Not me, necessarily. But plenty of other girls my size, and even larger.

But though Rachel and I have different priorities—she wants a boyfriend; I'd just take a BA, at this point—and can't seem to agree on what constitutes a meal—her, lettuce, no dressing; me, falafel, extra tahini, with a pita 'n' hummus starter and maybe an ice cream sandwich for dessert—we get along okay, I guess. I mean, Rachel seems to understand the look I shoot her about Mrs. Allington, anyway.

"Mrs. Allington," she says. "Let's get you home, shall we? I'll take you upstairs. Would that be all right, Mrs. Allington?"

Mrs. Allington nods weakly, her interest in my career change forgotten. Rachel takes the president's wife by the arm as Pete, who has been hovering nearby, holds back a wave of firemen to make room for her and Mrs. A. on the elevator they've turned back on especially for her. I can't help glancing nervously at the elevator's interior as the doors open. What if there's blood? I know they said they'd found her at the bottom of the shaft, but what if part of her was still on the elevator?

But there's no blood that I can see. The elevator looks the same as ever, imitation mahogany paneling with brass trim, into which hundreds of undergraduates have scratched their initials or various swear words with the edges of their room keys.

As the elevator doors close, I hear Mrs. Allington say, very softly, "The birds."

"God," Magda says, as we watch the numbers above the elevator doors light up as the car moves toward the penthouse. "I hope she doesn't throw up again in there."

"Seriously," I agree. That would make the ride up twenty flights pretty much suck.

Magda shakes herself, as though she's thought of something unpleasant—most likely Mrs. A.'s vomit—and looks around. "It's so quiet," she says, hugging herself. "It hasn't been this quiet around here since before all my little movie stars checked in."

She's right. For a building that houses so many young people—seven hundred, most still in their teens—the lobby is strangely still just then. No one is grumbling about the length of time it takes the student workers to sort the mail (approximately seven hours. I'd heard that Justine could get them to do it in under two. Sometimes I wonder if maybe Justine had some sort of secret pact with Satan); no one is complaining about the broken change machines down in the game room; no one is Rollerblading on the marble floors; no one is arguing with Pete over the guest sign-in policy.

Not that there isn't anybody around. The lobby is jumping. Cops, firemen, college officials, campus security guards in their baby blue uniforms, and a smattering of students— all resident assistants—are milling around the mahogany and marble lobby, grim-faced . . .

. . . but silent. Absolutely silent.

"Pete," I say, going up to the guard at the security desk. "Do you know who it was?"

The security guards know everything that goes on in the buildings they work in. They can't help it. It's all there, on the monitors in front of them, from the students who smoke in the stairwells, to the deans who pick their noses in the elevators, to the librarians who have sex in the study carrels . . .

Dishy stuff.

"Of course." Pete, as usual, is keeping one eye on the lobby and the other on the many television monitors on his desk, each showing a different part of the dorm (I mean, residence hall), from the entranceway to the Allingtons' penthouse apartment, to the laundry room in the basement.

"Well?" Magda looks anxious. "Who was it?"

Pete, with a cautious glance at the reception desk across the way to make sure the student workers aren't eavesdropping, says, "Kellogg. Elizabeth. Freshman."

I feel a spurt of relief. I have never heard of her.

Then I berate myself for feeling that way. She's still a dead eighteen-year-old, whether she was one of my student workers, or not!

"How did it happen?" I ask.

Pete gives me a sarcastic look. "How do you think?"

"But," I say. I can't help it. Something is really confusing me. "Girls don't do that. Elevator surf, I mean."

"This one did." Pete shrugs.

"Why would she do something like that?" Magda wants to know. "Something so stupid? Was she on drugs?"

"How should I know?" Pete seems annoyed by our barrage of questions, but I know it is only because he is as freaked as we are. Which is weird, because you'd think he's seen it all: He's been working at the college for twenty years. Like me, he'd taken the job for the benefits: A widower, he has four children who are assured of a great—and free—college education, which is the main reason he'd gone to work for an academic institution after a knee injury got him assigned to permanent desk duty in the NYPD. His oldest, Nancy, wants to be a pediatrician.

But that doesn't keep Pete's face from turning beet red every time one of the students, bitter over not being allowed into the building with their state-of-the-art halogen lamps (fire hazard), refers to him as a "rent-a-cop." Which isn't fair, because Pete is really, really good at his job. The only time pizza delivery guys ever make it inside Fischer Hall to stick menus under everyone's door is when Pete's not on duty.

Not that he doesn't have the biggest heart in the world.

When kids come down from their rooms, disgustedly holding glue traps on which live mice are trapped, Pete has been known to take the traps out to the park and pour oil onto them to free their little paws and let them go. He can't stand the idea of anyone—or anything—dying on his watch.

"Coroner'll run tests for alcohol and drugs, I'm sure," he says, trying to sound casual, and failing. "If he ever gets here, that is."

I'm horrified.

"You mean she . . . she's still here? I mean, it—the body?"

Pete nods. "Downstairs. Bottom of the elevator shaft. That's where they found her."

"That's where who found her?" I ask.

"The fire department," Pete says. "When someone reported seeing her."

"Seeing her fall?"

"No. Seeing her lying there. Someone looked down the crack—you know, between the floor and the elevator car— and saw her."

I feel shaken. "You mean nobody reported it when it happened? The people who were with her?"

"What people?" Pete wants to know.

"The people she was elevator surfing with," I say. "She had to be with someone. Nobody plays that stupid game alone. They didn't come down to report it?"

"Nobody said nothing to me," Pete says, "until this morning when a kid saw her through the crack."

I am appalled.

"You mean she could have been lying down there for hours?" I ask, my voice cracking a little.

"Not alive," Pete says, getting my drift right away. "She landed headfirst."

"Santa Maria," Magda says, and crosses herself.

I am only slightly less appalled. "So . . . then how'd they know who it was?"

"Had her school ID in her pocket," Pete explains.

"Well, at least she was thinking ahead," Magda says.

"Magda!" I'm shocked, but Magda just shrugs.

"It's true. If you are going to play such a stupid game, at least keep ID on you, so they can identify your body later, right?"

Before either Pete or I can reply, Gerald, the dining director, comes popping out of the cafeteria, looking for his wayward cashier.

"Magda," he says, when he finally spots her. "Whadduya *doing*? Cops said they're gonna let us open up again any minute and I got no one on the register."

"Oh, I'll be right there, honey," Magda calls to him. Then, as soon as he's stomped out of earshot, she adds, "Dickhead." Then, with an apologetic waggle of her nails at Pete and me, Magda goes back to her seat behind the cash register in the student cafeteria around the corner from the guard's desk.

"Heather?"

I look around, and see one of the student workers at the reception desk gesturing to me desperately. The reception desk is the hub of the building, where the residents' mail is sorted, where visitors can call up to their friends' rooms, and where all building emergencies are supposed to be reported. One of my first duties after being hired had been to type up a long list of phone numbers that the reception desk employees were to refer to in the event of an emergency of any kind (apparently, Justine had been too busy using college funds to buy ceramic heaters for all of her friends ever to get around to this).

Fire? The number for the fire station was listed.

Rape? The number for the campus's rape hotline was listed.

Theft? The number for the Sixth Precinct.

People falling off the top of one of the elevators? There's no number for that.

"Heather." The student worker, Tina, sounds as whiny today as she did the first day I met her, when I told her she couldn't put people on hold while she finished the round of Tetris she was playing on her Game Boy (Justine had never had a problem with this, I was told). "When're they gonna get rid of that girl's body? I'm losing it, knowing she's, like, still DOWN there."

"We saw her roommate." Brad—the guy with the misfortune to be the resident assistant on duty this weekend, meaning he has to stay in the building at all times, in case he's needed . . . like in the event of a student death—drops his voice conspiratorially as he leans across the desk toward me. "She said she didn't even know Beth—that's the dead girl—she said she didn't even know Beth *knew* about surfing. She said she had no idea Beth hung out with that crowd. She said Beth was kinda *preppie*."

"Well," I say, lamely. I can tell the kids are looking for some kind of words of comfort from me. But what do I know about helping kids cope with the death of a classmate? I'm as freaked as either one of them. "I guess it just goes to show you never really quite know someone as well as you think you do, doesn't it?"

"Yeah, but going for a joyride on top of an elevator?" Tina shakes her head. "She musta been crazy."

"Prozac candidate," Brad somberly agrees, exhibiting some of that sensitivity training the housing department has drilled so hard into their RAs' heads.

"Heather?"

I turn to see Rachel's graduate assistant, Sarah, coming toward me, a thick file in her hands. Garbed as always in the height of New York College graduate student chic—overalls and Uggs—she grabs my arm and squeezes.

"Ohmigod," Sarah says, making no attempt whatsoever to lower her voice so that it isn't audible to everyone on the entire first floor. "Can you believe it? The phones are ringing off the hook back in the office. All these parents are calling to make sure it wasn't their kid. But Rachel says we can't confirm the deceased's identity until the coroner arrives. Even though we know who it is. I mean, Rachel had me get her file and told me to give it to Dr. Flynn. And would you look at this file?"

Sarah waves the thickly packed manila file. Elizabeth Kellogg had a record in the hall director's office, which means that she'd either gotten in trouble for something or been ill at some point during the school year . . .

. . . which is odd, because Elizabeth was a freshman, and the fall semester had only just begun.

"Getta loada this." Sarah is eager to share all she knows with me, Brad, and Tina. The latter two are listening to her with wide eyes. Pete, over at the guard's desk, is acting like he's busy watching his monitors. But I know he's listening, too. "Her mother called Rachel, all bent out of shape because we allow residents to have any guests they want, and she didn't want Elizabeth to be able to sign in boys. Apparently Mom expected her daughter to remain a virgin until marriage. She wanted Rachel to make it so that Elizabeth was only to be allowed to sign in girls. Obviously there are issues at home, but whatever—"

It's the job of the GA—or graduate assistant—to assist the director in the day-to-day operations of the residence hall. In return, GAs receive free room and board and practical experience in higher education, which is generally their chosen field.

Sarah's getting a lot more practical experience in the field here in Fischer Hall than she'd bargained on, what with a dead girl and all.

"Clearly there was some major mother-daughter rivalry going on there," Sarah informs us. "I mean, you could tell Mrs. Kellogg was jealous because her looks are fading while her daughter's—"

Sarah's undergrad degree is in sociology. Sarah thinks that I suffer from low esteem. She told me this the day she met me, at check-in two weeks earlier, when she went to shake my hand, then cried, "Oh my God, you're *that* Heather Wells?"

When I admitted that I was, then told her—when she asked what on earth I was doing working in a college residence hall (unlike me, Sarah never messes up and calls it a dorm)—that I was hoping to get a BA one of these days, she said, "You don't need to go to college. What you need to work on are your abandonment issues and the feelings of inadequacy you must feel for being dropped from your label and robbed by your mother."

Which is kind of funny, since what I feel I need to work on most are my feelings of dislike for Sarah.

Fortunately Dr. Flynn, the housing department's on-staff psychologist, comes hurtling toward us just then, his briefcase overflowing with paperwork.

"Is that the deceased's file?" he demands, by way of greeting. "I'd like to see it before I talk to the roommate and call the parents."

Sarah hands him the file. As Dr. Flynn flips through it, he suddenly wrinkles his nose, then asks, "What is that smell?"

"Um," I say. "Mrs. Allington sort of—well, she, um . . ."

"She yorked," Brad says. "In the planter over there."

Dr. Flynn sighs. "Not again." His cell phone chimes, and he says, "Excuse me," and reaches for it.

At the same moment, the reception desk phone rings. Everyone looks down at it. When no one else reaches for it, I do.

"Fischer Hall," I say.

The voice on the other end of the phone isn't one I recognize.

"Yes, is this that dormitory located on Washington Square West?"

"This is a residence hall, yes," I reply, remembering, for once, my training.

"I was wondering if I could speak to someone about the tragedy that occurred there earlier today," says the unfamiliar voice.

Tragedy? I immediately become suspicious.

"Are you a reporter?" I ask. At this point in my life, I can sniff them out a mile away.

"Well, yes, I'm with the *Post*—"

"Then you'll have to get in touch with the Press Relations Department. No one here has any comment. Good-bye." I slam down the receiver.

Brad and Tina are staring at me.

"Wow," Brad says. "You're good."

Sarah gives her glasses a push, since they've started to slide down her nose.

"She ought to be," she says. "Considering what she's had to deal with. The paparazzi wasn't exactly kind, were they, Heather? Especially when you walked in and found Jordan Cartwright receiving fellatio from . . . who was it? Oh yes. Tania Trace."

"Wow," I say, gazing at Sarah with genuine wonder. "You really put that photographic memory of yours to good use, don't you, Sarah?"

Sarah smiles modestly while Tina's jaw drops.

"Heather, you went out with *Jordan Cartwright*?" she cries.

"You caught him getting head from *Tania Trace*?" Brad looks as happy as if someone's just dropped a hundred-dollar bill in his lap.

"Um," I say. It's not like I have much of a choice. They can easily Google it. "Yeah. It was a long time ago."

Then I excuse myself to go search for a soda, hoping a combined jolt of caffeine and artificial sweeteners might make me feel less like causing there to be yet another death among the building's student population.

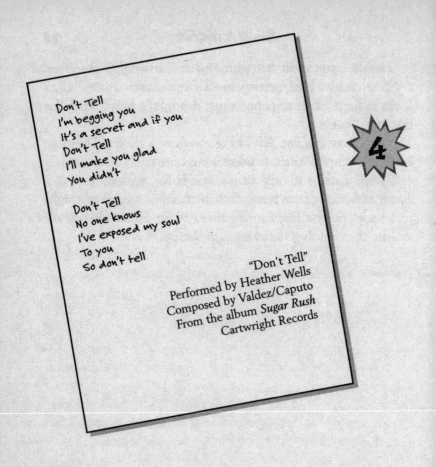

Don't Tell
I'm begging you
It's a secret and if you
Don't Tell
I'll make you glad
You didn't

Don't Tell
No one knows
I've exposed my soul
To you
So don't tell

"Don't Tell"
Performed by Heather Wells
Composed by Valdez/Caputo
From the album *Sugar Rush*
Cartwright Records

The closest soda machine is located in the TV lounge, where all of the college's crisis management people are congregated. I don't want to risk asking Magda for a free one from the caf when she's already in trouble with her boss.

I only recognize a few of the many administrators in the lounge, and then only from being interviewed by them when I'd applied for my job. One of them, Dr. Jessup, the head of the housing department, detaches himself from another administrator's side when he notices me, and comes over, looking very different in his weekend wear of Izod shirt and Dockers than he did in his usual charcoal suits.

"Heather," Dr. Jessup says, his deep voice gruff. "How's it going?"

"Okay," I reply. I've already jammed a dollar into the machine, so it's too late to run away—though I'd like to, since everyone in the room is staring at me, like, *Who is that girl? Don't I know her from somewhere? And what's she doing* here?

Instead of running, I make a selection. The sound of the can hitting the slot at the bottom of the machine is loud in the TV lounge, where conversation is muted out of respect for both the deceased and the grieving, and where the TV, which normally blasts MTV 2 24/7, has been turned off.

I retrieve my can from the machine and hold it in my hands, afraid to open it and attract more undue attention to myself by making noise.

"How do the kids seem to you?" Dr. Jessup wants to know. "In general?"

"I just got here," I say. "But everybody seems pretty shaken up. Which is, you know, understandable, considering the fact that there's a dead girl at the bottom of the elevator shaft."

Dr. Jessup widens his eyes and motions for me to keep my voice down, even though I hadn't been speaking above a whisper. I look around, and realize there are some administrative bigwigs in the TV lounge. Dr. Jessup is hypersensitive about his department being perceived as a caring, student-oriented one. He prides himself on his ability to relate to the younger generation. I realized this during my first interview, when he'd narrowed his gray eyes at me and asked the inevitable question, the one that makes me want to throw things, but that I can't seem to escape: "Don't I know you from somewhere?"

Everyone thinks they've seen me somewhere before. They

just can't ever figure out where. I get "Didn't you go to the prom with my brother?" a lot. Also, "Weren't you and I in one of the same classes in college?"

Which is especially weird, because I never attended a single prom, much less college.

"I used to be a singer" was what I'd said to Dr. Jessup, the day of my job interview. "A, um, pop singer. When I was, you know. A teenager."

"Ah, yes," Dr. Jessup had said. " 'Sugar Rush.' That's what I thought, but I wasn't sure. Can I ask you a question?"

I'd twisted uncomfortably in my seat, knowing what was coming. "Sure."

"Why are you applying for a job in a residence hall?"

I'd cleared my throat.

I wish VH1 would do a *Behind the Music* on me. Because then I wouldn't have to. Explain to people, I mean.

But it's not like I'm *Behind the Music* material. I was never famous enough for that. I was never a Britney or a Christina. I was barely even an Avril. I was just a teenager with a healthy set of lungs on her, who was in the right place at the right time.

Dr. Jessup had seemed to understand. At least, he'd tactfully dropped the subject after I mentioned the stuff about my mom fleeing the country with my manager—and oh yeah, my life's savings—my label dropping me, and my boyfriend, too, in that order. When I was offered the position of administrative assistant to Fischer Hall, at a starting salary that equaled what I used to earn in a week on the concert circuit, I accepted without hesitation. I wasn't seeing much of a long-term career in waitressing—which, for a girl who doesn't even like standing up to wash her hair, can be brutal—and getting a college education seemed like a good idea. I have to wait until I pass my six months' probation—just three more to go—but then I can start enrolling in as many courses as I want.

The first class I'm going to take is Psych 101 so I can see if I'm really as filled with neuroses as Rachel and Sarah seem to think.

Now Dr. Jessup is inquiring about Rachel's mental health. "How's she holding up?" Dr. Jessup wants to know.

"I guess she's okay," I say.

"You should buy her some flowers, or something," Dr. Jessup says. "Something to perk her up. Candy, maybe."

I say, "Oh, that's a good idea," even though I have no clue what he's talking about. Why should I buy flowers or candy for *Rachel*? Does Elizabeth Kellogg's death affect Rachel more than it affects Julio, the head of the maintenance staff, who'll probably be the person hosing Elizabeth's blood out of the elevator shaft later on? Is anybody buying candy for *Julio*?

Maybe I should just buy flowers for both of them.

"Rachel's not used to the city yet," Dr. Jessup is saying, by way of explanation, I suppose. "This is bound to shake her up a little. She's not a jaded New Yorker yet, like some of us. Right, Wells?" He winks.

"Right," I say, even though I still have no idea what he means. Would a Whitman Sampler be enough, or did he want me to go all the way to Dean & Deluca's and buy a bunch of those petits fours? Which would be okay, because then I can get myself some of those chocolate-covered orange peels.

Except . . . Rachel doesn't eat candy. It's not on the Zone. Maybe I should get her some nuts?

But our conversation comes to an abrupt end when President Allington comes striding into the lounge.

I'll tell you the truth. I never recognize Phillip Allington at first glance, even though I've been seeing him get off the elevators every weekday morning since last June, when I started working at Fischer Hall.

The reason I never recognize President Allington is because President Allington doesn't exactly dress like a college president. His ensemble of choice is white trousers—which he continues to wear well after Labor Day, regardless of Miss Manners—gold New York College T-shirt (tank top for really humid days), Adidas, and, in inclement weather, a gold and white New York College letter jacket. According to another article I found in Justine's files, the president feels if he dresses like a student, he'll be more accessible to them.

But I've never seen a New York College student dressed in the school colors. They all wear black, to blend in with the rest of the New Yorkers.

Today President Allington has opted for the T-shirt rather than the tank, even though the temperature outside is over seventy degrees. Well, maybe he had a meeting of the board of trustees to attend, and wanted to dress to impress.

It isn't until all the other administrators immediately rush over to him to make sure the president knows what an integral part he or she is playing in the resolution of what will no doubt be referred to on Monday in the student-run newspaper as "The Tragedy" that I'm like, "Oh, yeah. That's the president."

Ignoring everyone else, Dr. Allington looks directly at Dr. Jessup and says, "You should do something about this, Stan. This is not good. Not good at all."

Dr. Jessup looks as if he wishes *he* were the one at the bottom of the elevator shaft. I don't really blame him, either.

"Phil," he says to the president. "It happens. In a population this big, there are bound to be some deaths. We had three last year alone, and the year before that, there were two—"

"Not in my building," President Allington says. I can't help thinking that he is trying to sound like Harrison Ford in *Air Force One* ("Get off my plane").

But he sounds more like Pauly Shore in *Bio-Dome*.

This seems to me like an appropriate time to go back to my office. I find Sarah there sitting at my desk, talking on the phone. No one else is around, but there's still a disagreeable amount of tension in the room. It seems to be emanating from Sarah, who slams the phone down and glares at me.

"Rachel says we have to cancel the hall dance tonight." She is practically glowering.

"So?" This sounds like a reasonable request to me. "Cancel it."

"You don't understand. We've lined up a real band. We stand to lose about fifteen hundred dollars from this."

I stare at Sarah.

"Sarah," I say. "A girl is dead. *Dead*."

"And by veering from our normal routine because of her selfish act," Sarah says, "we will only cause her death to be romanticized by the student population." Then, coming down off her grad student high horse for a second, she adds, "I guess we can make back the lost revenue in T-shirt sales. Still, I don't see why we should cancel our dance, just because some nutcase took a dive off the top of an elevator."

And people say *show biz* is rough. They've obviously never worked in a dorm.

Excuse me, I mean, residence hall.

I don't see how
We could have drifted so far apart
Seems like just yesterday
You were calling me baby
Now I'm alone
And I can't help crying

Do Over
Baby I want a
Do Over
'Cause I'm not ready
To let you go

"Do Over"
Performed by Heather Wells
Composed by Dietz/Ryder
From the album *Sugar Rush*
Cartwright Records

5

Being this is New York City, where so many unnatural deaths occur every day, it ends up taking the coroner's office four hours to get to Elizabeth's body.

The coroner arrives at three-thirty, and by three thirty-five, Elizabeth Kellogg is declared dead. Cause of death, pending an investigation and autopsy, is recorded as acute trauma, in the form of a broken neck, back, and pelvic bone, in addition to multiple fractures to the face and extremities.

Call me a dreamer, but I don't think anybody in the student population will be romanticizing her death when they find *this* out.

Worse, the coroner says he thinks Elizabeth has been dead for nearly twelve hours. Which means she's been lying in the bottom of that elevator shaft since the night before.

And okay, he says she died on impact with the cement floor, so death was instantaneous. It's not like she'd lain there, alive, all night.

But still.

There's no hiding the coroner's van, or the body that is eventually trundled out of the building and into it. By four o'clock, the entire student population of Fischer Hall knows there's been a death. They also know, once the elevators are turned back on, and they are finally allowed to take them back to their floors, how she died. I mean, they're college students: They're not stupid. They can put together two and two and come up with four.

But I can't be too concerned with how the seven hundred residents of Fischer Hall are dealing with the news of Elizabeth's death. Because I am too busy being concerned with how Elizabeth's parents are dealing with the news of her death.

That's because it was decided by Dr. Jessup—a decision backed up by Dr. Flynn—that because of Rachel's previous contact with Mrs. Kellogg concerning Elizabeth's guest privileges, she should be the one to make the call to the dead girl's parents.

"It will be less of a shock," Dr. Flynn assures everyone, "for the Kelloggs to hear the news from a familiar voice."

Sarah is unceremoniously banished from the office once the decision is made, but Dr. Jessup asks me to stay.

"It'll be a comfort to Rachel," is what he says.

He clearly hasn't seen Rachel in action in the cafeteria,

cussing out the salad bar attendants for accidentally putting full-fat ranch dressing in the fat-free ranch dispenser, the way I had. Rachel is hardly the type who needs comforting.

But who am I to say anything?

The scene is excruciatingly sad, and by the time Rachel hangs up the phone, I have what feels like an oncoming migraine as well as an upset stomach.

Of course, it could be the eleven Jolly Ranchers and the bag of Fritos I'd had in lieu of lunch. But you never know.

These symptoms are made worse by Dr. Jessup. Chagrined by Dr. Allington's remarks, the assistant vice president has thrown caution and New York City health codes to the wind, and is smoking energetically, his rear end resting against the edge of Rachel's desk. No one offers to open a window. This is because our office windows are on the ground floor, and every time you open them, some wit walks up to them and yells, "Can I have fries with that?" into our office.

It is right then that it occurs to me that Rachel is finished with her phone calls, and that I am no longer needed to be a comfort to her. There is nothing more I can do to help.

So I stand up and say, "I'm going to go home now."

Everyone looks at me. Fortunately Dr. Allington has long since departed, as he and his wife have a house in the Hamptons and they head out there every chance they get.

Except that today Mrs. Allington wouldn't leave through the front door—not with the coroner's van parked out there on the sidewalk, behind the fire engine. I had to turn off the alarm so she could leave by the emergency exit off the side of the cafeteria, the same door through which the security guards usher the Allingtons' more prestigious guests—like the Schwarzeneggers—when they have dinner parties so that they don't have to be bothered by any students.

The Allingtons' only child, Christopher—a very good-looking guy in his late twenties, who wears a lot of Brooks Brothers, and is living in graduate student housing while attending the college's law school—was behind the wheel of their forest green Mercedes when they finally left. Dr. Allington solicitously placed his wife in the backseat, their overnight bags in the trunk, then hopped into the front seat beside his son.

Christopher Allington peeled out so fast that people attending the street fair—oh yes. The street fair went on, in spite of the fire engine and coroner's wagon—jumped up onto the sidewalk, thinking someone was trying to run them down.

I'll tell you something: If the Allingtons were my parents, I'd have tried to run people down, too.

Dr. Flynn recovers from my announcement that I'm leaving before anybody else. He says, "Of course, Heather. You go on home. We don't need Heather anymore, do we, Stan?"

Dr. Jessup exhales a stream of blue-gray smoke.

"Go home," he says to me. "Have a drink. A big one."

"Oh, Heather," Rachel cries. She leaps up from her swivel chair and, to my surprise, throws her arms around me. She has never been physically demonstrative with me before. "Thank you so much for coming over. I don't know what we would have done without you. You keep such a level head in a crisis."

I have no idea what she's talking about. I hadn't done a single thing. I certainly hadn't bought her those flowers Dr. Jessup had recommended. I'd calmed the student workers down, maybe, and talked Sarah out of having her dance, but that's it, really. Not exactly anything life-saving.

I look everywhere but at anyone else's face as Rachel hugs me. Hugging Rachel is a lot like hugging—well, a stick. Because she's so thin. I sort of feel bad for her. Because who wants to hug a stick? I know all those guys who go after models do. But I mean, what kind of normal person wants to hug, or be hugged by, a lot of pointy bones? It would be one thing if she were *naturally* pointy. But I happen to know that Rachel starves herself in order to be that way on *purpose*.

It's just not right.

To my relief, Rachel lets go almost immediately, and as soon as she does, I hurry from the office without another word, mostly because I am afraid I will start crying if I speak. Not because of her boniness, but because it all just seems like such a *waste*. I mean, a girl is dead, her parents devastated. And for *what*? A thrill ride on top of an elevator?

It just doesn't make any sense.

Since the alarm to the fire exit is still turned off, I leave the building through it, relieved that I don't have to pass the reception desk. Because I seriously think I might lose it if anyone says a single word to me. I have to walk all the way down to Sixth Avenue and around the block to avoid running into anyone I know—passing right by Banana Republic, which does carry size 12 clothing, but rarely has any in stock, because, being that it's the most common size, they can never keep enough of it on the racks for everyone—but it's worth it. I am in no shape for small talk with anyone.

Sadly, however, when I get to my front door, I discover that small talk is exactly what I'm in for. Because lounging on my front stoop is my ex-fiancé, Jordan Cartwright.

And I'd truly been convinced my day couldn't get any worse.

He straightens when he sees me, and hangs up the cell phone he'd been jawing into. The late-afternoon sunlight brings out the gold highlights in his blond hair, and I can't help noticing that in spite of the Indian summer heat, the lines pressed into his white shirt and—yes, I'm sorry to have to say it—matching white pants look perfectly crisp.

With the white outfit, and the gold chain around his neck, he looks like he's AWOL from a really bad boy band.

Which, sadly, is exactly what he is.

"Heather," he says, when he sees me.

I can't read his pale blue eyes because they're hidden by the lenses of his Armani sunglasses. But I suppose they are, as always, filled with tender concern for my well-being. Jordan is good at making people think he actually cares about them. It's one of the reasons his first solo effort, "Baby, Be Mine," went double platinum. The video was number one on *Total Request Live* for weeks.

"There you are," he says. "I've been trying to reach you. I guess Coop's not home. Are you all right? I came down as soon as I heard."

I just blink at him. What is he doing here? We broke up. Doesn't he remember?

Maybe not. He'd obviously been working out. Like majorly. There's actual definition to his biceps.

Maybe a dumbbell fell on his head or something.

"She lived in your building, didn't she?" he goes on. "The girl on the radio? The one who died?"

It is totally unfair that someone who looks so hot can be so . . . well, lacking in anything remotely resembling human emotion.

I dig my keys out of the front pocket of my jeans.

"You shouldn't have come down here, Jordan," I say. People are staring—mostly just the drug dealers, though. There are a lot of them in my neighborhood, because the college, in order to clean up Washington Square Park for the students (and, more importantly, their parents), puts all this pressure on the local police precinct to scoot all the drug dealers and homeless people out of the park and onto the surrounding streets . . . like, for instance, the one I live on.

Of course when I'd accepted Jordan's brother's offer to move in with him, I didn't know the neighborhood was so bad. I mean, come on, it's Greenwich Village, which had long ago ceased to be a haven for starving artists, after the yuppies moved in and gentrified the place and the rents shot sky high. I figured it had to be on par with Park Avenue, where I'd been living with Jordan, and where "those kind of people," as Jordan calls them, simply don't hang out.

Which is a good thing, because "those kind of people" apparently can't take their eyes off Jordan—and not just because of the prominently displayed gold chain.

"Hey!" one of them yells. "You that guy? Hey, are you that guy?"

Jordan, used to being harassed by paparazzi, doesn't bat an eye.

"Heather," he says, in his most soothing tone, the one he'd used during his duet with Jessica Simpson on their Get Funky tour last summer. "Come on. Be reasonable. Just because things didn't work out between us romantically is no reason why we can't still be friends. We've been through so much together. Grew up together, even."

This part, anyway, is true. I'd met Jordan back when I'd first been signed by his father's record label, Cartwright Records, when I'd been an impressionable fifteen years of age, and Jordan had been all of eighteen. Back then, I'd truly believed Jordan's whole tortured artist act. I'd believed him when he insisted that he, like me, hated the songs the label was giving him to sing. I'd believed him when he'd said he, like me, was going to quit singing them, and start singing the songs he'd written himself. I'd believed him right up to the point I'd told the label it was my songs or no songs, and the label had chosen no songs . . . and Jordan, instead of telling the label (also known as his dad) the same thing, had said, "Maybe we better talk about this, Heather."

I glance around to make sure his current performance isn't for the benefit of a hidden camera. I totally wouldn't put it past him to have signed up with some reality show. He's one of those people who wouldn't mind watching his own life broadcast on national television.

That's when I notice the silver convertible BMW parked by the hydrant in front of the brownstone.

"That's new," I say. "From your dad? A reward for taking up with Tania Trace?"

"Now, Heather," Jordan says. "I told you. The thing with Tania—it's not what you think."

"Right," I say with a laugh. "I suppose she fell down and just happened to land with her head in your crotch."

Jordan does something surprising then. He whips off his sunglasses and looks down at me very intently. I'm reminded of the first time I ever met him—at the Mall of America. The label—namely Jordan's dad—had arranged for Jordan's band, Easy Street, and me to tour together, in an effort to bring out the maximum number of preteens—and their parents, and their parents' wallets—possible.

Jordan had given me the same intent look then that he was giving me now. His "Baby, you got the bluest eyes" hadn't sounded a bit like a pickup line then.

But what did I know? I'd been yanked out of high school my freshman year and had been on the road ever since, heavily chaperoned and making contact with guys my own age only when they came up to ask for my autograph. How was

I supposed to know "Baby, you got the bluest eyes" was a pickup line?

I didn't realize it until years later, when "Baby, you got the bluest eyes" showed up as a line from one of the singles off Jordan's first solo album. It turns out he'd had a lot of practice saying it. With sincerity, even.

It had certainly worked on me.

"Heather," Jordan says now, as the rays of the sun, filtering through the treetops and apartment buildings to the west, play over the even planes of his handsome, still slightly boyish face. "We had something, you and I. Are you sure you really just want to walk away from that? I mean, I know I'm not exactly blameless in all this. That thing with Tania . . . well, I know how that must have looked to you."

I stare at him incredulously.

"You mean like she was giving you head? Because that's how it looked to me."

Jordan flinches as if I'd hit him.

"See?" He folds his arms across his chest. "See, that's exactly what I mean. When we first met, Heather, you never said crass things like that. You've changed. Don't you see? That's part of the problem. You're not the same girl I knew all those years ago—"

I decide that if he drops his gaze to my waistline, where I've changed the most since ten years ago, I was going to belt him.

But he doesn't.

"You've gotten . . . I don't know. Hard, I guess, is the word," he goes on. "And after what you've been through with your mom and your manager, who can blame you? But Heather, not everyone is out to steal all your money and flee to Argentina with it like they did. You've got to believe me when I say that I never meant to hurt you. We just drifted apart, you and I. We want different things. You want to sing your own songs, and you apparently don't care if doing so destroys your career—what's left of it. While I . . . well, I want—"

"Hey!" yells the drug dealer. "You're JORDAN CARTWRIGHT!"

I can't believe this is happening. First Elizabeth, now this.

What does Jordan want from me, anyway? That's what I can never figure out. The guy is thirty-one years old, six-two, and worth a *lot* of money—way more than the hundred thousand a year Rachel is looking for in her ideal mate. I mean, I know his parents weren't exactly thrilled when the two of us moved in together. It hadn't looked good, two of their most popular teen performers, shacking up . . .

But had our *entire* relationship just been an elaborate attempt to get back at Mr. and Mrs. Grant Cartwright for allowing their youngest son to audition for the Mickey Mouse Club, like he'd begged them to back when he was nine, to his everlasting shame? Because of course *serious* rockers don't have photos of themselves in Mickey Mouse ears being shown in *Teen People* every other week . . .

"Jordan," I say, cutting him off as he is listing the things he wants out of life, most of which have to do with bringing a little sunshine into people's lives, and why is that so wrong? Except that I never said it was. "Could you please just *go away*?"

I jostle past him, my keys in my hand. I guess my plan was to unlock the door and get inside before he could stop me.

With three locks to undo, though, a quick escape is kind of tough.

"I know you don't take me seriously as an artist, Heather," Jordan goes on. And on and on. "But I can assure you that just because I don't write the songs I sing, that doesn't make me any less creative than you are. I do practically all my own choreography now. That move I did on the 'Just Me and You Now' video? You know, this one?" He does a quick step-ball-change, accompanied by a pelvic thrust, on the front stoop of the brownstone. "That's all mine. I know to you that might not be much, but don't you think it's time you took a good look at your own life? I mean, what have *you* been doing that's so artistically fulfilling lately? This stupid dorm thing—"

Two locks down. One to go.

"—and living down here with drug addicts at your doorstep . . . and with *Cooper*! With *Cooper*, of all people! You know how my family feels about *Cooper*, Heather."

I do know how his family feels about Cooper. The same way they feel about Cooper's grandfather, who came out of the closet at the age of sixty-five, bought a bright pink stucco brownstone in the Village, then willed it to his black sheep grandson, who'd moved into the garden apartment, turned the middle floor into a detective agency, and offered the top floor to me, rent-free (in exchange for doing his billing), when he'd found out about my walking in on Jordan and Tania.

"I mean, I know there isn't anything going on between you two," Jordan is saying. "That's not what I'm worried about. You aren't Cooper's type."

He can say that again. Sadly.

"But I wonder if you're aware that Coop has a criminal record. Vandalism. And yeah, he was a juvenile, but still, for God's sake, Heather, he has no respect for public property. That was an Easy Street marquee he defaced, you know. I'm aware that he always resented my talent, but it's not my fault I was born with such a gift—"

The third lock springs open. I'm free!

"Good-bye, Jordan," I say, and slip inside, shutting the door carefully behind me. Because, you know, I don't want to slam it in his face and hurt him, or anything. Not because I still care, but because that would be rude.

Plus his dad might sue me, or something. You never know.

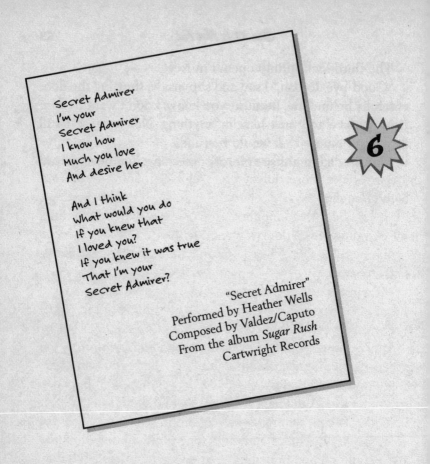

Secret Admirer
I'm your
Secret Admirer
I know how
Much you love
And desire her

And I think
What would you do
If you knew that
I loved you?
If you knew it was true
That I'm your
Secret Admirer?

"Secret Admirer"
Performed by Heather Wells
Composed by Valdez/Caputo
From the album *Sugar Rush*
Cartwright Records

6

Jordan is pounding on the door, but I'm ignoring him.

It's cool inside the brownstone, and smells vaguely of toner from the photocopier in Coop's office. I start up the stairs to my apartment, thinking Lucy—have I mentioned her? She's my dog—will want to be let out, when I happen to glance down the hall and see that the French doors to the back terrace are open.

Instead of going upstairs, I go down the hallway— Cooper's grandfather had it papered in black and white stripes, which was apparently all the rage in the seventies gay community—and find the man of the house sitting in a lawn chair on the back terrace, a bottle of beer in his hand, my dog at his feet, and a red mini-Igloo at his side.

He's listening—as he usually is, when he's home—to a jazz station on the radio. Cooper is the only member of his family who eschews the screeching of Easy Street and Tania Trace for the more dulcet tones of Coleman-Hawkins and Sarah Vaughn.

"Is he gone yet?" Cooper wants to know, when he notices me standing in the doorway.

"He will be soon," I say. Then it hits me. "Are you *hiding* back here?"

"You got that right," Cooper says. He opens the Igloo and takes a beer from it. "Here," he says, offering it to me. "I figured you'd need one of these."

I take the cold bottle gratefully, and sink down onto the green padded seat cushion of a nearby wrought-iron chair. Lucy immediately darts over and thrusts her head between my thighs, snuffling happily at me. I rub her ears.

That's the nice thing about having a dog. They're always so happy to see you. Plus, you know, there are health benefits. People's blood pressure goes down when they pet a dog. Or even a cat. It's a documented fact. I read it in *People* magazine.

Of course, pets aren't the only thing that can help keep your blood pressure down. Sitting in a really tranquil place can do it, too. Like, for instance, Cooper's grandfather's terrace and the garden below, which are totally two of the best-kept secrets in Manhattan. Leafy and green, surrounded by high, ivy-covered walls, the place is this tiny oasis carved from a former eighteenth-century stable yard. There's even this little fountain in the garden, which Cooper, I see, has turned on. It gurgles comfortingly in the late-afternoon stillness. As I stroke Lucy's ears, I can feel my heart rate returning to normal.

Maybe when I pass my six months' review, and I'm finally able to enroll in school, I'll become a pre-med major. Yeah, it'll be hard to do with a full time job—not to mention Cooper's billing. But I'll find a way to make it work.

And then maybe later I'll get like a scholarship or something to medical school. And then, when I graduate, I can take Lucy with me on rounds, and she can calm down all of my patients. I'll totally eradicate heart disease, just by having my patients pet my dog. I'll be famous! Like Marie Curie!

Only I won't wear uranium around my neck and die of radiation poisoning like I read that Marie Curie did.

I don't mention my new plan to Cooper. Somehow, I don't think he'd fully appreciate its many facets. Although he's a pretty open-minded guy. Arthur Cartwright, Cooper's grandfather, angered by the way the rest of the family had treated him after he'd revealed he was gay, had left the majority of his vast fortune to AIDS research; the entirety of his world-class art collection to Sotheby's to auction, with the provision that all proceeds from the sales go to God's Love We Deliver; and almost all the property he'd owned to his alma mater, New York College . . .

. . . all except his beloved pink brownstone in the Village, which he'd willed to Cooper—along with a cool million bucks—because Cooper had been the only member of the Cartwright family to have said, "Whatever floats your boat, Gramps," when he'd heard the news about his grandfather's new boyfriend, Jorge.

Not that Jordan and the rest of the Cartwrights had been overly worried by Arthur's cutting them off. There'd still been plenty of money left in the Cartwright family bank vault for everyone else.

Still, it hadn't exactly made Cooper, already the family scapegoat for getting himself thrown out of multiple high schools and choosing college over a place in Easy Street—not to mention his tendency to date highly attractive heart surgeons or art gallery owners named Saundra or Yokiko—the most popular member of the Cartwright clan.

Which truthfully doesn't seem to bother him. I've never met anyone who seems more content with his own company than Cooper Cartwright.

He doesn't even *look* like the rest of his family. Dark-haired, whereas the rest of them are blond, Cooper does have the requisite Cartwright good looks and ice blue eyes.

Though his eyes are where any resemblance to his brother Jordan ends. Both are tall, with gangling, athletic builds.

But whereas Jordan's muscles have been honed by a personal trainer several hours a day at his personal home gym, Coop's are from playing aggressive rounds of one-on-one down at the public basketball courts on Sixth and West Third, and from—though he won't admit this—high-speed on-foot pursuits through Grand Central on behalf of whatever client he's currently employed by. I know the truth because, being the one who does his client billing, I see the receipts. There is no way someone can go from a cab— a six-dollar trip ending at 5:01—to a Metro North ticket booth—round-trip ticket to Stamford, departing at 5:07— without running.

Because of all this—the niceness, the eyes, the weekend-hoops thing . . . not to mention the jazz—of course I've fallen madly in love with Cooper.

But I know it's completely futile. He treats me with the kind of friendly nonchalance you'd normally reserve for your kid brother's girlfriend, which is what I am apparently destined to remain to him, since, compared to the women he dates, who are all waiflike, gorgeous, and professors of Renaissance literature or microphysicists, I'm like vanilla pudding, or something.

And who wants vanilla pudding when they can have crème brûlée?

I'm going to fall in love with someone else just as soon as I can. I swear. But in the meantime, is it so wrong that I enjoy his company?

Taking a long sip from his beer, Cooper studies the tops of the buildings around us . . . one of which happens to be Fischer Hall. You can see the twelfth to twentieth floors, including the president's penthouse, from Arthur Cartwright's backyard garden.

You can also see the vents to the elevator shaft.

"So," Cooper says. "Was it bad?"

He doesn't mean my encounter with Jordan. This is obvious by the way he nods his head in the direction of the college campus.

I'm not surprised he knows about the dead girl. He would have heard all the sirens and seen the crowds. For all I know, he could even have a police scanner tucked away somewhere.

"It wasn't pretty," I say, taking a sip of my beer while massaging Lucy's pointed ears with my free hand. Lucy is a mutt I'd picked up from the ASPCA shortly after my mother took off. I'm sure Sarah would say I adopted Lucy as some sort of surrogate family member, since I'd been abandoned by all of mine.

But since I'd been touring all the time, I'd never been able to have a pet, and I just felt like the time had come to get one. Part collie and seemingly part fox, Lucy has a laughing face I'd been unable to resist—even though Jordan had wanted a pure breed, if possible a cocker spaniel. He hadn't been too happy when, instead of Lady, I'd come home with the Tramp.

But that had been all right, because Lucy never liked Jordan anyway, and had promptly shown her disapproval of him by eating a pair of his suede pants.

Strangely, she doesn't seem to have a problem with Cooper, a fact I attribute to Cooper's never having thrown a copy of *Us Weekly* magazine at her for chewing on his Dave Matthews Band CDs. Cooper doesn't even own any Dave Matthews Band CDs. He's a Wynton Marsalis fan.

"Anybody know how it happened?" Cooper wants to know.

"No," I say. "Or, if someone does, they aren't exactly coming forward with the information."

"Well." He takes a swig of beer. "They're just kids. Probably afraid they'll get into trouble."

"I know," I say. "It's just that . . . how could they have just *left* her there? I mean, she had to have been there for hours. And they just left her."

"Who left her?"

"Whoever she was with."

"How do you know she was with anybody?"

"Nobody goes elevator surfing alone. The whole point is that a bunch of kids climb on top of the elevator through the maintenance panel in the ceiling, and dare one another to jump off the roof of their car they're riding on, onto the roof of a second car as it passes by. If there's no one to dare you, there's no point."

It's easy to explain things to Cooper, because he's a very good listener. He never interrupts people, and always seems genuinely interested in what they have to say. This is another character trait that sets him apart from the rest of his family.

It's also one that I suspect aids him in his line of work. You can learn a lot from letting other people talk, and just listening to what they have to say.

At least, it said this once in a magazine I read.

"The whole point is that kids dare each other to make bigger and braver leaps," I say. "You would never elevator surf alone. So she had to be with someone. Unless—"

Cooper eyes me. "Unless what?"

"Well, unless she wasn't elevator surfing at all," I say, finally voicing something that's been nagging at me all day. "I mean, girls don't, generally. Elevator surf. At least, I've never heard of one, not at New York College. It's a drunk-guy thing."

"So." Cooper leans forward in his lawn chair. "If she wasn't elevator surfing, how did she fall to the bottom of the shaft? Do you think the elevator doors opened, but the car didn't come, and she stepped out into the shaft without looking?"

"I don't know. That just doesn't happen, does it? The doors won't open unless the car is there. And even if they did, who would be stupid enough not to look first?"

Which is when Cooper says, "Maybe someone pushed her."

I blink at him. It's quiet in the back of his brownstone—you can't hear the traffic from Sixth Avenue, or the rattling of bottles from Waverly Place as homeless people go through our garbage. Still, I think I might not have heard him correctly.

"Pushed her?" I echo.

"That's what you're thinking, isn't it?" Cooper's blue eyes reveal no emotion whatsoever. This is what makes him such an excellent PI. And why I continue to believe there might be hope for him and me romantically after all—because I've never seen anything in his eyes to lead me to believe otherwise. "Maybe she didn't slip and fall. Maybe she got pushed."

The thing is, that is EXACTLY what I'd been thinking.

But I'd also been thinking that this sounded . . . well, too nuts ever to mention out loud.

"Don't try to deny it," Cooper says. "I know that's what you're thinking. It's written all over your face."

It's a relief to burst out with, "Girls don't elevator surf, Coop. They just don't. I mean, maybe in other cities, but not here, at New York College. And this girl—Elizabeth—she was preppie!"

It's Cooper's turn to blink. "Excuse me?"

"Preppie," I say. "You know. Clean-cut. Preppie girls don't elevator surf. And let's say that they did. I mean, they just LEFT her there. Who would do that, to a friend?"

"Kids," Cooper says, with a shrug.

"They aren't kids," I insist. "They're eighteen years old."

Cooper shrugs. "Eighteen's still a kid in my book," he says. "But let's say you're right, and she was too, um, preppie to be elevator surfing. Can you think of anyone who'd have a reason to want to push her down an elevator shaft . . . providing they could figure out how to do this in the first place?"

"The only thing in her file," I say, "is that her mom called and asked her to restrict her guest sign-in privileges to girls only."

"Why?" Cooper wants to know. "She got an abusive ex-boyfriend the mom wanted PNG'd?"

A PNG, also known as a persona non grata memo, is issued to the dorm security guards whenever a resident—or her parents, or a staff member—requests that a certain individual be denied entry to the building. Since you have to show a student or staff ID, driver's license, or passport to be let into the hall, the guards can easily deny entry to anyone on the PNG list. Once, my first week, the student workers issued a fake PNG against me. As a joke, they said.

I bet they never did that to Justine.

Also, I can't believe Cooper has been paying such close attention to my ramblings about my crazy job at Fischer Hall that he even remembers what a PNG is.

"No," I say, flushing a little. "No boyfriend mentioned."

"Doesn't mean there isn't one. The kids have to sign guests in, right?" Cooper asks. "Did anyone check to see if Elizabeth had a boyfriend—maybe one Mom doesn't know about—over last night?"

I shake my head, not taking my gaze off the back of Fischer Hall, which is glowing red in the rays from the setting sun.

"She had a roommate," I explain. "She's not going to be having some guy spend the night with a roommate right there in the bed across the room."

"Because preppie girls don't do things like that?"

I squirm a little uncomfortably. "Well . . . they don't."

Cooper shrugs. "Roommate could've stayed the night with someone else."

I hadn't thought of this. "I'll check the sign-in logs," I say. "It can't hurt."

"You mean," Cooper says, "you'll tell the police to check the sign-in logs."

"Police?" I am startled. "You think the police are going to get involved?"

"Probably," is Cooper's mild reply. "If they harbor the same 'preppie girls don't do that' suspicions you seem to."

I make a face at him just as the doorbell rings and we hear Jordan bellow, "Heather! Come on, Heather! Open up!"

Cooper doesn't even turn his head in the direction of the front door.

"His devotion to you is touching," Cooper remarks.

"It's got nothing to do with me," I explain. "He's just trying to annoy you. You know, get you to throw me out. He won't be happy until I'm living in a cardboard box on the median of Houston Street."

"Sounds like it's over between you two, all right," Cooper says, wryly.

"It's not *that*. He doesn't still *like* me. He just wants to punish me for leaving him."

"Or," Cooper says, "for having the guts to do your own thing. Which is something he'll never have."

"Good point."

Cooper's a man of few words, but the words he does use are always the exactly right ones. When he heard about my walking in on Jordan and Tania, he called my cell and told me that if I was looking for a new place to live, the top-floor apartment of his brownstone—where his grandfather's houseboy had lived—was available. When I explained how broke I was—thanks to Mom—Cooper said I could earn my keep by doing his client billing and entering the piles of receipts he had lying around into Quicken, so he didn't have to pay his accountant $175 an hour to do it.

Simple as that, I left the Park Avenue penthouse Jordan and I had been sharing, and moved into Cooper's place. After only a single night there, it was as if Lucy and I had never lived anywhere else.

Of course, the work isn't exactly easy. Coop had said he thought it would total maybe ten hours a week, but it's more like twenty. I usually spend all day Sunday and several nights a week trying to make sense out of the piles of scrap paper, notes scribbled on matchbooks, and crumpled receipts in his office.

Still, as rent goes, twenty hours a week of data entry is nothing. We're talking a West Village floor-through that would easily go for three thousand a month on the open market.

And yeah, I know why he did it. And it's not because deep down inside he has a secret penchant for size 12 ex–pop stars. In fact—like Jordan's pounding on the door just now—it's got nothing to do with me at all. Cooper's motivation in letting me move in with him is that, in doing so, he's really bugging the hell out of his family—primarily his little brother. Coop revels in annoying Jordan, and Jordan, in return, hates Cooper. He says it's because Coop is irresponsible and immature.

But I think it's really because Jordan's jealous of the fact that Cooper, when his parents tried to pressure him into joining Easy Street by cutting him off financially, hadn't seemed to mind being poor in the least, and had in fact found his own way in the world without the help of Cartwright Records. I've always suspected that Jordan—much as he loves performing—wishes he'd told his parents where to go, the way Cooper—and eventually me, too—had.

Cooper obviously suspects the same thing.

"Well," he says, as in the background, we hear Jordan shout, "*Come on, I know you guys are in there.*" "Much as I'm enjoying sitting here listening to Jordan have a meltdown on my stoop, I have to get to work."

I can't help staring at him as he puts down his beer bottle and stands up. Cooper really is a choice specimen. In the fading sunlight, he looks particularly tanned. But it isn't, I know, a tan from a can, like his brother's. Coop's tan is from sitting for hours behind some bushes with a telephoto lens pointed at a motel room doorway . . .

Not that Cooper has ever told me what, exactly, he does all day.

"You're working?" I ask, squinting up at him. "On a Saturday night? Doing what?"

He chuckles. It's like a little game between us. I try to trick him into letting slip what kind of case he's working on, and he refuses to take the bait. Cooper takes his clients' rights to privacy seriously.

Also, he thinks his cases are way too kinky for his kid

brother's ex-girlfriend to hear about. To Cooper, I think I'll always be a fifteen-year-old in a halter top and ponytail, proclaiming from a mall stage that I'm suffering from a sugar rush.

"Nice try," Cooper says. "What are *you* going to do?"

I think about it. Magda is pulling a double at the cash register in the caf, and would want to go straight home afterward to wash the smell of Tater Tots out of her hair. I could call my friend Patty—one of my former backup dancers from the Sugar Rush tour, and one of the few friends I have left from back when I'd been in the music business.

But she's married now, with a baby, and doesn't have much time for her single friends anymore.

I realize I'm probably going to spend this night as I spend most other nights—either doing Cooper's data entry or twiddling around with my guitar, a pencil, and some blank sheet music, trying to compose a song that, unlike "Sugar Rush," doesn't make me want to puke every time I hear it.

"Oh," I say casually. "Nothing."

"Well, don't stay up too late doing *nothing*," Cooper says. "If Jordan's still out there when I leave, I'll call the cops and have that Beemer of his towed."

I smile at him, touched. When I *do* get my medical degree, one of the first things I'm going to do is ask Cooper out. He can't seem to resist super-educated women, so who knows? Maybe he'll even say yes.

"Thanks," I say.

"Don't mention it."

Cooper goes inside, taking his radio with him, leaving Lucy and me alone in the slowly creeping shadows. I sit there for a while after he's gone, finishing the rest of my beer, and gazing up at Fischer Hall. The building looks so homey, so tranquil. It's hard to believe it had been the scene of so much sadness a little earlier in the day.

It isn't until it has grown dark enough that lights begin appearing in the windows of Fischer Hall that I finally go inside.

And when I do, it hits me that Cooper's warning when I'd told him I was going to do nothing tonight had been a bit on the wry side. Is it possible that he knows that I hadn't really meant what I said? Is it possible that he *knows* what I do every night . . . and that it isn't nothing? Can he hear my guitar all the way downstairs?

No way.

But then why had he said the word *nothing* like that? So . . . I don't know. *Meaningfully?*

I can't figure it out.

But then, let's face it, guys have always been something of a mystery to me.

Still, when I get out my guitar that night, I play it extra softly, just in case Cooper does come home unexpectedly. I'm not about to let anyone—not even Coop—hear my latest stuff. Not after the way his dad laughed at me the day I played it for him, not too long before Jordan and I broke up.

Angry-girl rocker shit, Grant Cartwright called my songs. *Why don't you leave the songwriting to the pros*, he'd said, *and stick to doing what you do best, which is belting out top forty and power ballads? By the way, have you put on some weight?*

One of these days, I'm going to show Grant Cartwright what an angry-girl rocker *really* looks like.

Later, as I'm washing my face before bed, I look out the window and see Fischer Hall all lit up against the night sky. I can see the tiny forms of students, moving around in their rooms, and can hear, faintly, the sound of music being played from a few of those rooms.

It's true someone in that building died today. But it's also true that, for everyone else, life goes on.

And it's going on now, as girls primp in front of their bathroom mirrors in preparation for going out, and boys chug Rolling Rocks as they wait for the girls.

Meanwhile, through the vents along the side of the building, I see intermittent flashes of light as the elevators glide silently up and down their shafts.

And I can't help wondering what happened. What made her do it?

Or . . .

Who?

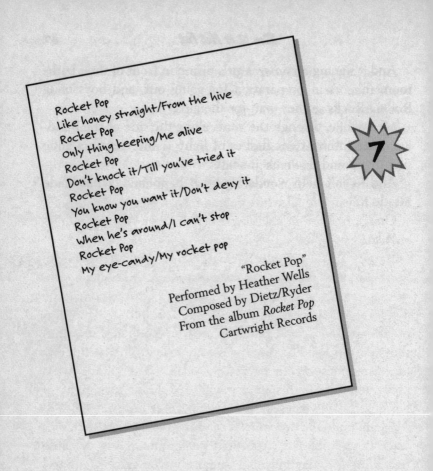

Rocket Pop
Like honey straight/From the hive
Rocket Pop
Only thing keeping/Me alive
Rocket Pop
Don't knock it/Till you've tried it
Rocket Pop
You know you want it/Don't deny it
Rocket Pop
When he's around/I can't stop
Rocket Pop
My eye-candy/My rocket pop

"Rocket Pop"
Performed by Heather Wells
Composed by Dietz/Ryder
From the album *Rocket Pop*
Cartwright Records

7

On Monday, Sarah and I let ourselves into Elizabeth's room to pack up all her belongings.

This is because her parents are too distraught to do it themselves, and ask that the residence hall director's office do it for them.

Which I can totally understand. I mean, the last thing you expect when you send your kid off to college is that three weeks later, you're going to get a call informing you that your daughter is dead, and that you need to come to the city to pick up all her stuff.

Especially when your kid is as straitlaced as Elizabeth seemed to be . . . at least, judging from her things, which Sarah inventoried (so that later, if the Kelloggs noticed something missing, they couldn't accuse us of having stolen it, something Dr. Jessup said had unfortunately happened before in cases of students' deaths), while I packed. I mean, the girl had seven Izods. Seven! She didn't even own a black bra. Her panties were all white cotton Hanes Her Way.

I am sorry, but girls who wear Hanes Her Way do not elevator surf.

Except that I am clearly in the minority in this belief. Sarah, as she records each item I pull from Elizabeth's dresser, pontificates on the finer points of schizophrenia, the disease she's currently studying in her psych class. Symptoms of schizophrenia don't generally show up in its sufferers until they are the age Elizabeth was at her death, Sarah informs me. She goes on to say it's probable that that's what prompted Elizabeth's uncharacteristic daring the night of her death. The voices she heard in her head, I mean.

Sarah could have a point. It certainly wasn't Elizabeth's alleged boyfriend, as Cooper had suggested. I know, because first thing Monday morning—before I even grabbed a bagel and coffee from the caf—I checked the sign-in logs from Friday night.

But there's nothing there. Elizabeth hadn't signed anyone in.

While Sarah and I spend the entire day packing Elizabeth's things—never encountering her roommate, who appears to spend every waking hour in class—Rachel is busy arranging the campus memorial service for the deceased, as well as getting the bursar's office to refund Elizabeth's tuition and housing fees for the year.

Not that the Kelloggs seem to appreciate it. At the memorial service in the student chapel later on that week (which I don't attend, since Rachel says she wants an adult presence in the office while she's out, in case a student needs counseling, or something—the residence hall staff is very concerned about how Elizabeth's death might affect the rest of the building's population, although so far they've shown no sign of being traumatized), Mrs. Kellogg assures all present, in strident tones, that the college isn't going to get away with causing her daughter's death, and that she herself isn't going to rest until the parties responsible are punished (at least according to Pete, who pulled a double and was guarding the chapel doors at the time).

Mrs. Kellogg refuses to believe that any sort of reckless behavior on Elizabeth's part might have brought about her own death, and insists that when her daughter's blood work is returned in two weeks, we'll see that she's right: Elizabeth never drank, and certainly never did drugs, and so was not hanging out with a bunch of trippy elevator surfers the night of her death.

No, according to Mrs. Kellogg, Elizabeth was pushed down that elevator shaft—and no one's going to tell her otherwise.

Mr. and Mrs. Kellogg weren't the only ones going through a hard time in the aftermath of their daughter's death, however. After seeing what Rachel went through that week, I started to understand what Dr. Jessup had meant. About the flowers, I mean. Rachel totally deserved some.

Really, what she deserves is a raise.

But, knowing the college's general stinginess—there's been a hiring freeze since the nineties, which is lifted only for emergency appointments, like my replacing Justine—I doubt a raise is forthcoming.

So on Thursday, the day after the memorial service, I slip out to the deli around the corner, and instead of buying myself a pack of Starburst, an afternoon pick-me-up latte, and a lottery ticket, as is my daily ritual, pick up instead their best bouquet of roses, which I then put in a vase on Rachel's desk.

It's actually scary how excited she gets when she walks in from whatever meeting she's been attending, and finds them.

"For me?" she asks, tears—I'm not kidding—practically springing from her eyes.

"Well," I say. "Yes. I feel bad about all you've been going through—"

The tears dry up pretty quick after that.

"Oh, they're from you," she says, in a different voice.

"Um," I say. "Yeah."

I guess maybe Rachel thought the flowers were from a guy, or something. Maybe she met one recently at the gym. Though if she had, I'm sure Sarah and I would have heard about it. Rachel's way serious about it—finding a guy to settle down with, I mean. She fully stays on top of her weekly manicure and pedicure appointments, and she gets her roots done twice a month (she's a brunette, so she says her gray really shows). And of course she exercises like a demon, either at the college gym, or by running around Washington Square Park. I guess four times around the park is a mile or something. Rachel can go around like twelve times in half an hour.

I have pointed out that she can get the same health benefits from walking around the park that she can from running around it, while avoiding shin splints and knee problems in later life. But every time I mention this, she just looks at me.

"It's been hard on *all* of us, Heather" is what Rachel says now, slipping an arm around my shoulders. "It hasn't been easy for you, either. Don't deny it."

She's right, but not for the reasons she thinks. She thinks it's been hard on me because I've had to do a lot of the grunt work—you know, begging for boxes from Maintenance to put Elizabeth's stuff in, then packing them, then dragging them to Mail Services to ship them, not to mention rescheduling all of Rachel's judicial hearings, dealing with the whiny student workers (who insist they should get bereavement days off from doing the mail, even though none of them actually knew the deceased—Justine would have given them time off, they claim).

But to tell the truth, none of that had been as hard as admitting to myself that Fischer Hall, which I'd come to think of, since I'd starting working there, as one of the safest places in the world, is actually . . . not.

Oh, not that I have any proof that Elizabeth did get pushed, the way Mrs. Kellogg thinks. But the fact that she'd died at all . . . that part has me fully wigging. The students who go to New York College are pretty spoiled, for the most part. They have no idea how good they have it, these kids . . . loving parents, a stable source of income, nothing to worry about except passing midterms and snagging a ride home for Thanksgiving break.

I myself haven't been as carefree as they are since . . . well, since the ninth grade.

And the fact that one of them did something so incredibly stupid as jump on top of an elevator and try to ride it—or worse, jump from the top of one car to another—and that someone else—someone in this building—was there at the time, and witnessed it—saw Elizabeth slip and fall to her death, and yet hadn't come forward . . .

That's what was really freaking me out.

Of course, Cooper is probably right. Probably, whoever was with Elizabeth at the time of her death doesn't want to come forward because he's afraid he'll get in trouble.

And I suppose it's even possible Sarah's right, and Elizabeth could have been suffering from the early stages of schizo-phrenia, or even a clinical depression, brought out by a hor-mone imbalance, or something, and that's what made her do it.

But we're never going to know. That's the thing. We're never going to know.

And that just isn't right.

But it doesn't seem to bother anybody but Mrs. Kellogg.

And me.

That Friday—nearly a week after Elizabeth's death—Sarah and I are sitting in the hall director's office, ordering stuff from Office Supply. Not ceramic heaters to give away to our friends, but actual stuff we need, like pens and paper for the copy machine and stuff.

Well, okay, *I'm* doing the ordering. Sarah is lecturing me about how my weight gain probably represents a subcon-scious urge to make myself unattractive to the opposite sex, so that none of them can hurt me again the way Jordan hurt me.

I am refraining from pointing out to Sarah that I am not, in fact, fat. I have already told her, several times, that size 12 is the size of the average American woman, something Sarah should well know, since she is, in fact, a size 12, too.

But it's pretty clear to me by now that Sarah just likes to talk to hear the sound of her own voice, so I let her go on, since she has no one else to talk to, Rachel being in the cafe-teria attending a breakfast reception for the New York Col-lege basketball team, the Pansies.

Yes, that's really their name. The Pansies. They used to be called the Cougars or something, but about twenty years ago a bunch of them got caught cheating, so the NCAA dropped them from Division I to Division III, and made them change their name.

As if being called the Pansies isn't embarrassing enough, President Allington is so hot to win the Division III championship this year that he's recruited the tallest players he can find. But since the good ones all went to Division I or II schools, he just got the leftovers, like the ones with the worst academic records in the country. Seriously. Sometimes the players write notes to me about things that are wrong with their rooms, in barely legible handwriting, with many spelling errors. Here's an example:

"Deer Heather. Theirs something wrong with my toilet. It wont flosh and keeps making this sond. Pleaze help."

Here's another:

"To who it conserns: My bed is not long enuf. Can I have new bed. Thanx."

I swear I am not making this stuff up.

Sarah and I don't hear the scream, although later we hear that she apparently screamed the whole way down.

What we do hear are running footsteps in the hallway, and then one of the RAs, Jessica Brandtlinger, skids into the office.

"Heather!" Jessica cries. Her normally pale face has gone white as paper, and she is breathing hard. "It happened again. The elevator shaft. We heard a scream. You can see her legs through the crack between the floor and the car—"

I am up before she's gotten half a sentence out.

"Call nine-one-one," I yell to Sarah, on my way out. "Then find Rachel!"

I follow Jessica down the hall toward the guard desk and the stairs to the basement. Pete, I see, is not at his desk. We find him already in the basement, standing in front of the elevator bank, shouting into his walkie-talkie as Carl, one of the janitors, is trying to pry open the elevator doors with a crowbar.

"Yes, another one," Pete is yelling into his walkie-talkie. "No, I'm not joking. Get an ambulance here fast!" Seeing us, he lowers the walkie-talkie, points at Jessica, and shouts, "You: Go back upstairs and call this car"—he slaps the door to the left-hand cab—"to the first floor and hold it there. Don't let anyone on or off, and whatever you do, don't let the doors close until the fire department gets here and turns it off. Heather, find the key."

I curse myself for not grabbing it on my way downstairs. We keep a set of elevator keys behind the reception desk: an override key, like the ones the Allingtons were issued when they moved in, so they can bypass floors on their way to the penthouse; a key to the motor room for repairs; and a key that opens the doors from the outside.

"Got it!" I yell, and tear back up the stairs, right behind Jessica, who has run back up the stairs to call the elevator to the first floor and hold it there.

When I get to the reception desk, I tear open the door and rush through it, heading straight for the key cabinet, which is supposed to remain locked at all times—only the desk worker on duty is allowed to hold the key.

But with the building maintenance staff, and resident assistants constantly borrowing keys so they can make repairs, clean, or let locked-out students into their rooms, the key cabinet is rarely, if ever, locked, the way it's supposed to be. I find the doors to it yawning wide open as I flash by Tina, the desk worker on duty.

"What's going on?" Tina asks, nervously. "Is it true there's another one? At the bottom of the elevator shaft?"

I ignore her. That's because I'm concentrating. I'm concentrating because I have found the elevator override key, and the key to the motor room.

But the key to the elevator doors is gone.

And when I check the sign-out sheet hanging on the door to the key cabinet, there is no signature for it, or any indication it was ever checked out in the first place.

"Where's the key?" I demand, swinging on Tina. "Who has the elevator door key?"

"I—I d-don't know," Tina stammers. "It wasn't there when I came on duty. You can check my duty sheet!"

Another change to the way Justine had run things that I'd implemented upon being hired—besides the key sign-out sheet—was forcing the desk workers to keep a log of what happened during the shift. If someone borrowed a key—even if they signed it out—the desk worker was still supposed to record the fact on his or her duty sheet. And the first thing a desk worker was supposed to do upon arriving at the desk was jot down which keys were in and which were out.

"Then who has it?" I cry, grabbing the logbook and flipping to the previous desk worker's duty sheet.

But while there are entries for every other key taken during the previous worker's shift, there's nothing about the elevator door key.

"I don't know!" Tina's voice is rising to dangerously hysterical levels. "I swear I didn't give it out to anyone!"

I believe her. But that doesn't help the situation.

I whirl around to run back downstairs and tell Carl to break down the doors, if he has to. But my way is blocked by President Allington who, along with some other administrative types, has come out of the cafeteria to see what all the commotion's about.

"We're trying to have an event in there, you know," is what he snaps to me.

"Yeah?" I hear myself snapping back. "Well, we're trying to save someone's life out here, you know."

I don't stick around to hear what he has to say in reply to

that. I've grabbed the first aid kit from the desk and am racing back down the stairs . . . only to encounter Pete, looking pale, making his way slowly back up them.

"I couldn't find the key," I say. "Someone's got it. He's going to have to force the doors open . . ."

But Pete is shaking his head.

"He already did," Pete says, taking my arm. "Come on back upstairs."

"But I've got the kit," I say, waving the red plastic case. "Is—"

"She's gone," Pete says. Now he's pulling on me. "Come on. And don't look. You don't want to look."

I believe him.

I let him steer me up the stairs. As we enter the lobby, I see that the president is still there, standing around with some basketball players and the same administrators in their gray suits. Beside them, Magda, who has emerged from behind her cash register to see what's going on, makes a bright splash of color in her pink smock and fuchsia hot pants.

Magda takes one look at my expression, and her face crumples. "Oh no! Not another of my movie stars!"

Pete ignores her, goes to the phone by the security desk, and holding up a key chain, on which is attached a student ID card—and a little rubber replica of the cartoon character Ziggy—begins reading the information from the ID card to his superiors at the security office.

"Roberta Pace," he reads tonelessly. "Fischer Hall resident. First year. ID number five five seven, three nine—"

I stand a little ways from both the security and the reception desks, feeling myself begin to shake. I don't know the name. I don't ask to see the photo on the ID. I don't want to know if I knew the face.

It's right then that Rachel rounds the corner from the ladies' room.

"What's going on?" she asks, her gaze going from my face to Pete's to President Allington's.

It's Tina, behind the desk, who speaks.

"Another one fell off the top of the elevator," she says, in a small voice. "She's dead."

Rachel's face drains of all its color beneath her carefully applied MAC foundation.

But when she speaks a few seconds later, there is no tremor in her voice. "I assume the authorities have been notified? Good. Do we have an ID? Oh, thank you, Pete. Tina, beep Maintenance, and have them turn off all the elevators. Heather, can you call Dr. Jessup's office, and let them know what's going on? President Allington, I am so sorry about this. Please, go back to your breakfast . . ."

Aware that I'm shaking and that my heart is beating a million times a minute, I slip back to my office to start making calls.

Only this time, instead of calling Dr. Jessup's office first, I call Cooper.

"Cartwright Investigations," he says, because I've called him on his office line, hoping he'd be there.

"It's me," I say. I keep my voice down, because Sarah is in Rachel's office next door, calling each of the resident assistants on their cell phones and telling them what's happened, then asking them to come back to their floors as soon as possible. "There's been another one."

"Another what?" Cooper asks. "And why are you whispering?"

"Another death by elevator," I whisper.

"Are you serious?"

"Yeah," I say.

"Dead?"

I think about Pete's face.

"Yeah," I say.

"Jesus, Heather. I'm sorry."

"Yeah," I say, for the third and final time. "Listen . . . could you come over?"

"Come over? What for?"

The firemen from Ladder #9 come striding past our office door just then, in their helmets and coats. One of them is carrying an axe. Obviously, no one told New York's bravest what the nature of the emergency was when they called.

"Downstairs," I say to them, pointing to the stairs to the basement. "Another, um, elevator incident."

The captain looks surprised, but nods and leads what has suddenly turned into a very grim procession past the reception desk and down the stairs.

To Cooper, I whisper, "I want to get to the bottom of what is going on over here, and I could use the help of a professional investigator, Cooper."

"Whoa," Cooper says. "Slow down there, slugger. Are the police there? Aren't they professional investigators?"

"The police are just going to say the same thing about this one that they did about the last one," I say. "That she was elevator surfing, and slipped."

"Because that's probably what happened, Heather."

"No," I say. "No, not this time. Definitely not this time."

"Why? Is this latest one preppie too?"

"I don't know," I say. "But that's not funny."

"I didn't mean it to be funny. I just—"

"She liked Ziggy, Coop." My voice cracks a little, but I don't care.

"She liked what?"

"Ziggy. That cartoon character."

"I've never heard of it."

"Because it's like the uncoolest cartoon character ever. No one who likes Ziggy is going to elevator surf, Coop. *No one*."

"Heather—"

"And that's not all," I whisper, as Sarah's voice drifts from Rachel's office, self-importantly intoning, "We need you to come back to the building as soon as possible. There's been another death. I am not at liberty to reveal the details just now, but it's imperative that you—"

"Someone took the key," I tell Cooper.

"What key?" he wants to know.

"The key that opens the elevator doors." I am losing it. I know I am. I am practically crying. But I struggle to keep my voice from shaking. "No one signed it out, Coop. You're supposed to sign it out. But they didn't. Which means whoever has it doesn't want anyone to know. Which means whoever has it can open the elevator doors anytime they want . . . even if there's no car there."

"Heather." Cooper says, in a voice I can't, even in my agitated state, help finding incredibly soothing. And sexy. "This is something you need to tell the police. Right away."

"Okay," I say, in a small voice. In Rachel's office, Sarah is going, "I don't care if it's your grandmother's birthday, Alex. There's been a *death* in the building. Which is more important to you: your grandmother's birthday, or your job?"

"Go tell the police exactly what you told me," Cooper's soothing, sexy voice is saying in my ear. "And then go get a big cup of coffee with lots of milk and sugar in it and drink it all while it's still hot."

This last part surprises me. "Why?" I say.

"Because I have found in my line of work that sweet milky drinks are good for shock when there is no whiskey available. Okay?"

"Okay. Bye."

I hang up, and then I call Dr. Jessup, and explain to his assistant—because she says Dr. Jessup is in a meeting—what's happened. Upon hearing the news, his assistant, Jill, says, in an appropriately panicked voice, "Oh my God. I'll let him know right away."

I thank her and hang up. Then I stare at the phone.

Cooper is right. I need to tell the police about the key.

I tell Sarah I'll be back in a minute, and leave the office. I walk out into the lobby—and find it a sea of confusion. Basketball players mingle with firemen. Administrators are on every available phone, including Pete's and the one at the reception desk, doing damage control. Rachel is nodding her head as the fire chief tells her something.

I glance toward the front door of the building. The same police officer who'd been there the day Elizabeth died is standing there again, not letting any of the kids outside back into the building.

"You'll get back in when I say you'll get back in," the cop is snarling at a skinhead with a lip ring who is going, "But I have to get to my room to get my project! If I don't turn in my project by noon, I'll get an F!"

"Excuse me," I say to the cop. "Can you tell me who is in charge here?"

The cop glances at me, then jerks a thumb in Rachel's direction.

"Near as I can tell, that one over there," he says.

"No," I say. "I mean, is there a detective, or—"

"Oh yeah." The cop nods toward a tall, gray-haired man in a brown corduroy jacket and plaid tie who is leaning against the wall—and, though he probably doesn't know it, getting glitter all down his back, since he's brushing up against a poster urging students to attend an audition for *Pippin* that is heavy on the Elmer's glued glitter. Except for an unlit cigar at the corner of his mouth that he appears to be chewing on, he is doing absolutely nothing at all.

"Detective Canavan," the cop says.

"Thanks," I say to the cop, who is telling another resident, "I don't care if you're bleeding out the eyes. You're not getting back into this building until I say so."

I approach the detective with my heart in my throat. I've never spoken to a detective before. Well, except for when I was pressing grand larceny charges against my mom.

"Detective Canavan?" I ask.

I realize at once that my first impression—that he is doing nothing—was totally wrong. Detective Canavan isn't doing nothing at all. He is staring fixedly at my boss's legs, which look quite shapely beneath her pencil skirt.

He rips his gaze from Rachel's legs and looks at me instead. He has a bristly gray mustache that actually looks quite good on him. Facial hair so rarely flatters.

"Yeah?" he says, in a smoke-roughened voice.

"Hi," I say. "I'm Heather Wells. I'm the assistant director here at Fischer Hall. And, um, I just want to tell someone— the elevator key is missing. It might not mean anything— keys go missing here all the time. But I just thought someone should know. Because it seems really weird to me, these girls dying from elevator surfing. Because, you know, girls just don't. Elevator surf. In my experience."

Detective Canavan, who has listened attentively to my whole speech, waits until my voice peters out before taking the cigar from his mouth and pointing it at me.

" 'Sugar Rush,' right?" he says.

I am so surprised, my jaw becomes unhinged. I finally manage to stammer, "Um, yes."

"Thought so." The cigar goes back between his teeth. "My

kid had a poster of you up on the door to her bedroom. Had to look at you in that damned miniskirt every time I went to tell her to turn down her damned stereo."

Since there is absolutely no reply I can make to this statement, I remain silent.

"What the hell are you doing," Detective Canavan asks, "working here?"

"It's a long story," I say, really hoping he's not going to make me tell it.

He doesn't.

"As my daughter would say," Detective Canavan says, "back when she was your biggest fan, *Whatever*. Now what's this about a missing key?"

I explain it to him again. I also mention, in passing, the part about Elizabeth being a preppie, and Roberta liking Ziggy, and how both of these facts made them highly unlikely candidates for elevator surfing. But mostly I dwell on the missing key.

"Lemme get this straight," Detective Canavan says, when I'm done. "You don't think these girls—who were both, if I understand it, freshmen, new to the city, and full of what my daughter, the French major, calls the *joie de vivre*—were going for joyrides on top of your building's elevator cars at all. You think someone is going around, opening the elevator doors when there's no car there, and pushing these girls down the shaft to their deaths. Have I got that right?"

Hearing it put like that, I realize how stupid my theory sounds. More than stupid. Idiotic, even.

Except . . . except Ziggy!

"Let's just say you're right," Detective Canavan says. "How did whoever is doing this get the elevator key in the first place? You said you guys keep it in a lockbox behind—what is it? That desk there?"

"Yeah," I say.

"And who has access back there? Anybody?"

"No," I say. "Just the student workers and building staff."

"So you think some guy who works for you is going around, killing girls? Which guy, huh?" He points at Pete, standing behind the guard's desk, speaking to one of the firemen. "That one there? Or what about that guy?" He points at Carl, who is still visibly pale, but is nevertheless describing what he'd seen at the bottom of the shaft to a uniformed police officer.

"Okay," I say, starting to feel like I want to die. Because I realize how stupid I was being. In about five seconds, this guy had shot so many holes in my theory, it looked like a big chunk of Swiss cheese.

But still.

"Okay, so, maybe you're right. But maybe—"

"Maybe you better show me where you keep this missing key," Detective Canavan says, and straightens up. I am delighted, as I follow him toward the reception desk, to see that I was right: There is pink glitter all over his shoulders, as if he's been fairy-dusted.

As we approach the reception desk, I see that Tina has disappeared. I throw a questioning look at Pete.

"Packages," Pete interrupts his conversation with the fireman to say to me, meaning that Tina is escorting the mail carrier to the room down the hall where we lock arriving packages until the students can be notified to come down to the desk to claim them.

I nod. Rain or shine, sleet or snow, the mail must get through . . . even if there's a girl lying dead at the bottom of the elevator shaft.

I slip behind the desk, ignoring the phones, which are ringing off the hook, and head straight for the key cabinet.

"This is where we keep the keys," I explain to Detective Canavan, who has followed me through the door to the reception desk and now stands with me behind the counter. The key box is large and metal, mounted to the wall. Inside the box is hanging rack after hanging rack of keys. There are three hundred of them, one spare for every room in the building, plus assorted keys that are for staff use only. They all look basically the same, except for the key to the elevator doors, which is shaped a little like an Allen wrench, and not a typical key at all.

"So to get at them, you have to get back here," Detective Canavan says. I don't miss the fact that his gray eyebrows have raised at the sight of all the mail bags, slumped haphazardly on the floor at our feet. The desk is hardly what you'd call the most secure area in the building. "And to get back here, you have to pass the security desk, which is manned twenty-four hours a day."

"Right," I say. "The security guards know who is allowed behind the desk and who isn't. They're not going to let someone go back here unless they work here. And usually there's a worker behind the counter, anyway, who wouldn't let anybody have access to the keys unless he or she was staff. And even then, we make them sign them out. The keys, I mean. But no one signed the elevator key out. It's just . . . gone."

"Yeah," Detective Canavan says. "You said that. Listen, I got some real crimes—including a triple stabbing in an apartment over a deli on Broadway—that I need to investigate. But please, show me where this elusive key, which could prove that the young lady in question didn't die accidentally, normally hangs."

I flip through the hanging racks, thinking that I'm going to kill Cooper. I mean, I can't believe he talked me into doing this. This guy doesn't believe me. It's bad enough he's seen that poster of me from *Sugar Rush*. If there's anything that can undermine a person's credibility, it's a life-sized poster of her in a pastel tiger print mini screaming into a microphone at the Mall of America.

And okay, my conviction that girls don't elevator surf—particularly preppie, Ziggy-loving girls—may not be what anyone could call rock-solid proof. But what about the missing key? What about THAT?

Except that, as I flip to the rack that normally holds the elevator door key, I see something that makes my blood run cold.

Because there, in the exact place it's supposed to go—the exact place it wasn't, just moments ago—is the elevator door key.

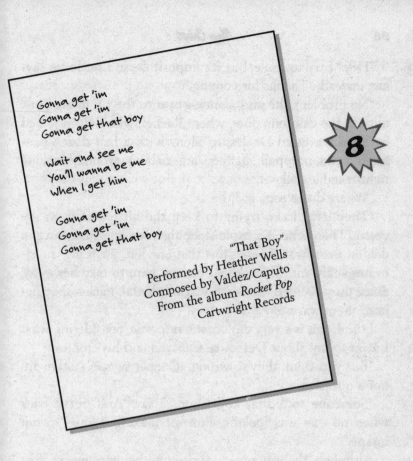

Gonna get 'im
Gonna get 'im
Gonna get that boy

Wait and see me
You'll wanna be me
When I get him

Gonna get 'im
Gonna get 'im
Gonna get that boy

"That Boy"
Performed by Heather Wells
Composed by Valdez/Caputo
From the album *Rocket Pop*
Cartwright Records

He says he'll be here in five minutes, but he's in the lobby in less than three.

He's never been inside the building before, and looks strangely out of place in it . . . maybe because he isn't tattooed or pierced like everyone else who passes by the desk.

Or maybe it's just because he's so much better-looking than everybody else, standing there with his bed-rumpled hair (although I know he's been up for hours—he runs in the morning) and his banged-up leather jacket and jeans.

"Hey," he says when he sees me.

"Hey." I try to smile, but it's impossible, so I settle for saying, instead, "Thanks for coming."

"No problem," he says, glancing over to the TV lounge, just outside the cafeteria door, where Rachel, who'd been joined by an ashen-faced Dr. Jessup, along with a half-dozen panicked residence hall staffers, are milling around, looking tight-faced and upset.

"Where'd the cops go?" he asks.

"They left," I say, trying to keep the bitterness from my voice. "There's been a triple stabbing in an apartment over a deli on Broadway. There's just that one left, guarding the elevator shaft until the coroner can get here to take her away. Since they decided her death was accidental, I guess they figured there was no reason to stay."

I think this is a very diplomatic response, considering what I *want* to say about Detective Canavan and his cronies.

"But you think they're wrong," Cooper says. A statement, not a question.

"Someone took that key, Coop," I say. "And put it back when no one was looking. I'm not making it up. I'm not insane."

Although, the way my voice rises on the word *insane*, that claim may actually be debatable.

But Cooper's not here to debate it.

"I know," he says gently. "I believe you. I'm here, aren't I?"

"I know," I say, regretting my outburst. "And thanks. Well. Let's go."

Cooper looks hesitant. "Wait. Go where?"

"Roberta's room," I say. I hold up the master key I've swiped from the key box. "I think we should check her room first."

"For what?"

"I don't know," I say. "But we have to start somewhere."

Cooper looks at the key, then back at me.

"I want you to know," Cooper says, "that I think this is a bad idea."

"I know," I say. Because I do.

"So why are we doing it?"

I am about five seconds from bursting into tears. I've felt this way since Jessica first burst into my office with the news about another death, and my humiliation in front of Detective Canavan hasn't helped the matter any.

But I struggle to keep the hysteria from my voice.

"Because this is happening in *my* building. It's happening to *my* girls. And I want to be sure it's happening the way these cops and everyone are saying it's happening, and that it's not . . . you know. What I'm thinking."

"Heather," he says. "Remember when 'Sugar Rush' first came out, and all that fan mail started arriving at the Cartwright Records offices, and you insisted on reading it all, and personally answering it?"

I bristle. I can't help it.

"Hello," I say. "I was fifteen."

"It doesn't matter," Cooper says. "Because in fifteen years, you haven't changed. You still feel personally responsible for every person with whom you come in contact—even people you've never met. Like the reason you were put on earth is to look out for everybody else on it."

"That's not true," I say. "And it's only been *thirteen* years."

"Heather," he says, ignoring me. "Sometimes kids do stupid things. And then other kids, because they are, in fact, just kids, imitate them. And they die. It happens. It doesn't mean a crime has been committed."

"Yeah?" I am bristling more than ever. "What about the key? What about *that*?"

He still doesn't look convinced.

"I want you to know," he says, "that I'm only doing this to keep you from making an even bigger mess out of things than they're already in—something, by the way, at which you seem to excel."

"You know, Coop," I say. "I appreciate that vote of confidence. I really do."

"I just don't want you to lose your day job," he says. "I can't afford to give you health benefits on top of room and board."

"Thanks," I say snarkily. "Thanks so much."

But it doesn't matter. Because he comes with me.

It's a long, long walk up to Roberta Pace's room at the six-teenth floor. We can't, of course, take the elevator, because they've been shut down. The only sound I hear, when we finally reach the long, empty hallway, is the sound of our own breathing. Mine, in particular, is heavy.

Other than that, it's quiet. Dead quiet. Then again, it's before noon. Most of the residents—the ones who hadn't been awakened by the ambulance and fire engine sirens—are still sleeping off last night's beer.

I point the way with my set of keys and start toward 1622. Cooper follows me, looking around at the posters on the hallway walls urging students to go to Health Services if they're concerned that they might have contracted a sexually transmitted disease, or informing them of a free movie night over at the student center.

The RA on sixteen has this thing for Snoopy. Cut-out Snoopys are everywhere. There's even this posterboard Snoopy holding a real little cardboard tray with an arrow pointing to it that says, "Free Condoms Courtesy of New York College Health Services: Hey, for $40,000 a year, students should get something free!"

The tray is, of course, empty.

On the door to 1622, there is a yellow memo board, the

erasable kind, with nothing written on it. There's also a Ziggy sticker.

But someone has given Ziggy a pierced nose and someone else has written in a balloon over Ziggy's head, "Where Are My Pants?"

I raise my set of keys and bang on the door, hard, with them.

"Director's Office," I call. "Anybody there?"

There's no response. I call out once more, then slide the key into the lock and open the door.

Inside, an electric fan on top of a chest of drawers hums noisily, in spite of the fact that the room, like all the rooms in Fischer Hall, has central air conditioning. Except for the fan, nothing else moves. There is no sign of Roberta's roommate, who is going to be in for quite a shock when she gets back from wherever she's gone, and finds herself with a single room for the rest of the year.

There's only one window, six feet across and another five feet or so high, with twin cranks to open the panes. In the distance, past the garden rooftops and water towers, I can see the Hudson, flowing serenely along its way, the sun's rays slanting off its mirrored surface.

Cooper's squinting at some family photographs on one of the girls' bedstands. He says, "The dead girl. What's her name?"

"Roberta," I say.

"Then this bed's hers." She's had her name done in rainbow letters on a sheet of scroll paper by a street artist. It is hanging over the messier bed, the one by the window. Both beds have been slept in, and neither roommate appears to have been much concerned with housekeeping. The sheets are tousled and the coverlets—mismatched, as roommates' coverlets so often are—are awry. There is a strong Ziggy motif in the decorating on Roberta's side of the room. There are Ziggy Post-it Notes everywhere, and a Ziggy calendar on the wall, and on one of the desks, a set of Ziggy stationery.

Both girls, I notice, are Jordan Cartwright fans. They have the complete set of Easy Street CDs, plus *Baby, Be Mine*.

Neither of them owns a single CD by yours truly. Which is no real surprise, I guess. I was always way more popular with the tween set.

Cooper gets down onto his knees and starts looking under the dead girl's bed. This is very distracting. I try to concentrate on snooping, but Cooper's butt is a particularly nice one. Seeing it so nicely cupped by his worn Levi's as he leans over, it is kind of hard to pay attention to anything else, even though, you know, this is very serious business, and all.

"Look at this," he says, as he pulls his head and shoulders from beneath Roberta's bed, his dark hair tousled. I quickly readjust my gaze so it doesn't look like I'd been staring below his waist. I hope he doesn't notice.

"What?" I ask intelligently.

"Look."

Dangling from the end of a Ziggy pencil Cooper pulled from the pencil jar on Roberta's desk is a pale, limp thing. Upon closer examination, I realize what it is.

A used condom.

"Um," I say. "Ew."

"It's pretty fresh," Cooper says. "I'd say Roberta had a hot date last night."

With his free hand, he picks up an envelope from the pack of Ziggy stationery sitting on Roberta's desk, then drops the condom into it.

"What are you doing?" I ask in alarm. "Isn't that tampering with evidence?"

"Evidence of what?" Cooper folds the envelope over a couple of times, and sticks it in the pocket of his coat. "The police already determined there hasn't been a crime committed."

"Well, so what are you saving it for?"

Cooper shrugs and tosses away the pencil. "One thing I learned in this line of work: You just never know."

He looks around Roberta's room and shakes his head. "It does seem weird. Who has sex, then goes elevator surfing? I could maybe see it if it were the other way around—you know, all the adrenaline, or whatever, from risking your life, making you randy. But before? Unless it's some kinky sex thing."

I widen my eyes. "You mean like the guy likes to have sex with a girl, then pushes her off the top of the elevator?"

"Something like that." Cooper looks uncomfortable. He doesn't like talking about kinky sex practices with me, and changes the subject. "What about the other girl? The first one. You said you checked, and she hadn't signed anyone in the night she died?"

"No," I say. "But I checked just before you got here, and Roberta didn't sign in anyone last night, either." Then I think of something. "If . . . if there'd been something like that in Elizabeth's room—a condom or something, I mean—the cops would have found it, right?"

"Not if they weren't looking for it. And if they were really convinced her death was accidental, like this last one, they wouldn't have even looked."

I chew my lower lip. "Nobody's moved into Elizabeth's space. Her roommate has the place to herself now. We could go take a look at it."

Cooper looks dubious.

"I will admit it's weird about this kid dying the way she did, Heather," he says. "Especially in light of the condom and the key thing. But what you're implying—"

"You implied it first," I remind him. "Besides, we can *look*, can't we? Who's it going to hurt?"

"Even if we did, it's been a week since she died," he points out. "I doubt we're going to find anything."

"We won't know unless we try," I say, starting for the door. "Come on."

Cooper just looks at me.

"Why is proving that these girls didn't cause their own deaths so important to you?" he demands.

I blink at him. "What?"

"You heard me. Why are you so determined to prove these girls' deaths weren't accidental?"

I can't tell him, of course. Because I don't want to sound like what Sarah would be bound to brand me if she knew— a psychopath. Which is how I know I *would* sound, if I told him what I feel . . . which is that I owe it to the building—to Fischer Hall itself—to figure out what's really going on in it. Because Fischer Hall has—like Cooper—saved my life, in a way.

Well, okay, all they've saved me from is waitressing for the rest of my life at a Senor Swanky's.

But isn't that enough? I know it doesn't make any sense— that Sarah would accuse me of transferring my affection for my parents or my ex onto a pile of bricks built in 1850—but I really do feel that I have a responsibility to prove what's happening isn't Fischer Hall's fault—the staff, for not notic- ing these girls were on a downward spiral, or whatever—or the girls, who seem too sensible to do something so stupid— or even the building itself, for not being homey enough, or whatever. The school newspaper had already run one "in- depth" report on the dangers of elevator surfing. Who knows what it was going to print tomorrow?

See. I said it's stupid.

Still, it's how I feel.

But I can't explain it to Cooper. I know there's no point in my even trying.

"Because girls don't elevator surf" is all I can come up with.

At first I think he's going to walk out, the way Detective Canavan did, without another word, furious at me for wasting his time.

But instead all he does is sigh and say, "Fine. I guess we've got another room to check."

9

Shake Your Pom-Pom
Shake Your Pom-Pom
Shake it, baby
All night long

"Shake It"
Performed by Heather Wells
Composed by O'Brien/Henke
From the album *Rocket Pop*
Cartwright Records

Elizabeth Kellogg's roommate opens the door to 1412 at my first knock. She's wearing a big white T-shirt and black leggings and she's holding a portable phone in one hand and a burning cigarette in the other.

I plaster a smile on my face and go, "Hi, I'm Heather. This is—"

"Hi," the roommate interrupts me to say, her eyes growing wide as she notices Cooper for the first time.

Well, and why not? She's a healthy red-blooded American girl, after all. And Cooper does bear more than a slight resemblance to one of America's most popular male heart-throbs.

"Cooper Cartwright," Cooper says, flashing the roommate a grin that, if I hadn't known better, I'd have sworn he'd practiced in the mirror and reserved only for extreme cases like this one.

Except Cooper is not a practicing-smiles-in-the-mirror type of guy.

"Marnie Villa Delgado," the roommate says. Marnie's a big girl like me, only larger in the chest than in the tush, with a lot of very dark, very curly long hair. I can tell she's sizing me up, the way some women will, wondering if I'm "with" Cooper, or if he's fair game.

"We were wondering, Marnie, if we could have a word or two with you about your former roommate, Elizabeth," Cooper says, revealing so many teeth with his grin, he nearly blinds me.

But not Marnie, since, apparently deciding Cooper and I are not an item (how could she tell? Really? How come other girls—like Marnie and Rachel and Sarah—know how to do this, but I don't?), she says, into the phone, "I gotta go," and hangs up.

Then, her gaze fastened hypnotically on Cooper, she says, "Come on in."

I slip past her, Cooper following me. Marnie, I see at once, has done a pretty fast job of redecorating after Elizabeth's death. The twin beds have been shoved together to form one king-sized bed, covered by a giant tiger-striped bedspread. The two chests of drawers have been stacked one on top of the other so Marnie now has eight drawers all to herself, instead of four, and Elizabeth's desk is currently being employed as an entertainment unit, with a TV, DVD player, and CD player all within arm's reach of the bed.

"I already talked to the police about her." Marnie flicks ashes onto the tiger-striped throw rug beneath her bare feet and turns her attention momentarily from Cooper to me. "Beth, I mean. Hey. Wait a minute. Don't I know you? Aren't you an actress or something?"

"Me? No," I answer truthfully.

"But you're in the entertainment industry." Marnie's tone is confident. "Hey, are you guys making a movie of Beth's life?"

Before Cooper can utter a sound, I ask, "Why? You think, uh, Beth's life has cinematic potential?"

Marnie's trying to play it cool, but I hear her cough as she takes a drag from her cigarette. She's definitely a for-dramatic-effect-only smoker.

"Oh yeah. I mean, I can see the angle you'd want to work from. Small-town girl comes to the big city, can't take it, gets herself killed on a stupid dare. Can I play myself? I totally have the experience . . ."

Cooper blows our cover, though, by going, "We're not with the entertainment industry. Heather's the assistant director of this building, and I'm a friend of hers."

"But I thought—" Marnie is really staring at me now, trying to remember where she's seen me before. "I thought you were an actress. I've seen you somewhere before—"

"At check-in, I'm sure," I say hastily.

"Your roommate," Cooper says, looking up from a survey he seems to be making of the small kitchen area, in which Marnie has stowed a microwave, hot plate, food processor, coffee maker, and one of those scales people on diets use to measure the weight of their chicken breasts. "Where was she from?"

"Well," Marnie says. "Mystic. You know, Connecticut."

Cooper is opening cupboards now, but Marnie is so confused, she doesn't even protest.

"Hey, I know. You were on *Saved by the Bell*, weren't you?" she asks me.

"No," I say. "You said Eliz—I mean, Beth—hated it here?"

"Well, no, not really," Marnie says. "Beth just didn't fit in, you know? I mean, she wanted to be a *nurse*."

Cooper looks at her. I can tell he doesn't hang around New York College students much, because he asks her, "What's wrong with nurses?"

"Why would anybody come to New York College to study to be a *nurse*?" Marnie's tone is scornful. "Why pay all that money to study here when you can go some place, you know, *cheap* to study to be a nurse?"

"What's *your* major?" Cooper asks.

"Me?" Marnie looks as if she wants to say the word *Duh*, but doesn't want to be rude. To Cooper. Instead, she grounds out her cigarette in an ashtray shaped like a human hand and says, "Acting." Then she sits down on her new king-sized bed and stares at me. "I know I've seen you somewhere before."

I pick up the hand ashtray to distract her—both from trying to place me and from noticing what Cooper is doing, which is some major snoopage.

"Is this yours or Elizabeth's?" I ask her, even though I already know the answer.

"Mine," Marnie says. "Of course. They took all of Beth's stuff away. Besides, Beth didn't smoke. Beth didn't do anything."

"What do you mean, she didn't do anything?"

"What I said. She didn't do anything. She didn't go out. She didn't have friends over. And her mother—what a trip! You hear what she did at the memorial service? The mother?"

Cooper is scouting out the bathroom. His voice, as he calls out from there, is muffled.

"What did she do?" he asks.

Marnie starts fishing around in this black leather backpack on the bed.

"Spent the whole thing saying she was going to sue New York College for not making the elevators more surf proof. And what are you doing in my bathroom?"

"I understand Elizabeth's mother wanted her daughter's guest privileges to extend only to females," I say, ignoring her question about Cooper's presence in her bathroom.

"Beth never said anything to me about that." Marnie finds her cigarette pack. It is, thankfully, empty. She tosses it on the floor and looks annoyed. "But I wouldn't be surprised. That girl was like from another century, practically. I don't think Beth'd ever even *kissed* a guy until a week or two before she died."

Cooper appears in the bathroom doorway. He looks way too big to fit through it, but he manages, somehow.

"Who?" I ask, before he has the chance to butt in. "What guy?"

"I don't know." Marnie shrugs, bereft without her cigarettes. They made nice props, since she was playing the grieving roommate, and all.

"There was this guy she was going on about, right before she . . . you know." Marnie makes a whistling sound and points at the floor. "Anyway, they'd just met. But when she talked about him, her whole face kinda . . . I don't know how to explain it."

"Did you ever see this guy?" I ask. "Do you know his name? Did he go to the memorial service? Was he the one who talked Elizabeth into elevator surfing?"

Marnie balks. "Jesus, you ask a lot of questions!"

Cooper comes to the rescue. As always.

"Marnie, this is really important. Do you have any idea who this guy was?"

For me, she balks. For Cooper, she is more than willing to try.

"Let's see." Marnie screws up her face. She isn't pretty, but she has an interesting face. Maybe good for character roles. The chubby best friend.

Why is the best friend always chubby? Why isn't the heroine ever chubby? Or, you know, not chubby, but a size 12? Or maybe even a 14? Why does the heroine always wear a size 2?

"Yeah, she said his name was like Mark, or something," Marnie says, breaking in on my thoughts on sizeism in the entertainment industry. "But I never saw him. I mean, they started going out just a week or so before she died. He took her to the movies. Some foreign film at the Angelika. That's why I thought it was so strange—"

"What?" I shake my head. "That what was so strange?"

"Well, I mean, that a guy who liked, you know, *foreign* films would be into elevator surfing. That's so . . . juvenile. The *freshmen* guys are into it. You know, the ones with the baggy pants, who look about twelve years old? But this guy was older. You know. Sophisticated. According to Beth. So what was he doing, encouraging her to jump around on top of an elevator?"

I sit down next to Marnie on the enormous bed.

"Did she tell you that?" I ask. "Did she tell you he wanted her to go elevator surfing with him?"

"No," Marnie says. "But he had to have, right? I mean, she'd never have gone alone. I doubt she even knew what it was."

"Maybe she went with some of those freshmen guys you mentioned," Cooper suggests.

Marnie makes a face. "No way," she says. "Those guys'd never have invited her along with them. They're too cool— or think they are—to be interested in someone like her. Besides, if she'd been with them, she wouldn't have fallen. Those guys wouldn't have let her. They're good at it."

"You weren't here, were you, the night she died?" I ask.

"Me? No, I had an audition. We aren't supposed to audition as freshmen, you know"—she looks sly—"but I figured I had a good shot. I mean, come on. It's Broadway. If I got into a Broadway show, I'd quit this place in a New York minute."

"So Elizabeth had the room to herself that night?" I ask.

"Yeah. She was having him over. The guy. She was real excited about it. You know, she was making a romantic dinner for two on the hot plate." Marnie looks suspicious. "Hey— you're not going to tell, are you? That we have a hot plate? I know it's a fire hazard, but—"

"The guy, Mark," I interrupt. "Or whatever his name was. Did he show? That night?"

"Yeah," Marnie says. "At least, I assume he did. They were gone by the time I got home, but they left the dinner plates in the sink. I had to do them, to keep them from attracting bugs. You know, you would think for what we're paying to live here, you guys would have regular exterminators—"

"Did anyone else meet him?" Cooper interrupts. "This Mark guy? Any of your mutual friends?"

"Beth and I didn't have any mutual friends," Marnie says, a bit scathingly. "I told you, she was a loser. I mean, I was her roommate, but I wouldn't have *hung out* with her. I didn't even find out she was dead until, like twenty-four hours after the fact. She never came back to the room that night. I just figured, you know, she was over at the guy's place."

"Did you tell this to the police?" Cooper asks. "About Elizabeth having the guy over the night she died?"

"Yeah," Marnie says, with a shrug. "They didn't seem to care. I mean, it's not like the guy murdered her. She died because of her own stupidity. I mean, I don't care how much wine you've had, you don't jump around on top of an elevator—"

I suck in my breath. "They were drinking? Mark and your roommate?"

"Yeah," Marnie says. "I found the bottles in the trash. Two of them. Pretty expensive, too. Mark must have brought them. They were, like, twenty bucks each. The guy's a big spender, for someone who lives in a hellhole like this."

I catch my breath.

"Wait—he lives in Fischer Hall?"

"Yeah. I mean, he'd have to, wouldn't he? 'Cause she never had to sign him in."

Good grief! I'd never thought of this! That Beth might actually have had a boy in her room, but that there was no record of her having signed one in, because he hadn't *had* to be signed in. He lives in the building! He's a resident of Fischer Hall, too!

I look up at Cooper. I'm not sure where all this was leading, but I have a pretty good idea that it's leading somewhere . . . somewhere important. I can't tell if he feels the same, though.

"Marnie," I say. "Is there anything, anything else at all that you can tell us about this guy your roommate was seeing?"

"All I can tell you," Marnie says, sounding annoyed, "is what I already said—that his name is Mark or something, he likes foreign films, has expensive taste in wine, and that I'm pretty sure he lives here. Oh, and Beth kept saying how cute he was. But how cute could he be? I mean, why would a cute guy be interested in *Beth*? She was a dog."

The student-run newspaper, the *Washington Square Reporter*, had run a photo of Elizabeth the Monday after her death, a photo from the freshmen class yearbook, and Marnie, I'm sorry to say, wasn't exaggerating. Elizabeth hadn't been a pretty girl. No makeup, thick glasses, outdated, Farrah Fawcett–style hair, and a smile that was mostly gums.

Still, photos by school-hired photographers are never all that flattering, and I had assumed that Elizabeth was actually prettier than this photo indicated.

But maybe my assumption was wrong.

Or maybe, just maybe, Marnie's jealous because her roommate had a boyfriend, and she didn't.

Hey, it happens. You don't need a sociology degree—or a private investigator's license—to know that.

Cooper and I thank Marnie and leave—though we couldn't escape without Marnie launching, once again, into a chorus of I-*know*-I-know-you-from-somewhere. By the time we make it out into the hallway, I'm cursing, as I do nearly every day, my decision—or, I should say, my mom's decision—to forgo my secondary education for a career in the music industry.

Trudging back down the stairs in silence, I wonder if Cooper is right. *Am* I crazy? I mean, do I *really* think there's some psycho stalking the freshwomen of Fischer Hall, talking them into elevator surfing with him after having his way with them, then pushing them to their deaths?

When we reach the tenth-floor landing, I say, experimentally, "I once read this article in a magazine about thrill killers. You know, guys who murder for the fun of it."

"Sure," Cooper says dryly. "In the movies. It doesn't happen so often in real life. Most crimes are crimes of passion. People aren't really as sick as we like to imagine."

I look at him out of the corner of my eye. He has no idea how sick my imagination is. Like how at that very moment I was imagining knocking him down and ripping off all his clothes with my teeth.

I wasn't. Well, not really. But I could have been.

"Somebody should probably speak to the other girl's roommate," I say, resolutely pushing away my fantasy about Cooper's clothes and my teeth. "You know, the one who died today. Ask her about the condom. Maybe she knows who it belonged to."

Cooper looks down at me, those ultra-blue eyes boring into me.

"Let me guess," he says. "You think it might belong to a guy named Mark who likes foreign films and has expensive taste in Bordeaux."

"It won't hurt to ask."

"You got a guy on your staff who fits that description?" Cooper wants to know.

"Well," I say, thinking about it. "No. Not really."

"Then how'd he get the key from behind the reception desk?"

I frown.

"Haven't worked that part out yet, have you?" Cooper asks, before I can reply. "Look, Heather. There's more to this detective stuff than snooping around, asking questions. There's also knowing when there's actually something worth snooping around about. And I'm sorry, but I'm just not seeing it here."

I suck in my breath. "But . . . the condom! The mystery man!"

Cooper shakes his head. "It's sad about those girls. It really is. But think about how you were when you were eighteen, Heather. You did crazy things, too. Maybe not as crazy as climbing onto the roof of an elevator on a dare, but—"

"They didn't," I say, fiercely. "I'm telling you, those girls did not do that."

"Well, they ended up at the bottom of a shaft somehow," Cooper says. "And while I know you'd like to think it's because some evil man pushed them, there are nearly a thousand kids who live in this dorm, Heather. Don't you think one of them might have noticed a guy shoving his girlfriend down an elevator shaft? And don't you think that person would have told someone what they'd seen?"

I blink a few more times. "But . . . but . . ."

But I can't think of anything else to say.

Then he looks at his watch. "Look. I'm late for an appointment. Can we play *Murder, She Wrote* again later? Because I've got to go."

"Yeah," I say, faintly. "I guess."

"Okay. See you," he says. And continues down the stairs at a clip so fast, there's no way I'll catch up with him.

Though on the landing below, he stops, turns, and looks up at me. His eyes are amazingly blue.

"And just so you know," he says.

"Yes?" I lean eagerly over the stair railing. *The reason I'm so against you investigating this on your own*, I am expecting—well, okay, hoping—he'll say, *is because I can't stand the thought of you putting yourself in harm's way. You see, I love you, Heather. I always have.*

"We're out of milk," is what he says instead. "Pick some up on your way home, if you remember, okay?"

"Okay," I say weakly.

And then he's gone.

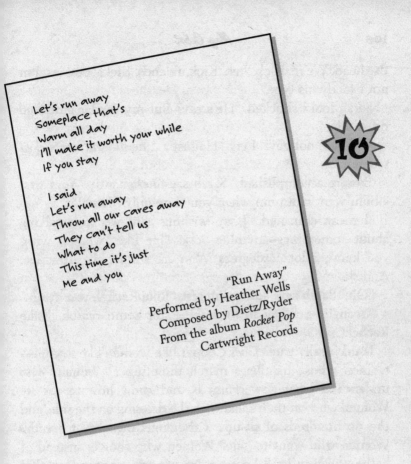

Let's run away
Someplace that's
Warm all day
I'll make it worth your while
If you stay

I said
Let's run away
Throw all our cares away
They can't tell us
What to do
This time it's just
Me and you

"Run Away"
Performed by Heather Wells
Composed by Dietz/Ryder
From the album *Rocket Pop*
Cartwright Records

10

"Who was that?" Sarah wants to know. "That guy who left just now?"

"That?" I slip behind my desk. "That was Cooper."

"Your *roommate*?" I guess Sarah has overheard me on the phone with him or something.

"Housemate," I say. "Well, landlord, really. I live in the top floor of his brownstone."

"So he's cute *and* rich?" Sarah is practically salivating. "Why haven't you jumped his bones?"

"We're just friends," I say, each word feeling like a kick in the head. We're. Kick. Just. Kick. Friends. Kick. "Besides, I'm not exactly his type."

Sarah looks shocked. "He's *gay*? But my gaydar didn't go off at all—"

"No, he's not gay!" I cry. "He just . . . he likes *accomplished* women."

"You're accomplished," Sarah says, indignantly. "Your first album went platinum when you were only fifteen!"

"I mean educated," I say, wishing hard we were talking about something—anything—else. "He likes women with, you know, a lot of degrees. Who are stunningly attractive. And skinny."

"Oh," Sarah says, losing interest. "Like Rachel, you mean."

"Yeah," I say, my heart sinking, for some reason. "Like Rachel."

Is that really true? *Does* Cooper like women like Rachel— women whose handbags match their shoes? Women who understand what PowerPoint is, and know how to use it? Women who eat their salad with the dressing on the side, and can do hundreds of sit-ups without getting out of breath? Women who went to Yale? Women who shower instead of bathe, the way I do, because I'm too lazy to stand up that long?

Before I have a chance to really think about it, Rachel comes running in, her dark hair mussed, but still sexy-looking, and says, "Oh, Heather, there you are. Where have you been?"

"I was upstairs with one of the investigators," I say. It's even true. Sort of. "They needed to get into the dead girl's room—"

"Oh," Rachel says, losing interest. "Well, now that you're back, could you call counseling services and see if they can see someone right away? Roberta's roommate is in a state—"

I perk right up.

"Sure," I say, reaching for my phone, my promise to Cooper that I would quit playing *Murder, She Wrote* promptly forgotten. "No problem. You want someone to walk her over there?"

"Oh, yes." Rachel may have been dealing with a tragedy, but you would never have known it to look at her. Her Diane von Furstenberg wrap dress clings to her lithe figure in all the right places, and none of the wrong ones (the way wrap dresses do on me) and there are bright spots of color in her cheeks. "Do you think you can find someone?"

"I'd be happy to help," I say.

Sure, I feel a twinge of guilt as I say it. I mean, that my willingness to lend a hand has more to do with a desire to question the dead girl's roommate than actually to help her.

But not enough to stop myself.

I call counseling services. Of course they've already heard about "the second tragedy," so they tell me to bring the roommate, Lakeisha Green, right over. One of my job responsibilities is personally to escort students who've been referred to counseling services to the building that houses it, because once a student who was sent over by herself got lost on the way and ended up in Washington Heights wearing her bra on her head and insisting that she was Cleopatra.

Seriously. You can't make this stuff up.

Lakeisha is sitting in a corner of the cafeteria under a kitten poster Magda had hung on the wall to brighten the place up, since, as Magda puts it, antique stained glass windows and mahogany wainscoting are just plain "ugly on the eye." Magda is there, too, trying to coax Lakeisha into eating some Gummi Bears.

"Just a few?" Magda is saying, as she dangles a plastic bag full of them in front of Lakeisha's face. "Please? You can have them for free. I know you like them, last night you bought a bag with your friends."

Lakeisha—just to be polite, you can tell—takes the bag. "Thank you," she murmurs.

Magda beams, then, when she notices me, whispers, "My poor little movie star. She won't eat a thing."

Then, in an even lower voice, Magda asks, "Who was that man Pete and I saw you with today, Heather? The handsome one?"

"That was Cooper," I say, since I've told Magda all about Cooper . . . as one does, naturally, discuss hotties over sloppy joes on one's lunch break.

"*That* was Cooper?" Magda looks aghast. "Oh, honey, no wonder—"

"No wonder what?"

"Oh, never mind." Magda pats me on the arm in a gesture that would have been comforting if I hadn't, you know, been terrified of being poked by one her nails. "It will turn out all right. Maybe."

"Uh, thanks." I'm not at all sure what she was talking about . . . or that I wanted to know. I turn my attention to Roberta Pace's roommate.

Lakeisha looks really, really sad. Her hair is done up in braids all over her head, and at the end of each braid is a brightly colored bead. The beads click together whenever Lakeisha moves her head.

"Lakeisha," I say, gently. "I understand you have an appointment to speak to someone at counseling services. I'm here to walk you there. Are you ready to go?"

Lakeisha nods. But she doesn't stand up. I glance at Magda.

"Maybe she wants a rest," Magda says. "Does my little movie star want a rest?"

Lakeisha hesitates a moment. Then she says, "No, it's okay. Let's go."

"You sure you don't want a DoveBar?" Magda asks. Because DoveBars are, actually, the solution to nearly every problem in the universe.

But Lakeisha just shakes her head, causing her hair beads to rattle musically.

Which is surely how she stays so skinny. Refusing Dove-Bars when offered, I mean. I can't remember ever turning down an offer of free ice cream. Especially a DoveBar.

Our walk out of the building is slow-paced and somber. They are letting students back into the building a few at a time, with the warning that they'll have to use the stairs to get to their rooms. As one might expect in such a small community, word of another death has spread fast, and when the students see Lakeisha and me leaving the building together, there is a lot of whispering—"That's the roommate," I hear, and someone else responding, "Oh, poor thing." Lakeisha either doesn't hear it or chooses to ignore it. She walks with her head held high, but her gaze lowered.

We're standing on the street corner, waiting for the crossing sign to change, when I finally get the courage to bring up what I want to know.

"Lakeisha," I say. "Do you know if Roberta had a date last night?"

Lakeisha looks over at me like she's seeing me for the first time. She's a tiny little thing, all cheekbones and knees. The little bag of Gummi Bears Magda had pressed on her, and which she still carries, seems to be weighing her down.

She says, "Excuse me?" in a soft voice.

"Your roommate. Did she have a date last night?"

"I think so. I don't really know," Lakeisha replies, in an apologetic whisper that's hard to hear above the sound of all the traffic. "I went out last night—I had dance rehearsal at eight. Bobby was asleep by the time I got back. It was real late, after midnight. And she was still asleep when I went down to breakfast this morning."

Bobby. Had they been close, Lakeisha and her Ziggy-loving roommate? They must have been, if she'd called her Bobby. What am I doing, interrogating the poor girl this way, after she's had such a shock?

Is Jordan right? About what he'd accused me the other day. Had I turned hard?

I guess so, since next thing I knew, I was trying again.

"The reason I ask, Lakeisha—" I feel like a total and complete heel. Maybe it's all right, you know, if you feel like a jerk. Know what I mean? I mean, I've read that crazy people—sorry, I mean mentally disturbed people—never consider themselves mentally disturbed. So maybe real jerks never consider themselves jerks. So the fact that I *feel* like a jerk means that I couldn't possibly *be* one . . .

I'll have to remember to ask Sarah.

"The reason I ask is that the police"—slight lie, but oh well—"the police found a used condom under Roberta's bed this morning. It was, uh, pretty fresh."

This seems to clear a little of the fog out of Lakeisha's head. She looks at me, and this time, I can tell she really sees me.

"Excuse me?" she asks, in a stronger voice.

"A condom. Under Roberta's bed. It had to have been from last night."

"No way," Lakeisha says, firmly. "There is no way. Not Bobby. She's never—" She breaks off and studies her Nikes. "No," she says, again, and shakes her head with such force that the beads on the ends of her braids click like castanets.

"Well, someone had to have left that condom," I say. "If it wasn't Roberta, who—"

"Oh my God" Lakeisha suddenly interrupts, with actual excitement in her voice. "It had to be Todd!"

"Who's Todd?"

"Todd is the man. Bobby's man. The new man. Bobby never had a man before."

"Oh," I say, somewhat taken aback by this information. "She was . . . um—"

"A virgin, yeah," Lakeisha says, distractedly. She's still trying to digest the information I've given her. "They must have— they must have done the deed after I left. He must have come over! She musta been so excited."

Then Lakeisha's excitement dies and she shakes her head again. "Then she had to go and do something so stupid—"

Okay. Now we were getting somewhere.

I slow down my pace, and Lakeisha slows hers as well, unconsciously. We are within two blocks of the counseling center.

"So elevator surfing wasn't something your roommate did regularly?" I ask, even though I already know the answer.

"Bobby?" Lakeisha's voice breaks. "Elevator surf? No! Never. Why would she go and do something so stupid? She's a smart girl—*was* a smart girl," she corrects herself. "Too smart for that, anyway. Besides," she adds. "Bobby was afraid of heights. She never even wanted to look out the window, she thought we were up too high as it was."

I knew it. I *knew* it. Someone had pushed her. It's the only explanation.

"So this Todd guy," I say, trying not to let my eagerness show. Also the fact that my heart had begun slamming a mile a minute inside my chest. "When did Roberta meet him?"

"Oh, last week, at the dance."

"Dance?"

"The dance in the cafeteria."

We'd ended up not canceling the dance that had been planned for the night of Elizabeth's death. Sarah hadn't been the only one to throw a fit at the suggestion—the student government had rebelled as well, and Rachel had caved. The dance ended up being very well attended and there'd only been a single moment of unpleasantness, and that was when some Jordan Cartwright fans got all riled up over the music selection, and nearly came to blows with some residents who preferred Justin Timberlake.

"Todd was there," Lakeisha says. "He and Bobby started hanging out together that night."

"This Todd," I say. "Do you know his last name?"

"No." Lakeisha looks momentarily troubled. Then her face brightens. "He lives in the building, though."

"He does? How do you know?"

" 'Cause Bobby never had to sign him in."

"And this Todd guy—" I'm practically holding my breath. "You met him?"

"Not met him, but Bobby pointed him out to me at the dance. He was kinda of far away, though."

"What'd he look like?"

"Tall."

When Lakeisha doesn't go on, I prompt, "That's it? He was tall?"

Lakeisha shrugs.

"He was white," she says, apologetically. "White guys . . . they all. You know."

Right. Everyone knows all white guys look the same.

"Do you think this Todd guy"—now Lakeisha is calling him "this Todd guy," too—"had something to do with . . . what happened to Bobby?"

"I don't know," I say. And as I say it, I realize we're at the building that houses the campus counseling services. So fast! I'm disappointed. "Oh. Well, Lakeisha, this is it."

Lakeisha looks up at the double doors without seeming

really to see them. Then she says to me, "You don't think—you don't think this Todd guy . . . *pushed* her, or anything, do you?"

My heart slows, then seems to stop altogether.

"I don't know," I say carefully. "Why? Do you? Did Roberta mention that he was . . . abusive?"

"No." Lakeisha shakes her head. The beads click and rattle. "That's just it. She was so happy. Why would she do something so dumb?" Lakeisha's eyes fill with tears. "Why would she do a thing like that, if she'd found the guy of her dreams?"

My feelings, exactly.

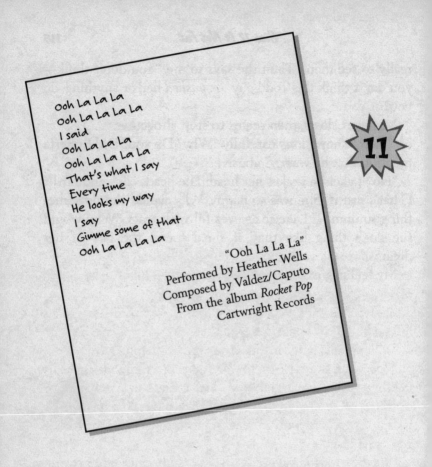

Ooh La La La
Ooh La La La La
I said
Ooh La La La
Ooh La La La La
That's what I say
Every time
He looks my way
I say
Gimme some of that
Ooh La La La La

"Ooh La La La"
Performed by Heather Wells
Composed by Valdez/Caputo
From the album *Rocket Pop*
Cartwright Records

I fill Magda and Pete in on the whole thing during our lunch break. I tell them what's going on, including the part about Cooper—

But not that I'm madly in love with him or anything. Which of course makes the story much shorter and far less interesting.

Pete's only response is to scoop up a forkful of chili and eye it dubiously.

"Are there carrots in this? You know I hate carrots."

"Pete, didn't you hear me? I said I think—"

"I heard you," Pete interrupts.

"Oh. Well, don't you think—"

"No."

"But you didn't even—"

"Heather," Pete says, carefully placing the offending carrot on the side of his plate. "I think you been watching way too much *Law and Order: Special Victims Unit.*"

"I love you, honey" is what Magda has to say about it. "But let's face it. Everyone knows you're a little bit"—she twirls a finger around one side of her head—"cuckoo. You know what I mean?"

I cannot believe a woman who would spend *five hours* having the Statue of Liberty air-brushed on her fingernails is calling *me* cuckoo.

"C'mon." I glare at them. "Two girls with no history of an interest in elevator surfing dying from it in two weeks?"

"It happens." Pete shrugs. "You want your pickle?"

"You guys, I'm serious. I really do think someone is pushing these girls down the shafts. I mean, there's a pattern. Both of these girls were late bloomers. They never had boyfriends before. Then, suddenly, a week before they died, they both got boyfriends—"

"Maybe," Magda suggests, "they did it because after saving themselves for the right man for all those years, they found out sex wasn't so great after all."

All conversation ceases after that, because Pete's choking on his Snapple.

The rest of the day is a blur. Because the two deaths occur so close together in the semester, we're bombarded by the press, mostly the *Post* and the *News*, but a *Times* reporter calls as well.

Then there's the memo Rachel insists on sending to all the residents, letting them know that a counselor will be on hand twenty-four hours a day this weekend to help them all through their grief. This means I have to make seven hundred photocopies, then talk the student worker into stuffing the memos into three hundred mailboxes, two for each double room, and three for the triples.

At first Tina, the desk worker, outright refuses. Justine, it seems, had always simply made one copy per floor, then hung them next to each set of elevators.

But Rachel wants each resident to receive his or her *own* copy. I have to tell Tina that I don't care how Justine had done things, that this is how *I* want things done. To which Tina actually replies, dramatically, "Nobody cares about what happened to Justine! She was the best boss in the world, and they fired her for *no good reason*! I saw her crying the day she found out! I *know*! New York College is so *unfair*!"

I want to point out that Justine was probably crying tears of relief that she'd only been fired and not prosecuted for what she'd done.

But I'm not supposed to mention the fact that Justine had been fired for theft in front of the students—kind of for the same reason we're not supposed to call the place we work a dorm. Because it doesn't foster a real feeling of security.

Instead, I promise to pay Tina time and a half to get the memos distributed. This cheers her right up.

By the time I get home—with milk—it's nearly six. There's no sign of Cooper—he's probably on a stakeout, or whatever it is private eyes do all day. Which is fine, because I have plenty to keep myself occupied. I've smuggled home a building roster, and I'm going through it, circling every resident named Mark or Todd. Later, I'm going to call each one, using the building phone book, and ask them if they knew Elizabeth or Roberta.

I'm not really sure what I'm going to say if any of them say yes. I guess I can't come right out and be all "So . . . did you shove her down the elevator shaft?" But I figure I will deal with that when the time comes.

I am just settling down in front of the roster with a glass of wine and some biscotti I found in the cupboard when the doorbell rings.

And I remember, with an almost physical jolt, that I volunteered to babysit for Patty's kid tonight.

Patty takes one look at me after I open the door and knows. She goes, "What happened?"

"Nothing," I assure her, taking Indy from her arms. "Well, I mean, something, but nothing happened to me. Another girl died today. That's all."

"Another one?" Frank, Patty's husband, looks delighted. There's something about violent death that makes some people very excited. Frank is evidently one of them. "How'd she do it? OD?"

"She fell off the top of one of the elevators," I say, as Patty elbows Frank, hard enough to make him go *unngh*. "Or at least, that's as close as we can figure out. And it's okay. Really. I'm all right."

"You be nice to her," Patty says to her husband. "She's had a bad day."

Patty has a tendency to get fussy when she's going out. She isn't comfortable in evening clothes—maybe because she still hasn't lost all of the baby weight yet. For a while, Patty and I tried going power walking through SoHo in the evenings, as part of our efforts to do our government-suggested sixty minutes of exercise per day.

But Patty couldn't seem to pass by a shop window without stopping, then asking, "Do you think those shoes would look good on me?" then going inside and buying them.

And I couldn't pass a bakery without going in and buying a baguette.

So we had to stop walking, because Patty's closets are full enough as it is, and who needs that much bread?

Besides, Patty has nowhere to wear all her new stuff. She's basically a homebody at heart, which, for a rock star's wife, is not a good thing.

And Frank Robillard is a rock star with a capital S. He makes Jordan look like Yanni. Patty met him when they were both doing Letterman—he was singing, she was one of those showgirls who stands around holding the cold cuts party platter—and it was love at first sight. You know, the kind you read about, but that never happens to you. That kind.

"Cut it out, Frank," Patty says to her one true love. "We're going to be late."

But Frank is prowling around the office, looking at Cooper's stuff.

"He shot anybody yet?" he asks, meaning Cooper.

"If he had, he wouldn't tell me," I say.

Since I've moved in with Cooper, my stock has gone way up with Frank. He never liked Jordan, but Cooper is his hero. He'd even gone out and bought a leather jacket just like Cooper's—used, so it's already broken in. Frank doesn't understand that being a private investigator in real life isn't like how it is on TV. I mean, Cooper doesn't even own a gun. All you need to do Cooper's job is a camera and an ability to blend with your environment.

Cooper's surprisingly good, it turns out, at blending.

"So, you two going out yet?" Frank asks, out of the blue. "You and Cooper?"

"Frank!" Patty screams.

"No, Frank," I say, for what has to be the three hundredth time this month alone.

"Frank," Patty says. "Cooper and Heather are roommates. You can't go out with your roommate. You know how that is. I mean, all the romance is gone once you've seen someone in their bathrobe. Right, Heather?"

I blink at her. I have never thought of this. What if Patty is right? Cooper is never going to think of me as date-worthy— even if I win a Nobel Prize in medicine. Because he's seen me too many times in sweat pants! With no makeup!

Patty and Frank say their good-byes, then Indy and I stand and wave to them as they go down my front steps and climb back into their waiting limo. The drug dealers on my street watch from a respectful distance. They all worship Frank's band. I am convinced that the reason Cooper's house is never graffitied or robbed is because everyone in the neighborhood knows that we're friends with the voice of the people, Frank Robillard, and so the place is off-limits.

Or maybe it's because of the alarm and the bars on all the ground and first floor windows. Who knows?

Indy and I spend a pleasant evening watching *Forensic Files* and *The New Detectives* on the TV in my bedroom, where I'm able to keep an eye on both my best friend's child and the back of Fischer Hall. Looking up at the tall brick building, with so many of its lights ablaze, I can't help remembering what Magda had said—her joke about Elizabeth and Roberta ending it all over discovering that sex isn't all it was cracked up to be. Bobby had been a virgin . . . at least according to her roommate. And it seemed likely that Elizabeth Kellogg had been one as well.

Is that it? Is that the link between the two girls? Is someone killing the virgins of Fischer Hall?

Or have I seen one too many episodes of *CSI*?

When Patty and Frank arrive to pick up their progeny just after midnight, I hand him over at the front door. He'd passed out during *Crossing Jordan*.

"How was he?" Patty asks.

"Perfect, as always," I say.

"For you, maybe," she says with a snort as she shifts the sleeping baby in her arms. Frank is waiting in the limo below. "You're so good with him. You should have one of your own someday."

"Twist the knife, why don't you," I say.

"I'm sorry," Patty says. "I love having you sit for us, but you do realize you've never once said you couldn't because you were busy? Heather, you've got to get back out there. Not just with your music, either. You've got to try to meet someone."

"I meet plenty of people," I say defensively.

"I mean someone who isn't a freshman at New York College."

"Yeah," I say. "Well, it's easy for you to criticize. You've got the perfect husband. You don't know what it's like in real life. You think Jordan was an anomaly? Patty, he's the *norm*."

"That isn't true," Patty says. "You'll find someone. You just can't be afraid to take a risk."

What is she talking about? I do nothing but take risks. I'm trying to keep a psychopath from killing again. Isn't that enough? I have to have a ring on my finger, too?

Some people are never satisfied.

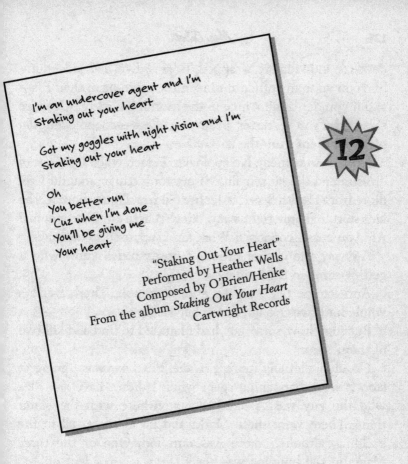

I'm an undercover agent and I'm
Staking out your heart

Got my goggles with night vision and I'm
Staking out your heart

oh
You better run
'Cuz when I'm done
You'll be giving me
Your heart

"Staking Out Your Heart"
Performed by Heather Wells
Composed by O'Brien/Henke
From the album *Staking Out Your Heart*
Cartwright Records

12

No matter how much I try to shake it, the thought stays with me all weekend. The Virgins of Fischer Hall.

I know it sounds insane. But I just kept thinking about it.

Maybe Patty's right, and the kids in the dorm—residence hall, I mean—are taking up the space in my heart where love for my own kids would be if, you know, I had any. Because I can't stop worrying about them.

Not that there can be that many more virgins left in the building—which I happen to be in a position to know. Ever since I swapped the Hershey's Kisses in the candy jar on my desk for individually wrapped Trojans, I've had kids stumbling down to my office at nine in the morning in their PJs—and if you don't think nine in the morning is early by college standards, you've never been in college—unapologetically plucking them from the jar.

No embarrassment. No apologies. In fact, when I run out of Trojans, and the jar remains empty for a day or so until I get more from Health Services, let me tell you, I hear about it. The kids start in on me right away: "Hey! Where are the condoms? Are you out of condoms? What am I supposed to do *now*?"

Anyway, the upshot of it is, I pretty much know who is getting some in my building.

And let me tell you, it's a *lot* of people. There aren't a whole lot of virgins left in Fischer Hall.

But somehow, some guy had managed to find and kill two of them.

I couldn't let any more girls die. But how was I going to stop it from happening again when I didn't have any idea who the guy was? I didn't get anywhere with the roster thing. There were three Marks and no Todds at all in the building, although there was one Tad. One of the three Marks in the building was black (he was a resident on Jessica's floor—I called her to ask) and another Korean (I called his RA as well), which ruled them both out, since Lakeisha had been sure the guy was white. Tad was so obviously gay that I just stammered an apology and said I'd gotten the wrong number when he picked up the phone.

The third Mark had gone home for the weekend, according to his roommate, but would be back on Monday. But according to his RA, he was only five foot seven, hardly what you'd call tall.

I guess you could call the investigation—such as it was—stymied.

And with Cooper in absentia all weekend, it wasn't like I could ask for his professional advice on the matter. I'm not sure if he was hiding from me, or busy working, or busy—well, doing something else. Since I moved in, Cooper hadn't had a single overnight guest—which for him, at least if Jordan is to be believed, might be a record dry spell. But given how frequently he was gone from the townhouse for days at a time, I could only assume he was crashing at the home of his current flame—whoever she might be.

Which was typical of him. You know, not to rub it in my face that he's getting some, while I'm most definitely not.

Still, I had a hard time appreciating his courteousness as the weekend wore on, and I was still no closer to figuring out who was killing the Virgins of Fischer Hall. If, um, anyone was.

Which might be why, when Monday morning finally rolls around, I'm the first one in the office, latte and bagel already ingested, deeply engrossed in Roberta Pace's student file.

The file's contents are remarkably similar to Elizabeth's, although the two girls came from different sides of the country—Roberta was from Seattle. But they'd both had interfering mothers. Roberta's mother had called Rachel to complain that Roberta needed a new roommate.

Which startles me. How could anyone not like Lakeisha?

But according to the "incident report"—one of which is filled out whenever a staff member has an interaction with a resident—when Rachel spoke to Roberta, it turned out to be Mrs. Pace, not her daughter, who had the problem with Lakeisha. "It's not that I don't like black people," Mrs. Pace had told Rachel, according to the report. "I just don't want my daughter to have to *live* with one."

This is the kind of stuff, I've discovered, that people in higher ed have to deal with every day. The good thing is, usually it's not the kids with the problem, but their parents. As soon as the parents go back home, everything ends up being okay.

The bad thing is—well, that people like Mrs. Pace exist at all.

I force myself to read on. According to the report, Rachel called Roberta down to the office and asked her if she wanted a room change, the way her mother said she did. Roberta said no, that she liked Lakeisha. Rachel reports that then she let Roberta go and called the mother back, gave her our standard speech in such cases—"Much of a college education takes part outside the classroom, where our students experience new cultures and ways of life. Here at New York College, we do everything we can to encourage cultural diversity awareness. Don't you want your son/daughter to be able to get along with every sort of individual when he/she enters the workforce?"

Then Rachel told Mrs. Pace that her kid wasn't getting a room change and hung up.

And that was it. That was the only thing in Roberta's file. The only sign at all that she'd had any sort of trouble adjusting to college life.

Except, of course, that now Roberta is dead.

I hear the ding of an elevator, and then Rachel's heels clacking on the marble floor outside our office. A second later, she appears in the doorway, a steaming mug of coffee that she's brought down from her apartment in one hand, and the morning's *Times* in the other. She looks startled to see me at my desk so early. Even though I live four minutes away from it, I'm almost always five minutes late to work.

"Oh my goodness," Rachel says, looking pleased to see me. "Aren't you here early! Did you have a nice weekend?"

"Yeah," I say, closing Roberta's file, and kind of sliding it under some other stuff on my desk.

Not that I don't have every right to be reading it. It's just that I feel kind of reluctant to tell Rachel what I suspect—about the girls being pushed, and all. I mean, technically, I probably should have said something about the key, or the condom, at least, or that both girls had recently met a guy . . .

But I can't help wondering—what if Cooper is right? What if Elizabeth and Roberta really did fall, but I make this big stink about how I think they'd been murdered? Would Rachel mark down in my employment file that I suffer from paranoid delusions? Could something like that keep me from passing my six months' probation? Could they fire me for it, the way they had Justine—even though I'd fully kept my hands off the ceramic heaters?

I'm not about to risk it. I decide to keep my suspicions to myself.

"Mostly," I say, in reply to Rachel's question about my weekend. Because, aside from calling about the Marks and Todds, I'd done nothing but walk Lucy, watch TV, and fiddle around with my guitar. Hardly anything worth reporting. "You?"

"Terrible," Rachel says, shaking her head. Although for someone who's had such a bad weekend, she looks really great. She has on a new suit, really well-cut. The black brings out the ivory in her skin, and makes her hair seem an even deeper chestnut. "Roberta's parents came in," Rachel goes on, "to pick up their daughter's things. It was just a nightmare. They plan on suing, of course. Though on what grounds, I can't imagine. Those poor people. I felt so sorry for them."

"Yeah," I say. "That had to suck."

The phone on Rachel's desk starts ringing. "Oh, hello, Stan," she says, when she answers it. "Oh, thank you so much, but I'm fine, really. Yes, it's been just awful—"

Wow. Stan. So Rachel's on a first-name basis with Dr. Jessup now. Well, I guess if a couple of kids in your dorm—oops,

I mean, residence hall—die, you get to know the head of your department pretty well.

I start going through the briefing forms the weekend desk attendants have left me. I can generally get payroll, the budget, any memos that need to be typed, and the desk coverage schedules done by eleven in the morning. Then I have the rest of the day free for cruising the Net, gossiping with Magda or Patty, or trying to figure out who might be killing girls in my place of work, which is how I've already decided I'm going to spend this particular Monday.

I just haven't quite figured out how.

I'm just finishing up the payroll when this pair of Nike-encased feet appear in my line of vision. I lift my head, expecting to see a basketball player—hopefully with a semilegible note I can add to my collection.

Instead, I see Cooper.

"Hey," he says.

Is it my fault my heart flips over in my chest? I mean, I haven't seen him in a while. Like almost seventy-two hours. Plus, you know, I'm totally man-starved. That has to be why I can't take my eyes off the front of the jeans he's wearing, white in all the places where the denim's been stressed, like at his knees and other, more interesting places.

He also has on a blue shirt beneath his rumpled leather jacket—the exact same blue as his crinkly eyes.

"Wh—" is the only sound I can get to come out of my mouth, on account of the jeans . . . and the my-being-a-total-loser-who-is-completely-in-love-with-him part.

I watch as he takes a newspaper out from beneath his arm, unfolds it, and places it in front of me.

"Wh—" I say again. At least, that's how it sounds to my ears.

"I wanted to make sure you knew about this," Cooper says.

"You know, before *Us Weekly* starts calling, and catches you by surprise."

I look down at the paper. It's the *New York Post*. On the front page is a large, blown-up photo of my ex-fiancé and Tania Trace dining at some outdoor café in SoHo. Underneath their images are the words, in eighteen-point type at least:

THEY'RE ENGAGED!

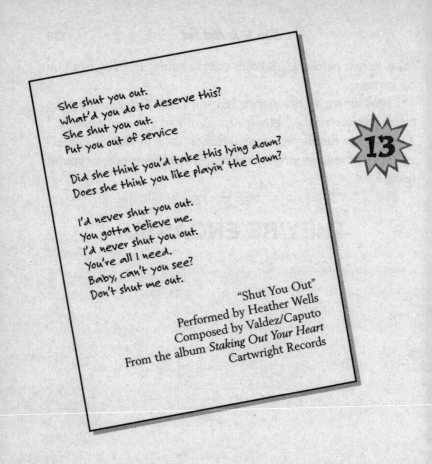

She shut you out.
What'd you do to deserve this?
She shut you out.
Put you out of service

Did she think you'd take this lying down?
Does she think you like playin' the clown?

I'd never shut you out.
You gotta believe me.
I'd never shut you out.
You're all I need.
Baby, can't you see?
Don't shut me out.

"Shut You Out"
Performed by Heather Wells
Composed by Valdez/Caputo
From the album *Staking Out Your Heart*
Cartwright Records

13

Wow. That didn't take long. I mean, considering we've only been broken up for, what? Four months? Five, maybe?

"Wh—" seems to be the only sound I am capable of making.

"Yeah," Cooper says. "That's what I thought you'd say."

I just sit there, looking down at the photo of Tania's ring. It looks just like MY ring. The one I'd ripped off my finger and thrown at them when I'd caught them going at it in our bedroom.

But it can't be the same ring. Jordan is cheap, but not THAT cheap.

I open the paper, and flip to the page with the article on it.

Look at that. They aren't just engaged. They're going on tour together, too.

"You okay?" Cooper wants to know.

"Yeah," I say, glad I've gotten back the ability to say something besides "wh."

"If it's any comfort to you," he says, "her new single got retired from *TRL*."

I know better than to ask Cooper what he's been doing watching *Total Request Live*. Instead, I say, "They retire videos when they've spent too long on the list. That means the song's still totally popular."

"Oh."

Cooper looks around, clearly seeking a way to change the subject. My office is sort of the reception area for Rachel's office, which is separated by an attractive metal grate that I've been trying to get the maintenance department to replace since I arrived. I'd decorated my area with Monet prints upon my arrival, and even though Rachel had wanted to replace the Giverny water lilies with anti–date rape and community development posters, I had held my ground.

I read in a magazine once that Monet is soothing. That's why you see prints of his work in so many doctors' offices.

"Nice place," Cooper says. Then his gaze falls on the jar of condoms on my desk.

I feel myself turning crimson.

Rachel chooses that moment to hang up the phone and lean out of her office to ask, "May I help you?"

When she sees that the visitor to our office is of the male persuasion, over six feet and under forty—not to mention totally hot—she says, in a completely different voice, "Oh. *Hello*."

"Good morning," Cooper says politely. Cooper is unfailingly polite to everyone but members of his immediate family. "You must be Rachel. I'm Cooper Cartwright."

"Nice to meet you," Rachel says. She shakes the hand he offers and smiles beatifically. "Cooper . . . Cooper . . . Oh yes, Cooper! Heather's friend. I've heard so much about you."

Cooper glances in my direction, his blue eyes crinkling more than ever. "You have?"

I wish the floor would open up and swallow me whole. I try to remember what I've ever said to Rachel about Coop. Besides the fact that he's my landlord, I mean. Because what if I said something really indiscreet, like that Cooper's my idea of a perfect mate and that sometimes I fantasize about ripping his clothes off with my teeth? I've been known to say things like that sometimes, when I've had too many Krispy Kremes combined with too much caffeine.

But all Rachel says is "I suppose you've heard about our troubles here."

Cooper nods.

"I have."

Rachel smiles again, a little less beatifically this time. I can tell she's mentally calculating how much Cooper's watch must cost—he wears one of those gadget-heavy black plastic ones—and deciding he can't possibly be worth a hundred grand a year.

If only she knew.

Then the phone on her desk rings again, and she goes to answer it. "Hello, Fischer Hall. This is Rachel. How may I help you?"

Cooper raises his eyebrows at me, and I remember, in a rush, what Magda had said, about Rachel being Cooper's type.

No! It isn't fair! Rachel is EVERYONE'S type! I mean,

she's attractive and athletic and well put together and successful and went to Yale and is making a difference in the world. What about ME? What about girls like me, who are just . . . well, nice? What about the *nice* girls? How are *we* supposed to compete with all of these competent, athletic, shower-taking girls, with their diplomas and their Palm Pilots and their teeny tiny butts?

Before I have a chance to say anything in defense of my kind, however, one of the maintenance workers comes rushing in.

"Haythar," Julio cries, wringing his hands. He's a little guy, in a brown uniform, who without being asked to, daily cleans the bronze statue of Pan in the lobby with a toothbrush.

"Haythar, that boy is doing it again."

I blink at him. "You mean Gavin?"

"Sí."

I glance over at Rachel. She's gushing into the phone, "Oh, President Allington, please don't worry about me. It's the *students* I feel for—"

I sigh resignedly, push back my chair, and stand up. I'm just going to have to face that fact that where Cooper is concerned, I'm always going to look like the world's biggest spaz.

And there's nothing I can do about it.

"I'll take care of it," I say.

Julio glances at Cooper, and, still wringing his hands, asks nervously, "You want I should come with you, Haythar?"

"What is this?" Cooper looks suspicious. "What's going on?"

"Nothing," I say to him. "Thanks for dropping by. I have to go now."

"Go where?" Cooper wants to know.

"I just have to deal with this one thing. I'll see you later."

Then I hurry out of the office and head for the service elevator, which is reserved for use of the maintenance staff only, and has one of those metal gates inside the doors to keep students out . . .

Only I know which lever to push to throw the gate back. Which I push, then turn to say, "Ready when you are" to Julio—

Only it isn't Julio who's followed me. It's Cooper.

"Heather," he says, looking annoyed. "What's this all about?"

"Where's Julio?" I squeak.

"I don't know," Cooper says. "Back there, I guess. Where are you going?"

From inside the elevator shaft, I can hear whooping. Why me? Why, God, why?

There's nothing I can do about it, though. I mean, it's my job. And it will mean a free medical degree, eventually, if I can stick it out.

"Can you work a service elevator?" I ask Cooper.

He looks even more annoyed. "I think I can figure it out."

More whooping from inside the shaft.

"Okay," I say. "Let's go then."

Cooper, looking curious as well as annoyed now, follows me inside, ducking so as not to hit his head on the low jamb, and I pull the grate shut and yank back the power lever. As the elevator lurches upward with a groan, I put a foot on the siderails and, with a heave, grab the sides of the wide opening in the elevator's roof where a ceiling panel has been removed. Through it, I can see the cables and bare brick walls of the elevator shaft, and high overhead, patches of bright light where the sun peeks in through the fire safety skylights.

Cooper's curiosity quickly fades, so that all that's left is annoyance.

"What," he asks, "do you think you're doing?"

"Don't worry," I say. "I'm okay. I've done this before." My head and shoulders are already through the hole in the elevator's ceiling, and with another heave, I wiggle my hips through it, too.

Then I have to rest. Because that's a lot of upper body lifting for a girl like me.

"*This* is what you do all day?" Cooper, down below me, demands. "Where does it say in your job description that you are responsible for chasing after elevator surfers?"

"It doesn't say it anywhere," I reply, looking down at him in some surprise through the opening between my knees. The dark walls of the elevator shaft slip past me like water as we rise. "But somebody's got to do it." And if I don't, how am I ever going to pass my six months' probation? "What floor are we on?"

Cooper glances through the grate, at the painted numbers going by on the back of each set of elevator doors.

"Nine," he says. "You know, one slip, and you could end up like those dead girls, Heather."

"I know," I say. "That's why I have to stop them. Somebody might get hurt. Somebody else, I mean."

Cooper says something under his breath that sounds like a curse word . . . which is surprising, because he so rarely swears.

One floor later, two walls of the shaft open up, so that I can see into the shafts of the building's other elevators. One of the elevators is waiting at ten, and by craning my neck, I can see the other about five floors overhead.

The whooping is getting louder.

Right then, Elevator 2 starts to descend, and I see, perched on the cab's roof, amid the cables and empty bottles of

Colt .45, Gavin McGoren, junior, film major, diehard *Matrix* fan, and inveterate elevator surfer.

"Gavin!" I yell, as Elevator 2 slides past me. Unlike me, he's standing upright, preparing to leap onto the roof of Elevator 1 as it goes by. "Get down from there right now!"

Gavin throws me a startled glance, then groans when he recognizes me between the cables. I see several flailing arms and legs as the friends he's surfing with dive back down through the maintenance panel and into the elevator car, to save themselves from being ID'd by me.

"Aw, shit," Gavin says, because he hadn't been quick enough to escape, like his friends. "Busted!"

"You are so busted you're gonna be sleeping in the park tonight," I assure him, even though no one's ever gotten thrown out of the hall for elevator surfing . . . at least until now. Who knew, in light of recent events, if the board of trustees would get a backbone? You have to do something really bad—like hurl a meat cleaver at your RA, as a kid had done last year, according to a file I'd found—to be asked to leave the residence halls.

And even then, the kid was allowed back the following fall, after proving he'd spent the summer in counseling.

"Goddammit!" Gavin screams into the shaft, but I don't worry. That's just Gavin.

"Do you think this is funny?" I ask him. "You know two girls died doing this in the past two weeks. But you just woke up this morning and thought you'd go for a joyride anyway?"

"They was amateurs," Gavin says. "You know I got the creds, Heather."

"I know you're a jackass," I reply. "And stop talking like you come from Bed-Stuy, everyone knows you grew up in Nantucket. Now get down. And if you aren't in Rachel's office by the time I'm downstairs, I'm having the locks changed on your door and confiscating all your stuff."

"Shit!" Gavin disappears, slithering through the elevator cab's roof and scraping the ceiling panel back into place behind him.

Elevator 2 begins its long descent to the lobby, and I sit for a minute, enjoying the darkness and the lack of noise. I really like the elevator shafts. They are the most peaceful places in the whole dorm—I mean, residence hall.

When people aren't falling down them, anyway.

When I let myself down—and no judge would give me a ten for my dismount—Cooper is standing in one corner of the car, his arms folded across his broad chest, his features twisted into a scowl.

"What was that?" he asks, as I reach for the control lever and start bringing us back down to the main floor.

"That was just Gavin," I say. "He does that all the time."

"Don't give me that." Cooper sounds genuinely angry. "You did that on purpose. To show me what a *real* elevator surfer is like, and how much the two dead girls don't fit the bill."

I glare at him. "Oh, right," I say. "You think I prearranged that whole thing with Gavin? You think I knew in advance you were going to come over to shove my ex's engagement announcement in my face, and I called Gavin and was like, 'Hey, why don't you take a spin on Elevator Two and I'll come up and bust you to prove to my friend Cooper the difference between real elevator surfers and wannabes'?"

Cooper looks slightly taken aback . . . but not for the reason I think.

"I didn't come over to shove it in your face," he says. "I wanted to make sure you saw it before some reporter from the *Star* sprang it on you."

Realizing I'd maybe been a little harsh, I say, "Oh yeah. You said that."

"Yeah," Cooper says. "I did. So. Do you do that a lot? Climb on top of elevator cars?"

"I wasn't climbing. I was sitting," I say. "And I only do it when someone reports hearing someone in the shafts. Which is another reason it's so weird about Elizabeth and Roberta. No one reported hearing them. Well, until Roberta fell—"

"And you're the one who has to go after them?" Cooper asks. "If someone hears them?"

"Well, we can't ask the RAs to do it. They're students. And it isn't in the maintenance workers' union contract."

"And it's in yours?"

"I'm nonunion," I remind him. I can't help wondering what he's getting at. I mean, is he actually worried about me? And if so, is it just as a friend? Or as something more? Is he going to throw on the brake and stop the elevator and snatch me into his arms and whisper raggedly that he loves me and that the thought of losing me makes his blood run cold?

"Heather, you could seriously injure, if not kill, yourself doing something that stupid," he says, making it pretty obvious that the snatching me into his arms thing isn't going to happen. "How could you—" Then his blue eyes crinkle into slits as he narrows them at me. "Wait a minute. You *like* it."

I blink at him. "What?" Yeah, that's me. Miss Ready with a Comeback.

"You do." He shakes his head, looking stunned. "You actually enjoyed that just now, didn't you?"

I shrug, not sure what he's talking about. "It's more fun than doing payroll," I say.

"You like it," he goes on, as if I hadn't even said anything, "because you miss the thrill of standing up in front of thousands of kids and singing your guts out."

I stare at him for a second or two. Then I burst out laughing.

"Oh my God," I manage to get out, between guffaws. "Are you serious with this?"

Except that I can tell by his expression that he is.

"Laugh all you want," he says. "You hated singing the schlock the label gave you to sing, but you got a kick out of performing. Don't try to deny it. It gave you a thrill." His blue eyes crackle at me. "That's what all this is about, isn't it? Trolling for murderers and chasing elevator surfers. You miss the excitement."

I stop laughing and feel color heating up my face again. I don't know what he's talking about.

Well, okay, maybe I did. It's true I'm not one of those people who get nervous about performing in front of a crowd. Ask me to make small talk with thirty people at a cocktail party, and you might as well ask me to define the Pythagorean theorem. But give me a song set and stick me in front of a microphone? No problem. In fact . . .

Well, I sort of enjoy it. A lot.

But do I miss it? Maybe a little. But not enough to go back. Oh no. I can never go back.

Unless it's on my terms.

"That's not why I went after Gavin," I say. Because really, I don't see the connection. Chasing after elevator surfers is nothing like performing in front of three thousand screaming preteens. Nothing at all. Besides, don't I get enough psycho-analyzing from Sarah every day? Do I really need it from Cooper, too? "He could have killed himself up there—"

"You could have killed *yourself* up there."

"No, I couldn't," I say, in my most reasonable voice. "I'm really careful. And as for—what did you call it? Trolling for murderers?—I told you, I don't believe those girls were—"

"Heather." He shakes his head. "Why don't you just give your agent a call and ask him to schedule a gig for you?"

My jaw drops.

"What? What are you talking about?"

"It's obvious you're aching to get out there again. I respect the fact that you want to get a degree, but college isn't for everyone, you know."

"But—" I can't believe what I'm hearing. My hospital ward! My Nobel Prize! My date with him! Our joint detective agency and three kids—Jack, Emily, and baby Charlotte!

"I . . . I couldn't!" I cry. Then latch on to my one excuse: "I don't have enough songs for a gig."

"Could have fooled me," Cooper says, his gaze on the numbers of the floors we're passing at a dizzying speed, 14, 12, 11. . . .

"What—what do you mean?" I stammer, my blood suddenly running cold. It's true, then. He *can* hear me practicing He can!

It's Cooper's turn to look uncomfortable, though. From his scowl, it's clear he wishes he hadn't said anything.

"Never mind," he says. "Forget about it."

"No. You meant something by it." Why won't he just admit it? Admit that he's heard me?

I know why. I know why, and it makes me want to die.

Because he hates them. My songs. He's heard them, and he thinks they suck.

"Tell me what you meant."

"Never mind," Cooper says. "You're right. You don't have enough songs for a gig. Forget I said anything. Okay?"

The cab hits the main floor. Cooper yanks back the gate and holds it open for me, looking less polite than murderous.

Great. Now he's mad at me.

We're standing in the lobby, and since it's still pretty early in the morning—for eighteen-year-olds, anyway—we're the only ones around, with the exception of Pete and the reception desk attendant, the former engrossed in a copy of the *Daily News*, the latter listening enraptured to a Marilyn Manson CD.

I should just ask him. Just come out and ask him. He's not going to say it sucks. He's not his father. He's not Jordan.

But that's just it. I can take criticism from Cooper's father. I can take it from his brother. But from Cooper?

No. No, because if *he* doesn't like it—

Oh God, stop being such a baby and DO IT. JUST ASK HIM.

"Heather," Cooper says, running a hand through his dark hair. "Look. I just think—"

But before I have a chance to hear what Cooper just thinks, Rachel rounds the corner.

"Oh, there you are," Rachel says when she notices us. "Gavin's in my conference room. I'm going to have a word with him in a minute. Thanks so much for making him come down. In the meantime, Heather, I was wondering if you could have the student worker go around and tape up these fliers."

Rachel hands me a sheaf of papers. I look down at them, and see that they are announcements for a lip-synch contest the student government has decided to throw in the Fischer Hall cafeteria after dinner.

"At first I wasn't going to let them," Rachel seems to feel the need to explain. "I mean, holding something as silly as a lip-synch contest, in light of two such tragic deaths . . . but Stan thinks the kids can use something to take their minds off it. And I couldn't help but agree."

Stan. Wow. Rachel sure is getting chummy with the boss.

"Sounds good to me," I say.

"I was just heading into the cafeteria for a refill before tackling Gavin." Rachel holds up her American Association for Counseling and Development coffee mug. "Anybody care to join me?"

She says it to both of us, but her gaze is on Cooper.

Oh my God. Rachel has just asked Cooper to have coffee with her. *My* Cooper.

Of course, she doesn't know he's *my* Cooper. He's *not* my Cooper. And the way things seem to be going, he'll probably never be . . .

Say no. I try to send my thought waves into his brain, like on *Star Trek. Say no. Say no. Say no. Say*—

"Thanks, but I can't," Cooper says. "I've got work to do."

Success!

Rachel smiles and says, "Maybe some other time, then."

"Sure," Cooper says.

And Rachel click-clacks away.

When she's gone, I say, showing no sign that I had, seconds before, been using Vulcan mind control on him, "Look. I gotta get back to work." I hope he isn't going to bring up what we'd been talking about in the elevator. I don't think I could handle it. Not on top of the announcement of Jordan's engagement. There's only so much a girl can take in one day, you know?

Maybe Cooper senses this. Either that or the fact that I won't meet his gaze tips him off.

In any case, all he says is, "Gotcha. I'll see you later, then. And Heather—"

My heart gives a lurch. No. Please, not now. So close. I'd been so close to escaping—

"The ring," he says.

Wait. What? "Ring?"

"Tania's."

Oh! Tania's engagement ring! The one that looks exactly like the one I threw back in his brother's face!

"Yeah?"

"It's not yours," Cooper says.

Then he leaves.

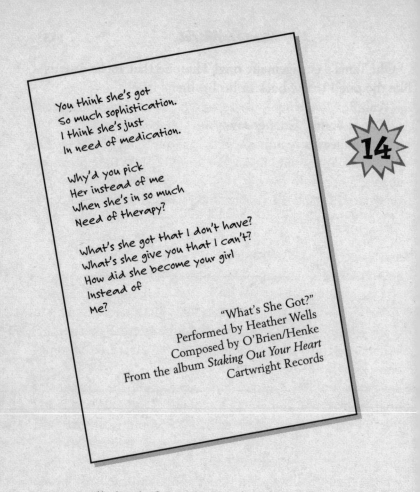

14

You think she's got
So much sophistication.
I think she's just
In need of medication.

Why'd you pick
Her instead of me
When she's in so much
Need of therapy?

What's she got that I don't have?
What's she give you that I can't?
How did she become your girl
Instead of
Me?

"What's She Got?"
Performed by Heather Wells
Composed by O'Brien/Henke
From the album *Staking Out Your Heart*
Cartwright Records

It's actually kind of appropriate that the student government decides to throw a lip-synch contest at Fischer Hall. Because, let's face it, New York College is primarily filled with kids who, like me, love to perform.

Which is probably why they asked me to be one of the judges, an honor I readily accepted. But not because I needed to—as Cooper had suggested—feel the thrill of performing again, but because I figured if I were ever going to find the mysterious Mark/Todd (if he existed at all), it was going to be at some Fischer Hall social function, since the guy evidently lived in the building.

And possibly worked there, as well, as Detective Canavan had—teasingly, I know—suggested to me.

It seemed pretty impossible to believe that any of the people I work with could be a killer. But how else to explain the apparent access to the key cabinet? Not to mention the fact that both of the dead girls had had files in the hall director's office. Not that that necessarily had anything to do with their deaths. But, as Sarah would no doubt put it, both Elizabeth and Roberta had had issues . . .

And those issues had been recorded in their files.

The thing is, all fifteen RAs, as well as the maintenance staff, have keys to the office Rachel and I share. So if there really is some guy cruising the files for potentially fragile, inexperienced girls he can easily seduce, then it has to be someone I know.

Only who? Who did I know who could be capable of doing something so awful? One of the RAs? Out of the fifteen of them, seven are boys, none of whom I consider real particular swingers, much less psychopathic killers. In fact, in the tradition of RAs, all of them are kind of nerdy—the sort who actually believe their residents when they insist they were smoking clove cigarettes, not pot. They seriously can't tell the difference.

Besides which, everybody in the whole building knows who the RAs are. I mean, the staff performs safer sex skits and stuff at dinnertime. If Mark or Todd had been an RA, Lakeisha would have known him by sight.

As far as the maintenance staff is concerned, forget it. They're all Hispanic and over fifty, and only Julio speaks enough English to be understood by someone not bilingual.

Plus they've all worked in Fischer Hall for years. Why would they suddenly start killing people *now*?

Which, of course, leaves just the women on the staff. I should, in light of diversity awareness, include them on my list of suspects . . .

Only none of them could have left that condom in Roberta's room.

But I guess I'm the only one who considers it odd that two girls—who each had a file in my office, and who each happened to have found a boyfriend within a week of each other—both happened randomly to decide to go elevator surfing, then plunged to their deaths at around the same time the key to the elevator doors went missing, only to reappear shortly after the discovery of at least one of their bodies.

Which is why at seven o'clock that night, I slip from the brownstone—I haven't heard a peep from Cooper since the elevator incident that morning, which is fine with me, because frankly, I don't know what I'm going to say to him when I *do* see him again.

It's also why I consequently walk right into Jordan Cartwright, who is just coming up the front stoop.

"Heather!" he cries. He has on one of those puffy shirts— you know, like the kind they made fun of on *Seinfeld*—and a pair of leather pants.

Yes. I am sorry to have to say it. Leather pants.

What's worse is, he really does look quite good in them.

"I was just coming to see how you are," he says, in a voice that drips with concern for my mental health.

"I'm fine," I say, pulling the door closed and working the locks. Don't ask me why we have so many locks when we also have a burglar alarm and a dog and our own Rastafarian community watch program. But whatever.

"Have a nice evening," one of the drug dealers urges us.

"Thank you," I say to the drug dealer. To Jordan, I say, "I'm sorry, I really don't have time to chat. I've got somewhere to go."

Jordan trots down the steps behind me.

"It's just," he says, "I don't know if you've heard. About Tania and me. I meant to tell you the other day, but you were so adversarial—I didn't want you to find out this way, Heather," Jordan says, keeping pace with me as I tear down the sidewalk. "I swear. I wanted you to hear it from me."

"Don't worry about it, Jordan," I say. *Why* won't he go away? "Really."

"Hey." One of the drug dealers blocks our path on the sidewalk. "Aren't you that guy?"

"No," Jordan says to the drug dealer. To me, he says, "Heather, slow down. We've got to talk."

"There's nothing to talk about," I assure him, in my most cheerful voice. "I'm good. Everything's good."

"Everything's *not* good," Jordan cries. "I can't stand to see you hurting like this! It's tearing me up inside—"

"Oh, hey," I say to the drug dealer who is trailing after us. "This is Jordan Cartwright. You know, from Easy Street."

"The dude from Easy Street!" the drug dealer cries, pointing at Jordan. "I knew it! Hey, look!" he calls to his friends. "It's the dude from Easy Street!"

"Heather!" Jordan is swallowed up in a crowd of autograph seekers. "Heather!"

I keep right on walking.

Well, what exactly was I supposed to do? I mean, he's engaged. ENGAGED. And not to me.

What more is there to say? It's not like I don't have more pressing concerns right now, too.

Rachel seems kind of surprised to see me walk through the

doors of Fischer Hall at night. She's standing in the lobby just as I come in, and her eyes get kind of big.

"Heather," she exclaims. "What are you doing here?"

"They asked me to judge," I say.

For some reason, she looks relieved. I realize why a second later. "Oh good! Another judge for the lip-synch! How great! I was hoping Sarah and I wouldn't have to judge on our own. What if there's a tie?"

"Heather." Jordan comes bursting into the lobby.

And all around us, breaths are sucked in as he is immediately recognized. Then the whispering begins: *"Isn't that—no, it couldn't be. No, it is! Look at him!"*

"Heather," Jordan says, striding up to Rachel and me. His gold necklaces rise and fall beneath the puffy shirt as he pants. "Please. We've got to talk."

I turn to Rachel, who is staring at Jordan with eyes that are even bigger than when I'd walked in.

"Here's another judge for you," I say to her.

Which is how Jordan and I end up sitting in the front row of about three hundred cafeteria chairs, facing the closed-off grill and salad bar, clipboards in our laps. You can imagine how difficult this makes it for Jordan to talk to me about our relationship, as he is so desperately longing to.

But this is just fine by me. I mean, the truth is I'm only here to hunt for the mysterious Mark and/or Todd, and my being a judge isn't exactly helpful in this capacity.

But if it keeps me from having to listen to Jordan as he tries to make excuses for his behavior—though why he should care what I think of him, when he's made it so perfectly obvious he doesn't want to be with me anymore, I can't imagine . . . maybe Sarah can explain it—it's fine.

The kids are all in a dither about Jordan. They hadn't known there was going to be a celebrity judge. (I don't count.

The few kids who'd recognized me at check-in could not have cared less. Tonight, it's all about Jordan . . . even though I'm afraid some of them are making fun of him, on account of the puffy shirt and Easy Street and everything.) Jordan's presence does seem to give the contest an air of legitimacy it lacked before.

It also seems to make the competitors even more nervous.

There's an elaborate sound and light system set up over by the salad bar, and all sorts of students are milling around, chatting and noshing on free soda and chips. I look for couples, trying to single out any boys and girls in close conversation, thinking that if Mark or Todd is going to strike again, there is a bevy of freshwomen here for him to choose from.

But all I see are groups of kids, boys and girls, white, African American, Asian, you name it, in baggy jeans and T-shirts, screaming happily at one another, and tossing back Doritos.

Mmmm. Doritos.

Sarah, seated next to Jordan, can't take her eyes off him. She keeps asking him searching questions about the music industry, the same ones she'd asked me when she'd first met me. Like, had he felt like a sellout when he'd done that Pepsi ad? And hadn't he felt that performing at the Super Bowl halftime show had been degrading to his calling as a musician? And what about that calling? Did it bother him that he knew how to sing, but not how to play a single instrument? Didn't that, in a way, mean that he wasn't a musician at all, but merely a mouthpiece through which Cartwright Records could deliver their message of corporate greed?

By the time the lights go down, and the hall president, Greg, gets up to welcome everyone, I'm feeling a little sorry for Jordan.

Then the first act comes on, a trio of girls lip-synching Christina's latest, with choreography and everything. With the lights down, I'm able to scan the audience without looking too obvious.

There are a *lot* of students there. Nearly every seat is filled, and the cafeteria can hold four hundred. Plus there are people lining the back of the room, hooting and applauding and, in general, acting like eighteen-year-olds away from home for the first time. Beside me, Jordan is staring at the Christina wannabes, his clipboard clutched tightly in his hands. For someone who's been shanghaied into the job, he seems to be taking it way seriously.

Or maybe he's only acting interested in order to keep Sarah from asking him any more questions.

The first act comes to a hip-grinding stop, and a quartet of boys leaps into the spotlight. Heavy bass begins to shake the cafeteria walls—they're performing "Bye Bye Bye" by 'N Sync—and I feel pity for Fischer Hall's neighbors, one of which is an Episcopalian church.

The boys throw themselves into their act. They have the choreography down pat—so much so I practically wet my pants, I'm laughing so hard.

I notice Jordan isn't laughing at all. He doesn't seem to understand that the boys are making *fun* of boy bands. He is carefully scoring them on originality and how well they know the lyrics.

Seriously.

Glancing over my clipboard as I score the boys' act—I give them mostly fives out of ten, since they don't have costumes—I notice a tall man wander into the dining hall, his hands buried deep in the pockets of his khakis.

At first I think it's President Allington. But the president never wears khakis, preferring, as I think I've mentioned before, white Dockers. The newcomer is entirely too well-dressed to be the school's president.

When he moves into a shaft of light that spills from the Coke machine, however, I realize that it's Christopher Allington, the president's son. So my confusion is understandable.

It isn't unusual for Christopher to drop by. I mean, even though he has his own place at the law school dorm, his parents do live upstairs. He'd probably come over to visit them, then stopped in the caf to see what all the noise was about.

But when he moves toward a group of students leaning against a far wall and begins chatting casually to them, I start to wonder. What *is* Christopher doing here, exactly? He's a law student, not an undergrad.

Pete had told me that when the Allingtons first arrived from the college somewhere in Indiana where President Allington had worked before, there'd been a big hush-up over the fact that Christopher hadn't scored high enough on his LSATs to get into New York College. Apparently his father had pulled some major strings, and gotten him in anyway.

But then, with an alcoholic mother and a father who wears tank tops in public, the poor kid probably doesn't have much in the way of gifts from the Allington gene pool anyway, and needed the extra help.

'N Sync pounds to a finish, and then an Elvis impersonator gives it a go. During his rendition of "Viva Las Vegas," for want of anything better to do, I watch Christopher Allington mingle. He works his way through the crowd until he's settled himself in a chair behind a whole row of girls. They're all freshmen—you can tell by their giggly awkwardness. They aren't quite in the New York College groove yet, as their unpierced faces and undyed hair and Gap clothing prove. One of them, a bit more sophisticated than the rest, turns in her seat and begins talking to Christopher, who leans forward to hear her better. The girl sitting next to her resolutely refuses to join in the conversation, keeping her face forward.

But you can tell she's eavesdropping like anything.

Elvis finishes to respectable applause, and then Marnie Villa Delgado—yes, Elizabeth Kellogg's roommate—takes the stage. Everyone gives her an extra hand. I try not to let myself think that the ovation is for having scored herself a single room for the rest of the semester.

Marnie, wearing a long blond wig and a pair of low-ride jeans, bows politely. Then she launches into a song that sounds vaguely familiar. I can't place it, at first. All I know is that it's a song I don't like very much. . .

And then it hits me. "Sugar Rush." Marnie is giving her all to the song that had made mine a household name . . . thirteen years ago. And only if that household contained a pre-adolescent girl.

Jordan, beside me, guffaws. Some of the students who know about my past laugh along with him. Marnie herself even gives me a sly look while she mouths the line, "Don't tell me stay on my diet/You have simply got to try it."

I smile and try not to look as uncomfortable as I feel. It helps to look back at Christopher, instead. He's still chatting up the girls in the row ahead of him. He has finally attracted the attention of the shy girl, who, while not pretty, has a more interesting face than her more vivacious companion. She has turned in her seat and is timidly smiling at Christopher, hugging her knees to her chest and pushing back wayward tendrils of reddish hair.

Up front, Marnie is tossing her blond wig—not to mention her hips—around in a manner that the crowd seems to find hilarious, and which I can only hope is not supposed to be an accurate imitation of me.

And that's when it hits me—out of the blue—that Christopher Allington could be Mark.

Or Todd.

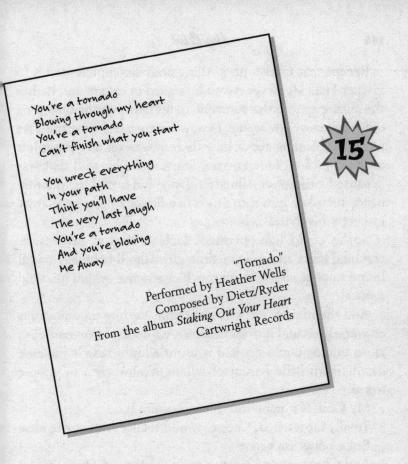

You're a tornado
Blowing through my heart
You're a tornado
Can't finish what you start

You wreck everything
In your path
Think you'll have
The very last laugh
You're a tornado
And you're blowing
Me Away

"Tornado"
Performed by Heather Wells
Composed by Dietz/Ryder
From the album *Staking Out Your Heart*
Cartwright Records

I guess you can say my blood went cold.

Okay, it didn't really. But it does feel kind of like someone has spilled some really cold Diet Coke down my back, or something.

All of a sudden, my palms are so sweaty I can hardly hold on to the clipboard. My heart starts hammering unsteadily, the way it had that time I'd sung those songs I'd written myself for Jordan's dad, and he'd laughed at me.

Christopher Allington? Christopher Allington? No way!
Except . . .

Except that Christopher Allington has complete access to Fischer Hall. He never has to be signed in or out, and he has the authority to order someone to let him into the director's office whenever he wants. I know because one time the RAs were complaining about how there was never any paper left in the copier on Monday morning and Rachel said that was because Christopher Allington always has one of the maintenance men key him into our office Sunday night so that he can copy his friends' class notes.

So he could have perused Rachel's files at his leisure, combing them for likely victims, girls who'll fall easily under his persuasion, girls without much experience, whom he could seduce.

And then he set out to meet them, starting up innocuous conversations and introducing himself under a fake name . . . all so that he could get laid without a lot of fuss. It's like he has his own little harem of willing freshwomen to choose from!

My God. It's diabolical. It's ingenious. It's . . .

Totally far-fetched. Cooper would totally scoff at the idea. But Cooper isn't here . . .

And Christopher Allington *is* way charming. Over six feet tall, with kind of longish blond hair that he wears feathered back, he has the boyish good looks of . . . well, a guy from a boy band. What freshman girl wouldn't be flattered by his attentions . . . so flattered that she'd have sex with him on a comparatively short acquaintance? My God, he's cute, older, sophisticated . . . Any eighteen-year-old girl would go ga-ga over him. Any *twenty-eight*-year-old girl would go ga-ga over him. The guy is fine.

But why did he *kill* them? Scoring babes is one thing, but killing them afterward? Doesn't that kind of defeat the purpose? If they're dead, you can't score with them again.

More importantly, *how* did he kill them? I mean, I know how—if, indeed, they were being killed—but how was he managing to push full-grown women down an elevator shaft when, undoubtedly, they'd be struggling against him? Drugs? But wouldn't the coroner's office have found some evidence of that?

My face feels hot. I fan it with my clipboard, turning my attention back toward Marnie. She's just winding up for her big finish, which involves hip gyrations the likes of which I haven't seen since Shakira's last performance on the MTV Music Video Awards. She *definitely* isn't imitating me. I've always been a rotten dancer, the despair of every choreographer I've ever met. I had difficulties, as they liked to point out, detaching my brain from my body, and just letting go.

Marnie pulls some kind of Carly Patterson back handspring thingie that ends in a set of splits and has the entire cafeteria on their feet, cheering. I rise to my feet as well . . . then start toward her. Lakeisha may have gone home, but Marnie's still here, and might be able to confirm whether or not her roommate had ever hooked up with Christopher Allington.

But Jordan grabs me by the arm before I've gone two steps.

"Where are you going?" he asks worriedly. "You aren't trying to sneak out of here before we've had our talk, are you, Heather?"

Jordan smells of Drakkar Noir, which is distracting. He'd worn Carolina Herrera for Men when he'd been with me, so clearly the Drakkar Noir is courtesy of Tania.

"I'll be back in a minute," I say, patting him reassuringly on the arm—his very buff arm. He's been bulking up for his next tour, and it shows. In a good way. "I promise."

"Heather," Jordan begins, but I won't let him finish.

"I promise," I say. "When this thing is over, we'll have a nice, long chat."

Jordan looks placated.

"All right," he says. "Good."

I see Marnie cross to the side of the dining hall where all the other acts have gathered to await the decision of the judges, and while the next group sets up for their performance, I hurry over to her.

Marnie has pulled off her blond wig and is wiping sweat from beneath her eyes. She smiles when she sees me approach.

"Marnie," I say. "Nice performance."

"Oh, thanks," she simpers. "I was worried you'd be mad. I finally figured out who you were, as you can see."

"Yeah," I say. "Look, I have to ask you something. Could that guy Elizabeth was seeing right before she died . . . could his name have been Chris?"

Marnie, clearly disappointed that the only reason I've sought her out is to talk about her dead roommate some more, shrugs unconcernedly.

"I don't know. It was something like that. Chris or Mark."

"Thanks," I say. She turns to say something slighting about one of the other acts to the trio of Christina wannabes, and I have to reach out and tug on her sleeve. "Uh, Marnie?"

She glances back at me. "Yeah?"

"See that girl over there in the fifth row, about ten seats over, talking to that blond guy?"

Marnie looks. Her eyebrows raise.

"That guy's a babe. Who is he?"

"So you don't know him?"

"Not yet," she says, making it clear she intends to rectify that situation.

I try to hide my disappointment. Maybe if I can get my hands on a photo of Christopher Allington, I could waylay Lakeisha outside one of her classes and get her to make an ID that way . . .

Then I think of something.

"Do you know the girl?" I ask Marnie.

She purses her lips.

"Kinda. She lives on the twelfth floor. I think her name is Amber or something."

Amber. Perfect. I have a name now, and a floor to go with it.

I get back to my seat just as two guys in drag launch into a rendition of "Dude Looks Like a Lady." Jordan leans over and whispers into my ear, "What was that all about?"

I just smile and shrug. There's no point trying to scream above the sound system, and besides, Sarah is eyeing me critically from over her clipboard. I don't think she appreciates me fraternizing with the contestants, since it might render me less than impartial in my judging.

So I sit helplessly in my chair while Christopher Allington is possibly—probably—schmoozing with his next victim. Amber—from what I can tell, given that I'm only able to catch brief glimpses of her, not wanting to look as if I'm staring—seems to be coming to life under Christopher's attentions. She fiddles with her red-brown hair and squirms in her seat, grinning nonstop and generally acting like a girl who has never had a handsome boy pay attention to her in her life. I watch worriedly, chewing my lower lip, wondering if tomorrow morning, we're going to find Amber at the bottom of the elevator shaft.

Except that I can't really see Christopher as the murdering type. The deflowering type, yeah. But a murderer?

Then again, Evita Peron's husband had been a notorious letch, and I read somewhere that he killed a bunch of people in Argentina, which is why Madonna didn't want people to cry for her in that song.

Finally the lip-synch ends. Greg, the hall president, comes out and announces that the judges should begin deliberating. Everyone else gets up and heads for the Doritos (luckies). Rachel scoots her chair around so that she is facing me and Jordan and Sarah.

"Well," she says, smiling at me. "What did you think?"

I think we've got a problem, I want to say. A really big problem. And not with the contest.

But instead I say, "I liked Marnie."

Jordan interjects, "You would! No, those guys who did the 'N Sync song were much better. They really had the choreography down. I gave 'em tens."

Sarah says, "Their ironic take on the boy band *was* deeply amusing."

"Um," I say. "I liked Marnie."

"And she's been through so much," Rachel agrees, earnestly. "It's the least we can do, don't you think?"

Just wanting to get the whole thing over with as soon as possible so I can make up an excuse to go talk to Chris, I say, "Yeah, okay. So let's give Marnie first place, 'N Sync second, and the Christina trio third."

Jordan looks a little peeved by the fact that we've basically ignored his input, but he doesn't argue.

Rachel goes off to tell Greg our decision, and I turn in my seat to spy on Christopher some more . . .

. . . just in time to see him leaving, one arm draped casually over Amber's shoulders.

I'm out of my chair like a shot, without a word to Jordan or anybody. I hear him call after me, but I don't have any time to waste with explanations. Christopher and Amber are already halfway through the TV lounge. If I don't act fast, that girl might end up as a stain on the elevator motor room floor.

But then, to my astonishment, instead of turning toward the elevators, Amber and Christopher actually walk out the front doors of the building.

I follow, darting past the groups of kids congregated in the lobby. Nighttime is when the hall really comes alive. Residents I've never seen before are leaning against the reception desk, chatting with the student worker on duty. The guard—not Pete, who works days—is harassing a clique of kids who claim to know someone on the fifth floor whose name they couldn't remember. Why can't the guard just be a pal and let them in?

I bolt past all of them, throwing open the doors and stumbling out into the warm autumnal evening.

Washington Square Park is crawling with cops at night, cops and tourists and drug dealers and chess players, who sit at the benches in the chess circle until the park closes at midnight, playing by the light of the street lamps. High school kids from Westchester, in their parents' Volvos, tool down the street, playing their radios too loudly and occasionally having their cars impounded for creating a public nuisance. It's a wild scene, and one of the reasons why so many kids request rooms overlooking the Square . . . when there's nothing on TV, there's always the park to watch.

Which is precisely what Christopher and Amber are doing. They're leaning against one of Fischer Hall's outdoor planters, smoking cigarettes, and watching the NYPD make a bust across the street. Christopher has his arms folded across his chest, and is puffing away like Johnny Depp or someone, while Amber twitters like a little bird, holding her cigarette like someone who isn't used to holding one at all.

There isn't a moment to lose, I can see that. I approach them, trying to look casual. I imagine that's how Cooper would have handled the situation, anyway.

"Hey," I say amiably to Christopher. "Can I bum a smoke?"

"Sure," says Christopher. He draws a pack of Camel Lights from his shirt pocket and hands me one.

"Thanks," I say. I put the cigarette between my lips, then lean down so Christopher can light it with the Zippo he's brandished.

I've never been a smoker. For one thing, if you're a singer, it messes up your vocal cords. For another, I just don't get how a cigarette could ever be better than a Butterfinger, so if you're going to indulge, why not go the way of delicious peanut buttery crisp?

But I stand there and pretend to inhale, wondering what I should do next. What would Nancy Drew do? Jessica Fletcher? That other one, what was her name? On *Crossing Jordan*? God, I totally suck as a detective. What's going to happen after Cooper and I get together—you know, after I get my degree and all? How are we going to be all Nick and Nora Charles, when Nora can't hold up her share of the detecting? This is a very distressing thought. I try to push it from my mind.

Across the street, the cops are busting some drunk who thought it would be amusing to expose himself to the people sitting in the chess circle. I don't know why some men feel this compulsion to show off their genitalia. It's invariably the guy with the least interesting appendage, too.

I say as much to Christopher and Amber. You know, to make conversation. She looks startled, though Christopher laughs.

"Yeah," he says. "There should be a law. Only drunks with at least six inches should be allowed to drop trou."

I look at him, my eyebrows raised. Trou. He's kind of funny, Christopher Allington. Did Ted Bundy have a sense of humor? He did when Mark Harmon played him in that movie I saw on Lifetime the other night . . .

Across the street, the drunk is hurling insults at the cops who've cuffed him, and a few people in the chess circle are shouting back at him. Chess players are not anywhere near as mild-mannered as they've been made out to be by the media, you know.

"Oh my," Amber says, when one particularly colorful epithet reaches us. "They sure don't talk like that to the police back home."

"And where's home?" I ask her, nonchalantly flicking my ash on the sidewalk. At least, I hope I look nonchalant.

"Boise, Idaho," Amber says, as if there's more than one Boise.

"Boise," I echo. "Never been there." Total lie. I'd performed at the Boise Civic Center before five thousand screaming preteens during the Sugar Rush tour. "How about you?" I ask Christopher.

"Nope," he says. "Never been to Boise. Hey, don't I know you from somewhere?"

"Me?" I try to look surprised. "I don't think so."

"Yeah," he says. "I do. Hey, you in law school?"

"No," I say, flicking more ash. They may give you cancer and everything, but cigarettes really do make great props if you're trying to look casual. For instance, while catching a possible murderer.

"Really?" Christopher blows pale smoke from his nostrils. No fair! He knows smoke tricks! " 'Cause I swear I've seen you somewhere before."

"Probably right around here. I've seen you lots. You're President Allington's son, Christopher, aren't you?"

You'd have thought I'd smacked him in the face with a sack full of Gummi Bears, he looks so surprised. For a second I think he's going to swallow his cigarette.

But he recovers himself pretty quickly.

"Uh, yeah," he says. His eyes are gray, and at the moment, still friendly. "How'd you know?"

"Someone pointed you out," I say. "Do you live here? With your folks?"

That stings. He says quickly, "Oh no. Well, I mean, I have my own place, but it's in the law school dorm, over there—"

"You're not an undergrad?" Amber asks. She clearly isn't very swift on the uptake. "You're a law student?"

"Yeah," Christopher said. He doesn't look quite as comfortable as he had before I'd mosied over and dropped my little bomb. Poor guy. He doesn't know I have even more ammunition up my (capped) sleeve.

"I didn't know you were President Allington's son," Amber says, with something like reproachfulness in her little Minnie Mouse voice.

"Well, it's not something I like to advertise," Christopher mutters.

"And I thought you said your name was Dave."

"Did I?" Christopher finishes his cigarette, drops the butt on the sidewalk, and stamps it out. "You must not have heard me right. It was kind of loud in there. I'm sure I said my name's Chris."

Across the street, the cops haul the pantless drunk into a squad car. Now they're all standing around, filling out forms attached to clipboards and drinking coffee somebody's bought from the deli around the corner. The drunk bangs on the car window, wanting some coffee, too.

Everyone ignores him.

Okay, this sucks. I'm turning out to be world's worst detective. I'm definitely going to have to take some courses in criminal justice. You know, when I pass my six months' probation and can start taking classes free.

"It's so sad, isn't it?" I ask, in a voice even *I* think sounds way too chipper—sort of like Less Than Zero's voice from the jean store the other day. "All the losers there are in this city, I mean. Like that pants-dropping drunk getting hauled away right across the street. Oh, and those stupid girls here in the buildings. The ones that died—what was it, again? Oh, yeah. Elevator surfing. Can you believe anyone would do anything that dumb?"

I glance at Chris to see how he's taking this direct reference to his victims. But he doesn't look disturbed at all . . .

. . . unless you can call pulling out another cigarette and lighting it disturbed.

Which, uh, I guess it is. In a way. But not in the way I meant.

"Oh," gasps Amber, in a valiant attempt to hold up her end of the conversation. "I know! That was so sad. I knew that last girl, sort of. One time I got stuck in the elevator with her. It was only for about a minute, but she was freaking out, because she hated heights. When I heard how she'd died, I was like, 'What?' 'Cause why would somebody that scared of heights do something so dangerous?"

"Roberta Pace, you mean?" I slide my gaze toward Chris, to see how he reacts to the name.

But he's busy checking his watch—a Rolex. A real one, too, not one of those ones you can buy on the street for forty bucks, either.

"Yeah, that was her name. God, wasn't that sad? She was so nice."

"I know," I nod gravely. "And what's even weirder than her being afraid of heights, but elevator surfing anyway, is that I heard just the day before she died, she'd met some guy—"

I don't get to finish my sentence, though. Because just then iron fingers close around my upper arm, and I suddenly find myself yanked from behind, hard.

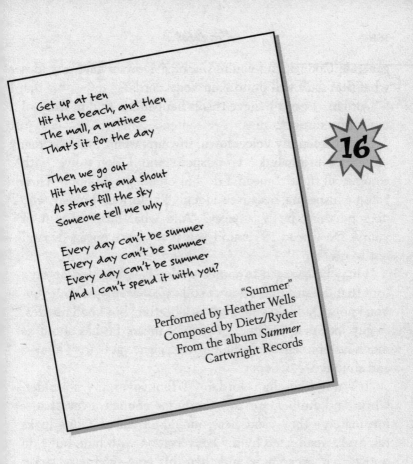

Get up at ten
Hit the beach, and then
The mall, a matinee
That's it for the day

Then we go out
Hit the strip and shout
As stars fill the sky
Someone tell me why

Every day can't be summer
Every day can't be summer
Every day can't be summer
And I can't spend it with you?

"Summer"
Performed by Heather Wells
Composed by Dietz/Ryder
From the album *Summer*
Cartwright Records

Stumbling, I put out a hand to steady myself, and feel the un-mistakable ripple of rock-hard—and gym-formed—abdominal muscles beneath my fingers.

Is there any part of Jordan Cartwright that isn't hard?

Including, apparently, his head?

He drags me a few feet away from Chris and Amber.

"What do you think you're doing?" Jordan demands, ripping the cigarette from my fingers and stomping on it. "You're *smoking* now? A few months of living with that degenerate Cooper, and you're *smoking*? Do you have any idea what that stuff will do to your vocal cords?"

"Jordan." I can't believe this is happening. And in front of my prime suspect!

I try to keep my voice down, so Chris won't overhear me.

"I wasn't inhaling," I whisper. "And I don't live with Cooper, all right? I mean, I do, but on a separate floor." Then I stop whispering, because suddenly I'm furious. I mean, who does he think he is, anyway? "And what business is it of yours? Do I need to remind you that you're engaged? And not to me?"

"I may be engaged to someone else, Heather," Jordan says, "but that doesn't mean I don't still care—deeply—about you. You know, Dad said you'd hit rock bottom, but I had no idea. A guy like that, Heather? *Really*? I mean, he has about as much fashion sense as"—he throws a glance at Chris's khakis, and shudders—"Cooper!"

"It's not like that, Jordan." I look over my shoulder. Chris and Amber are still there, far enough away that— fortunately—they can't hear our raised voices. Chris looks relatively unaffected by my conversation with him, but I do notice that every now and then, his gray-eyed gaze strays toward us. Is he afraid? Afraid that the jig is up at last?

Or is he just wondering where Jordan bought his puffy shirt?

"Don't look," I say softly to Jordan. "But that guy I was talking to? I think he might be a murderer."

Jordan looks over at Chris. "Who? That guy?"

"I said don't look!"

Jordan tears his gaze from Chris and stares down at me instead. Then he reaches out and crushes me to his chest.

"Oh, you poor, sweet girl," he says. "What's Cooper done to you?"

I struggle to break free of his smothering embrace—or at least to speak without getting chest hair in my mouth.

"This doesn't have anything to do with Cooper," I say, conscious that the student worker at the desk is trying to hide a smirk as she watches us through the window. "Girls are dying in this building, and I think—"

"So this is where you two disappeared to!"

We both spin around and stare wide-eyed at Rachel, who'd slipped outside unnoticed by either of us.

"You missed the awards ceremony," Rachel chastises us, jokingly. "Marnie was so thrilled to win that she cried."

"Wow," I say, without the slightest enthusiasm. "Neat."

"I came looking for you two," Rachel says, "because I thought you might want to join me for a drink in my place . . ."

Jordan and I exchange glances. There is a desperate glint in his. I don't know what he sees in mine. Probably confusion. Rachel had invited me up to her place only once before, for a glass of wine after the first freshmen check-in of the semester, and I'd been totally uncomfortable not only because, well, she's my boss, and I was desperate to do whatever I had to do to make sure I passed my six months' probation, but also because . . .

Well, Rachel's apartment is really clean. Not that I'm messy, or anything, but . . .

Okay, I'm a little messy. I will admit there's a lot of stuff jammed in my closets and under my bed and sort of, well, all over the place.

But at Rachel's, everything had been put neatly away. There were no stray copies of *Us Weekly* next to the toilet, like at my place, or bras hanging off any doorknobs, or wadded-up Ho Ho wrappers on the nightstand. It was like she'd been expecting company.

Either that, or she keeps her place that clean all the time . . .

But no. That can't possibly be true. That just isn't even *human*.

Plus, I'd noticed that the few CDs she *did* have—neatly stacked, in alphabetical order—were by artists such as Phil Collins and Faith Hill.

PHIL COLLINS. AND FAITH HILL.

Not that there's anything wrong them. They're actually very talented artists. I totally loved that "Circle of Life" song the first fifty times I heard it . . .

"Actually, Rachel," I say carefully, "I'm kinda tired."

"Me, too," Jordan chimes in quickly. "It's been a really long day."

"Oh," Rachel says, looking distinctly disappointed. "Maybe another time, then."

"Sure," I say, not looking at Jordan—because really, this whole thing is all his fault. Rachel would never have invited me up for drinks if it hadn't been for Jordan. She had pretended not to recognize him, but I'd overheard one of the RAs tipping her off. Tomorrow she'll probably be all over me with questions about his eligibility.

Because he's worth WAY more than a hundred grand.

"Well," I say. "See you in the morning."

"Right. Good night!" Rachel smiles. To Jordan, she says, "Nice meeting you, Jordan!"

"Likewise," says Jordan, almost as if he means it.

Then, taking Jordan's arm, I steer him back toward Waverly Place, before the conversation can get any more awkward, and he can embarrass me any more in front of the people I work with.

"Oh my God," I say to him, as we walk. "What do you think I should do? About Amber, I mean? What if she turns out to be his next victim? I'll never forgive myself . . . although I totally busted him in front of her, with the whole 'Dave' thing. Don't you think I busted him? Don't you think she'll be a little wary of him now? Oh God. Do you think I should go to the police? I don't have any proof it's him, though. Except . . . except Cooper probably still has the condom! I could use it as some kind of leverage—like, 'Confess or I'll take it to the cops.' Or something."

Jordan, beside me, sounds horrified.

"*Condom?* Heather, what are you—"

"I told you," I say, stomping a foot. "I'm trying to catch a killer. Or at least I think he's a killer. I can't be sure. Your brother thinks I've got an overactive imagination. But you think it's weird, don't you, Jordan? Two girls dead in as many weeks, neither of them with a reputation for elevator surfing, and both of them just having a boyfriend for the first time? I mean, doesn't that sound suspicious to you?"

We turn the corner onto Waverly Place, and one of the Rastafarians approaches, hoping, I guess, that I'd change my mind at last and would take him up on his offer of "Smoke? Smoke?"

Instead of ignoring him and answering my question, Jordan snarls, "Back off!" at the drug dealer, who really isn't a very threatening presence. I mean, I'm way taller and probably twenty pounds heavier than he is. No wonder the poor guy looks so surprised at Jordan's outburst.

Which is when I realize who's really standing in front of me. Not a friend. Not even an acquaintance. But my ex-boyfriend.

"Oh, just forget it," I say, and drop his arm before heading home.

The only problem is, Jordan follows me.

"What'd I do?" he wants to know. "Heather, just tell me. I'm sorry. It's just that I don't know how you expect me to react. Dead girls and condoms and drug dealers. And you *smoke* now. What kind of life is this, Heather? What kind of life?"

I start up the steps to Cooper's brownstone, fumbling for my keys in the light from the street lamp.

"Look," I say. I'm working the locks as fast as I can, conscious that Jordan has come up the stairs behind me, and is blocking all the light from the street lamp with his big, puffy shirt. "It's *my* life, okay? Sorry it's such a mess. But you know, Jordan, you had a hand in making it that way—"

"I know," Jordan cries. "But you wouldn't go to counseling with me, remember? I begged you—"

Both of his heavy hands land on my shoulders, this time not to shake me, but to turn me around to face him. I blink up at him, unable to see his features because the street lamp behind him has made a halo around his head, casting everything within it into dark shadows.

"Heather," Jordan goes on, "every couple has problems. But if they don't work through them together, they won't last."

"Right," I say sarcastically. "Like we did."

"Right," Jordan says, looking down at me. I can't see his eyes, but I can still feel his gaze burning into me. Why's he looking at me like that, anyway? Like he . . . like he . . .

"Oh no," I say, taking a hasty step backward—right into the door. The knob presses hard against my back. "Jordan . . . what are you doing here? I mean, what are you *really* doing here?"

"My parents are throwing an engagement party for me," he says, in a voice that suddenly sounds hoarse. "For Tania and me, I mean. Back home. At the penthouse. Right now."

Mr. and Mrs. Cartwright hadn't thrown an engagement party when Jordan and I had gotten engaged. Instead, Mrs. Cartwright had asked if I was pregnant.

I guess she couldn't think of any other reason her son would bother to get himself engaged to a girl whose career was on the wane and waistline on the rise.

"Well, shouldn't you be there, then?" I ask him.

"I should," Jordan says. And suddenly I realize he doesn't just sound hoarse. He sounds miserable. "I know I should. Only . . . only all I've been able to think of all day is you."

I swallow hard and try to think rationally. After all, I'm a girl detective. That is what girl detectives do. We think rationally.

But there's something about Jordan's proximity—not to mention the misery . . . and raw need . . . in his voice—that's making this really difficult.

And the weight of his hands on my shoulders is very pleasant. And suddenly, I don't even mind the smell of Drakkar Noir so much.

And in the dark, of course, I can see neither the gold necklace nor the ID bracelet he's wearing.

I know! ID bracelet!

"I just," I babble, trying to keep down this wave of hysteria that's threatening to engulf me. "I just think maybe the excitement of it all—the announcement, the reporters—is getting to you. Maybe if you just go home and have an Advil—"

"I don't want an Advil," Jordan murmurs, drawing me close. "All I want is you."

"No," I say, feeling panicky at the touch of puffy shirt to my cheek. "No, you don't. Remember? You keep telling me I've changed. Well, I *have* changed, Jordan. We both have. We've got to move on, and start living our own—separate— lives. That's what you're doing with Tania, and that's what I'm doing with . . . with . . . " With who? I don't have anybody! It isn't fair that he has somebody, and I don't.

"Well, with Lucy," I finish—quite bravely, in my opinion.

"Is that what you want?" Jordan asks me, his lips alarmingly close to mine all of a sudden. "For me to be with Tania?"

I can't believe what I'm hearing.

"*Now* you're asking?"

And the next thing I know, he's stooped down low and is pressing his mouth over mine.

Ordinarily I'm pretty clear-headed in situations like this. I mean, usually when a guy starts kissing me—not that this happens very often—I have the presence of mind to either tell him to stop if I don't like it, or kiss him back if I do.

But in this particular case, I'm so surprised, I just sort of freeze. I mean, I'm still conscious of the doorknob pressing into my back, and the fact that all the lights in the house are out, which means Cooper isn't home yet—thank God!

But beyond that, and some mild embarrassment that the drug dealers, out on the street, are whooping encouragingly, "Go for it, mon!" I don't feel . . . anything.

Anything but good, I mean.

I know as well as the drug dealers that it's been a while since I'd gotten any.

It must have been a while for Jordan, too (either that, or Tania isn't quite pulling her weight in bed . . . which isn't surprising, given that she can only weigh like one-ten, tops), because all I do is slide my arms up around his neck—force of habit, I *swear*—and the next thing I know, he's slammed my body back against the door, the front of his leather pants molded to me so closely that I can feel the individual rivets on his fly . . .

. . . not to mention the thickening, er, muscle beneath those rivets.

Then his tongue is inside my mouth, and his hands in my hair . . .

And all I can think is *OH NO*.

Because he's engaged. And not to me. And I—well, really, I am NOT that type of girl. I'm NOT.

But this little voice inside my head keeps going, *Maybe this is how it's meant to be*, and *Hmmm, I remember how this feels*, and *Well*, he *certainly doesn't seem to mind those added pounds*, which makes it VERY hard to do the right thing, which is push him away.

As a matter of fact, well . . . the little voice is making it *impossible* to push him away.

I guess all those choreographers were wrong. You know, about me having trouble turning off my brain and just letting my body go. Because my body is humming along just fine, without any support from my brain at all . . .

It begins to look as if it would behoove us to get indoors, considering the supportive shouts of the drug dealers, so I twist around and finally get the door open, and we kind of fall into the dark foyer . . .

. . . where I press both my hands against his chest and use my one last moment of sanity to say, "You know, Jordan, I really don't think we should be doing this—"

But it's too late. He's already pulled my shirt from the waistband of my jeans. Next thing I know, his hands are cupping my breasts through the lace of my bra while he kisses me. Deeply. Like he means it, even.

And okay, yeah, I do think—briefly—of reminding him that just that morning, I had been reading all about his engagement—to someone else—in the paper.

But you know, sometimes your body just takes up where your mind leaves off.

And my body seems to be on autopilot, remembering all the good times it had once had with the body that's currently pressed up against it.

And it's pretty much begging for more.

Then it's like I can't think at all for a while. Except . . .

Well, I do have this one thought, toward the end. This thought I really wish I hadn't had.

And that's *Wrong brother*.

That's all. Just that I'm definitely, positively rolling around on the floor with the *wrong brother*.

And I'm not real proud of it.

The worst part of it is, it isn't even that good. I guess the best I can say is that it's quick—thank God, because the hallway runner is beneath me, not the most comfortable carpet in the house. And it's safe—Jordan came prepared, like any good Easy Street member.

Other than that, it doesn't end up being much different than the sex we used to have every Monday, Wednesday, and Saturday . . .

. . . with the obvious exception being that, this time, *I'm* the other woman.

I wonder if Tania ever felt as guilty about it as I do. Somehow, I doubt it. Tania doesn't strike me as someone who ever feels guilty about anything. I once saw her throw a Juicy Fruit wrapper on the ground in Central Park. She doesn't even feel guilty about *littering*.

Another notable difference to our post-breakup sex, as opposed to our pre-breakup sex, is that Jordan gets up almost immediately after we're finished and starts getting dressed. Back when we'd been dating, he'd just roll over and go to sleep.

When I sit up and stare at him, he says, "I'm sorry, but I gotta go," like someone who just remembered a real important dental appointment.

Here's the *really* embarrassing part: I feel kind of sad.

Like there'd been this part of me that had been sure he'd roll over and say he was going to call Tania and break up with her RIGHT NOW because he wants to be with me forever.

Not, you know, that I'd have gone back to him if he had. Probably not.

Okay, definitely not.

But it's . . . well, it's *lonely*, when you don't have anyone. I mean, I don't want to come off sounding like Rachel. I'm not saying that if I had a boyfriend—even Cooper, the man of my dreams—it would cure all my problems.

And I'm not about to start eating salad with no dressing if that's what I have to do to get one—I'm not *that* desperate.

But . . . it would be nice to have *someone* care.

I don't mention any of this to Jordan, though. I mean, I have *some* pride. Instead, when he says he's leaving, I just go, "Okay."

"I mean, I would stay," he says, tugging his shirt over his head, "but I got a real early press junket tomorrow. For the new album, you know."

"Okay," I say.

"But I'll call you tomorrow," he says, fastening the buttons of his fly. "Maybe we can have dinner, or something."

"Okay," I say.

"So, I'll call you," Jordan says, from the foyer.

"Sure," I say. I think we both know he's lying.

After he leaves, and I've locked up behind him, I creep up the stairs to my apartment, where I'm met by an extremely exuberant Lucy, eager for her evening walk. As I look for her leash, I glance through the windows of my kitchen, and see the upper floors of Fischer Hall.

I wonder if Christopher Allington has managed to talk his

way into Amber's pants as easily as Jordan Cartwright talked his way into mine.

Then I remember that said pants are still downstairs, and I hurry down to get them before Cooper comes home and finds the proof of my profound stupidity on the hallway runner.

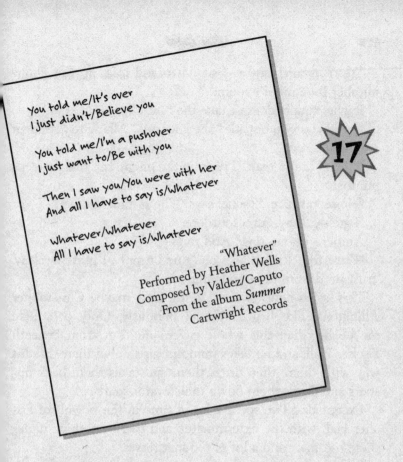

You told me/It's over
I just didn't/Believe you

You told me/I'm a pushover
I just want to/Be with you

Then I saw you/You were with her
And all I have to say is/Whatever

Whatever/Whatever
All I have to say is/Whatever

"Whatever"
Performed by Heather Wells
Composed by Valdez/Caputo
From the album *Summer*
Cartwright Records

17

I'm right about one thing:

Rachel is *totally* curious about Jordan, and the nature of my relationship with him.

The minute I walk into the office the next morning—wet hair, mug of steaming coffee from the caf in my hand, big scarlet letter on my blouse (just kidding about that last part), Rachel is all "So you and your ex-boyfriend seemed to be getting along pretty well last night."

She has *no* idea how true this statement really is.

"Yeah" is all I say, as I sit down and look up the phone number for Amber's room.

Rachel totally doesn't take the hint.

"I saw you two outside," she goes on. "Talking to President Allington's son."

"Chris," I say. "Yeah." I pick up the phone and dial Amber's number.

"He seems nice," Rachel says. "The president's son."

"I guess," I say. For a murderer.

Amber's phone rings. And rings.

"Cute, too," Rachel goes on. "And I hear he's quite wealthy. Trust fund from his grandparents."

This last is news to me. Oh my God, maybe Christopher Allington's like Bruce Wayne! Seriously. Only evil. Like maybe he's had this whole cavern dug out from beneath Fischer Hall, and he takes innocent girls down there, has his way with them, then drugs them and takes them back upstairs and drops them down the elevator shaft . . .

Except that I've spent a lot of time in the bowels of Fischer Hall with the exterminator, and there's nothing under there but mice and a lot of old mattresses.

Someone picks up the phone in Amber's room. A girl's voice says sleepily, "Hello?"

"Hello," I say. "Is this Amber?"

"Uh-huh," the sleepy voice says. "This is Amber. Who's this?"

"No one," I say. Just wanted to make sure you were still alive. "Go back to sleep."

"Okay," Amber says groggily, and hangs up the phone.

Well, Amber's still alive, anyway. For now.

"So are you and Jordan getting back together?" Rachel wants to know. She doesn't seem to think my calling students and waking them up for no apparent reason at all strange.

Which actually says a lot about the weirdness of the place where we work, and our jobs there. "You make the cutest couple."

Fortunately I'm saved from having to reply by my phone, which begins ringing right then. I answer it, wondering if Amber has caller ID and wants to know what the hell I'm doing, waking her up at nine in the morning on a school day.

Only it isn't Amber on the other end. It's Patty, going, "Okay, tell me everything."

"About what?"

I'm not actually feeling very good. All I wanted to do when I woke up this morning was pull the covers back over my head and stay in bed forever and ever.

Jordan. I slept with *Jordan*. Why, God, why?

"Whadduya mean *about what?*" Patty sounds shocked. "Haven't you seen the paper today?"

I feel my blood run cold for the second time in twenty-four hours.

"What paper?"

"The *Post*," Patty says. "There's a photo of you two kissing right on the cover. Well, you can't really see that the woman's you, but it's definitely not Tania Trace. And it's definitely Cooper's front stoop—"

I say a word that sends Rachel skittling out of her office, asking if everything is all right.

"Everything's fine," I say, placing a shaking hand over the receiver. "It's nothing, really."

Meanwhile Patty is busy squawking in my ear.

"The headline says *Sleazy Street*. I guess they mean because Jordan's scamming on his fiancée. But don't worry, they call you the 'unidentified woman.' God, you'd think they'd be able to figure it out. But it's obviously an amateur shot, and your head is in shadows. Still, when Tania sees it—"

"I don't really want to talk about this right now," I interrupt, feeling queasy.

"Don't want to?" Patty sounds surprised. "Or can't?"

"Um. The latter?"

"I gotcha. Lunch?"

"Okay."

"You are such a dope." But Patty is chuckling. "I'll swing by around noon. Haven't seen Magda in a while. Can't wait to hear what SHE has to say about this."

Neither can I.

I hang up. Sarah comes in, full of eager questions about—what else? Jordan. All I want to do is curl up into a ball and cry. Why? WHY? WHY had I been so WEAK?

But since you can't cry at work without seventy people coming up to you and going, "What's wrong? Don't cry. It'll be okay," I pull out a bunch of vending machine refund requests and started processing them instead, bending over my calculator and trying to look super busy and responsible.

It isn't like Rachel doesn't have plenty to do herself. She found out earlier in the week that she'd been nominated for a Pansy. Pansys are these medals, in the shape of a flower, that the college gives out to staff and administrators every semester when they've done something above and beyond the line of duty. For instance, Pete has one for ramming this girl's door down when she barricaded herself behind it and turned on the gas in her oven. He completely saved her life.

Magda has one, too, because—weird as she is, with the movie star thing—the kids, for the most part, just adore her. She makes them feel at home, especially every December, when, in disregard of all campus regulations, Magda decorates her cash register with a stuffed Santa, a miniature crèche, a menorah, and Kwanzaa candles.

I personally think it's nice that Rachel got nominated.

She's dealt with a lot since she started here at Fischer Hall, including two student deaths in two weeks. She's had to notify two sets of parents that their kid is dead, pack up two sets of belongings (well, okay, I did that, both times), and organize two memorial services. The woman deserves a pansy-shaped medal, at the very least.

Anyway, because of her Pansy nomination, Rachel is automatically invited to the Pansy Ball, this black-tie affair held annually on the ground floor of the college library, and she's all aflutter about it, since the ball is tonight and she keeps insisting she has nothing to wear. She says she's going to have to go hit some sample sales at lunch to see if she can find something suitable.

I know what this means, of course. She'll be coming back with the most beautiful gown any of us has ever seen. When you're a size 2, you can just pop into any store and find hundreds of totally stunning options.

When I'm finished with the refund requests, I announce that I'm going to disbursements to get them cashed, and Rachel waves me away, thankfully not commenting on the fact that I hate waiting on line at Banking (which was Justine's favorite place) and usually send a student worker to do it.

Of course, on my way to disbursements, I swing by the caf to see Magda. She takes one look at my face and informs her supervisor, Gerald, that she's taking a ten-minute break, even though Gerald's like, "But you just went on break half an hour ago!"

Magda and I walk out into the park, sit on a bench, and I pour out the whole stupid Jordan story.

When she's done laughing at me, Magda wipes her eyes and said, "Oh, my poor baby. But what did you expect? That he was going to beg you to come back?"

"Well," I say. "Yes."

"But would you have gone with him?"

"Well . . . no. But it would have been nice to be asked."

"Look, baby, you know and I know that you are the best thing that has ever happened to him. But him? He just wants a girl who will do whatever he say. And that is not you. So you let him stay with Miss Bony Butt. And you wait for a *nice* man to come along. You never know. He might be closer than you think."

I know she's talking about Cooper.

"I told you," I say, miserably. "I'm not his type. I'm going to have to get like four degrees just to compete with his last girlfriend, who discovered a dwarf sun, or something, and got it named after her."

Magda just shrugs and says, "What about this Christopher you were telling me about, then?"

"Christopher *Allington*? Magda, I can't date him! He's a possible murderer!"

When I reveal my suspicions concerning Christopher Allington, Magda gets very excited.

"And no one would suspect him," she cries, "because he is the president's son! It's like in a movie! It's perfect!"

"Well, almost perfect," I say. "I mean, why would he go around killing innocent girls? What's his motive?"

Magda thinks about that for a while, and comes up with several theories based on movies she'd seen, like that Chris has to kill people as an initiation rite into some kind of secret law school society, or that possibly he has a split personality or a deranged twin. Which brings her around to the fact that Chris Allington is probably going to be at the Pansy Ball, and if I really want to play detective, I should wrangle myself a ticket and go observe him in his natural element.

"Those tickets cost like two hundred dollars, unless you're nominated for a Pansy," I inform her. "I can't afford one."

"Not even to catch a murderer?" Magda asks.

"He's only a *potential* murderer."

"I bet Cooper could get a pair." I'd forgotten that Cooper's grandfather was a major New York College benefactor, but Magda hasn't. Magda never forgets anything. "Why don't you go with him?"

I haven't had much to smile about lately, but the thought of Cooper putting on a tuxedo does make me kind of laugh. I doubt he's ever even owned one.

Then I stop smiling at the idea of my asking him to go with me to the Pansy Ball. Because he'd never agree to it. He'd want to know why I want to go so badly, then lecture me for sticking my nose where it doesn't belong.

Magda sighs when she hears this.

"Okay," she says, regretfully. "But it could have been just like a movie."

I spend my time at Banking carefully *not* thinking about the night before—which had definitely been nothing like a movie. If it had been like a movie, Jordan would have showed up this morning with a big bouquet of roses and two tickets to Vegas.

Not, you know, that I'd have gone with him. But like I said, it would have been nice to be asked.

I'm walking back across the park, toward Fischer Hall, mentally rehearsing the "I'm sorry, but I just can't marry you" speech I decide I'm going to give to Jordan in case, you know, he *does* turn up with the flowers and the tickets, when I look up, and there he is.

No, seriously. I practically bump into him on the sidewalk in front of the building.

"Oh," I say, clutching an envelope filled with dollar bills to my chest protectively, like it might be able to ward him off. "Hi."

"Heather," Jordan says. He's standing beside a black stretch limo parked—not exactly unobtrusively—in front of the dorm. He's obviously just come from his press junket. He doesn't have any roses with him, but he does have on multiple platinum chains and a very hang-dog look.

Still, I don't feel too sorry for him. After all, *I'm* the one with the rug burns on my ass.

"I've been waiting out here for you," Jordan says. "Your boss said you'd be back within the hour, but—"

Oops. It's eleven-thirty, and I'd left the office at ten. Rachel probably hadn't anticipated my heading out to the park to chat with Magda.

"Well," I say. "I'm back." I look around, but I still don't see any flowers. Which is fine, since I've forgotten my speech anyway. "What's up?"

You are not getting back together with him, I tell myself, firmly. You are *not* getting back together with him. Even if he crawls on his knees . . .

Well, maybe if he crawls on his knees.

No! Not even then! He's the wrong brother, remember? The wrong brother!

Jordan looks around uncomfortably. "Listen. Can we go somewhere and talk?"

"We can talk right here," I say. Because I know if I go off somewhere alone with him, I might do something I'll regret later.

Might? I already *had*.

"I'd feel better," he says, "if we could talk inside the limo."

"*I'd* feel better," I say—stay strong, stay strong—"if you'd just say what you have to say."

Jordan looks surprised at the firmness of my tone. It surprises me, too.

That's when I realize that he probably believes I think we're getting back together or something.

Ahem.

Next thing I know, he's spilling his guts right there on the sidewalk.

"It's just that . . . I'm . . . I'm really confused right now, Heather," he says. "I mean, you're so . . . well, you're just great. But Tania . . . I talked it over with Dad, and I just . . . well, I can't break up with Tania right now. Not with the new album coming out. My dad says—"

"*What?*" I can't believe what I'm hearing. I mean, I believe it. I just can't believe he's actually saying it.

"Seriously, Heather. He's really pissed about that photo in the *Post*—"

"You don't think that *I*—"

"No, no, of course not. But it looks really bad, Heather. Tania's got the best-selling album on the label right now, and my dad says, you know, if I were to leave her, it'd really hurt *my* new album's chances of—"

"Okay," I say. I don't think I can bear to hear any more. This so isn't anything I'd rehearsed a speech for. "It's all right. Really, Jordan. It is."

And the weirdest thing is that, at that moment, it kind of *is* all right. Somehow, hearing Jordan tell me that he can't get back together with me because his dad won't like it completely snuffs out whatever romantic feelings I still have for him.

Not that I had any. Anymore.

Jordan's mouth kind of falls open in astonishment. He'd clearly been expecting tears of some kind. And in a way, I *do* feel like crying. But not because of him.

I don't see any point in telling Jordan that, though. I mean, the guy has enough problems as it is. Sarah would probably have a field day diagnosing all his deep-seated neuroses . . .

Jordan returns my smile with almost childlike relief, and says, "Wow. Okay. That's just . . . that's really sweet of you, Heather."

Strangely enough, all I can think of at that moment is Cooper. Not, you know, how sad it is that I think he's so hot, and he barely knows I'm alive . . . except, you know, for the fact that the pile of receipts on his desk keeps slowly disappearing.

No, I find myself actually praying that Cooper, wherever he is, doesn't happen to pick up a copy of this morning's *Post*. Because the last thing I want is him knowing I'd been making out with—and thank God this was all the *Post* had photographic evidence of—his brother on his front stoop . . .

I don't know if it's because I've been working in Fischer Hall for so long that I've sort of developed a sixth sense about these things or what. But it's right about then that I feel something. A sudden rush of air, a shadow out of the corner of my eye, and I let go of Jordan's hand fast and yell, "Look out!" before I'm even completely aware of what's happening.

Then the next thing I know, there's a sickening thudding sound, then a crash. Then dirt and sharp things are flying through the air.

When I take my arms away from my head and uncover my eyes, I'm horrified to see Jordan sprawled across the sidewalk next to his limo, a huge gash on the side of his head from which blood is pumping steadily, making a soup out of the fine layer of dirt, geraniums, and cement shards that litter the area.

I'm transfixed with shock for a second or two.

Then I'm on my knees at Jordan's side.

"Ohmigod!" A girl who'd been standing a few feet away, trying to hail a taxi, comes running up. "Ohmigod, I saw the whole thing! It was a plant! A potted plant! It came flying down from that penthouse up there!"

"Go inside," I say to her, in a calm voice I don't recognize as my own, "and tell the security guard to call an ambulance and the police. Then ask the desk attendant for the first aid kit."

The girl does as I say, wobbling on her high heels. She's all dressed up for a job interview, but doesn't seem to realize that she's going to be very, very late for it.

What had that instructor said, way back when I'd first trained for this position, about CPR?

Oh, right. Stop. Look. And listen.

I stop and see with relief that Jordan's chest is rising and falling. He's still breathing. A pulse beats in his neck, hard and steady. He's unconscious, but not near death—yet. The planter has struck a glancing blow, sliding down the side of his head, behind his ear, and causing a huge welt on his shoulder. His shirt is torn right through.

Blood is still coursing from the open wound on his head, though, and I'm considering whipping off my own shirt to use as a bandage—that wouldn't make me *too* popular with the guys in the chess circle—when the limo driver comes running around the car, at the same time that Pete comes bursting through the front door of the residence hall.

"Here, Heather." He thrusts the reception desk first aid kit at me, his dark eyes wide. "I got an ambulance on the way, too."

"Is he dead?" the limo driver asks nervously, a cell phone to his ear. Undoubtedly he's on with Jordan's dad.

I hand over my envelope from Banking to Pete, then rummage through the first aid kit, find a rolled up Ace bandage, and shove that into the wound. It turns dark red almost immediately.

"Go get me a towel, or something," I say to Pete, still in this strange, calm voice that sounds so unlike my own. Maybe it's my future voice. You know, the voice I'm going to use in my medical practice, after I get my degree. "There are some linens left over from summer conference housing in the package room. Go get me a couple towels."

Pete is off like a shot. People have started to gather around, Fischer Hall residents as well as people from the chess circle in the park. They all have plenty of medical advice to offer.

"Lift up his head," one of the drug dealers urges me.

"No, lift up his feet," someone else says. "If the face is red, raise the head. If the face is pale, raise the tail."

"His face is red, mon."

"That's just from all the blood."

"Hey, isn't that Jordan Cartwright?"

Pete returns with several clean white towels. The first turns red after only a minute or so. The second seems to do the trick. Blood stops gushing out so alarmingly as I press the towel to Jordan's head.

"How did it happen?" everyone keeps asking.

A man from the chess circle volunteers: "I saw the whole thing. You're lucky you weren't killed, lady. That thing was heading straight for you. If you hadn't jumped outta the way—"

The police arrive before the ambulance, take one look at what I'm doing, and apparently approve, because the next thing I know, they've started shooing people away, telling them the show is over.

I say, urgently, "Take statements from the witnesses! This thing didn't just fall, you know. Somebody pushed it!"

Everyone gathers eagerly around the policemen, wanting to tell their story. It's right around then that Rachel comes running out of the building, her high heels clacking on the pavement.

"Oh, Heather!" she cries, picking her way through the shards of cement and clods of dirt and geranium. "Oh, Heather! I just heard. Is he—is he going to be—"

"He's still breathing," I say. I keep the towel pressed to the wound, which has finally stopped bleeding. "Where's that ambulance?"

But right then it pulls up, and the EMS workers leap out and, thankfully, take over. I'm more than happy to get out of the way. Rachel puts an arm around my shoulders as we watch them take Jordan's vital signs. One of the cops, meanwhile, goes inside, while the other one picks up one of the larger chunks of planter and looks at me.

"Who's in charge here?" he wants to know.

Rachel says, "I guess that'd be me."

"Any idea where this came from?" the cop asks, holding up the slab.

"Well, it looks like one of the cement planters from the Allingtons' terrace," Rachel replies. She turns and points up, toward Fischer Hall's facade. "Up there," she says, craning her neck. "Twentieth floor. The penthouse. There are planters like this lined all around the terrace." She quits pointing and looks at me. "I can't imagine how it could have happened. The wind, maybe?"

I feel really cold, but it isn't from any wind. It's as warm a day in fall as any.

Magda, who has joined us, seems to agree.

"There is no wind today," she says. "On New York One they said it would be mild all day long."

"None of those planters ever blew over before," Pete says. "And I been here twenty years."

"Well, you can't be suggesting someone pushed it," Rachel says, looking horrified. "I mean, the students don't even have access to the terrace—"

"Students?" The cop squints at us. "This some kind of dorm, or something?"

"Residence hall," both Rachel and I correct him automatically.

The EMS workers load Jordan onto a backboard, then onto a stretcher, and then into the back of the ambulance. As they are closing the doors, I glance at Rachel.

"I should go with him," I say to her.

She gives me a little push toward the vehicle. "Of course, you should," she says kindly. "You go. I'll take care of things here. Call me and let me know how he is."

I tell her I will, and hurry after the EMS guys, asking them if I can hitch a ride to the hospital with them. They're totally cool about it, and let me take the passenger seat of the cab.

From the front seat, I can look back through this little door and see what the paramedic who isn't driving is doing to Jordan. What he is doing to Jordan is asking him what day of the week it is. Apparently, Jordan's regaining consciousness. He doesn't know what day of the week it is, though, and only grunts in response, like someone who'd really like to go back to sleep.

I think about suggesting that they ask him who he's engaged to, but then decide this would be too mean.

As we pull away from the hall, I notice that Rachel, Sarah, Pete, and Magda are all huddled on the sidewalk, gazing worriedly after me.

I realize then, with a kind of pang, that yeah, okay, maybe I don't have a boyfriend.

But I do have a family.

A weird one, maybe.

But I've got one.

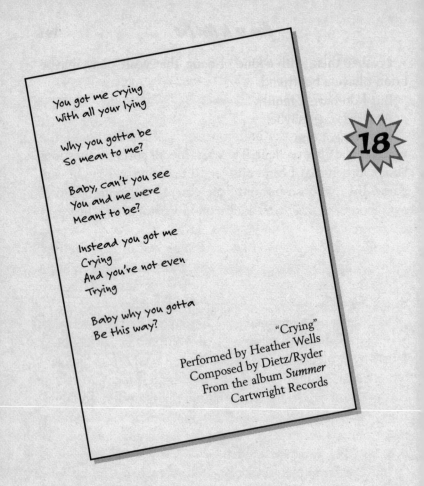

You got me crying
With all your lying

Why you gotta be
So mean to me?

Baby, can't you see
You and me were
Meant to be?

Instead you got me
Crying
And you're not even
Trying

Baby why you gotta
Be this way?

"Crying"
Performed by Heather Wells
Composed by Dietz/Ryder
From the album *Summer*
Cartwright Records

18

In the nearly four months since I started working at New York College, I've been to just about every emergency room in Manhattan with various sick or injured students. St. Vincent's isn't really one of my favorites. There's a TV in the waiting room and everything, but it's always turned to soap operas, and the candy machine is always out of Butterfingers.

Also, a lot of junkies go there to try to convince the triage nurse that they really need some morphine for these mysterious pains in their feet. The junkies are entertaining to watch for a while, but when they start withdrawing they get hostile, and then the security guard has to throw them out and then they beat on the windows and in general make it very hard to concentrate on *Jane* magazine or whatever I happen to be reading.

But though the waiting room at St. Vincent's sucks, the medical staff is excellent. They ask me all sorts of questions about Jordan that I can't answer. But as soon as I say his full name, they whoosh him into the emergency room ahead of everybody, because, you know, even doctors have heard of Easy Street.

Visitors aren't allowed in the ER except during the first five minutes of every hour, so I'm banished to the waiting room. But I employ my time there wisely by calling Jordan's dad to give him the details about the accident.

Mr. Cartwright is understandably upset by the news that his most popular male solo artist—oh, and son—has been felled by a geranium planter, so I don't take it personally when he is very curt on the phone with me. Our most recent conversation before that hadn't gone very smoothly, either— the one where he'd told me that he'd get Jordan to dump Tania and "fly right" if I'd just quit demanding to sing my own songs on my next album.

Mr. Cartwright is kind of a jerk. Which might be why Cooper hasn't spoken to him in almost a year.

After I hang up with Jordan and Cooper's dad, I can't think of anyone else to call. I guess I could let Cooper know his brother's been hurt.

But Cooper is bound to ask what Jordan was doing at Fischer Hall in the first place. And the truth is, I'm not the world's greatest liar. I just have this feeling Cooper will see right through any attempt on my part to pull the wool over his eyes.

So I sink into a plastic chair in one corner of the waiting

room and have fun watching other emergency patients being carted in instead of making any more phone calls. It's just like *Trauma in the ER*, on the Learning Channel, only, you know, live. I see a jovial drunk with a bleeding hand, a frazzled mom with a baby she's spilled her cappuccino on, a kid in a school uniform with a big cut on his chin being steered around by a nun, a construction worker with a broken foot, and a bunch of Spanish women with no visible problems who talk very loudly and get yelled at by the triage nurse.

I sit for twenty more minutes, and then the security guard announces that everyone waiting has five minutes to see their loved ones in the ER. So I herd along with the nun and the nervous mom and the Spanish ladies through the double doors and look around for Jordan.

He is unconscious again, or at least his eyes are closed, the white bandage around his head contrasting startlingly with the deep tan of his skin. (His parents have a really nice summer place in the Hamptons. The pool has a waterfall and everything.) They'd put his gurney in a pretty secluded, quiet section of the ER, and when I ask, the nurse tells me a bed is being prepared for him upstairs. They're still waiting for his X-rays, but it looks as though a concussion is likely.

I guess I must look really worried or something since the nurse smiles at me and puts her hand on my arm and says, "Don't worry. I'm sure he's going to be back to doing dance moves in no time."

In spite of the nurse's assertion, I can't bring myself to leave him there all alone. I can't believe no one from his family has shown up yet! So when my five minutes of standing there and staring at Jordan are up, I go back to my plastic seat in the waiting room. I'll stay, I decide, until he's moved upstairs, or until a member of his family arrives. I'll just hang out till they get here. And then—

And then I don't know what I'll do. I'm convinced—one hundred percent convinced, surer than I've ever been about anything, which I realize isn't saying much, but whatever—that someone has just tried to kill me.

Right? I mean, hadn't that been what the guy from the chess circle had said? "Good thing you moved, lady, or you'd have been the one it hit," or something like that?

And the someone who pushed that planter over could only have been Christopher Allington. Who else had access to his parents' terrace? Who else had reason to knock geranium planters onto my head? It wasn't a premeditated attempt at murder—it couldn't have been. How could he have known I'd be on my way back into the building right then?

No, he must have just looked down and decided fate was on his side and given that planter the heave-ho. If I hadn't ducked, it would have hit me, and not Jordan. And it probably would have killed me, because, you know, my head isn't anywhere near as hard as an ex-member of Easy Street's.

But why does Chris want to kill me? Just because I suspect him of being a murderer? Suspecting someone of being a murderer and actually having proof of someone being a murderer are two entirely different things. What possible proof could Chris think I have? I mean, aside from the condom—which only proves he's randy, not a killer—I have nothing on him. I don't even have proof that there've actually *been* any murders.

So why is he trying to kill me? Isn't he putting himself more at risk by trying to kill me than by just laying low? Especially since foul play isn't suspected in the deaths of Elizabeth and Roberta—

By anyone but me, anyway.

A deep, familiar voice breaks in on my meditations. I look

away from the snoring junkie I've been staring at unseeingly, and up into Cooper's calm, smiling face . . .

. . . and suddenly feel like throwing up.

"Heather," he says, with friendly nonchalance, as he folds himself into the plastic chair beside me.

"Um." That's all I can think of to say. Swift, huh? After a lot of mental turmoil, I finally add, "Hi."

Cooper gazes with mild interest at the snoring junkie. He looks, in his scruffy but form-fitting jeans and black leather jacket, good enough to eat. Better than Ho Hos, even. Cooper, I mean. Not the junkie.

"So," he says, in the same conversational tone. "What's new with you?"

I go cold all over, then hot. It's totally unfair, the hold this guy has over me. And he's never so much as asked me out! Okay, he asked me to move in with him, but, hello, that was out of pity. And I live on a whole separate floor. With a whole separate set of locks on the door. Which I've never actually used, but has he ever bothered to find that out? No!

"Nothing much," I say to him, hoping he can't see how my heart is leaping around inside my T-shirt. "Did, um, your dad call you?"

"No," Cooper says. "Your friend Patty did. When she came to your office to pick you up for lunch, Magda told her what happened. Patty had the baby with her, or she'd have come herself."

"Oh," I say. I'd forgotten all about my lunch appointment with Patty. Glancing at the waiting room clock, I see that it's after two. "Well."

"What she couldn't quite explain," Cooper says, "is what, precisely, happened."

Which is when it all comes spilling out.

I don't want for it to. I don't mean for it to. It's just . . .

well, I guess that's why Cooper's such a good detective. There's something in his deep voice that just makes you blurt out everything you know . . .

Well, okay, not *everything*. I did manage to keep the whole part about what Jordan and I had done on Cooper's hallway runner under wraps. Wild horses aren't going to drag *that* information out of me.

Oh, and the part about me wanting to, you know, peel off Cooper's clothes with my teeth, of course.

But the rest of it just comes out in this giant gush, the way the hot chocolate in the dorm cafeteria does sometimes, right after Magda's poured the mix in but before anybody's stirred it . . .

I tell him, starting with the lip-synch the night before, when I'd first begun to suspect that Christopher Allington was Elizabeth and Roberta's killer, and ending with the geraniums cracking Jordan's head open, skipping over the part in between where his brother and I made the beast with two backs in his foyer.

I've overheard Cooper in action with his clients a couple of times. The washer/dryer is on the same floor as his office, just off the kitchen, and I've been in there washing my control top underwear (I only wear it on special occasions, like customer service training seminars or cultural diversity awareness workshops) when he's met with people who've hired him. He talks to them in this totally calm, careful voice . . .

. . . a completely different voice, it turns out, than he uses on his nonpaying clientele.

"Heather, are you insane?" He looks really mad. He *sounds* really mad. "You went and *talked* to the guy?"

It would be nice to think that the reason he's so angry with me is because my near brush with death has finally made him realize his true feelings for me.

But I think all it did was reinforce his suspicions that I'm a complete and total whacko.

"Why are you yelling at *me*?" I demand. "I'm the victim here!"

"No, you're not. Jordan is. And if you'd just listened to me—"

"But if I'd listened to you, I wouldn't know that Chris Allington is the dangerous psychopath we've been looking for!"

"A fact of which you still don't have any proof." Cooper shakes his head. He has dark, thick hair that he hardly ever gets cut and that is always growing past his collar, giving him a distinctly nonconformist air, even without the whole private eye thing. "That planter could have been knocked over by anyone. How do you know the Allingtons' gardener wasn't watering the plants and accidentally knocked the thing over?"

"Directly onto me? Isn't that just a bit of a coincidence? Considering the fact that I was just questioning Chris Allington the night before?"

I swear I see the corners of Cooper's mouth twitch at this.

"I'm sorry, Heather, but I doubt your interrogation skills are such as to goad Chris Allington into a murderous frenzy."

Okay, Miss Marple I may not be. But he doesn't have to rub it in.

"I'm telling you, he tried to kill me. Why don't you believe me?" I hear myself cry, before I can shut my mouth. "Can't you see that I'm not a stupid little teen pop star anymore, and that I might just know what I'm talking about?"

Even as the words are coming out, I'm wishing them unsaid. What am I doing? *What am I doing?* This is the guy who, without my even asking, offered me a place to live when I had nowhere to go . . . well, okay, except the guest room in Patty and Frank's loft.

But, you know. Besides that. How ungrateful can I be?

"I'm so sorry," I say, feeling dry-mouthed with panic. "I didn't mean it. I don't know where that came from. I'm just—I think maybe I'm just upset. You know. From the stress."

Cooper is just sitting there, looking at me with a totally unreadable expression.

"I don't think of you as a stupid little teen pop star" is all he says, in a tone suggesting mild surprise.

"I know," I say quickly. Oh God, why can't I ever seem to keep my mouth shut? WHY?

"I just worry about you sometimes," Cooper goes on, before I can say anything else. "I mean, you get yourself into things. . . . That whole thing with my brother—"

What whole thing? Did he mean . . . my *relationship* with his brother? Or last night? Oh please, don't let him have seen the *Post*. . . .

"And it's not like you have anyone." He shakes his head again. "Any family, or anyone to look after you."

"But neither do you," I remind him.

"That's different," he says.

"I don't see how," I say. "I mean, except that I'm younger than you." But what's seven years, really? Prince Charles and Lady Diana were twelve years apart . . . and okay, that didn't turn out so well, but how likely are we to repeat their mistakes as a couple? If Cooper and I ever were to become one, I mean. Neither of us even likes polo.

"Besides," I say, remembering what I'd seen out of the ambulance window. "I do have a family. Sort of. I mean, there's Rachel and Magda and Pete and Patty and you—"

I didn't mean to add that last word. But there it is, floating in the air between us. You. You're part of my family, Cooper. My new family, now that my real family members are all incarcerated or on the lam. Congratulations!

Cooper just looks at me like I'm crazy (how unusual). So I add lamely, "And Lucy, too."

Cooper exhales slowly.

"If you really feel strongly that what happened wasn't an accident," he says at last, pointedly ignoring the We Are Family speech (don't think I don't notice), "and you really think someone is trying to kill you, then I suggest we go to the police."

"I tried that," I remind him. "Remember?"

"Yes. But this time I'm going with you, and I'm going to make sure—"

His voice trails off as a petite, attractive brunette comes rushing up to the waiting room desk, all breathless and leather-skirted, her left hand weighted down by a massive diamond ring.

Okay, so I can't actually see the ring from where I'm sitting. I still know who she is. I've seen her with her mouth around my ex's you-know-what. Her image will be forever burned onto my retina.

"Excuse me," she breathes to the stony-faced receptionist. "But I believe my fiancé is here. Jordan Cartwright. When can I see him?"

Tania Trace, the woman who'd taken my place in Jordan's heart and penthouse—not to mention my position on the music charts.

"Funny," Cooper observes. "She looks as if she's handling the pain quite well."

I glance at him curiously, then remember that he's referring to something I'd told him some time ago, after I'd first moved in.

"Oh sure," I say. "Because she's strung out on painkillers. But I'm telling you, Coop, you can't have that much plastic surgery and expect to live a pain-free life. I mean, she's been almost completely reconstructed. In reality, she's a size eighteen."

"Right," Cooper says. "Looks like my brother's in good hands now. Shall we go?"

We go.

And none too soon, if you ask me.

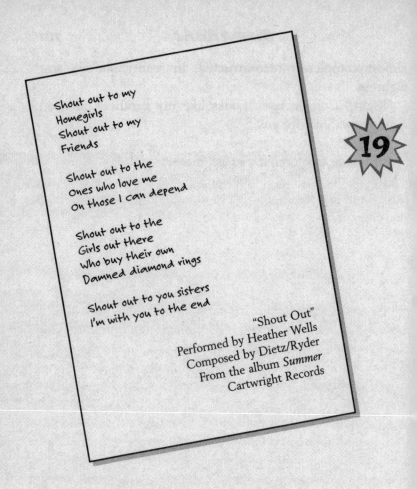

19

Shout out to my
Homegirls
Shout out to my
Friends

Shout out to the
Ones who love me
On those I can depend

Shout out to the
Girls out there
Who buy their own
Damned diamond rings

Shout out to you sisters
I'm with you to the end

"Shout Out"
Performed by Heather Wells
Composed by Dietz/Ryder
From the album *Summer*
Cartwright Records

The first person at the Sixth Precinct I tell my story to is a pretty but tired-looking woman at the front desk. She has her long black hair in a bun, which I assume is regulation hairstyle for policewomen.

I make a mental note not to major in criminal justice.

The woman directs us to a pudgy guy at a desk, to whom I repeat my story. Like the receptionist, he looks bored . . .

. . . until I get to the part about Jordan. Everybody perks up at the mention of Easy Street.

The pudgy guy has us wait a few minutes, and then we're

ushered into someone's extremely tidy office. We sit across from a very neat desk for a minute or two before the owner of the office walks in, and I see that he is none other than cigar-chomping Detective Canavan.

"You!" I nearly shout at him.

"You!" he nearly shouts back. He's holding a Styrofoam cup of coffee and—what else?—a doughnut. Krispy Kreme glazed, from the look of it. Lucky duck.

"To what do I owe the pleasure this time, Miss Wells?" he asks. "Wait, don't tell me. This wouldn't happen to be about somebody crowning a Backstreet Boy, would it?"

"Easy Street member," I correct him. "And yes, it would."

Detective Canavan sits down at his desk, removes the unlit cigar from his mouth, tears off a piece of his doughnut, and dunks it in his coffee. He then puts the coffee-soaked piece of doughnut in his mouth, chews, swallows, and says, "Pray enlighten me."

I glance at Cooper, who had remained silent at my side through two recitations of my tale. Seeing that he isn't going to be any help this time, either, I launch into it for a third time, wondering, not for the first time, what it is I find so attractive about Cooper anyway, since he can be so uncommunicative sometimes. Then I remember the whole being-so-hot-and-kind-and-generous-to-me-without-asking-anything-in-return thing, and I know why.

Detective Canavan clasps his hands behind his head as he listens, tipping his chair back as far as it will go. Either he has forgotten his Mitchum for Men or he is just a very profuse sweater, because he has large perspiration stains underneath his arms. Not that this seems to bother him.

"So," Detective Canavan says, to the water-stained ceiling panels, when I'm through talking. "Now you think the president of New York College's kid is a murderer."

"Well," I say, hesitantly. Because when he puts it that way, it sounds so . . . dumb. "Yes. I guess I do."

"But you got no proof. Sure, this guy here's got a condom. A condom we could probably prove is his. But which wouldn't be admissible in court. But you got no proof any crime has actually been committed, with the exception of this planter over the side of the terrace, which could have been accidental—"

"But those planters have been up there for years," I interrupt. "And none of them ever fell down until today—"

"Coroner's report on both dead girls states cause of death was accidental." Detective Canavan quits gazing at the ceiling and looks at me. "Listen, miss—is it still miss?"

Unaccountably, I feel myself blushing. Maybe because if it hadn't been for Tania Trace, by now it would have been Mrs. Although I sort of doubt it would have remained that way for long.

"It's Ms.," I say firmly.

Detective Canavan nods. "My wife's a Ms. now, too. Anyway, listen, Ms. Wells. Kids that age? They're dopes. Accidents are the leading cause of death for people ages seventeen to twenty-five. Kids are trying to find themselves, taking stupid risks—"

"Not those girls," I say, firmly.

"Maybe not. The point is, Ms. Wells, you got nothing on this guy. You don't even have a definite murder to pin on him. If the Backstreet Boy dies, then maybe we'll have something. Maybe. But the coroner could just as easily rule that one as accidental as well."

"Well," I say. I have to admit, I feel very let down. Detective Canavan hadn't laughed outright in my face this time, I'll admit, but he hadn't taken a single note, either. I pick up my backpack.

"Sorry to have wasted your time. Again." I get up, and Detective Canavan looks at me like I was nuts.

"Where do you think you're going?" he demands. "Sit down. I'm not through with you yet."

I sit back down, perplexed.

"What's the point?" I ask Detective Canavan, with more asperity than is, perhaps, necessary. "You obviously think I'm some kind of nutcase. What do I need to stick around here for? I can get laughed at by my own friends"—I keep my gaze averted from Cooper's face. "I don't need to go to the police for that."

Detective Canavan finishes the rest of his doughnut, then picks up his cigar. He looks at Cooper.

"She's a fiery one," he comments, nodding at me.

"Oh, she's that," Cooper agrees, gravely.

"Wait." I glance from one man to the other, suspicion dawning. "You two know each other?"

Cooper shrugs. "I've seen him around the neighborhood," he says, referring to Detective Canavan.

"Can't swing a dead cat without running into this guy behind a parked car or mailbox, shooting film of some poor schmuck whose wife is leaving him," says Detective Canavan, referring to Cooper.

"Great," I say, feeling more inadequate than ever. "That's just great. Well, I hope you two are enjoying your little laugh at my expense—"

"Do I look like I'm laughing?" Detective Canavan demands. "Do you see so much as a smile upon my face? Your boyfriend over there, I don't see him laughing, either."

"I see absolutely nothing amusing about the situation," Cooper says.

I look at him. He isn't smiling. And he hasn't, I noticed, objected to being called my boyfriend. I look back at Detective Canavan.

"He's not my boyfriend," I point out loudly—to what purpose, I cannot imagine. But I'm sure my cheeks are crimson.

Detective Canavan nods at me as if I'd said something along the lines of *The sky is blue.*

"Now, Ms. Wells," he says. "We do have a very high number of nutcases, as you call them, who come in here to report various crimes that may or may not actually have occurred. Some of these so-called nutcases are honest citizens who want to help the police to do their job. I would put you in this category. You have done your duty by relating your beliefs in this matter to me, and I, in due course, will investigate them."

"Really?" I perk right up. "You really will? You're gonna question Chris?"

"I will do so." Detective Canavan sticks his cigar back in his mouth. "Discreetly. That is my job. It is not, however, *your* job. I strongly advise you, Ms. Wells, not to involve yourself any further in this matter."

"Because you think Christopher Allington might try to kill me, too?" I ask, breathlessly.

"Because I think Christopher Allington might try to sue you for making false accusations, and he'd have a pretty good case, too." Detective Canavan ignores my crestfallen expression. "What you're suggesting, Ms. Wells, is that Christopher Allington is not only a serial killer, but a killer of such intelligence and skill that he not only leaves no evidence linking him to his crimes—save for an alleged condom—but leaves no trace that a crime has even been committed. I hate to disappoint you, but in my experience, killers aren't that smart. They are, in fact, remarkably stupid people. That is why they have killed: They are so limited intellectually, they saw no other way out."

Detective Canavan's dark gray eyebrows furrow together in thought as he goes on. "And despite all the media hoopla around them, I have yet to meet an actual serial killer myself, and I have investigated over seven hundred homicides. So I suggest you keep a low profile as far as Christopher Allington is concerned, Ms. Wells. I'd hate for you to lose your job over something like this."

I'm so disappointed that I don't think there's anything I can do to hide it. My shoulders slump, and my head sinks down between them as I murmur, "Thank you, Detective."

Detective Canavan hands me his card, tells me to call him if I think of anything else that might be helpful to his investigation, and, after asking Cooper a question or two about some case or other he's seen him snooping around the neighborhood over, sends us on our way.

Cooper hails us a cab, and maintains an air of extreme seriousness all the way back to the house. He seems to have taken my accusation—that he thinks of me as a teen pop star—to heart, and is doing everything in his power to prove it isn't true. He even tells me, in the cab, that he considers Detective Canavan a good man and a fine investigator, and says if there's something to get to the bottom of at Fischer Hall, Detective Canavan is the man to do it.

Which makes me feel better. A little.

Once back at the brownstone—I know I really ought to head back to the office, but seeing as how I'm home now anyway, I decide I'll just give Lucy a quick walk—I pause briefly in front of the antique, gilt-framed mirror in the front hallway to reapply my lip gloss, while Cooper goes back to his office to replay his messages. I've already glanced around to make sure that there are no signs of the love tussle Jordan and I shared on the runner the night before.

Still, when Cooper comes out of his office a second later and asks, "What exactly is going on with you and Jordan?" I nearly have a heart attack.

"Wh-what do you mean?" I stammer.

"Well, what was he doing outside Fischer Hall today, anyway?"

"Oh," I say, relaxing. "That. Nothing. Just talking."

"I see." Cooper leans against the doorframe, his blue eyes brighter than normal. "So you wouldn't happen to know anything about that blond he was photographed by the *Post* kissing on my doorstep?"

I almost swallow my tongue.

I can't believe he's seen it! Are things *ever* going to go my way? Or had I used up all my luck already? You know, those ten years of good luck I once read that everybody gets—one magical decade where nothing goes wrong . . . or at least, nothing major.

Had my decade of luck already gone by? And if so, can I have a do-over? Because if someone had asked me, "Hey, Heather, do you want your decade of luck between ages fourteen and twenty-four or twenty-four and thirty-four?" I'd have chosen the latter. I really would have.

Because who wants the best years of their life to be the ones they spent in *high school*?

I guess my extreme consternation must show on my face, since a second later Cooper has straightened and is going, "What's the matter?" in a voice that—almost—sounds like he actually cares.

Which just makes me want to start sobbing, right then and there.

"It's nothing," I say. "Really."

It isn't nothing, though. I mean, everyone else can deny it, but I know—I *know*—someone is trying to *kill* me. I had sex with my ex, who is engaged to someone with a way better career—and much smaller butt—than mine. And, worst of all, Cooper's seen the photographic evidence of my indiscretion . . . or at least, of what led up to it.

"Something's wrong," Cooper says, coming to stand beside me in front of the mirror. "Don't deny it. I'm a trained observer, remember? There's this little line you get between your eyebrows when you're upset—" He points at my reflection. "See it?"

God. He's right. I have a little worry line between my eyebrows. My God, if I keep this up, I'll have wrinkles by the time I'm thirty.

With an effort, I force my face to relax.

"It's nothing," I say, quickly, averting my gaze from my reflection. "Really. That thing with Jordan last night—it was just a good-bye kiss."

Cooper looks at me. Skeptically.

"A good-bye kiss," he says.

"Yeah. Because it's, you know, really over between us. Jordan and me." I clear my throat. "You know. Really, *really* over."

Cooper nods, though he still looks dubious.

"Right," he says. "Well, if you say—"

"We're both ready to move on," I interrupt, warming to my story, "at last. You know, we needed to have some closure, because the way things ended—with me storming out like that, and all—well, it wasn't healthy. Things are good now between us. We both know it's really . . . over."

"So if things are really, really over between the two of you," Cooper asks, "what was Jordan doing in front of Fischer Hall this morning when that planter fell on him?"

Dang! I forgot about that!

But it's okay. I have the situation under control.

"Oh, that?" I say, with a breezy laugh. Yes! I even manage a breezy laugh. Maybe I, like Britney and Mandy, have a film career in my future. Maybe I should be a theater major, like Marnie. Maybe someday I'll have an Oscar to put on the shelf next to my Nobel Prize. Wait. Is a Nobel Prize a statue or a medal? I can't remember.

"Yeah," I say. Still breezy. "He was just returning a, um, CD that I'd left at our place. You know, when I moved out."

"A CD," Cooper says.

"Uh-huh," I say. "My, um, *Tank Girl* soundtrack. You can't find it anymore. It's very rare."

"I see," Cooper says. I try not to notice how, now that he's taken off his leather jacket, his biceps—barely visible beneath the short sleeves of his plain gray T-shirt—are just as defined as his brother's. . . .

Only from actual work, not working *out*, I know. It's not all sneaking around with a camera when you're a PI. I imagine Cooper has to . . . you know. Lift things. And stuff. I wonder if maybe he ever gets sweaty doing it and has to take his shirt off completely, you know, because he's so hot . . .

Whoa. I so need to go back to work.

But all this detective stuff has reminded me of something.

"Yeah," I say. Now that the danger of tears has been averted, I'm feeling a little more daring. "In fact, now that Jordan and I have everything settled, I feel, you know, like celebrating."

"Celebrating," Cooper echoes tonelessly.

"Yeah. You know. I never go out anymore. So I thought, Hey, why not go to the, um, Pansy Ball tonight."

"The *Pansy* Ball?" Cooper's gaze doesn't stray from my face. I hope he isn't checking to see if I'm lying. I really *do* want to go to the Pansy Ball. Just not, you know, for the reasons I'm telling him.

"Yeah," I say. "It's a ball to honor the trustees and people who've been given Pansys. You know, for service to the college. Rachel's getting one."

It isn't my imagination. At the sound of my boss's name,

Cooper abruptly loses interest in the conversation. In fact, he walks over to the mail that has just slid through the drop slot—to Lucy's intent interest—and, after wrestling it from her, starts sorting through it.

"Rachel, huh?" he says.

"Yeah," I say. "The tickets are like two hundred bucks, though. To the ball. And God knows I can't afford one. But I was thinking, your grandfather was an alumnus, right? So I bet you have access to some free ones. Tickets, I mean."

"Probably," Cooper says, giving Lucy, who is whining piteously, a J. Crew catalog to chew on.

"So could I, maybe, have one?" I ask. Subtle. That's me. Miss Subtle.

"So you can spy on Christopher Allington?" Cooper doesn't even look up from the mail. "Not a chance."

My jaw drops.

"But—"

"Heather, didn't you hear a word that detective said? He's going to look into it. Subtly. In the meantime, stay out of it. At best, the only thing you're going to get for your efforts is sued."

"I swear I'm not gonna talk to him," I insist, raising my right hand and making the Girl Scout's honor symbol with three fingers. Except, of course, I never was a Girl Scout, so it doesn't count. "I won't go near him."

"Correct me if I'm mistaken," Cooper says, "but aren't you convinced he tried to kill you today?"

"Well, that's what I'm trying to find out," I say. "C'mon, Cooper, what could possibly happen at the *Pansy Ball*, for God's sake? He's not going to try to do anything to me there, in front of everybody . . ."

"No, he isn't," Cooper says. "Because I'm not letting you out of my sight."

I blink. Wait. What did he just say?

"You—you want to go with me?"

"Only because if I don't keep an eye on you, who knows what'll fall on your head next time." Cooper puts down the mail. His blue-eyed gaze bores into me like a pair of head-lights. "And because I can see by the look in your eyes that you're going to get your hands on a ticket somehow, even if it means seducing some unsuspecting rube in the geology de-partment."

I'm stunned. Cooper is taking me to the Pansy Ball! Cooper Cartwright is taking me out! It was almost like a . . .

Well, a *date*.

"Oh, Cooper!" I breathe. "Thank you so much! You don't know how much this means to me—"

Cooper is already moving back toward his office, shaking his head. He keeps his thoughts to himself, but I have a pretty good idea that he isn't, as I am, frantically trying to fig-ure out what he's going to wear.

Guys have it so easy.

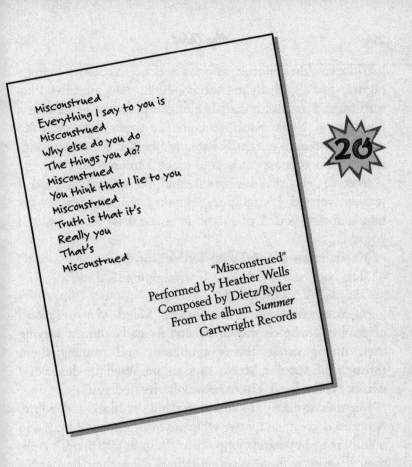

Misconstrued
Everything I say to you is
Misconstrued
Why else do you do
The things you do?
Misconstrued
You think that I lie to you
Misconstrued
Truth is that it's
Really you
That's
Misconstrued

"Misconstrued"
Performed by Heather Wells
Composed by Dietz/Ryder
From the album *Summer*
Cartwright Records

I can't get through the remainder of the workday fast enough.

Everyone asks after Jordan's health, causing me to realize guiltily that I don't even know how he's doing, since I've been slightly distracted since leaving the hospital, what with meeting with detectives and getting asked out (sort of) by the man of my dreams, and having to figure out what I'm going to wear on our date to the Pansy Ball, and all.

So I call St. Vincent's and after being transferred about a

half-dozen times because of privacy concerns, Jordan being a big star and all, finally get someone who tells me, after I assure them I am not a member of the press and even sing a few bars of "Sugar Rush" to convince them that I'm really me, that Jordan is currently listed as being in good condition, and that doctors expect him to make a full recovery.

When I relay this news to Rachel, she goes, "Oh, good! I was so worried. It's so lucky, Heather, that the planter hit him and not you. You might so easily have been injured yourself."

Magda is less pleased with Jordan's prognosis.

"Too bad," she says baldly. "I was hoping he'd die."

"Magda!" I cry, horrified.

"Look at my byootiful movie stars," Magda says to a group of students who've shown up for an early dinner, waving their dining cards. Taking the cards and running them through the scanner, Magda says, to me, "Well, he deserves a whack on the head, after the way he treated you."

Magda's so lucky. To her, everything is black and white. America is great, no matter what anybody else might say, and members of boy bands who cheat on their girlfriends? Well, they deserve to have planters dropped on their heads. No questions asked.

Patty is relieved to hear from me when I call her. I guess when she'd crossed the park and seen all the blood on the sidewalk in front of Fischer Hall, she'd gotten really freaked out. She'd been convinced something had happened to me. She'd had to sit down in the cafeteria with her head between her knees for twenty minutes—and eat two DoveBars Magda pressed on her—before she finally felt well enough to flag down a cab and go home.

"Are you really sure about this college degree thing, Heather?" she asks now, worriedly. "Because I'm sure Frank could set up an appointment for you with people from his label—"

"That'd be nice," I say. "Except, you know, I'm not sure how impressed Frank's label would really be about the fact that most of my past performances took place in malls—"

"They wouldn't care about that," Patty cries. Which is really sweet of her, and all, but that's exactly the kind of thing record labels *do* care about, I've discovered.

"Maybe we can get you a part in a musical, you know, like on Broadway," Patty says. "Debbie Gibson's doing it. Lot's of stars are—"

"Operative word being star," I point out. "Which I am not."

"I just don't think you should work in that dorm anymore, Heather," Patty says worriedly. "It's too dangerous. Girls dying. Flower pots falling down on people—"

"Oh, Patty," I say, touched by her concern. "I'll be all right."

"I'm serious, Heather. Cooper and I discussed it, and we both feel—"

"You and Cooper discussed *me*?" I hope I don't sound too eager. What had they talked about? I wonder. Had Cooper revealed to Patty that he has a deep and abiding love for me that he dares not show, since I'm his brother's ex and sort of an employee of his?

But if he had, wouldn't she have told me right away?

"Cooper and I just feel—and Frank agrees—that if—well, if it turns out this whole murder thing is true, you might be putting yourself in some kind of danger—"

This doesn't sound to me like Cooper had said anything at all about harboring a deep and abiding love for me. No wonder Patty hadn't called me right away to dish.

"Patty," I say, "I'm fine. Really. I've got the best bodyguard in the world." Then I tell her about the Pansy Ball, and Cooper's escorting me there.

Patty doesn't sound as excited about it as I expect her to, though. Oh, she says I can borrow her dress—the red Armani she'd worn to the Grammys when she'd been seven months' pregnant with Indy, and which I hope will consequently fit me—and all, but she isn't exactly shrieking, "Ooooh he asked you out!"

Because I guess he hasn't, really. Maybe it isn't a *real* date when the guy is just going out with you to make sure no one kills you.

God. When did Patty get so mature?

"Well, just promise me to be careful, okay, Heather?" Patty still sounds worried. "Cooper says he thinks the whole murder thing is kind of . . . unlikely. But I'm not so sure. And I don't want you to be next."

I do my best to reassure Patty that my safety is hardly in jeopardy—even though, of course, I'm pretty sure the exact opposite is true. Someone in Fischer Hall wants me dead.

Which means I am definitely on to something with my Elizabeth-Kellogg-and-Roberta-Pace-were-murdered theory.

It isn't until I've hung up with Patty that I feel someone's gaze on me. I look up and see that Sarah is sitting at her desk, stuffing Tootsie Rolls into little plastic bags as a surprise for each of the RAs, all of whom she feels need a pick-me-up after the rocky start their semester had gotten off to, given the dead girls and all.

Only I can't help noticing that Sarah has stopped stuffing, and is instead staring at me owlishly through her thick glasses—she only wears her contacts on special occasions, such as check-in (potential to meet cute single dads) or poetry readings at St. Mark's Church (potential to meet cute penniless poets).

"I didn't mean to listen in on your conversation," Sarah

says, "but did I just hear you say you think someone's trying to *kill* you?"

"Um," I say. How can I put this so as not to cause her undue alarm? After all, I get to go home every night, but Sarah has to live here. How comfortable is she going to feel knowing there's a dangerous psychopath stalking the floors of Fischer Hall?

Then again, Sarah lost her virginity on an Israeli kibbutz the summer of her freshman year—or so she'd told me—so it isn't like she's a potential victim.

So I shrug and say, "Yes."

Then—because Rachel is upstairs in her apartment getting ready for the ball (she'd managed to find something to wear, but wouldn't show it to us on account of "not wanting to ruin the surprise")—I tell her my theory about Chris Allington and the deaths of Elizabeth Kellogg and Roberta Pace.

"Have you told any of this to Rachel?" Sarah asks me, when I'm done.

"No," I say. "Rachel has enough to worry about, don't you think?" Besides—I don't mention this part to Sarah—if it turns out I'm wrong, it won't look so good at my six months' employment review . . . you know, my suspecting the son of the president of the college of a double homicide.

"Good," Sarah says. "Don't. Because has it occurred to you that this whole thing—you know, with your thinking that Elizabeth and Roberta were murdered—might be a manifestation of your own insecurities over having been betrayed and abandoned by your mother?"

I just blink at her. "What?"

"Well," Sarah says, pushing up her glasses. "Your mother stole all your money and fled the country with your manager.

That had to have been the most traumatic event in your life. I mean, you lost everything—all your savings, as well as the people on whom you thought you could most depend, your father having been absent most of your life to begin with due to his long-term incarceration for passing bad checks. And yet whenever anyone brings it up, you dismiss the whole thing as if it were nothing."

"No, I don't," I say. Because I don't. Or at least, I don't think I do.

"Yes, you do," Sarah says. "You even still speak to your mother. I heard you on the phone with her the other day. You were chatting with her about what to get your dad for his birthday. In *jail*. The woman who stole all your money and fled to Argentina!"

"Well," I say, a little defensively. "She's still my *mother*, no matter what she's done."

I'm never sure how to explain about my mom. Yes, when the going got tough—when I let Cartwright Records know I was only interested in singing my own lyrics, and Jordan's dad, in response, unceremoniously dropped me from the label—not that my sales had been going gangbusters anymore anyway—my mom got going.

But that's just how she is. I was mad at her for a while, of course.

But being mad at my mom is kind of like being mad because it's raining out. She can't help what she does, any more than clouds can.

But I suppose Sarah, if she heard that, would just say I'm in denial, or worse.

"Isn't it possible that you're displacing the hostility you feel about what your mother did to you onto poor Chris Allington?" Sarah wants to know.

"Excuse me," I say. I'm getting kind of tired of repeating

myself. "But that planter didn't just fall out of the sky, you know. Well, okay, it did, but not by itself."

"And could it be that you miss the attention you used to receive from your fans so much that you've latched on to any excuse to make yourself feel important by inventing this big important mystery for you to solve, where none actually exists?"

I remember, with a pang, what Cooper had said outside the service elevator. Hadn't it been something along these same lines? About me wanting to relive the thrill of my glory days back at the Mall of America?

But wanting to find out who's responsible for killing people in your place of work is totally different from singing in front of thousands of busy shoppers.

I mean, isn't it?

"Um" is what I say in response to Sarah's accusation. "Maybe. I don't know."

All I can think is, Sarah's lucky she met Yael when she did. The kibbutz guy, I mean. Otherwise, she's just the kind of girl Chris would go for next.

Well, except for that habit she has of psychoanalyzing people all the time. I could see how that might get annoying.

I haven't been to a dressy party in ages, so when I finally get off work that night, I have a lot of preparations to make. First I have to go to Patty's to get the dress—which fits, thank God, but barely.

Then I have to give myself a pedicure and manicure, since there isn't time to have my nails done by professionals. Then I have to wash and condition my hair, shave my legs (and under my arms, since Patty's dress is strapless), and, then, just to be on the safe side, I shave my bikini line as well, because, even though it's highly unlikely I'm going to get lucky twice in two days, you never know. Then I have to apply a facial

mask, and moisturize all over. Then I have to shape my eyebrows, dry and style my hair, apply makeup, and layer
fragrance.

Then, noticing that the heels of my red pumps have obviously met with an unfortunate accident involving a subway
grate, I have to go over them with a red Magic Marker.

And of course, through all of that, I have to pause occasionally to snack on Double-Stuff Oreos so that I won't get
light-headed from not having had anything to eat since this
afternoon, when Magda smuggled that Reuben from the caf
for me.

By the time Cooper taps on my apartment door, I'm just
struggling to zip up Patty's dress and wondering why it had
fit two hours ago in her loft but doesn't fit now—

"Just a second," I yell, trying to figure out what on earth I'm
going to wear if I can't get Patty's dress to close properly. . . .

Finally the zipper moves, though, and I grab my wrap and
bag and clatter down the stairs, thinking it's a shame there's
no one who can open the door for me and say, "She'll be
down in a minute," so I can make a sweeping entrance, like
Rory Gilmore or whoever. As it is, I have to knee Lucy out of
the way just so I can get to the door.

I regret to say I don't register Cooper's reaction to my
appearance—if he even had one, which I kind of doubt—
because I'm so completely taken aback by his. Cooper does
own a tuxedo, it turns out . . . a very nice one, in fact.

And he looks more than a little sexy in it.

What is it about men in tuxedos? Why do they always
look so *good* in them? Maybe it's the emphasis on the width
of the chest and shoulders. Maybe it's the startling contrast
of crisp white shirt front and elegant black lapel.

Whatever it is, I don't think I've ever seen a guy in a tux

who didn't look great. But Cooper is the exception. He doesn't look great.

He looks *fantastic*.

I'm so busy admiring him that I nearly forget I'm attending this event to catch a killer. For a second—just one—I really do delude myself into thinking Cooper and I are on a date. Especially when he says, "You look great."

Reality returns, though, when he looks at his watch and says distractedly, "Let's go, all right? I've got to meet someone later, so if we're going to do this, we need to get a move on."

I feel a pang of disappointment. Meet someone? Who? Who does he have to meet? A client? A snitch?

Or a *girlfriend*?

"Heather?" Cooper raises his eyebrows. "You okay?"

"Fine," I say, faintly.

"Good," Cooper says, taking me by the elbow. "Let's go."

I follow him down the stairs and out the door, telling myself that I'm being an idiot. Again. So what if he has to meet someone later? What do I care? This isn't a date. It *isn't*. At least, not with him. If I have any kind of date at all tonight, it's a date with the killer of Elizabeth Kellogg and Roberta Pace.

I repeat this to myself all the way through the park, past the Washington Square monument, and even as we cross the street to the library, where the event is being held and which has been transformed, by strategic placement of red carpets and colored lights and banners, into a ballroom for the occasion.

We have to dodge a few stretch limos and a bunch of uniformed campus security guards (Pete had been asked to pull a double for the occasion, but he'd said no, since his daughter Nancy had a science fair that night), all of whom wear white gloves and have whistles in their mouths, just to approach the massive, clay-colored building. There are velvet ropes to keep out the riffraff . . . only there doesn't seem to be either riff or raff expressing much interest in crashing the party, just some graduate students standing there, clutching their backpacks, looking angry that the party is preventing them from getting to their study carrels.

Cooper shows his tickets to a guy by the door, and then we're ushered inside and immediately assailed by waiters wanting to ply us with drinks and crab-stuffed mushroom caps. Which are actually quite tasty. The Oreos turn out not to be sitting very well beneath my control top panties, anyway.

Cooper snags two glasses for us—not of champagne, but of sparkling water.

"Never drink on the job," he advises me.

I think about Nora Charles, and the five martinis she'd downed in *The Thin Man*, trying to keep up with Nick. Imagine how many murders he might have solved if he'd followed Cooper's advice, and stayed sober!

"Here's to homicide," Cooper says, tapping the side of my glass with his. His blue eyes glint at me—almost taking my breath away, as always, with their brilliance.

"Cheers," I reply, and sip, glancing around the wide room for faces I recognize.

There's an orchestra playing a jazzed up version of "Moon River" over by the reference section. Banquet tables have been set up in front of the elevators, from which jumbo shrimp are disappearing at an alarming rate. People are milling around, looking unnaturally amused by each other's conversation. I see Dr. Flynn speaking rapidly to the dean of undergraduates, a woman whose eyes are glazed over with either boredom or drink—it's hard to tell which.

I spot a cluster of housing administrators bunched under a gold New York College banner, like a family of refugees at Ellis Island, huddled under the shadow of the Statue of Liberty. College administrators, I've noticed, don't seem to be hugely respected by either the student body or the academic population. For the most part, the building directors at New York College seem to be viewed as little more than camp counselors, and Dr. Jessup and his team of coordinators and associate directors aren't given much more respect than that. Which is unfair, because they—well, okay, we—work super hard—way harder than a lot of those professors, who breeze in to teach a one-hour class once a week, then spend the rest of their time backstabbing their colleagues in literary reviews.

While Cooper is being sucked into conversation with a trustee—an old Cartwright family friend—I study my supervisors over the rim of my glass. Dr. Jessup is looking uncomfortable in his tux. Standing beside him is a woman I take to be his statuesque wife, since she appears to be exchanging pleasantries with a woman who could only be Dr. Flynn's better half. Both women look lean and lovely in sparkly sheath dresses.

But neither one of them looks as good as Rachel. Rachel stands beside Dr. Jessup, her eyes sparkling as brightly as champagne winking in the glass she holds. She looks resplendent in form-fitting silk. The midnight blue of her gown contrasts startlingly with her porcelain skin, which in turn seems to glow against the darkness of her hair, piled on top of her head with jeweled pins.

For someone who'd declared she'd had "nothing to wear" to the ball, Rachel had done really well for herself.

So well, in fact, that I can't help feeling sort of self-conscious about the way I'm kind of spilling out of Patty's dress. And not in a good way, either.

It takes me a while to locate the college's illustrious leader, but I finally spot him over by one of the library check-out kiosks. President Allington has ditched the tank top for once, which might be part of the reason it takes me so long to find him. He's actually wearing a tuxedo, and looks surprisingly distinguished in it.

Too bad I can't say the same for poor Mrs. Allington, in her black velour, bell-bottomed pantsuit. Its wide sleeves fall back every time she lifts a glass to her mouth . . . which I must say she's doing with alarming alacrity.

But where, I wonder, is the Allingtons' progeny, the suave Chris/Todd/Mark? I don't see him anywhere, though I'd been positive he'd show up, being a cute guy in his twenties, and all. What cute guy in his twenties can resist an event like this one? I mean, come on. Free beer?

Cooper is talking about lipstick cameras or something with an older gentleman who called me "miss" and said he liked my dress (in so sincere a tone that I looked down to make sure the zipper is still holding) when suddenly a very slender, very attractive woman dressed all in black walks up and says Cooper's name in a very surprised voice.

"Cooper?" The woman, who manages to look glamorous and professorial at the same time, takes his arm in an unmistakably territorial manner—as if in the past, she's touched him in other, more intimate places, and has every right to grab his arm—and says, "What are *you* doing here? It seems like it's been months since I last heard from you. Where have you been keeping yourself?"

I can't say Cooper looks panic-stricken, exactly.

But he does look a little like a guy who is wishing very hard that he were somewhere else.

"Marian," he says, placing a hand on her back and leaning down to kiss her. On the cheek. "Nice to see you." Then he makes introductions, first to the old guy, then to me. "Heather, this is Professor Marian Braithwaite. Marian teaches art history. Marian, this is Heather Wells. She works here at New York College as well."

Marian reaches out and shakes my hand. Her fingers flutter like a tiny bird trapped between my own gargantuan mitts. In spite of this, I'm willing to bet she works out regularly at the college gym. Also that she's a showerer, and not a bather. She just has the look.

"Really?" Marian says, brightly, smiling her perfect Isabella Rossellini smile. "What do you teach?"

"Um," I say, wishing someone would shove a potted geranium on my head and spare me from having to reply. Sadly, no one does. "Nothing, actually. I'm the assistant director of one of the undergraduate dormitories. I mean, residence halls."

"Oh." Marian's perfect smile never wavers, but I can tell by the way she keeps looking at Cooper that all she wants to do is drag him away and rip all his clothes off, preferably with her teeth, and not stand around chatting with the assistant director of an undergraduate residence hall. I can't say I really blame her, either. "How nice. So, Cooper, have you been out of town? You haven't returned a single one of my calls. . . ."

I don't get to hear the rest of what Marian is saying because suddenly my own arm is seized. Only when I turn to see who is doing the seizing, instead of an ex—which would, of course, have been impossible, mine being in the hospital— I find Rachel.

"Hello, Heather," she cries. Twin spots of unnaturally bright color light her cheeks, and I realize that Rachel has been hitting the champagne. Hard. "I didn't know you were coming tonight. How are you? And Jordan? I've been so worried about him. How is he?"

I realize, with a guilty start, that I hadn't thought of Jordan all night. Not since I'd opened my door and laid eyes on Cooper, as a matter of fact. I stammer, "Um, he's all right. Good condition, in fact. Expected to make a full recovery."

"What a semester we've had, huh?" Rachel elbows me chummily. "You and I definitely need a few weeks' vacation after all we've been through. I can't believe it. Two deaths in two weeks!" She glances around, worried someone might have heard her, and lowers her voice. "I can't believe it."

I grin at her. Rachel is definitely drunk. Most likely, she hadn't had anything to eat, and the champagne has gone right to her head. Most of the hors d'oeuvres they're passing around, stuffed mushroom caps and shrimp in puffed pastries, don't look as if they're all that low carb, so Rachel's probably been eschewing them.

Still, it's nice to see Rachel happy for a change—although it's surprising that something like this, which seems kind of stodgy and boring to me, is all it takes to bring out the party girl in her. But then, I didn't go to Yale, so maybe that's why.

"Neither can I," I agree with her. "You look really nice, by the way. That dress suits you."

"Thanks so much!" Rachel sparkles. "I had to pay full price, but I think it was worth it." Then her gaze falls on Cooper, and her eyes light up even more. "Heather," she whispers, excitedly. "You're here with Cooper? Are you and he—"

I glance over my shoulder at my "date," who is still apparently trying to explain to the professor where he's been for the past few months (which, as far as I knew, is right on Waverly Place. I kind of wonder if maybe Cooper has been trying to give Marian the old heave-ho. Why else hadn't he called her? Although why any guy would dump a catch like her, I can't imagine. She's successful, intelligent, gorgeous, thin, a showerer . . . geez, *I*'d date her).

"Um," I say, feeling my cheeks warm up a little at the thought of Cooper and me being, you know. Together. "No. He just had a spare ticket, so I tagged along. We're just friends."

And destined to remain no more than that. Apparently.

"Like you and Jordan," Rachel says.

"Yeah," I say, managing a smile—though I don't know how. "Like me and Jordan."

It isn't her fault. I mean, she doesn't know she's just rubbing salt in the wound.

"Well, I better get going," she says. "I promised Stan I'd snag one of those crab cakes for him. . . ."

"Oh," I say. "Sure. Bye."

Rachel glides away on her very own cloud nine. I wonder if the rumor Pete heard, about Rachel getting a big fat promotion, was true. I wouldn't be surprised. Nobody else on campus had had to feel for two different pulses in as many weeks. What could the college do to show its appreciation, other than promote her? A Pansy Award isn't enough. After all, Magda said Justine had been nominated for a Pansy once because she'd let a student borrow her phone book.

"Hey, blondie!"

I ignore the voice from behind me, and stare at Cooper instead. He's still talking to Marian Braithwaite, who's looking up at him adoringly and laughing every now and then at whatever it is he's saying. How do they know each other? Maybe Marian had hired him. Maybe she'd suspected her professor husband was cheating on her, and she'd hired Cooper, and he'd proved that she had nothing to worry about, and *that's* why she's so glad to see him, and keeps reaching out to touch his arm—

"Blondie!"

Someone taps my shoulder, and I turn in surprise, expecting to see one of the president's aides, demanding to see my ticket . . .

. . . and find myself staring instead into his son's laughing gray eyes.

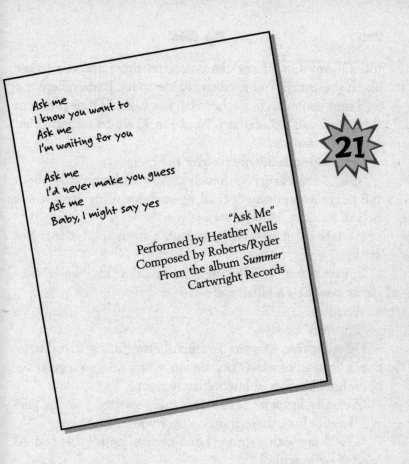

Ask me
I know you want to
Ask me
I'm waiting for you

Ask me
I'd never make you guess
Ask me
Baby, I might say yes

"Ask Me"
Performed by Heather Wells
Composed by Roberts/Ryder
From the album *Summer*
Cartwright Records

21

"Hey," Chris says, smilingly. "Remember me?"

I stare at him, so freaked out that I can't utter a sound.

Christopher Allington. Christopher Allington had sought me out. *Chris Allington* is holding on to my upper arm and smiling down at me like we're old friends bumping into one another at the bowling alley or whatever. He's even offering me a glass of champagne!

Well, it would be rude to say no.

I take the flute from him mutely, my heart hammering hard in my ears. Christopher Allington. Christopher Allington. Oh my God. How can you stand there and talk to me like it's nothing? You tried to kill me today. Remember?

"I met you outside Fischer Hall last night," Chris prompts, thinking I can't place him. As if I'm likely to forget! "That *was* you, wasn't it?"

I pretend to suddenly recover my memory.

"Oh," I say, vaguely—though there's nothing vague about the tingly awareness I feel all up and down my arm, where he still holds it. "Sure. How are you?"

He lets go of me. His grip hadn't been unpleasant. Not at all.

But isn't that weird? I mean, *shouldn't* it have been? Seeing as how he's a killer, and all?

Weird.

"I'm fine," he says.

He *looks* fine. His tux is much better-fitting than his father's. Instead of a bow tie, though, Chris wears a regular tie. Somehow, on him, it looks exactly right.

"Actually, I'm a lot better now that I spotted you," he goes on. "I really hate these things. Don't you?"

"Oh," I say with a shrug. "I don't know. It isn't that bad. At least there's alcohol."

I down the champagne he'd offered me in a single swallow, despite Cooper's warning about drinking on the job. After the shock Chris has given me, sneaking up on me like that, I feel like I sort of deserve it.

Chris, watching me, laughs.

"So, who're are you here with?" he wants to know. "Those tickets aren't cheap. Are you one of the student reps?"

I shrug again. Detective Canavan had said that in his experience, people who kill are excessively stupid, and I'm beginning to think that in Chris's case, this might actually be true. The fact that I'm almost ten years older than your average student government representative doesn't seem to register on him . . .

. . . which is fine by me. I mean, seeing as how I'm trying to be all sneaky and undercover to get him to slip up and confess and stuff. Not that I have any idea how I'm going to do this, of course.

And at least Chris, unlike some people, seems to appreciate how I look in my borrowed dress. I see his gaze stray toward my cleavage several times. And not because my zipper is coming apart in the back and everything is hanging loose. I know because I check.

The band starts playing a slow tune. To my surprise, some couples actually wander out onto the library's main floor and begin to dance . . . Chris's mom and dad among them. I see President Allington lead his wife out onto the dance floor with a sweeping bow that has the trustees laughing and applauding.

It's kind of sweet, actually.

At least until Mrs. Allington trips on her bell-bottoms and almost falls flat on her face. Fortunately President Allington whirls her around and makes it look like it was a fancy step he'd engineered on purpose.

Which is even sweeter. Maybe Chris isn't as unlucky as I'd originally thought. In his parentage, I mean.

"Hey," Chris says, surprising me yet again, this time by taking the champagne glass from my hand and setting it down on the tray of a passing waiter. "Wanna dance?"

My head whips around so fast to look at him, a long strand of my hair smacks me in the mouth and sticks to my lip gloss.

"What?" I ask, desperately trying to remove it. The hair, I mean. From my mouth.

"Do you wanna dance?" Chris asks. His grin is slightly mocking, to show me that he knows as well as I do that dancing at the New York College Pansy Ball is kind of . . . well, goobery. Still, he wants to let me know he's game . . .

His grin is infectious. It's the grin of the high school football captain, the handsomest boy in school, so sure of himself and his good looks that it never even occurs to him that some girl might say *No way, Jose* to his invitation. Probably because no girl ever has.

And I'm not about to be the first one.

And not just because I want to find out whether or not Chris is the one who killed Elizabeth and Roberta.

So I smile and say, "Sure," and follow Chris out onto the dance floor.

I'm not the world's greatest dancer, but it doesn't matter, because Chris is good. He's probably been to one of those prep schools where they teach all the guys the box step, or whatever. He's so good, he can talk while he dances. I have to count inside my head. One-two-three. One-two-three. Step ball change . . . oh wait, that's a different dance.

"So," Chris says, conversationally, as he presses my body to his and swings me expertly around, hardly wincing when I accidentally stomp on his toes. "What's your major?"

I'm trying to look—surreptitiously—for Cooper. I mean, he's supposed to be keeping an eye on me, right?

But I don't see him anywhere. I don't see Marian, either, for that matter. Have I been ditched for an ex-girlfriend? After that fuss Cooper made about potentially risking my life in my pursuit of the killer of Fischer Hall, has he run out on me?

Well! Nice to know how much he cares!

Although, you know, seeing as how he's letting me live in his house rent-free—well, virtually—I guess I haven't got any right to complain. I mean, how many people in Manhattan have such easy access to a washer/dryer?

In answer to Chris's question about my major, I say, "Um . . . I'm undeclared."

Well, that much is true.

"Oh, really?" Chris looks genuinely interested. "That's good. Keep your options open. I think too many people go into college with their mind already made up about what career they want to pursue when they graduate. They stick to the core curriculum for that major and don't give themselves the opportunity to try new things. You know, find out what they're really good at it. It could be something they never thought of. Like jewelry making."

Wow. I didn't know you could take jewelry making for college credit. You could actually *wear* your final. How practical.

"What are you leaning toward?" Chris asks.

I'm going to say pre-med, but changed my mind at the last second.

"Criminal justice," I lie, to see how he reacts.

But he doesn't run away to cower in fear, or anything. Instead, he says breezily, "Yeah, fascinating stuff, criminal justice. I've been thinking about heading into criminal law myself."

I bet you have. Aloud I ask, putting on a playful tone, "So what was a great big law student like yourself doing hanging around an undergraduate residence hall?"

At least Chris has the grace to look embarrassed. "Well," he says, in an aw shucks voice, "my parents do live there."

"And so do a lot of attractive coeds," I remind him. Remember? You've killed two of them?

He grins. "That, too," he says. "I don't know. The girls in my program aren't exactly—"

Over Chris's shoulder, I finally catch a glimpse of Cooper. He appears to be exchanging words with Professor Braithwaite. Really. They are having what looks like a heated conversation over by the raw bar. I see Cooper fling a glance at me.

So he hasn't forgotten. He's still keeping an eye on me.

Fighting with his ex, too, it appears.

But also keeping an eye on me.

Since I realize he doesn't know what Chris looks like, he might not know I'm dancing with my lead suspect. So I point to Chris's back, and mouth, *This is Chris* to him.

But this doesn't work out quite the way I expect it to. Oh, Cooper gets the message, and all.

But so does Marian, who, seeing that she no longer has his full attention, follows the direction of Cooper's gaze, and sees me.

Not knowing what else to do, I wave, lamely. Marian looks away from me coldly.

Whoa. Sorry.

"The girls in law school—"

I swivel my head around and realize that Chris is talking. To me.

"Well, let's just say they consider sitting in a carrel in the law library studying till midnight every night a good time," he says, with a wink.

What is he talking about?

Then I remember. Undergrad coeds versus law school students. Oh, right. The murder investigation.

"Ah," I nod, knowingly. "Law school girls. Not like those fresh-from-the-farm first years in Fischer Hall, huh?"

He laughs outright.

"You're pretty funny," he says. "What year are you?"

I just shrug and try to look like it wasn't, um, let's see, seven or so years since my first legal drink.

"At least tell me your name," he urges, in this low voice that I'm sure some former girlfriend had told him was sexy.

"You can just keep calling me Blondie," I purr. "That way you'll be able to keep me straight from all your other girl-friends."

Chris lifts his eyebrows and grins. "What other girlfriends?"

"Oh, you," I cry, giving him a little ladylike smack on the arm. "I've heard all about you. I was friends with Roberta, you know."

He looks at me like I've lost my mind. The eyebrows have furrowed. "Who?"

God, he's good. There isn't a hint of guilt in his silver gray eyes.

"Roberta," I repeat. I have to admit, my heart is pounding at my daring. I'm doing it. Detecting! I'm really doing it! "Roberta Pace."

"I don't know who you're talking about."

I seriously can't believe this guy. "Bobby," I say.

Suddenly, he laughs. "*Bobby*? You're friends with *Bobby*?"

I didn't miss both the strange emphasis on the *you're* and the use of the present tense. I am, after all, a trained investi-gator. Well, at least, I do the data entry for one.

"I *was* friends with Roberta," I say, and I'm not smiling or pretending to be less than twenty-one anymore. Because I can't believe the guy can be so cold. Even for a killer. "Until she fell off the top of that elevator last week."

Chris stops dancing. "Wait," he says. "What?"

"You heard me," I say. "Bobby Pace and Beth Kellogg. Both of them are dead, allegedly from elevator surfing. And you slept with both of them right before they did it."

I hadn't meant to just blurt it out like that. I'm pretty sure Cooper would have been more subtle. But I just . . . well, I got kind of mad, I guess. About him being so flippant about it. Roberta's and Elizabeth's deaths, I mean.

I guess a real investigator doesn't get mad. I guess a real investigator keeps a level head.

I guess I'm not destined for that partnership in Cooper's business after all.

Chris seems to have frozen, his feet rooted onto one black and one white tile.

But his grip on my waist doesn't loosen. If anything, it tightens until suddenly, we're standing hip to hip.

"What?" he asks, and his eyes are so wide that the blue-gray irises look like marbles floating in twin pools of milk. "What?" he asks, again. Even his lips have drained of color.

My face is only inches beneath his. I see the incredulity in his eyes, coupled with—and, shoddy investigator that I might have been, even I can see this—a slowly dawning horror.

That's when it hits me:

He doesn't know. Really. Chris had no idea—not right up until I'd told him just then—that the two dead girls in Fischer Hall were the ones with whom he'd, um, dallied just days before.

Is he really such a man-slut that he'd known only the first names—the nicknames—of the women he'd seduced?

It certainly looks that way.

The effect my announcement has on Chris is really pretty profound. His fingers dig convulsively into my waist, and he begins to shake his head back and forth, like Lucy after a good shampoo.

"No," he says. "That's not true. It can't be."

And suddenly I know that I've made a horrible mistake.

Don't ask me how. I mean, it's not like I have any experience in this kind of thing.

But I know anyway. Know it the way I know the fat content in a Milky Way bar.

Christopher Allington didn't kill those girls.

Oh, he'd slept with them, all right. But he hadn't killed them. That was done by someone else. Someone far, far more dangerous . . .

"Okay," says a deep voice behind me. A heavy hand falls on my bare shoulder.

"Sorry, Heather," Cooper says. "But we have to go now."

Where'd he come from? I can't go. Not *now*.

"Um," I say. "Yeah, just a sec, okay?"

But Cooper doesn't look too ready to wait. In fact, he looks like a man who's getting ready to run for his life.

"We have to go," he says, again. "*Now*."

And he slips a hand around my arm, and pulls.

"Cooper," I say, wriggling to get free. I can see that Chris is still in shock. It's totally likely that if I stick around awhile longer, I'll get something more out of him. Can't Cooper see that I'm conducting a very important interview here?

"Why don't you go get something to eat?" I suggest to Cooper. "I'll meet you over at the buffet in a minute—"

"No," Cooper says. "Let's go. Now."

I can understand why Cooper is so anxious to leave. Really, I can. After all, not everybody deals with their exes by, you know, sleeping with them on the foyer floor.

Still, I feel like I can't leave yet. Not after I've made this total breakthrough. Chris is really upset—so upset that he doesn't even seem to notice that there's a private eye looming over his dance partner. He's turned away, and is sort of stumbling off the dance floor, in the general direction of the elevators.

Where's he going? Up to the twelfth floor, to his father's office, to hit the real liquor—or just to use the phone? Or up to the roof, to jump off? I feel like I have to follow him, if only to make sure he doesn't do anything stupid.

Except when I start to go after him, Cooper won't let me.

"Cooper, I can't go yet," I say, struggling to free myself from his grip. "I got him to admit he knew them! Roberta and Elizabeth! And you know what? I don't think he killed them. I don't think he even knew they were dead!"

"That's nice," Cooper says. "Now let's go. I told you I have an appointment. Well, I'm late for it as it is."

"An appointment? An *appointment*?" I can hardly believe what I'm hearing. "Cooper, don't you understand? Chris said—"

"I heard you," Cooper says. "Congratulations. Now let's go. I said I'd bring you here. I didn't say I could stay all night. I do have actual paying clients, you know."

I realize it's futile. Even if Cooper did change his mind and let me go, I don't have any idea where Chris has disappeared to. And how smart would it have been, really, for me to follow him? I mean, considering what happened to the last couple of girls with whom he'd—how had I put it? Oh yeah, dallied. Hey, maybe I should be an English major. Yeah. A novelist, AND a doctor. AND a detective. AND a jewelry designer . . .

Cooper and I slip outside. I don't even have a chance to say good-bye to anyone, or congratulate Rachel on her Pansy. I've never seen a guy so eager to get out of one place.

"Slow down," I say, as Cooper hustles me to the curb. "I got heels on, you know."

"Sorry," Cooper says, and drops my arm. Then he put his fingers to his mouth and whistles for a cab that's cruising along West Fourth.

"Where are we going?" I ask curiously, as the cab pulls to the corner with a squeal of its brakes.

"You're going home," Cooper says. He opens the rear passenger door and gestures for me to get inside, then gives the driver the address of his grandfather's brownstone.

"Hey," I say, leaning forward in the seat. "It's just right across the block. I could've walked—"

"Not alone," Cooper says. "And I have to head in the other direction."

"Why?" I don't miss the fact that Marian the Art Historian has just slipped out the library doors behind us.

But instead of walking over and joining Cooper on the curb, she shoots him an extremely unfriendly look, then hurries off on foot toward Broadway.

Cooper, whose back is to the library, doesn't see the professor, or the dirty look.

"I've got to see a man," is all Cooper will say to me, "about a dog. Here." He shoves a five-dollar bill at me. "Don't wait up."

"What dog?" The cab starts to move. "Cooper, what dog? Are you getting another dog? What about Lucy? What's wrong with Lucy?"

But we're already gliding out into traffic. Cooper has turned and strode off towards West Third Street. Soon I can't see him at all.

What had all that been about? I mean, really. I know Cooper's clients are important to him, and stuff. And I know he thinks this whole thing with me and the deaths in my building is like a figment of my imagination, or whatever.

But still. He could at least have listened to me.

That's when the cab driver, who appears to be Indian—like from India, not Native American—says, helpfully, "I believe that's an expression."

I look at his reflection in the rearview mirror. "What is?"

"See a man about a dog," the cab driver says. "It's an American expression. Like rolling stone gathers no moss. You know?"

I slump back into my seat. No, I didn't know. I don't know anything, apparently.

Well, I guess I knew that. I mean, isn't that why I'm working at New York College? To get an education?

Well, I'm getting one, all right. And I haven't even started classes yet.

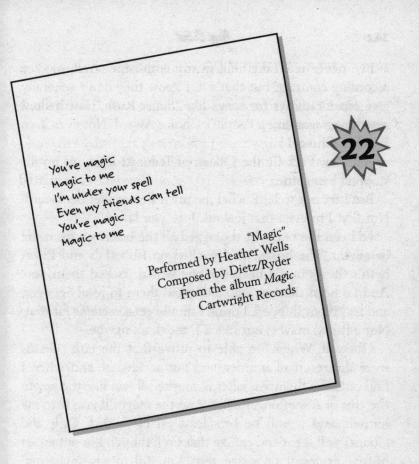

22

You're magic
Magic to me
I'm under your spell
Even my friends can tell
You're magic
Magic to me

"Magic"
Performed by Heather Wells
Composed by Dietz/Ryder
From the album *Magic*
Cartwright Records

After Cooper and I—and Chris Allington—left the Pansy Ball, Rachel Walcott was awarded a Pansy for exemplary service to the college.

She shows me the little flower-shaped pin the next morning, pride gleaming in her pretty brown eyes. She wears it on the lapel of her black linen suit jacket as if it were a medal of valor or something.

I guess maybe to her it kind of is. I mean, in a single semester, she's had to deal with way more tragedy than most administrators have to face in their entire careers.

I've never won anything in my entire life. Well, okay, a recording contract, but that's it. I know they don't generally give out Grammys for songs like "Sugar Rush." But hello, I never even won like a People's Choice Award. Not even *Teen* People's Choice.

And I was totally the Queen of Teen. At least, up until I stopped being one.

But I try not to let Rachel see my jealousy over her award. Not that I'm even that jealous. Just, you know.

I'd been the one who'd dragged all the boxes up from the basement. The boxes we'd packed up Roberta's and Elizabeth's things in. I'd been the one who'd packed them, too. And I'd been the one who'd dragged them to Mail Services, and had them shipped. I think I should get *something* for that. Not a Pansy, maybe, but like a Dandelion, maybe.

Oh well. When I'm able to prove that the girls' deaths were the result of murder, and not accidental, and when I find out who their real killer is, maybe I'll win like the key to the city, or something. Really! And the mayor'll give it to me himself, and it will be broadcast on New York One, and Cooper will see it and realize that even though I'm not an art history professor or a size zero, I'm still totally smart and cute, and he'll ask me out and we'll get married and have Jack, Emily, and Charlotte Wells-Cartwright . . .

Well, a girl can dream, right?

And I *am* happy for Rachel. I congratulate her and sip my coffee as she describes what it had been like, winning this prestigious award in front of all her peers. She tells me how Dr. Jessup had hugged her and how President Allington had personally thanked her for services above and beyond the call of duty. She chatters excitedly about how she's the first administrator in the history of New York College to receive seven separate nominations for the award, the most any one person has ever garnered—and she'd gotten them all in just her first four months of employment! She says how glad she is that she'd gone into higher education instead of business or law, like so many of her fellow Yale grads.

"Doesn't it feel good," she asks me, "to know you're making such a difference in people's lives, Heather?"

"Um," I say. "Sure."

Although I'm pretty sure the people whose lives I'm making the biggest difference in—the student workers—just wish Justine would come back.

While Rachel winds down from her Pansy-induced high, I get on the phone and take care of a few things that I feel I've been neglecting.

First I call Amber in her room. When her sleepy voice croaks, "Yeah?" into the phone, I gently put the receiver back into the cradle. Okay, Amber's still alive. Check.

Then I call St. Vincent's to see how Jordan is doing. He is, I learn, doing better, but they still want to hold him for observation for another night. I don't really want to, but I figure I should speak to him—you know, seeing as how it's my fault he got hurt in the first place.

But when the switchboard puts my call through to his room, a woman answers. Tania. I can't deal with fiancées early in the morning, so I hang up. I feel guilty about it though, and order a half-dozen get well balloons from a local florist, instructing them to be delivered to St. Vincent's with the highly personal message, *Get Well Soon, Jordan. From Heather*. Likely they will get lost in all of the other gifts his fans are no doubt sending him—an overnight candlelight vigil also took place outside St. Vincent's ambulance bay, apparently—but at least I can say I tried.

Thinking about Jordan and his cracked skull reminds me

of Christopher Allington. A real detective would, of course, follow up on the conversation we'd had the night before.

So I decide to take another crack at him. I tell Rachel I'm going to the bathroom. But really I go to the elevator and take it up to the twentieth floor.

No one's supposed to go up to the twentieth floor but the Allingtons and their guests, which is why the carpet in the hallway outside the penthouse is really one big motion detector that goes off whenever somebody steps on it, including the Allingtons. This alarm causes a camera to be switched on, which then conveys an image of the interloper on a viewing screen at the guard's desk in the lobby.

But since the guard on duty that day is Pete, I'm not too worried about being busted. We've caught any number of freshmen on the twentieth floor, most of whom have been sent there by conniving upper classmen in search of the "Fischer Hall pool." The elusive Fischer Hall pool did once exist, but in the basement, not the penthouse, and it's a favorite senior prank to send unsuspecting first-years to the twentieth floor in search of it, knowing they'll trigger the motion detectors and get busted for being outside the president's apartment.

I step boldly onto the nondescript carpeting and lift a finger to poke at the doorbell to the Allingtons' apartment. I can hear a strange whistling sound beyond the door, and realize that this must be Mrs. Allington's birds, the cockatoos about whom she worries so incessantly when she's had too much to drink. When I press on the doorbell, the whistling turns into maniacal shrieking, and for a minute, I panic. Really. I forget all about being a detective slash novelist slash physician slash jewelry designer, and want to run back to the elevator . . .

But before I have a chance to ding and ditch, the door

swings open, and Mrs. Allington, bleary-eyed and dressed in a green velour caftan, blinks at me.

"Yes?" she demands, in a remarkably unfriendly manner, considering the fact that just two weeks or so ago, I'd held her hand while she barfed into one of the lobby planters. Behind her, I catch a glimpse of a six-foot-tall wicker cage, within which two large white birds scream at me.

"Uh, hi," I say brightly. "Is Christopher here?"

Mrs. Allington's puffy eyelids widen a little, then go back to normal. "What?"

"Chris," I repeat. "Your son, Christopher. Is he here?"

Mrs. Allington looks truly pissed off. At first I think it's because I've woken her up, but it turns out that's only part of it.

No, what I've really done is outrage Mrs. Allington's sense of propriety.

I know! Who even knew she had one? But it turns out she does.

She says, enunciating as carefully as if I were a foreigner, "No, Chris is not here, Justine. And if you had been raised properly, you'd know that it is considered highly inappropriate for young women to pursue boys so avidly."

Then she slams the door very hard, causing her birds to shriek even more loudly in surprise.

I stand staring at the closed door for a minute or so. I have to admit, my feelings are kind of hurt. I mean, I'd thought Mrs. Allington and I were close.

And yet she's *still* calling me Justine.

I probably should have just gone away. But, you know. I still needed to know where Chris was.

So I reach out and ring the bell again. The birds' screaming rises to fever-pitch, and when Mrs. Allington pulls open the door this time, she looks not only pissed off, but practically homicidal.

"*What?*" she demands.

"Sorry," I say, as politely as I can. "I really don't mean to bother you. But could you just tell me where I might find Chris?"

Mrs. Allington has a lot of loose skin on her face. A lift here and there might have done the trick, but she really isn't the nip-and-tuck type. She's more the never-move-your-mouth-when-you-speak old money New England type. Kind of like Mrs. Cartwright. Only scarier.

Anyway, some of that loose skin beneath her chin trembles a little as she glares at me.

Finally she says, "Can't you girls just leave him alone? You're always chasing after him, causing him trouble. Can't you just go after some other boy? Aren't there plenty in this dorm?"

"Residence hall," I correct her.

"*What?*"

"It's a residence hall," I remind her. "You said dorm. But it's actually a—"

"Go to hell," Mrs. Allington says, and she slams the door in my face again.

Wow. Talk about hostile. Instead of psychoanalyzing *me* all day, Sarah should maybe turn her attention to the Allingtons. They have *way* more problems.

Sighing, I turn around and press the down button for the elevator. I can't be sure, but I think Mrs. Allington has maybe already been at the bottle . . . and it isn't even ten o'clock in the morning yet! I wonder if she's always soused this early, or if this is a special occasion. Like to celebrate Rachel's Pansy Award, maybe.

When I get back downstairs, I nearly ram into this skinny girl in the hallway. She's headed into Rachel's office, so I start to ask if I can help her, but when she turns around, I see that it's Amber.

That's right.

Chris Allington's Amber, from Idaho. The one I just woke up.

"Oh," she says, recognizing me. "Hi." Her *hi* is less than en-thusiastic. That's on account of her still being half asleep. She's even in her pajamas. "You're not—you're not the hall director, are you?"

"No," I say. "I'm her assistant. Why?"

" 'Cause I just got a call saying I have to come down here this mornin' for a mandatory meeting with Rachel Walcott—"

At that moment, Rachel comes click-clacking out of our office, clutching a file folder to her chest.

"Oh, Heather, there you are," she says, brightly. "Cooper's here."

I think I must have made some sort of disbelieving noise, because Rachel peers at me curiously and says, "Yes, he is." Then her attention turns to the girl next to me. "Amber?" Rachel asks.

"Yes, ma'am." Amber sounds subdued. Well, and what eighteen-year-old freshman who'd been forced to wake up at ten o'clock in the morning for a meeting with the residence hall director wouldn't sound subdued?

"This way, Amber," Rachel says, laying hold of Amber's elbow. "Heather, if you could just hold all my calls for a few minutes—"

"Sure," I say, and go into our office. Where, sure enough, I find Cooper shaking his head at the jar of condoms on my desk.

"Hi, Cooper," I say, a little warily. Which I think is under-standable, given, you know, that the last time he'd shown up in my office, it had been to tell me that my ex-boyfriend was engaged to someone else. What could have happened now?

Then I feel a stab of panic, remembering Marian Braith-waite. Oh God. She and Cooper have made up. They've made up, and are getting married, and Cooper is here to tell me he needs the apartment back because they're going to put the nanny in there—

"Hi, Heather," Cooper says, looking much more like his normal self in jeans and his leather jacket than he had in that tux. "Got a minute?"

Hi, Heather, got a minute? Hi, Heather, got a minute? What kind of way is THAT to start a conversation? Could there be three other words in the English language more effective at striking terror deep within the heart than *Got a minute?* No. No, I do NOT have a minute! Not if you're going to tell me what I think you're going to tell me. Why her? WHY? Just because she's smart and accomplished and pretty and thin—

"Sure," I say, in what I hope sounds like a cool, assured voice, but which I'm pretty sure comes out sounding more like a bleat. I gesture for Cooper to sit down, and curl up in my desk chair, wishing I could have a bottle of whatever it was Mrs. Allington had been nipping at all morning.

"Listen, Heather," Cooper says. "About last night . . ."

No! Because if there are three words in the English language worse than *Got a minute?* they can only be *About last night . . .*

And now I've had all six of them, one right after the other. It isn't fair!

And what had even happened last night? Nothing! I'd gotten out of the cab Cooper had put me in and gone straight inside to bed.

Okay, maybe I'd stayed up for an hour or so working on a new song.

And maybe that song had been about him.

But he couldn't have heard it. I played super softly. And I never even heard him come in.

Oh, why me? WHY ME???

"I think I owe you an explanation" is the next unexpected thing out of his mouth.

But wait. *I owe you an explanation*? That doesn't sound like a prelude to asking me to move out. In fact, it almost sounds like an apology. But what on earth does Cooper have to apologize for?

"I met with a friend from the coroner's office last night after we left the ball," he begins. "And she said—"

Wait a minute. *She* said? Cooper ditched me for another girl?

"*That's* where you went?" I blurt out, before I can stop myself. "To meet a *girl*?"

Oh . . . my . . . God. What's wrong with me? Why can't I be cool and self-assured like . . . well, like Rachel? Why do I have to be such a complete spaz all the time?

Fortunately Cooper, being completely ignorant of my plans for him (you know, the fact that he's going to marry me and be the father of my three as yet unborn children and the inspiration for my Nobel Prize–winning medical career), doesn't catch on that I'm jealous. He seems to think I'm still angry because he made me leave the party early.

"I didn't want to say anything to you before," he says. "You know, in case she didn't have anything to tell me. But the fact is, there *was* something a little strange about those girls' bodies."

I just stare at him. Because I can't believe it. Not that his "friend" in the coroner's office had found something strange about Elizabeth's and Roberta's bodies. But that he'd bothered to consult with her on my behalf in the first place.

"B-but," I stammer. "But I thought . . . you thought . . . I was just making the whole thing up. Because of missing the thrill of performing . . ."

"I do," Cooper says, with a shrug. "I mean, I did. But I figured it wouldn't hurt to ask."

"And?" I lean forward eagerly. "What is it? Drugs? Were they drugged? Because I thought Detective Canavan said no drugs were detected in their systems."

"None were," Cooper says. "It wasn't drugs. It's burns."

I stare at him. "Burns? What kind of burns? Like . . . cigarette burns?"

"No," Cooper says. "Angie isn't sure." Angie? Cooper knows someone in the coroner's office named *Angie*? Just how had he and Angie met, anyway? Angie didn't sound like the kind of name a medical examiner would have. An exotic dancer, maybe. But not a doctor . . .

"And you have to take into account that those bodies," Cooper goes on. "Well, they're kind of a mess. But Angie says they did find burn marks on both girls's backs, marks they can't explain. It's not enough for them to change the coroner's ruling—you know, that the deaths weren't accidental. But it is . . . strange."

"Strange," I repeat.

"Yeah," Cooper says. "Strange."

"So . . ." I can't look him in the eye. Because I can't believe he's actually taking me seriously. *Me*, Heather Wells, of "Sugar Rush" fame!

And all it had taken were a couple of murders . . .

"So maybe I'm not just making it all up out of displaced aggression toward my mother?" I ask.

Cooped looks taken aback. "I never said you were."

Oh, right. That had been Sarah.

"But you believe me now?" I prod him. "I'm not just your little brother's crazy ex-girlfriend? But maybe, like, a rational human being?"

"I've never thought of you as anything but," Cooper says, a flash of annoyance in his blue eyes. Then, seeing my expression, he says, "Well, crazy, maybe. But I never thought of you as irrational. Honest, Heather, I don't know where you get this stuff. I've always thought of you as one of the—"

Most beautiful, ravishing creatures you've ever met? Most intelligent, stunningly gorgeous women of your acquaintance?

Sadly, before he gets a chance to tell me what he's always thought of me—or to fall to one knee and ask me to be his bride (I know. Still, a girl can dream), the phone rings.

"Hold that thought," I say to Cooper, and pick up the receiver. "Fischer Hall, this is Heather."

"Heather?" It's Tina, the desk worker on duty. "Hold on, Julio wants to talk to you."

Julio gets on the line. "Oh, Haythar, I sorry," he says. "But he's doing it again."

"Who's doing what again?" I ask.

"That boy, Gavin. Ms. Walcott told me—"

"Okay, Julio," I say, careful not to let Cooper catch on, considering what happened last time. "I'll meet you at the usual place." Then I hang up.

Talk about bad timing! Right when Cooper had been about to tell me what he really thinks about me!

Although, come to think of it, I'm not sure I want to know. Because most likely it's going to be something like "one of the best data-entry typists I've ever known."

"Stay right here," I say to Cooper.

"Is something wrong?" Cooper asks, looking concerned.

"Nothing I can't handle in a jiffy," I say. Oh my God, did I just say jiffy? Well, whatever. "I'll be right back."

Before he can say another word, I hightail it from the office, running for the service elevator, where I tell Julio, who meets me there, to take the control lever, and *Go, go, go!*

Because the sooner we get back, the sooner I can find out if, you know, there's a chance for me where Cooper is concerned, or if I should just give up on men already. Maybe

New York College offers a major in being a nun. You know, giving up guys completely, and embracing celibacy. Because that's seriously starting to look like it might be the way to go for me.

As Julio takes me up to the tenth floor, I climb the elevator walls and slide through the open ceiling panel. Up in the elevator shaft, it's warm and quiet, as usual.

Except that I can't actually hear Gavin laughing, though, which is *not* usual. Maybe he's finally gotten his head cut off by a snapping cable, as Rachel has so often warned him he might. Or maybe he's fallen. Oh, God please don't tell me he's at the bottom of the shaft . . .

I'm reflecting upon this—what I'm going to do if all I find on top of Elevator 1 is Gavin's headless corpse—as the service elevator approaches the two other cars, which are both sitting in front of the tenth floor.

As we rise above them, I see no sign of Gavin—not even his headless corpse. No empty beer bottles, no chortling laughter, nothing. It's almost as if Gavin had never been there . . .

The next thing I know, a thunderclap shakes the shaft, leaving a roaring in my ears, like the sound of ocean waves, only magnified a thousand times.

I've stood up—a little unsteadily—to get a better look at the roofs of the cabs below, and when I feel the explosion rip beneath my feet, I grab instinctively—but blindly—for something—anything—to hold on to.

Something that feels like a thousand razor blades slices my hands, and I realize I'm holding a metal rope that's vibrating crazily from the force of the explosion. Still, I hold on to the bucking steel cable, because it's the only thing that separates me from the oblivion of the dark shaft below. Because there's nothing else beneath my feet. One minute I'm standing on the roof of the service cab, and the next, the roof has caved in beneath my feet, crumpling like a can of Pringles.

Hmmm. Pringles.

It's funny what you end up thinking about right before you die.

I avoid getting hit by the rain of steel from above by sheer luck alone. The cable I've grabbed hold of continues to buck wildly, but I cling to it with both my hands and legs, wrapping one foot around the other.

Something strikes me hard enough on the shoulder as it plunges past to make me loosen my grip on the cable, stunned breathless by the impact.

That's when I look down, wild-eyed, and see that the service car is gone.

Well, not gone, exactly. It's free-falling below me like a soda can someone has thrown down a trash chute, the loosened cables—all but the one I'm holding—trailing behind it like ribbons on a bridal veil.

It can't crash, is all I could think to myself. I'd asked the elevator repairmen once if what had happened in the movie *Speed* could ever happen in real life. And they'd said no. Because even if all the cables connected to an elevator car snap at the same time (something they asserted could never, ever happen. But, um, hello), there's a counterweight built into the wall that would never let the car crash to the ground below.

I feel the deafening impact of that counterweight as it slams into place, saving the elevator car from colliding with the basement floor.

But when the broken cables rain down onto the cab's roof, the noise is unbelievable. Impact after impact shakes the shaft. I struggle to retain my grip on the one remaining cable, thinking only that with all that noise, I haven't heard a peep out of Julio. Not a single sound. I know he's still inside that car. While he'd been saved by the counterweight from being crushed, accordion style, against the cement floor of the basement, those cables have literally flattened the cab's roof. He's under that tangle of steel . . .

But God only knows if he's still alive.

The silence that follows the crash of the falling elevator cab is even more frightening than the shuddering impact of the split cables. I've always loved the elevator shafts because they're the only parts of the dorm—I mean, residence hall— that are ever totally quiet. Now, that quiet is like an impenetrable canopy between me and the ground. The quieter it gets, the higher this little bubble of hysteria rises in my throat. I hadn't had a chance to be frightened before.

But now, hanging more than ten stories with my feet dangling above nothing, I'm seized with terror.

That's when the bubble turns into a fountain, and I start to scream.

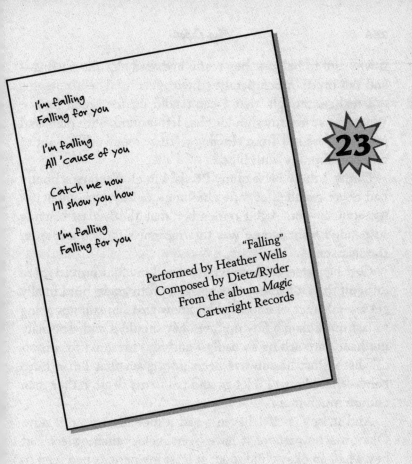

I'm falling
Falling for you

I'm falling
All 'cause of you

Catch me now
I'll show you how

I'm falling
Falling for you

"Falling"
Performed by Heather Wells
Composed by Dietz/Ryder
From the album *Magic*
Cartwright Records

23

Though it seems like hours, I think I'm only screaming for like a minute or so before I hear a distant, masculine voice shouting my name from far below.

"Here!" I shriek. "I'm up here! Tenth floor!"

The voice says something, and then, below me to my left, the two remaining elevator cabs both start moving down.

If I'd had any presence of mind, I'd have jumped for it, leaping to the roof of the nearest cab.

But it's a distance of more than five feet—the same distance Elizabeth and Roberta would have jumped, and missed, if we were to believe they really had died elevator surfing—and I'm pretty much paralyzed with fear.

I realize, though, that I can't hold on for much longer. Whatever struck my shoulder has left it numb with pain, and my palms are raw from clinging to rusty metal cable—not to mention slippery with blood.

Dimly, I think back to my PE days in elementary school. I had never excelled at rope climbing—or any physical activity, actually—but I did remember that the key to hanging suspended from a rope was to wrap one's foot in a loop in the slack end.

Getting a steel cable to wrap around my foot proved more difficult than it had ever been back in fifth grade, but I finally get a semblance of a foothold. I know that I'm still not going to last more than a few minutes. My shoulder and especially my hands are aching so badly—and my threshold for physical discomfort has always been low, given that I'm a huge baby—that I know I'll let go and fall to my death rather than endure much more.

And it isn't as if I haven't had a nice life up until now. Okay, maybe parts of it have been rockier than others. But hey, I had an okay childhood; at least my parents had seen to it that I'd never gone to bed hungry.

And I was never abused or molested. I had had a successful career—granted, it had peaked at age eighteen or so.

But still, I've gotten to eat in a lot of awfully good restaurants.

And I know that Lucy will be well taken care of. Cooper will look after her if anything happens to me.

But thinking of Cooper reminds me that I don't really want to die, not now, when things were just getting interesting. I'm never going to know what it is he really thinks of me! He'd been about to tell me, and now I'm going to die, and miss it!

Unless, of course, when you die you attain all the knowledge in the universe.

But what if you don't? What if you just die?

Well, then I guess it won't matter.

But what about those repairmen? They'd assured me elevator cables don't just snap. Okay, maybe one of them snaps, but not all of them, all at once. Those cables hadn't broken accidentally. Someone had deliberately booby-trapped them. Judging from the ball of flame that had erupted beneath my feet, I'm thinking bomb.

That's right, bomb.

Someone's trying to kill me.

Again.

Reflecting on who could possibly want to kill me takes my mind off my aching shoulder and throbbing hands—and even Cooper and the what-he-thinks-of-me thing—for a minute or so. Well, of course there's Christopher Allington, who may or may not have already tried to shove a geranium planter on my head because I suspect him of murder. He'd better have a really good alibi for this one.

But how would Christopher Allington have known that I'd be on that elevator? I rarely ride the service elevator. In fact, the only time I ever ride it is when I'm chasing elevator surfers.

Could Gavin McGoren somehow be involved in the deaths of Beth Kellogg and Bobby Pace? This seems far-fetched, but what other explanation could there be? Julio can't be the murderer. For all I know, he's dead down there. Why would he want to kill himself *and* me?

Suddenly, the elevator closest to me returns, and this time, there's somebody on the roof. But it isn't Gavin McGoren. Blinking—the shaft is filled with smoke—I see through the mist that a grim-faced Cooper is coming to my rescue.

Which must mean he likes me. At least a little. I mean, if he's willing to risk his own life to save mine . . .

"Heather," Cooper says. He sounds as cool and authoritative as ever. "Don't move, all right?"

"Like I'm going anywhere," I say. Or that's what I try I say. What I hear is actually a string of hysterical blubbering. But surely it isn't coming from me.

"Listen to me, Heather," Cooper says. He's climbed onto the roof of Elevator 1, and is hanging on to one of its cables. His face, I can see through the smoke, is pale beneath his tan. Now why is that? I wonder. "I want you to do something for me."

"Okay," I say. Or I try to, anyway.

"I want you to swing over here. It's okay, I'll catch you."

"Um," I say. And make the mistake of looking down. "No." Well, that came out definitively enough.

"Don't look down," Cooper says. "Come on, Heather. You can do it. It's just a few feet—"

"I'm not swinging anywhere," I say, clinging more tightly to my cable. "I'm waiting right here until the NYFD arrives."

"Heather," Cooper says, and some of the old familiar impatience with me is back in his voice. "Push off from the wall and swing over here. Let go of the cable when I say so. I swear I will catch you."

"Boy, you have really lost it." I shake my head. My voice sounds funny. It's kind of high-pitched. "No wonder your family cut you off without a cent."

"Heather," Cooper says. "The janitor told me that that cable you're holding on to probably isn't stable. It could break at any minute, like all the others—"

"Oh," I say. Well, that's different.

"Now do what I say." Cooper has leaned out as far from his elevator car as he can, and still have something to hold on to.

"Push off the wall with your foot and swing over here. I'll catch you, don't worry."

From the top of the service shaft comes a groaning sound. I'm almost sure it didn't come from me. More likely from the cable I'm holding on to.

Great.

Closing my eyes, I heave on the cable, forcing it to swing toward the wall on the far side of the shaft. I unwrap my foot from the dangling end and shove, as hard as I can, at the crumbling brick. Like a stone from a slingshot, I'm propelled in the direction of Cooper's waiting arms . . .

. . . but not close enough for my liking.

Still, he shouts, "Let go! Heather, let go now!"

That's it, I think. I'm dead. Maybe they'll do a *Behind the Music* on me *now* . . .

I let go.

And know, for a second, how Elizabeth and Roberta must have felt—the sheer terror of careening through the air with no net or body of water below me to break my fall . . .

Only instead of plummeting to my death, as they had, I feel hard fingers close around both my wrists. My arms are practically yanked out of their sockets as the rest of my body slams against the side of the elevator cab. I have my eyes screwed shut, but I feel myself being lifted, slowly . . .

I don't stop scrambling for a foothold until the seat of my jeans finally rest on something solid.

It's only then that I open my eyes and see that Cooper has managed to pull me to safety. We're both panting from mingled exertion and fear. Well, me from fear, anyway.

But we're alive. *I'm* alive.

Above our heads comes the groaning sound again. Next thing I know, the cable I'd been holding on to—along with the pulley it had been connected to—rips loose from its supports and plummets down the shaft, to crash into the roof of the cab below.

When I'm able to lift my gaze from the wreckage at the bottom of the shaft, I see that I'm clinging to Cooper's shirtfront, and that his arms are around me protectively. His face has gone the color of the smoke around us. There are streaks of blood and rust all over his shirt from where I'd grabbed at him with my cut hands.

"Oh," I say, releasing the now crumpled and greasy cotton. "Sorry."

Cooper's arms drop away from me at once.

"No problem," he says.

His voice, like my own, is steady enough. But there's something in his blue eyes I've never seen before . . .

But before I have a chance to put my finger on just what, exactly, it is, a familiar voice from inside the cab we're sitting on demands, "So is she okay or what?"

I look down through the open panel in the cab's ceiling and see relief wash over Pete's face.

"You had us shittin' our pants back there, Heather," he says. And indeed, his burly Brooklynese has a tremor in it. "You okay?"

"I'm fine," I say, and prove it by climbing shakily down from the roof of the cab virtually unaided. My shoulder twinges a painful warning at one point, but Pete's steadying hand on one elbow, and Cooper's careful grip on my belt, keep me from losing my balance. I find, once I'm safely inside the elevator car, that it's difficult to stand without leaning against something since my knees are shaking pretty badly.

But I manage all right, by sagging against the wall.

"What about Julio?" I ask.

Cooper and Pete exchange looks.

"He's alive," Cooper says, but his jaw is strangely clenched.

"Leastways, he was a minute ago." Pete yanks around the key he'd inserted in the override switch. "But as to whether he'll still be alive by the time they get him out—"

I feel dizzy. "Get him out?"

"They're gonna hafta to use cutters."

I look to Cooper for a more detailed explanation, but he isn't forthcoming with one.

Suddenly, I'm not so sure I want to know.

For the second time in two days, I end up in St. Vincent's emergency room.

Only this time, I'm the patient.

I'm lying on a gurney, waiting to get my shoulder X-rayed. Cooper has gone in search of a tuna salad sandwich for me, since fear has made me famished.

While I wait, I gaze mournfully at my ragged fingers and palms, wrapped in gauze and smarting from numerous stitches. It will be weeks, an irritatingly young attending physician has informed me, before I have normal use of them again. Forget guitar playing. I can barely hold a pencil.

I'm glumly considering how I'm going to do my job properly when I have little or no use of my hands—undoubtedly Justine would have found a way—when Detective Canavan shows up, the unlit cigar still clenched between his teeth. I'm not sure it's the same cigar. But it sure looks like it.

"Hey there, Ms. Wells," he says, as casually as if we'd just bumped into one another at Macy's or something. "Heard you had quite an eventful morning."

"Oh," I say. "You mean the part where somebody tried to kill me? Again?"

"That'd be the one," Detective Canavan says, removing the cigar. "So. You sore at me?"

I am, a little. But then again, it hadn't been his fault, really. I mean, that planter could have fallen over accidentally. And Elizabeth and Roberta really could have died while elevator surfing.

Except that it hadn't. And they hadn't, either.

"Can't say as I blame you," Detective Canavan says, before I have a chance to reply. "Now we got a Backstreet Boy with a busted head and a janitor in intensive care."

"And two dead girls," I remind him. "Don't forget the two dead girls."

Detective Canavan sits down on an orange plastic chair that's bolted to the wall outside the X-ray lab.

"Oh, yeah," he says. "And two dead girls. Not to mention a certain administrative assistant who should, by rights, be dead as well." He puts the cigar back in his mouth. "We think it was a pipe bomb."

"What?" I yell.

"A pipe bomb. Not particularly sophisticated, but effective. In an enclosed space, like the brick elevator shaft, it did a lot more harm than it would have if it had been in a suitcase or a car or something." Detective Canavan chews on the cigar. "Somebody seems to want you dead in a big way, honey."

I stare at him, feeling cold again. Cooper had thrown his leather jacket over my shoulders as soon as we'd gotten down into the lobby, because I'd started shivering for some reason. And then when the paramedics had arrived, they'd added a blanket.

But I'd been freezing ever since seeing the wreckage that had once been the service elevator, crumpled at the bottom of that shaft. Firefighters had tried to pry the doors open with massive pliers—the jaws of life, they called them—but the twisted metal just shrieked in protest. Lying in that wreckage was Julio, who I later learned had suffered multiple broken bones, but was expected to survive. I had started shivering just looking at the mangled cab, and my hands have felt like ice ever since.

"A pipe bomb?" I echo. "How would somebody—"

"Slipped it on top of the elevator car. Easy to make, if you have the know-how. All you need is a steel pipe, threaded on both ends so you can cap it. Drill a couple holes in the side for twin fuses, slip a couple firecrackers through the holes, epoxy them in place, tack on some cigarettes, then fill the thing with gunpowder. Easy as pie."

Easy as pie? That sounds worse than the SATs!

Noting my raised eyebrows, Canavan removes the cigar and says, "Excuse me. Easy as pie if you know how to do it. Anyway, somebody lit that thing a few minutes before you and—what's his name?" He refers to his notebook. "Oh yeah, Mr. Guzman—went for the ride. Now, if you don't mind my asking, what the hell were you doing on top of that thing?"

Confused, I think back. A pipe bomb, with twin cigarette fuses? I have no idea what such a thing would look like, but I certainly hadn't noticed anything like it when I'd been up on the elevator car's roof.

Then again, with all the gears and machinery up there, a small bomb would be easy to hide.

But a pipe bomb? A pipe bomb, in Fischer Hall?

Behind the double doors to the waiting room, a nurse is calling, "Sir, you can't go in there! Sir, wait—"

Cooper bursts through the swinging doors, his arms full of paper bags. A pretty nurse trails after him, looking mad.

"Sir, you can't be barging back here," she insists. "I don't want to have to call security—"

"It's all right, nurse," Detective Canavan says, flipping open his wallet and showing her his badge. "He's with me."

"I don't care if he's with the Royal Academy of Medicine," the nurse snaps. "He can't be barging back here."

"Have a cannoli," Cooper says, producing one from a bag. The nurse stares at him like he's insane.

"No, really," Cooper says. "Have one. On me."

Disgusted, the nurse takes the cannoli, chomps off a large bite, then leaves, still chewing. Cooper shrugs, then eyes the detective with undisguised hostility.

"Well, if it isn't the NYPD's biggest dick," he says.

"Cooper!" I'm surprised. "Detective Canavan was just telling me—"

"What, that it's all in your head?" Cooper laughs bitterly, then stabs an index finger at the wide-eyed detective. "Well, let me tell you something, Canavan. There is no way all six cables to an elevator cab could snap at the same time unless someone deliberately—"

"Cooper!" I cry, but Detective Canavan is chuckling.

"Simmer down, Romeo," he says, waving his cigar at us. "We already established that a second attempt was made on the life of your girlfriend here. Nobody's sayin' what happened with the elevator was an accident. Keep your shirt on. I'm on your side."

Cooper blinks a few times, then looks at me. I expect him to say something like, "She's not my girlfriend." Only he doesn't. Instead he says, "The tuna salad didn't look fresh. I got you salami instead."

"Wow," I say. Cooper hands me a sandwich that has to be a foot long, at least. Not that there's anything wrong with that.

Detective Canavan peers at the many bags Cooper has scattered about. "Got any chips in there?" he wants to know.

"Sorry." Cooper unwraps my sandwich and begins breaking it up into bite-sized pieces, since I can't hold anything real well. "Olive?"

Detective Canavan looks disappointed.

"No, thanks. So," he says, as if there'd been no interruption. "Who told you to get on that elevator?"

I say, speaking with my mouth full because I'm too hungry to wait, "All I know is, I got a call from the reception desk that Gavin—he's this kid that lives in the hall—was elevator surfing again, and so I went with Julio to try and chase the kid down."

"Yeah? And when you got up there, what?"

I describe the explosion, which had occurred almost simultaneously with my realization that Gavin wasn't up there after all.

"So," Detective Canavan says. "Who told the kid at the desk to call you?"

"We all know who did this," Cooper says. The barely suppressed fury is back in his voice. "Why are you just sitting there, Canavan, instead of arresting him?"

"Arresting who?" Canavan wants to know.

"Allington. He's the killer. It's obvious Heather's got him running scared."

"I'll say," Canavan shakes his head. "The kid left town last night. He's parked himself out at his folks' place in the Hamptons. No way he could have planted that bomb, not without some help. Kid's three hours away by LIE. Somebody wants your girlfriend dead, all right. But it ain't Chris Allington."

Tonight is the night
Tonight we'll get it right
Baby, I feel like I've been waiting
All my life for this night
So glad I waited
Anticipated
Tonight's the night
For loving you

"Tonight"
Performed by Heather Wells
Composed by Dietz/Ryder
From the album *Magic*
Cartwright Records

24

Getting X-rayed is way painful, since the technician has to twist my body into several unnatural positions in order to get the angle he wants to photograph. But aside from some Motrin, I'm not offered a single thing for the pain.

Hello. You can buy Motrin over the counter. Where's the Vicodin? Where's the morphine? What kind of hospitals do they run these days, anyway?

After they X-ray me, they wheel me into this waiting room with a lot of other patients who are lying on gurneys.

Most of them look to be in way worse shape than me. All of them seem to have much better painkillers.

Thankfully they let me keep my sandwich. It's my only source of comfort. Well, that and some Fritos I get out of the candy machine at the end of the ward. It's no joke getting those quarters in the slot with my bandaged fingers, believe me.

Still, even Fritos don't make me feel better. I mean, by rights, I should be dead. I really should have been killed by that bomb. But I hadn't died.

Not like Elizabeth Kellogg and Roberta Pace. What had gone through their minds when they'd been suspended above the hard ground sixteen, fourteen floors below? Had they struggled before they were pushed? There were no signs that they'd done so, just some burn marks, apparently.

But what *kind* of burn marks?

And why had *I* lived, while they had died? Is there some reason I'd been spared? Is there something I'm supposed to do? Find their murderer, maybe?

Or had I been allowed to live for some other, even higher purpose? Like to pursue my own medical career, and ensure that future pipe bomb victims would get better drugs when brought to local area hospitals?

A doctor who couldn't have been any older than me finally shows up just as I'm finishing off the last of the Fritos, holding my X-rays and smiling. At least until he gets a good look at me.

"Aren't you—" He breaks off, looking panicky.

I'm too tired to play games.

"Yes," I say. "I'm Heather Wells. Yes, I sang 'Sugar Rush.' "

"Oh," he says, looking disappointed. "I thought you were Jessica Simpson."

Jessica Simpson! I'm so appalled that I can't utter another

word, even when he blithely informs me that there isn't anything seriously wrong with my shoulder, other than some deep tissue bruising. I need bed rest, and no, he can't prescribe anything for the pain.

I swear I hear him humming the chorus from "With You" as he leaves.

Jessica Simpson? I don't look anything like Jessica Simpson! Okay, we both have long blond hair. But there the resemblance ends.

Doesn't it?

I find a ladies' room and go inside. Peering at my reflection in the mirror above the sink, I'm relieved to find that I do not in the least resemble Jessica Simpson.

But nor do I resemble a human being. Much. My jeans are torn and covered with grease and my own blood. I'm clutching Cooper's leather jacket as well as a bright orange blanket around my shoulders. There's blood and dirt all over my face, and my hair hangs in greasy tangles. There isn't a trace of lipstick anywhere in the vicinity of my mouth.

In short, I look hideous.

I try to rectify the situation as best I can. Still, the results aren't anything to write home about.

But it's a good thing I'd elected to freshen up a little, because when I wander out into the waiting room, my hospital bill—all seventeen hundred dollars of it, to be paid by New York College—in my back pocket, I'm almost blinded by the number of flashbulbs that go off. More than a dozen people I don't know are calling out, "Miss Wells! Miss Wells, over here! Just one question, Miss Wells—" and the hospital security guard is trying desperately to keep more reporters from spilling into the lobby from the street.

"Heather!" A familiar voice sounds from somewhere in the throng, but not before a woman with a lot of pancake makeup and very big hair shoves a microphone in my face and demands, "Miss Wells, is it true that you and former flame ex–Easy Street member Jordan Cartwright are back together?"

Before I can open my mouth to reply, another reporter pounces.

"Miss Wells, is it true that this is the second time in two days that someone has tried to kill you?"

"Miss Wells," a third reporter asks. "Is there any truth to the rumor that this bomb was part of an elaborate terrorist plot to eradicate America's most beloved former teen pop sensations?"

"Heather!"

Above the microphone props and shoulder-held cameras towers Cooper. He gestures to me, indicating a side door that says *Hospital Personnel Only* on it.

But before I can duck toward it, someone grabs me by my sore shoulder and shouts, "Heather, is it true that you'll be making your singing comeback representing Calvin Klein's new fragrance for his fashion company's fall line?"

Thankfully, a cop shows up, breaking through the wall of reporters and taking hold of my good arm. He physically propels me from the middle of the throng, using his nightstick as a prod to hasten our progress.

"All right, all right," he says over and over again, in the flat Brooklyn accent I've come to know and trust since moving to New York City. "Let the lady through now. Show a little compassion for the patient, folks, and get out of her way."

The anonymous officer steers me through the *Hospital Personnel Only* door, then posts himself in front of it like a Marvel comic book superhero, guarding Fort Knox.

Once inside what turns out to be the very same hallway where I'd left Cooper and Detective Canavan when I'd gone to get X-rayed, I see that they'd been joined by a number of people, including Patty and Frank, Magda and Pete, and, for some reason, Dr. Jessup.

Both Patty and Magda let out wails of dismay when they see me. I don't know why. I thought I'd cleaned myself up pretty good.

Nevertheless, Patty springs out of her plastic chair and grabs me in a hug I'm sure she means to be friendly, but which actually hurts quite a bit. She's crying and saying things like, "I told you to find a different job! This job is no good for you, it's too dangerous!"

Meanwhile, Magda's staring at my hands, her jaw moving in a weird way. I've never seen her eyes so big.

"Oh my God," she keeps saying, throwing accusing looks in Pete's direction. "You said it was bad, but you didn't say how bad."

"I'm okay," I insist, trying to extricate myself from Patty's impossibly long arms. "Really, Patty, I'm okay—"

"Jesus, Pats, you're hurting her." Frank tries to pry his wife off me. He peers down at me anxiously as he untangles Patty's arms from mine. "You really okay, kid? You look like hell."

"I'm okay," I lie. I'm still shaken up, not so much from my ordeal in the elevator shaft as from my ordeal at the hands of those reporters. Where had they come from? And how had they found out about the bomb so fast? New York College appeared in the press rarely, and positively, if at all. How was this going to reflect upon my six months' performance review? Would it be held against me?

Then Dr. Jessup coughs, and everyone looks at him. In his arms is an enormous bouquet of sunflowers. For me. Dr. Jessup has brought *me* flowers.

"Wells," he says, in his gravelly voice. "Always hafta be in the spotlight, dontcha?"

I smile, moved beyond speech. After all, Dr. Jessup is very busy, being assistant vice president and all. I couldn't believe he'd taken time out to come down to the hospital to give me flowers.

But Dr. Jessup isn't done. He leans down and kisses my cheek, saying, "Glad you're all in one piece, Wells. These are from the department." He thrusts the flowers at me, and when I helplessly raise my bandaged hands, Magda steps in, taking the bouquet for me. Dr. Jessup doesn't see her scowl, or if he does, he ignores it. He also doesn't hear her mutter, "He gives her flowers, when what he should be giving her is a big fat raise . . ."

"Rachel said to tell you she's sorry she couldn't come, but somebody has to hold down the fort." Dr. Jessup grins, showing all of his teeth. " 'Course, she didn't know about all the paparazzi. Bet she'll be sorry she missed that when she hears about it. So, who you gonna sell the story to, *Entertainment Tonight* or *Access Hollywood*?"

"The *Post*'ll offer you top dollar," Magda informs me, not aware that Dr. Jessup is kidding. "Or the *Enquirer*."

"Don't worry," I say with a smile. "I won't be talking to the press."

Dr. Jessup doesn't look convinced. His expression has gone from one of friendly concern to one of worried suspicion. I realize suddenly that the only reason he even showed up at the hospital was to see if I intended to go public with my story.

I should have known, I guess. I mean that Dr. Jessup wasn't there out of concern for me. Dr. Jessup was there for one reason, and one reason only:

Damage control.

I think he suspected it was going to be bad—why else would he have braved the traffic this far into the West Village?—but

I don't think he ever thought it was going to be *this* bad. A bomb going off in a New York College dormitory—I mean, residence hall—is news with a capital N. Something similar had happened at Yale, and it had made CNN, and been a lead story on all the local networks, even though it had turned out to have nothing to do with terrorism.

And the fact that one of the victims of this bomb is a former teen pop sensation? Well, that just makes the story that much juicier. My disappearance from the world of music had not gone unnoticed, and the reason behind it—including my mother's new Argentinian cattle ranch—had been made graphically public. I could just see the cover of the *Post*:

BLOND BOMBSHELL

Former Pop Star Heather Wells
Nearly Blown to Bits
at low-paying job she was forced to take at New York College in order to support herself after her music career tanked and she was thrown out by former fiancé, Easy Street member Jordan Cartwright.

Still, I can understand Dr. Jessup's concern. Having two of his employees injured in an elevator accident is one thing.

But a bomb in one of his dormitories—I mean, residence halls? Worse, a bomb in the building in which the president of the college lives? What's he going to tell the trustees? The poor guy probably thinks he's watching his vice presidency slip away.

I don't blame him for being more worried about his own skin than mine. After all, he's got kids. All I've got is a dog.

"Heather," Dr. Jessup begins again. "I'm sure you understand. This thing is a PR nightmare. We can't have the public thinking our residence halls are out of control—"

To my surprise, it's Detective Canavan who interrupts the assistant vice president. Noisily clearing his throat, then looking around unsuccessfully for a place to spit, Detective Canavan sighs, then swallows.

Then he says, "Hey. Hate to break this up, but the longer Ms. Wells here sticks around, the harder it's gonna be for my boys to maintain crowd control out there."

I feel an arm slip around my shoulders. Looking up, I'm surprised to see that the arm belongs to Cooper. He isn't looking at me, though. He's looking at the door.

"Come on, Heather," he says. "Frank and Patty brought their car. They parked it down below, in the garage. They'll give us a lift home."

"Oh yes, let's go," Patty urges. Her beautiful face is filled with distaste. "I hate hospitals, and I hate reporters even more." Her dark, almond-shaped eyes slide toward Dr. Jessup, and she looks as if she's about to add, *And I hate uptight bureaucrats most of all*, but she refrains, entirely for my sake, I'm sure, since I choose that moment to step on her foot sort of hard, causing her to let out a little yelp of pain.

After I say good-bye to Pete and Magda—who promise to stick around the hospital until they get to see Julio—a hospital administrator gladly shows us the way down to the parking garage, as if any sacrifice she can make to get rid of us—and ergo, all the reporters—will be well worth it.

All I can think the whole way to the car is, *Oh God. I am so fired.* When I'm not thinking, *Oh God, what's with the arm?* about Cooper, that is.

Except that once we're safely in the car, Cooper removes his arm. So then I just have the one thing to worry about.

"Oh God," I can't help saying miserably, a catch in my

throat, from the backseat. "I think Dr. Jessup is going to fire me."

"Nobody's going to fire you, Heather," Cooper says. "The guy's just looking out for his own interests."

"That man even crosses his eyes at you, baby, he's gonna hafta deal with me," Patty growls, from behind the wheel. Patty is an assertive—one might almost say aggressive—driver, which is why she, instead of Frank, does all the driving when they're in the city. She leans on the horn as a yellow cab cuts her off. "Nobody messes with my best girlfriend."

Frank, looking back at me from the front passenger seat, says, "Cooper give you his jacket?"

I look down at the leather coat still wrapped around my shoulders. It smells of Cooper, like leather and soap. I never want to take it off, not ever again. But I know I'm going to have to, when we get home.

"No," I say. "I mean, just to borrow."

"Oh," Frank say. "Because, you know, you've got your blood all over it."

"Frank," Patty says. "Shut up."

"It's all right," Cooper says, as he studies the many weirdos out his window who make up the street life of the West Village.

It's all right! My heart swells. Cooper had said it's all right that I got my blood all over his leather jacket! Probably because, you know, we'll be dating after this, and he's just going to give the coat to me anyway. And I'll have it—and Cooper—always, to keep me warm.

But then Cooper adds, "I know of a dry cleaner who's good at getting bloodstains out."

You know, it just isn't my day.

25

Hello
Do I have the right number?
Hello
Yes, I'm looking for my lover
Hello
Can you get him
On the line for me?
Hello
I know he used to live there
Hello
I know he used to care
Hello
Please get my lover on the line
For me

"Hello"
Performed by Heather Wells
Composed by Jones/Ryder
From the album *Magic*
Cartwright Records

Patty drops us off at the brownstone, even though Frank insists it isn't safe there, what with somebody wanting to kill me and all.

All I want to do is take a bath and crawl into my own bed and sleep for a thousand years. I don't want to have a big long discussion about whether whoever is trying to kill me knows where I live. Frank wants me to go stay with him and Patty.

Until Cooper points out that that might put Indy at risk.

At first I'm kind of shocked, you know, that Cooper would

say something so horrible. It's only when I see how swiftly Frank says that he thinks it would be better if I just stay at Cooper's, after all, what with Cooper being a trained crime fighter, that I realize what Cooper was up to. He knows I just want to go home. He knows I don't want to stay in Frank and Patty's guest room.

And because he's Cooper, and he's always doing nice things for me—giving me a free apartment when I have nowhere else to go, and no money for rent anyway; taking me to a party he doesn't really want to go to, since he might run into a former flame, with whom things had ended badly; risking his own life to save mine; that kind of thing—he'd done his best to get me what he knew I wanted.

Except, of course, the one thing I want more than anything.

But apparently that, for reasons I'll probably never know—and am pretty sure I don't want to, anyway—he's not prepared to give me.

Which is totally fine. I mean, I understand. I'll just open my OWN doctor's office/detective agency/jewelry shop, without his help.

Of course, having the kids on my own might be harder, but I'm sure I'll manage somehow.

Fortunately, I have an unlisted number, so there aren't any reporters lurking on my front stoop when we pull up. Just the usual drug dealers.

Lucy is wild with joy to see me—though I have to ask Cooper to walk her for the time being, since there's no way I can hold a leash with my torn-up hands. Once the two of them are gone, I slip upstairs to my apartment, where I peel off my grimy clothes and slide, at long last, into the tub.

Although it turns out that bathing with stitches in your hands is no joke. I have to get out of the tub and go into the kitchen, pull out some rubber gloves, and put those on before

I can wash my hair, because the doctor warned me that if I got the stitches wet, my hands might fall off, or something.

Once I get all the elevator grime and blood off me, let the bath refill, and I just lay there, soaking my sore shoulder for a while, wondering what I'm going to do now.

I mean, things aren't exactly looking good. Someone is trying to kill me . . . probably the same someone who'd already killed two people, at least. The only common denominator between the dead girls appears to be the president of the college's son.

But, at least according to the police, it's unlikely that Chris Allington was the one who'd tried to blow me up, because he'd been out of town at the time.

Which means that someone besides Chris is trying to kill me. And maybe that someone, and not Chris, killed the two girls.

But who? And why? Why would someone have killed Elizabeth Kellogg and Roberta Pace in the first place? What could they have possibly done to deserve to die? I mean, besides move into Fischer Hall. Oh, and date—albeit briefly— Chris Allington.

Is *that* it? Is *that* what had caused their deaths? The fact that they'd dated Chris? Had Magda been right? Not about the girls having killed themselves because, after waiting so long to have sex, they'd found out it really isn't the earth-shattering thing they'd been led to believe. But about the girls dying *because* of the sex—not at their own hand, but the hand of someone who didn't approve of what they'd just done.

Someone like Mrs. Allington, maybe? What was it that Chris's mother had said to me, just before the elevator incident? Something about "you girls."

"You girls are forever bothering him," she'd said. Or something like that.

You girls. There'd been something deeply antagonistic in Mrs. Allington's manner, an emotion far stronger than simple annoyance over my waking her up. Is Mrs. Allington one of those jealous mothers, who thinks no other woman is good enough for her precious son? Did *Mrs. Allington* kill Elizabeth and Roberta? And did she then try to kill me when I got too close to discovering her secret?

Oh my God! That's it! Mrs. Allington is the killer! Mrs. Allington! I'm brilliant! Perhaps the most brilliant detective mind since Sherlock Holmes! Wait. Is he even real? Or fictional? He's fictional, right?

Well, okay, then. I am the most brilliant detective mind since . . . since . . . Eliot Ness! He's real, right?

"Heather?"

I start, sloshing hot water and soap suds over the side of the tub.

But it's just Cooper.

"Just checking you're okay," he says, through the closed door. "You need anything?"

Um, yes. You. In here with me, naked. Now.

"No, I'm fine," I call. Should I tell him that I'd figured out who'd done this to me? Or wait until I'm out of the tub?

"Well, when you're through, I thought I'd order something to eat. Indian okay with you?"

Hmmmm. Vegetable samosas.

"Fine," I call.

"Okay, well, come out soon. There's something I need to talk to you about."

Something he needs to talk to me about? Like what? Like his true feelings for me? *I've always thought of you as one of the*— He never had finished telling me what he's always thought of me as.

Is he going to tell me now? Am I sure I want to know?

Two minutes later I slide into my usual seat at my kitchen table, bundled in my terry-cloth robe, with a towel wrapped around my wet hair. Oh, I want to know. I want to know all right.

Across the table from me, Cooper says, "That was fast."

Then he opens up his laptop.

Wait a minute. His *laptop*? What kind of guy uses audio-visual aids to tell a girl what he thinks of her?

"How much do you know," Cooper asks, "about Christopher Allington?"

"Christopher Allington?" My voice cracks. Maybe because it was hoarse from all the screaming I'd done earlier in the day. Or maybe because I'm in shock over the fact that what Cooper wants to talk to me about isn't his true feelings for me, but his suspicions about Chris. Hello. Annoying.

"But it couldn't have been Chris," I say, to get Cooper off that subject, and back onto, you know, me. "Detective Canavan said he—"

"When I investigate a case," Cooper interrupts calmly, "I investigate it from all angles. Right now, Christopher appears to be the common link between all the victims. What I'm asking is, what do you know about him?"

"Well," I say. Maybe Vulcan mind control would work again. WHAT HAVE YOU ALWAYS THOUGHT ABOUT ME? "Not much."

"Do you know where he went for undergrad?"

"No," I say. WHAT HAVE YOU ALWAYS THOUGHT ABOUT ME? Then, glancing at his face, I ask, "Why? Do you know where Chris went as an undergrad?"

"Yes," Cooper says. "Earlcrest."

"Earl what?" I ask. Vulcan mind control does not appear to

be working! Instead of telling me what he's always thought about me, he's blathering about Chris Allington. Who cares about Chris? What about how you feel about ME?

"Earlcrest College," Cooper says. "Chris went there for undergrad."

"What are you talking about, Cooper?" I wish the Indian food would hurry up and come. My stomach is growling. "And how do you even know where Chris went?"

Cooper shrugs his broad shoulders. "SIS." he says.

"S.O.S?" I echo, confused.

"No, SIS. Student Information System." When I continue to look blank, he sighs. "Ah, yes. How could I forget? You're computer illiterate."

"I am not! I surf the Net all the time. I do all your bills—"

"But your office is still antiquated. SIS hasn't been extended to the dormitory director's offices yet."

"Residence hall," I correct him, automatically.

"Residence hall," he says. Cooper is a flurry of activity. He's striking keys on the computer way faster than I can change chords on my guitar. "Here, look. I'm accessing SIS now to show you what I mean about Christopher Allington. Okay." Cooper turns the screen to face me. "Allington, Christopher Phillip. Take a look."

I peer at the tiny monitor. Christopher Allington's entire academic record is there, along with a lot of other personal information, like his LSAT scores and his course schedule and stuff. Chris, it turns out, has been through a lot of prep schools. He'd been thrown out of one in Switzerland for cheating, and another one in Connecticut, reason for expulsion unspecified. But he had still managed to get into the University of Chicago, which I've heard is quite selective. I wonder what strings his dad had pulled to help him out there.

But Chris's sojourn in the Windy City didn't last long. He'd dropped out after only a single semester. Then he'd seemed to take some time off . . . a good four years, as a matter of fact.

Then suddenly he'd shown up at Earlcrest College, from which he'd graduated last year somewhat older than the rest of his class, but with a B.A., just the same.

"Earlcrest College," I say. "That's where his dad used to be president. Before he got hired at New York College."

"Ah, nepotism," Cooper says, with a grin. "As alive and well in the halls of academia as ever."

"Okay," I say, still confused. "So he got kicked out of a few places as a kid, and could only get into a college his dad's president of. What does that prove? Not that he's a psychopathic murderer." I can't believe *I'm* the one arguing for Chris's innocence now. Is his mom really that much more appealing as a murderer? "And how did you access his file, anyway? Isn't it supposed to be private?"

"I have my ways," Cooper says, turning the computer screen back in his own direction.

"Oh my God." Is there no end to this man's fabulousness? "You hacked into the student system!"

"You were always curious about what I do all day," he says with a shrug. "Now you know. Part of it, anyway."

"I can't believe it," I say. "You're a computer nerd!" This changes everything. Now we're going to have to open a doctor's office slash detective agency slash jewelry shop slash computer hacking service. Oh, wait, what about my songs?

Cooper ignores me. "I think there's got to be something here," he says, tapping the laptop. "Something we're missing. The only connection between the girls seems to be Allington. He's the only one we know about, but, given what I see here, there must be something else. I mean, besides the fact that both girls were virgins with residence hall records before Chris got his hands on them . . ."

Mrs. Allington. It's on the tip of my tongue to say *What about Mrs. Allington?* I mean, she had the motive. She obviously had—what was it that Sarah would call it? An Oedipus complex? Only the opposite, because she had it for her son, not her dad . . .

Well, okay, Mrs. Allington has that thing where she thinks her son is hot, and she resents the girls who pursue him. Resents them enough to kill them, though? And could Mrs. Allington really have made that bomb? The one on top of the elevator? I mean, if you could just go out and buy a bomb at Saks, I totally think Mrs. Allington would.

But you can't. You have to make a bomb. And to make a bomb, you have to be sober. I'm pretty sure, anyway.

And Mrs. Allington has never once been sober—that I could tell—since she'd moved in to Fischer Hall.

I sigh and glance out the window. I can see the lights on in the president's penthouse. What are the Allingtons doing up there? I wonder. It's close to seven o'clock. Probably watching the news.

Or, perhaps, plotting to kill more innocent virgins?

The front door buzzer goes off, making me jump.

"That's dinner," Cooper says, and gets up. "I'll be right back."

He goes downstairs to get the Indian food. I keep on looking out the window while I wait for him to get back. Below the penthouse, lights appear in windows on other floors of Fischer Hall as the residents got home from class or dinner or their workouts or rehearsals. I wonder if any of the tiny figures I can see in any of the windows is Amber, the little redhead from Idaho. Is she sitting in her room, waiting for a call from Chris? Does she know he's hiding out in the

Hamptons? Poor little Amber. I wonder what she did to get in trouble with Rachel this morning.

That's when it hits me.

My lips part, but for a minute, no sound comes out from between them. Amber. I had forgotten all about Amber, and her meeting with Rachel this morning. What had Rachel needed to see Amber about? Amber herself hadn't known why she'd been scheduled for a mandatory meeting with the dorm director. What had Amber done?

Amber hadn't done anything. Anything except talk to Chris Allington.

That's all Amber had done.

And Rachel knew it, because she'd seen me with the two of them in front of the building after the lip-synch contest.

Just like she'd seen Roberta and Chris at the dance. And Elizabeth and Chris—where? Where had she seen them together? At orientation, maybe? A movie night?

Except that it didn't matter. Like it didn't matter that it was Rachel who'd told Julio to get me because Gavin was elevator surfing again.

Like it didn't matter that it was Rachel who'd snuck onto the penthouse roof and tried to push that planter onto my head.

Like it didn't matter that when the second girl died, Rachel hadn't been in the cafeteria, like she was supposed to have been. No, I'd met her coming from the ladies' room . . . around the corner from the stairs she'd been hurrying down, after pushing Roberta Pace to her death.

And the reason the elevator key had been missing, and then reappeared in such a short space of time that day? Rachel had had it. Rachel, the one person in Fischer Hall no desk attendant would ask to sign out a key, or even question the presence of behind the desk. Because she's the hall director.

And the girls who'd died—they hadn't died because they had files in Rachel's office.

They had files in Rachel's office because she'd singled them out to die.

"Hope you're hungry," Cooper says, returning to my apartment holding a big plastic *I ♥ NY* bag. "They messed up and gave us chicken *and* shrimp dansak . . ." His voice trails off. "Heather?" Cooper is peering at me strangely, his blue eyes concerned. "Are you okay?"

"Earlcrest," I manage to grunt.

Cooper puts the bag on the kitchen table and stares down at me.

"Yeah," he says. "That's what I thought you said. What about it?"

"Where is it?"

Cooper bends over to refer to his computer screen. "Uh, I don't—oh, Indiana. Richmond, Indiana."

I shake my head, so hard the towel slips from it, and my damp hair falls down over my shoulders. No. NO WAY.

"Oh my God," I breathe. "Oh my *God*."

Cooper is staring at me like I've lost my mind. And you know what? I think I *have*. Lost my mind, I mean. Because how could I not have seen it before now, even though it had been staring me right in the face. . . .

"Rachel worked there," I manage to rasp. "Rachel worked at a dorm in Richmond, Indiana, before she moved here."

Cooper, who'd been pulling white paper containers from the *I ♥ NY* bag, pauses. "What are you talking about?"

"Richmond, Indiana," I repeat. My heart is thumping so hard that I can see the lapel of my terry-cloth robe leaping over my breast with every beat. "The last place Rachel worked was in Richmond, Indiana . . ."

Comprehension dawns across Cooper's face.

"Rachel worked at Earlcrest? You think . . . you think *Rachel*'s the one who killed those girls?" He shakes his head. "Why? You think she was that desperate to win a Pansy Award?"

"No." No way is Rachel going around pushing people down the elevator shafts of Fischer Hall in order to get herself a Pansy, or even a promotion.

Because it isn't a promotion Rachel is after.

It's a man.

A heterosexual man, worth more than a hundred thousand dollars a year, if you count the trust fund he's supposed to have.

Christopher Allington. Christopher Allington is that man.

"Heather," Cooper says. "Heather? Look. I'm sorry. But there's no way. Rachel Walcott is not a killer."

I suck in my breath.

"How do you know?" I ask. "I mean, why not? Why not her, as opposed to someone else? Because she's a woman? Because she's pretty?"

"Because it's crazy," Cooper says. "Come on, it's been a long day. Maybe you should get some rest."

"I am not tired," I say. "Think about it, Cooper. I mean, *really* think about it. Elizabeth and Roberta met with Rachel before they died—I bet the stuff in their files, the stuff about their moms calling, isn't even true. I bet their mothers never called. And now Amber . . ."

"There are seven hundred residents of Fischer Hall," Cooper points out. "Are all the ones who had meetings with Rachel Walcott dead?"

"No, just the ones who also had relationships with Christopher Allington."

Cooper shakes his head.

"Heather, try to look at this logically. How could Rachel

Walcott have the physical strength to throw a full-grown, struggling young woman down an elevator shaft? Rachel can't weigh more than a hundred and twenty pounds herself. It's just not possible, Heather."

"I don't know how she's doing it, Cooper. But I do know that it's a bit of a coincidence that both Rachel and Chris were at Earlcrest last year, and now they're both here at New York College. I would bet cash money that Rachel followed Christopher Allington—and his parents—here."

When he continues to look hesitant, I stand up, push back my chair, and say, "There's only one way we'll ever know for sure."

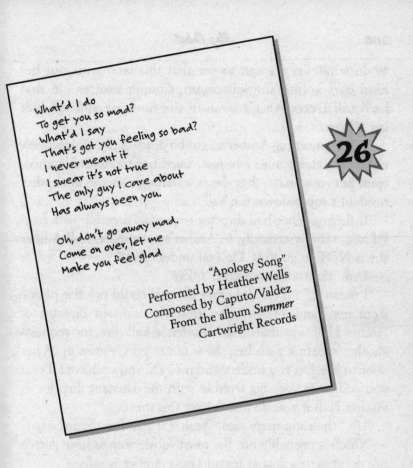

What'd I do
To get you so mad?
What'd I say
That's got you feeling so bad?
I never meant it
I swear it's not true
The only guy I care about
Has always been you.

Oh, don't go away mad.
Come on over, let me
Make you feel glad

"Apology Song"
Performed by Heather Wells
Composed by Caputo/Valdez
From the album *Summer*
Cartwright Records

26

Not surprisingly, Cooper balks at the idea of driving all the way to the Hamptons at seven o'clock on a weeknight just to have a word with a man the police themselves won't even haul in for questioning.

When I remind him that Chris is more likely to talk to either of us than the police, Cooper is still not convinced. He insists that after the injuries I'd sustained that morning, what I need is a good night's sleep, not a six-hour drive to East Hampton and back.

When I remind him that it is our duty as good citizens

to do whatever we can to see that this woman is put behind bars before she kills again, Cooper assures me that he'll call Detective Canavan in the morning and tell him my theory.

"But by morning Amber might be dead!" I cry. I know she's not dead yet, because I've just called her room and learned, from her roommate, that she is watching a movie in another resident's room down the hall.

"If the residence hall director requests a meeting with her," I'd said, semihysterically, to Amber's roommate, "tell Amber she is NOT to go to it. Do you understand?"

"Um," the roommate said. "Okay."

"I mean it," I'd cried, before Cooper could pry the phone from my hand. "Tell Amber that the assistant director of Fischer Hall says that if the residence hall director requests another meeting with her, she is not to go. Or even open her door to her. Do you understand me? Do you understand that you will be in very big trouble with the assistant director of Fischer Hall if you do not deliver this message?"

"Uh," the roommate said. "Yeah. I'll give her the message."

Which is probably not the most subtle way to have gotten my point across. But at least I know Amber is safe.

For the time being.

"We've got to go, Cooper!" I urge him, as soon as I've put the phone down. "I've got to know, now!"

"Heather," Cooper says, looking frustrated. "I swear to God, of all the people I've ever met, you have got to be the most—"

I suck in my breath. He's going to say it! Whatever it was he'd been about to say in my office! He's going to say it now!

Except that back then—in my office, I mean—it had sounded like what he'd been about to say was complimentary. Judging from the way his jaw is clenched now, though,

I don't think he's about to say something nice about me. In fact, I'm pretty sure I don't *want* to hear his next words.

Because, truthfully, the thing with Rachel is more important.

Which is why I say, "This is stupid. You know, there are trains to the Hamptons. I'll just go look up the schedule online and—"

I don't know if he gave in because he realized it was the only way to shut me up, or if he was genuinely concerned that I might do myself harm on the LIRR. Maybe he was just trying to placate the crazy injured girl.

In any case, in the time it takes me to get dressed, Cooper has retrieved his car—a '74 BMW 2002, a vehicle that invariably causes the drug dealers on my street to hoot tauntingly, because, in their opinion, the only good BMW is a new one—from its parking garage. He isn't happy about it, or anything. In fact, I'm pretty sure he was cursing whatever impulse had prompted him to ask me to move in with him in the first place.

And I feel bad about it. I really do.

But not enough to tell him to forget the whole thing. Because, you know, a girl's life is at stake.

It's easy to find the Allingtons' weekend place. I mean, they're in the East Hampton phone book. If they didn't want people to drop in, they'd have had an unlisted number, right?

And okay, there's this big wrought-iron gate at the end of their driveway, with a built-in intercom and everything, that might lead the average person to believe visitors were unwelcome.

But I for one didn't fall for it. I hop out of the car and go to press on the buzzer. And even when no one answers, I'm not discouraged. Well, very much.

"Heather," Cooper says, from the driver's window of his car, which he's rolled down. "I don't think anybody's going to—"

But then the intercom crackles, and a voice that is unmistakably Chris's says, *"What?"*

I can understand why he's so testy. I'd sort of been leaning on the buzzer, knowing that eventually the person inside would be driven insane and have to answer. It's a trick I'd picked up from the reporters who used to stake out the place Jordan and I had shared.

"Um, hi, Chris," I say into the intercom. "It's me."

"Me who?" Chris demands, still sounding annoyed.

"You know," I say, trying to sound girlishly flirtatious. "Let me in."

Then I add the three little words I'd learned from Justine's files that few students—and that's what Chris is, after all—can resist: "I brought pizza."

There's a pause. Then the gate slowly starts to open.

I hurry back to the car, where Cooper is sitting, looking— even if I do say so myself—vaguely impressed.

"Pizza," he echoes. "I'll have to remember that one."

"Works every time," I say. I don't mention how I knew. I'm kind of sick of Justine, to tell the truth.

We pull into the circular driveway, and Villa d'Allington, in all its white stucco glory, looms ahead of us.

I've been to the Hamptons before, of course. The Cartwrights have a house there, right on the water, surrounded on three sides by a federally protected bird sanctuary, so no else can build there, and ruin the view.

I've been to other people's homes there as well—houses that were considered architectural marvels and once even a chateau that had been transported, brick by brick, from the south of France. Seriously.

But I've never seen anything quite like the Allingtons' house. Not in the Hamptons, anyway. Stark white and massive, filled with airy, Mediterranean archways and bright, flowering plants, the place is lit up as brightly as Rockefeller Center.

Only instead of a great big gold guy looming over a skating rink, there's a great big white house looming over a swimming pool.

"How about," Cooper says, as we get out of the car, "you let me do the talking for a change."

I narrow my eyes at him. "You aren't going to hit him, are you?"

"Why would I do that?" Cooper asks, sounding surprised.

"Don't you hit people? I mean, in your line of work?"

"Can't remember the last time I did," Cooper says, mildly.

A little bit disappointed, I say, "Well, I think Christopher Allington's the type of guy you'd like to hit. If you hit people."

"He is," Cooper agrees, with a faint smile. "But I won't. At least, not right away."

We hear them first, and see them as soon as we part the morning glories that hang like a curtain over one of the archways. Ducking through the sweet-smelling vines, we end up in the backyard. To the left of the shimmering pool is a hot tub, steaming in the cool night air.

In the hot tub are two people, neither of whom, I'm thankful to see, is President Allington or his wife. I think that might have killed me, the sight of President Allington in a Speedo.

They don't notice us right away, probably because of all the steam and the bright floodlights that light the deck around the pool, but cast the hot tub area in shadow. Scattered here and there along the wide wooden planks of the patio are lounge chairs with pale pink cushions. Off to one side of the pool is a bar, a real bar with stools in front of it and a back-lit area that's filled with bottles.

I approach the hot tub and clear my throat noisily.

Chris lifts his face from the girl whose breasts he was nuzzling and blinks at us. He is clearly drunk.

The girl is, too. She says, "Hey, she hasn't got any pizza." She sounds disappointed about it, even though the two of them seemed to have been doing just fine for themselves in the extra cheese department.

"Hi, Chris," I say, and I sit down on the end of one of the lounge chairs. The cushion beneath me is damp. It has rained recently in the Hamptons.

It seems to take a few seconds for Chris to recognize me. And when he does, he isn't too happy.

"Blondie?" He reaches up to slick some of his wet hair back from his eyes. "Is that you? What are *you* doing here?"

"We just dropped by to ask you a few questions," I say. Lucy has come with us—I couldn't leave her cooped up in the brownstone all night—and now she butts her head against my knees and sits down, panting happily. "How are you, anyway?"

"I'm okay, I guess," Chris replies. He looks up at Cooper. "Who's he?"

"A friend," Cooper says. Then adds, "Of hers," I guess so there won't be any confusion.

"Huh," Chris says. Then, in an apparent attempt to make the best out of a bad situation, he goes, "Well. Care for a drink?"

"No, thank you," Cooper says. "What we'd really like is to talk to you about Elizabeth Kellogg and Roberta Pace."

Chris doesn't look alarmed. In fact, he doesn't even look surprised. Instead he says graciously, "Oh, sure. Sure. Oh, hey, where are my manners? Faith, honey, go inside and rustle up some grub for us, will you? And grab another bottle of wine while you're in there, why don't you?"

The girl in the hot tub pouts. "But, Chris—"

"Go on, honey."

"But my name's Hope, not Faith."

"Whatever." Chris slaps her on the backside as she climbs, dripping like a mermaid, from the hot tub. She has on a bathing suit, but it's a bikini, and the top is so skimpy and her boobs so large that the tiny Lycra triangles seem like mere suggestions.

Cooper notices the bikini phenomenon right away. I can tell by his raised eyebrows. It so pays to be a trained investigator.

Her rear proves as impressive as her front. Not an ounce of cellulite. I wonder if she, like Rachel, had StairMastered it all away.

"So, Chris," Cooper says, as soon as the girl is gone. "What's the deal with you and Rachel Walcott?"

Chris chokes on the sip of Chardonnay he'd been taking.

"Wh-what?" he coughs, when he can speak again.

But Cooper's just looking down at Chris the way he might have looked down at a really interesting but kind of gross bug that he'd found in his salad.

"Rachel Walcott," he says. "She was the director of the dorm—I mean, residence hall—you lived in your senior year at Earlcrest. Now she's running Fischer Hall, where your parents live, and where Heather here works."

Fumbling for a pack of cigarettes and a lighter he had left by the side of the Jacuzzi, Chris pulls one out with trembling fingers and lights it. He inhales, and in the semidarkness, the tip of the cigarette glows redly.

"Shit" is all he says.

I'm not a trained detective and all, but even I think this answer is kind of . . . suspicious.

"So what gives between the two of you?" Cooper asks. "You and Rachel. I mean, you might not have noticed, but people are dying—"

"I've noticed," Chris says sharply. "Okay? I've noticed. What the fuck do you think?"

Cooper apparently doesn't think this last part is all that necessary. You know, the bad language.

Because he says to Chris, in a much harsher voice than he's spoken in before, "You *knew*? How long?"

Chris blinks up at him through the steam from the bubbling jets. "What?" he asks, like someone who isn't sure he was hearing things right.

"*How long?*" Cooper demands again, in a voice that makes me glad it's Chris he's talking to, and not me. It also makes me doubt his story. You know, about not hitting people in his line of work. "How long have you known that Rachel was the one killing those girls?"

I can see that Chris has gone as pale as the watery lights beneath the surface of the pool, and it isn't from the cigarette smoke.

I don't blame him. Cooper's scaring me a little, too.

"I didn't know," Chris says, in a choked voice that is quite different from the cocky one he'd used previously. "I didn't put it together until last night, when you"—he looks at me "when you and I danced, and you told me Beth and Bobby were . . . were the ones who—"

"Oh, c'mon, Chris," Cooper says. "You expect us to believe that with all the publicity on campus after those supposed accidents—"

"I didn't know!" Chris splashes one hand into the water to emphasize his words, and gets Lucy's paws wet. She looks down at them quizzically, then goes to work with her tongue. "I swear to God, I didn't know. I don't exactly have a lot of free time, and what I do have I'm not going to waste reading the newspapers. I mean, of course I heard two girls in Fischer Hall had died, but I didn't know they were *my* two girls."

"And you didn't notice that neither of the girls was returning your calls?"

Chris ducks his head. Shamefacedly, I think.

"Because you never called them again." Cooper's voice is cold as ice.

Chris looks defensive. "Do *you?*" he demands, of Cooper. "Do you always call the next day?"

"If I want there to be a next time," Cooper replies, without missing a beat.

"Exactly." Chris's voice drips with meaning. At first I don't get what he means.

Then I do.

Oh.

Cooper shakes his head, looking as disgusted as I feel. Well, almost, anyway. "You expect me to believe that you never knew those girls were dead until you heard it from Heather the other night?"

"That's right," Chris says, and suddenly he flicks his cigarette into the rhododendrons and hauls himself out of the Jacuzzi. All he has on is a pair of baggy swim trunks. His frame is lean but muscular, his skin tanned to a light gold. There isn't a single patch of body hair on him, unless you count what curls out from beneath his arms.

"And when I heard about it, the first thing I did was, I came here." Chris stands up, wrapping himself in a wide, pale pink towel. "I needed to get away, I needed to think, I needed to—"

"You needed to avoid being hauled in for questioning by the cops," Cooper finishes for him.

"That, too. Look, so I slept with 'em—"

I can stand it no longer. Really. I feel sick—and not just because of all the Indian food we'd eaten in the car on the way over, either.

No, this isn't just indigestion. It's disgust.

"Don't act like it's no big deal, Chris," I say. "Your sleeping with those girls, then not calling them again. Not even telling them your real name in order to keep them from knowing who your father is. Because it *is* a big deal. Or it was, to them. You used them. You used them because you know you . . . you know you've got . . . well, performance inadequacies."

"What?" Chris looks shocked. "I do not!"

"Of course you do," I say, knowing I sound like Sarah, and not caring. "Why else were you looking for girls who don't have any sexual experience—until Hope here—so they don't have anything to measure your performance by?"

Chris looks as stunned as if I'd hit him.

And maybe, in a way, I have.

Cooper tugs on my sleeve and whispers, "Whoa, tiger. Simmer down. Let's not get our roles here confused. I'm the bad cop. You're the good one."

Then, patting me gently on the back—the way I pat Indy when I want him to calm down—Cooper says to a red-faced Chris, "Listen, nobody's accusing you of murdering anybody. What we want to know about is your relationship with Rachel Walcott."

"Why?" Chris is over being scared, and back to being surly. My remark about performance inadequacies has upset him. Undoubtedly because it's true.

Chris strides past Cooper, heading for the pool. "What about it?"

"Was there one?" Cooper wants to know.

"A relationship?" Dropping the towel, Chris climbs onto the diving board. A second later, he's sprung into the pool, hardly making a splash as his long, lean body arcs through the water. He swims up to the side of the pool we're standing on, then surfaces, seeming to have had a change of heart under water.

"All right," he says. "I'll tell you everything I know."

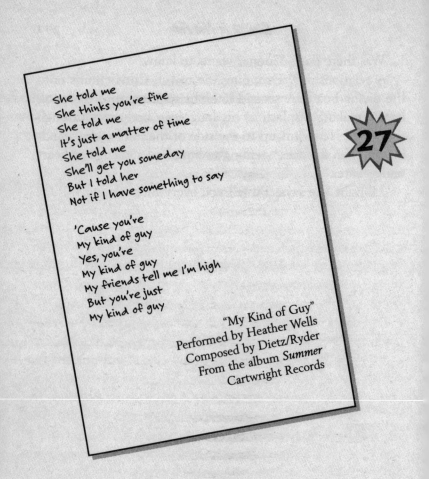

She told me
She thinks you're fine
She told me
It's just a matter of time
She told me
She'll get you someday
But I told her
Not if I have something to say

'Cause you're
My kind of guy
Yes, you're
My kind of guy
My friends tell me I'm high
But you're just
My kind of guy

"My Kind of Guy"
Performed by Heather Wells
Composed by Dietz/Ryder
From the album *Summer*
Cartwright Records

27

"Okay," Chris says, through chattering teeth. "Okay. So I slept with her for a few months. It's not like I asked her to marry me, or anything. But she went fucking psycho on me, okay? I thought she was going to cut my balls off."

I scoop up Chris's towel and drape it over his shivering shoulders. He doesn't seem to notice. He's on a roll. He's climbed from the pool and has started walking toward the house, Cooper and Lucy and I following behind, like an entourage after . . .

Well, some famous rock star.

"It started my junior year," Chris says. Now that he's started talking, it's like he can't stop. Or even slow down. You have to admire Cooper's technique. Not hitting the guy had done the trick. "A bunch of guys and I got in trouble for smoking pot in the dorm, you know, and we had to go see the dorm director—Rachel—for sanctioning. We all thought we were gonna get kicked outta school. So some of the guys, they were like, 'Chris, put the moves on her,' 'cause, I dunno, I was a little older than they were, and I had this reputation with the girls, you know?"

I envision Rachel—in her Manolo Blahniks and tailored Armani—being hit on by this smooth-talking, golden-haired Adonis. No, he isn't the suave businessman she'd been hoping to attract with her rock-hard glutes and blown-out hair.

But he has to have been the closest thing she was likely to get to it in Richmond, Indiana.

"Anyway, she let us off. For the pot-smoking thing, you know? Said it would be our little secret." There's a smirk in Chris's voice. But it isn't a happy smirk. "At first I thought it was because of whom my father is. But then we started running into each other in the cafeteria and stuff. More like—well, she'd run into me, you know? And the guys were like, 'Go for it, man. You start going with the dorm director, we can get away with anything we want.' And I had nothing else going on, you know, lady-wise, so I figured, 'Why not?' And one thing led to another, and then, well, we were an item, I guess."

He ducks under an archway, and we follow, through an open sliding glass door and into a dimly lit, sunken living room, where the primary decorating theme appears to be black leather. The couches are black leather. The ottomans are black leather. Even the mantel appears to be encased in black leather.

But surely not. I mean, wouldn't that catch on fire?

"Turns out, I was her first," Chris explains, going to the mantel and twisting a dial. Suddenly the room is bathed in an unearthly pink light. If I hadn't known better, I'd have thought we'd walked into a bordello. Or maybe one of those oxygen bars in SoHo. "She wasn't always as . . . put together as she looks now. She was actually kinda . . . well, when I knew her, back in Richmond, Rachel was kinda fat."

I blink at him. "What?"

Cooper throws me a warning glance. Chris is on a roll, and Cooper doesn't want me interrupting.

"You know." He shrugs. "She was fat. Well, not fat, really. But like . . . chubby. And she wore sweats all the time. I don't know what happened to her, you know, between now and then, but she slimmed down, majorly, and got, I don't know, like a makeover, or something. Because back then . . . I don't know."

"Wait." I am having trouble processing this. "Rachel was *fat?*"

"Yeah." He shrugs. "Maybe you're right. Maybe there is less . . . pressure being with someone who doesn't have anyone else to measure you by. There was definitely something— I dunno—exciting about being with this older chick who was so smart in some ways, and so dumb in others . . ."

"She was *fat?*" I am seriously stunned. "She runs like four miles a day! She eats nothing but lettuce. With no dressing!"

"Well," Chris says, with another shrug. "Maybe now. Not back then. She told me she'd been heavy her whole life, and that's why she'd never . . . you know. Had a guy before."

Whoa. Rachel had still been a virgin post–grad school? Hadn't she met *anyone* in high school? In college, even?

Apparently not.

"So how long did this go on? This affair," Cooper asks, apparently in an effort to get me off the *Rachel was fat?* thing.

Chris sinks down onto one of the black leather couches, not seeming to care whether he got the cushions wet. When you're as rich as he is, I guess things like that don't matter.

"Till midway through my senior year. That's when I realized I had to start really studying, you know, to get decent scores on my LSATs. After letting me goof off through most of my twenties, my parents were riding me, you know, to get into law school. I told her—Rachel—that I was going to hafta play it cool for a while. It seemed like a good time to break it off. I mean, it wasn't like it could go anywhere, her and me, after I graduated. No way was I sticking around Richmond."

"Did you tell her that?" Cooper asks.

"Tell her what?"

I see a muscle in Cooper's jaw twitch. "Did you tell Rachel that it couldn't go anywhere?" he elaborates, with forced patience.

"Oh." Chris doesn't meet either of our gazes. "Yeah."

"And?"

"And she flipped on me, man. I mean, really flipped. Started screaming, tearing stuff up. She picked up my computer monitor and threw it across the quad, no joke. I was so scared, I moved in with some buddies of mine off-campus for the rest of the year."

"And you never saw her again?" A part of me can't believe Chris's story. Another part of me believes it all too well. Not that I can picture Rachel throwing a computer monitor across the room.

But I can't picture her killing two girls—and almost killing three other people—either.

"No," Chris says. "Not till a couple weeks ago, when I got back from Richmond. I spent the summer there, doing volunteer stuff, as part of the deal I had with my dad about law school. Then I walked into Fischer Hall, and the first thing I see is Rachel, up at the reception desk, bawling some kid out for something or other. Only, you know, she's all . . . skinny. I nearly passed out, let me tell you. But she just smiled, cool as can be, and asked how I'd been. No hard feelings, and all that."

"And you believed her." Cooper's voice is toneless.

"Yeah." Chris sighs. "She seemed cool with it. I thought—you know, the weight loss, her new hairstyle, the clothes . . . I thought it was a good sign, you know. That she was moving on."

"And the fact that she had purposefully set out to get a job managing the building your parents live in," Cooper says. "That didn't raise a red flag that she might not be as 'cool with it' as you thought?"

"Obviously not," Chris says. "Until . . . well, what I found out last night."

A bell-like voice cries out, "Oh, there you are! I looked all over outside. I didn't know you'd come in."

Hope comes traipsing down the stairs, holding a tray of what looks—and smells—like spinach pastry puffs in one hand, and the hem of a floor-length, leopard print robe in the other.

"The canapés are ready," she says. "Do you want them in here, or out by the pool?"

"Out by the pool, okay, honey?" Chris smiles weakly at her. "We'll join you in a minute."

Hope smiles good-naturedly and detours toward the sliding glass doors.

"Don't be long," she warns us. "They'll get cold."

As soon as she's gone, Chris says, "I've gone over it and over it—since talking to you the other night, I mean—trying to figure out if Rachel could have done it. Killed those girls, I mean. Because I'm good, you know . . . but not exactly anybody worth killing over."

He smiles weakly at his own little joke. Cooper doesn't

smile back. I guess we are still playing good cop/bad cop. Since I'm apparently the good cop, I smile back. It isn't even hard. I mean, in spite of everything, I still sort of like Chris. I can't help it. He's just . . . Chris.

"I mean, when she and I broke up," Chris goes on, as if there'd been no interruption, "I told you she was—well, violent. She threw my computer across the quad. That's like a hundred and fifty feet. She's pretty strong. A girl—a small girl, like Beth or Bobby. Well, that'd be nothing for Rachel. If she was mad enough."

"And you believe that's what happened to those girls?" Cooper seems to be making sure. "Not that they died accidentally, but that Rachel killed them?"

Chris is sinking deeper and deeper into his parents' leather couch. You can tell he totally wants to disappear.

"Yes," he says, in a small voice. "I mean . . . that's the only explanation, isn't it? Because that whole elevator surfing thing . . . Girls don't elevator surf."

I throw Cooper an *I told you so* look. But he doesn't see it. He is too busy staring stonily at Chris.

In the silence that falls after this, I can hear a cricket start to chirp loudly outside. I have to admit, I'm kind of . . . well, moved by Chris's speech. Oh, I still think he's a pig and all of that. But at least he freely admits it. That's something, anyway.

Cooper doesn't look nearly as impressed as I am, however.

"Chris," he says. "You're coming back to the city with us now, and tomorrow morning, we're going to the police."

It isn't a request. It's a command.

Chris grimaces. "Why? What good will it do? They'll just arrest me. They'll never believe it was Rachel. Never."

"Not if you've got alibis for the times of the murders," Cooper says.

"I do," Chris says, brightening suddenly. "I was in class when the second girl—Bobby, I mean—died. I know, 'cause we all heard the sirens and looked out the windows. Fischer Hall is right down the street from the law building . . ."

Then Chris shakes his head. His hair is drying like a golden helmet on top of his head. "But they aren't seriously going to believe that Rachel Walcott is killing the girls I've slept with. I mean, c'mon. Rachel just won a fucking Pansy Award for Good Samaritanism, or whatever."

Cooper just stares at him. "Are there any girls you've slept with this year who *aren't* dead?"

Chris looks uneasy. "Well, no, but—"

I look over my shoulder, at the archways that lead out to the pool. "What about Hope?"

"What about her?"

"Do you want her to end up dead, too?"

"No!" Chris looks appalled. "But . . . I mean, she's the au pair from next door. How's Rachel even going to—"

"Chris," Cooper says. "Have you ever thought about taking a sabbatical from dating?"

Chris swallows.

"To tell you the truth," he says. "I'm starting to think that might not be such a bad idea."

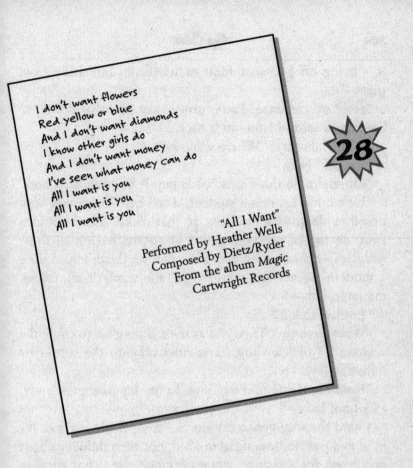

I don't want flowers
Red yellow or blue
And I don't want diamonds
I know other girls do
And I don't want money
I've seen what money can do

All I want is you
All I want is you
All I want is you

"All I Want"
Performed by Heather Wells
Composed by Dietz/Ryder
From the album *Magic*
Cartwright Records

28

"Think about it," I say to Patty. "Rachel meets this guy, this really handsome guy, who acts like he genuinely likes her, and maybe there's a part of him that really does . . ."

"Yeah," Patty agrees sarcastically. "The part he keeps in his briefs."

"Whatever. This guy, he's the first guy she's ever come across who is interested in her, let alone meets all of her qualifications for a boyfriend. You know, he's hot, he's rich, he's hetero. Okay, maybe he's a bit of a ne'er-do-well"—I lift up the glass of orange juice that's sitting by my bed and sip it—"living off his trust fund or whatever. But aside from that—"

"Hold on a minute." Patty turns to say, "Put that down," to her son. A second later, she's back.

"Right," she says. "Where were we?"

"Rachel," I say.

"Oh, right. So this Christopher guy. Is he really that hot?"

"He's hot. Plus he's a student," I tell her. "You aren't supposed to sleep with students, so that makes him forbidden fruit, on top of everything else. She starts having all these fantasies—I mean, why not? She's hit her thirties. And she's a modern twenty-first-century gal, she wants it all: career, marriage, kids—"

"License to kill."

"What have you. Then just as she's getting set to circle the wagons, li'l ol' Cowboy Chris rides off into the sunset by himself."

"Hold on, Heather," Patty says. To her son, she goes, "Indy! I said no! Indy—"

I hold the receiver to my ear as Patty yells at her kid. It's nice, in a way, to be snug in my bed, not even thinking about murderers for a change, while everyone else is out running around, actually doing something about them. I'd wanted to go with Cooper and Chris to see Detective Canavan. Really. I'd told him last night, as I'd stumbled up to bed in my apartment, to wake me up before he left in the morning.

But I guess the shock from all the excitement of the day before—the explosion, the trip to the hospital, the drive to Long Island and back—had finally taken its toll, because when Cooper had tapped on my bedroom door to see if I was up, I'd yelled at him to go away.

Not that I remember doing this. I mean, I would never have been so rude if I'd actually been conscious. Cooper left a note explaining the situation, and ending with the words, *Do* not *go to work today. Stay home and rest. I'll call you.*

And okay, he didn't sign it *Love, Cooper.* Just *Cooper.*

But still. He has to at least, you know, respect me more now. Now that it turns out I wasn't making it all up. About how someone had been trying to kill me, and all. I mean, he has to be thinking what a fantastic partner I'd make, to detect things with.

And who knows where that might lead? I mean, wouldn't the next rational step be for him to fall madly in love with me?

So yeah. I'm in a good mood. It's pouring rain outside, but I don't care. I'm snug in my bed, watching morning cartoons with Lucy by my side. Maybe it's only because I'd come so close to losing it, but life is seeming really, really good.

Or so I'm excitedly telling Patty. She seems very impressed by my theory—the one I'm hoping will send Detective Canavan, when he hears what Chris has to say, directly to Fischer Hall with an arrest warrant.

"I'm back," Patty says. "Where were we?"

"Rachel. Suddenly she's left holding the reins to the chuck wagon all by her lonesome," I say. "So what does a modern twenty-first-century gal like Rachel do?"

"Oh, wait, wait, let me try," Patty says, excitedly. "Rounds up a—what do they call it? Oh yes. A posse?"

"Gets rid of the competition," I correct her. "Because in Rachel's twisted mind, she thinks if she kills all Chris's girlfriends, she'll get him back through default. You know, if there aren't any other girls left, he'll have no choice but to return to her."

"Wow." Patty sounds impressed. "So how's she doing it?"

"What do you mean, how's she doing it? She's pushing them down the elevator shaft."

"Yeah, but how, Heather? How is a skinny bitch like Rachel pushing full-grown women—who surely don't want to die—down the elevator shaft? I mean, I can't even get my sister's damn chihuahua into his carrier, and he's just a tiny dog. Do you have any idea how hard it must be to push someone who doesn't want to die down an elevator shaft? You have to open the doors first. What are these girls doing while she's doing that? Why aren't they fighting back? Why doesn't Rachel have scratches on her face or on her arms? My sister's damned dog scratches me *hard* when I try to put him in his Sherpa."

I think back to my formative years of television viewing. "Chloroform," I say, simply. "She must be using chloroform."

"Wouldn't the coroner be able to find traces of this?"

Wow. Patty is good. Especially for someone who claims not to have time to watch *CSI*.

"Okay, okay," I said. "Maybe she conks them on the head with a baseball bat and slings 'em down the shaft while they're unconscious."

"The coroner wouldn't have noticed this?"

"They've just fallen sixteen stories," I say. "What's another bump?"

Beep.

My call waiting is going off.

"Oh, that's gotta be Cooper, Pats," I say. "Listen, I'll call you later. Want to go out for a celebratory brunch tomorrow? I mean, after they've incarcerated my boss?"

"Sure. Be there with bells on." Patty hangs up. I push down on the receiver, then say, "Hello?" after I hear the line click.

But the voice I hear isn't Cooper's. It's a woman's voice.

And it sounds like whoever it belongs to is crying.

"Heather?"

It takes me a second, but then I realize who it is.

"Sarah?" I say. "Is that you?"

"Y-yes." Sarah sniffles.

"Are you okay?" I sit up in bed. "Sarah, what's the matter?"

"It's . . . it's Rachel," Sarah say.

Whoa. Had the cops gotten there and arrested her already? It's going to be a blow, I know, for the building staff, what with Justine turning out to be a ceramic heater thief, and now Rachel turning out to be a homicidal maniac.

But they'll get over it. Maybe I'll bring in Krispy Kremes for everyone tomorrow.

"Yeah?" I say. Because I don't want to let on that I'd had anything to do with the arrest. Yet, anyway. "What about Rachel?"

"She . . . she's *dead*."

I nearly drop the phone.

"*What?*" I cry. "Rachel? Dead? What—"

I can't believe it. It isn't possible. Rachel? Dead? How on earth . . .

"I think she killed herself," Sarah says with a sob. "Heather, I just came into the office, and she's . . . she's *hanging* here. From that grate between our office and hers."

Oh my God.

Rachel's hanged herself. Rachel realized that the jig was up, but instead of going quietly, she killed herself. Oh my God.

I have to remain calm. For the building's sake, I realize. I have to be the one in charge now. The director is gone. That leaves me, the assistant director. I'm going to have to be the strong one. I'm going to have to be everybody's beacon of light in the dark times ahead.

And it's okay, because I'm totally prepared. It won't be any different, really, than if Rachel had been hauled off to jail. She's really just going to a different place. But she's gone, just the same.

"I don't know what to do," Sarah says, her voice rising to a hysterical pitch. "If anyone walks in and sees this—"

"Don't let anyone in," I cry. Oh God. The RAs. This is the last thing they need. "Sarah, don't let anyone come in. And don't touch anything." Isn't that right? Isn't that what they always say on *Law & Order*? "Call an ambulance. Call the police. Right away. Don't let anyone into the office but the police. Okay, Sarah?"

"Okay," Sarah says, with another sniffle. "But, Heather?"

"Yeah?"

"Can you come over? I'm . . . I'm so scared."

But I've already sprung from my bed and am reaching for my jeans.

"I'll be right there," I tell her. "Hold on, Sarah. I'll be right there."

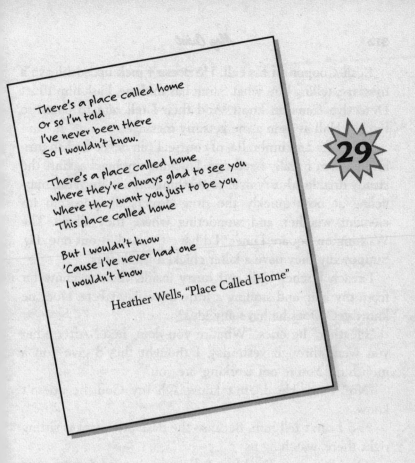

There's a place called home
Or so I'm told
I've never been there
So I wouldn't know.

There's a place called home
Where they're always glad to see you
Where they want you just to be you
This place called home

But I wouldn't know
'Cause I've never had one
I wouldn't know

Heather Wells, "Place Called Home"

29

It's my fault.

Rachel's death, I mean.

I should have known. I should have known this would happen. I mean, clearly she wasn't mentally stable. Of course at the slightest provocation, she was going to snap. I don't know how she figured it out—that we suspected her—but she had.

And she'd taken the only way out she felt she could.

Well, there's nothing I can do about it now. Nothing except be there for the people Rachel's death is likely to affect the most—the building staff.

I call Cooper on his cell. He doesn't pick up, so I leave a message, telling him what Sarah has told me. I ask him to let Detective Canavan know. And then I tell him to come to Fischer Hall as soon as he gets my message.

I can't find an umbrella, of course. I can never find an umbrella when I really need one. Ducking my head against the steady drizzle, I hurry over to Washington Square West, marveling at how quickly the drug dealers disappear in inclement weather, and wondering where they all go. The Washington Square Diner? I'd have to check it out one day. Supposedly they have a killer chicken-fried steak.

I reach Fischer Hall and hurry inside, flicking rainwater from my hair, and smiling a little queasily at Pete. Does he know yet? Does he have any idea?

"Heather," he cries. "What're you doin' here? After what you went through yesterday, I thought they'd give you a month off. You're not working, are you?"

"No," I say. He doesn't know. Oh my God, he doesn't know.

And I can't tell him. Because the desk attendant is sitting right there, watching us.

"Oh," Pete says. "And hey, Julio's doing good, by the way. They're letting him out in a few days."

"Great," I say, with as much enthusiasm as I can. "Well, see you later."

"See you."

I hurry down the hallway to the director's office door. To my surprise, it's partly open, even though I'd specifically told Sarah to close it. Anyone can walk in and see Rachel hanging there . . . unless maybe she's done it on her side of the grate. Yes, that would make more sense, actually. Her desk is pushed up against the wall beneath the grate, so it would have been easy for her to climb up there, then jump . . .

"Sarah?" I say. I push the door open all the way. No sign of Rachel. The exterior office is empty. Sarah—and the body— have to be in Rachel's office. "Sarah? Are you there?"

"In here," I hear Sarah's voice warble.

I glance at the grate. There's nothing tied around it. Sarah must have cut her down. Horrific as it had to have been to find her like that, she still shouldn't have messed with the body. That's tampering with evidence. Or something.

"Sarah," I say, hurrying through to Rachel's office, "I told you not to . . ."

My voice trails off. That's because I'm not greeted by the sight of a weeping Sarah cradling Rachel's lifeless form. Instead, I'm greeted by the sight of a perfectly healthy Rachel—wearing a new, very attractive cashmere sweater set and charcoal trousers—leaning against her desk, one booted foot balanced on her office chair . . .

. . . onto which she's tied Sarah with the phone cord and some computer cables.

"Oh, hi, Heather," Rachel says brightly. "You got here fast."

"Heather." Sarah is sobbing so hard now that her glasses have steamed up. "I'm so sorry. She made me call you—"

"Shut up." Rachel, annoyed, slaps Sarah, hard, across the face. The sound of the smack makes me jump.

It also wakes me up.

Trap. I've just walked into a trap. Automatically I turn towards the door—

"Stop or I'll kill her." Rachel's voice rings coldly through the room. Even Monet's water lilies couldn't soften it.

I freeze where I am. Rachel brushes past me and goes to the outer office door, pulling it all the way closed.

"There," she says, when the lock clicks into place. "That's more like it. Now we can have some privacy."

I stare at her, my grip tightening on the strap of my backpack, despite my stitches. Maybe, I think, I can hit her with it. My backpack, I mean. Although there isn't anything heavy in it. Just a hairbrush, my wallet, and some lipstick. Oh, and a Kit Kat bar, in case I get hungry later.

How had she known? How had she known we were on to her?

"Rachel," I say. My voice sounds funny. I realize it's because my throat has gone dry. I'm not feeling very good, all of a sudden. My fingers have gone ice cold, and the cuts on them ache.

Then I remember.

There's a canister of pepper spray in my backpack. It's several years old and the nozzle is all gunked up with sand from a trip to the beach. Will it still work?

Play it cool, I tell myself. What would Cooper do if he was faced with a killer? He'd play it cool.

"Wow," I say, hoping I sound cool, like Cooper. "What's this all about, Rachel? Is this some kind of trust game, or something? Because, if you don't mind me saying so, Sarah doesn't look like she's having a very good time."

"Cut the crap, Heather." Rachel speaks in a hard voice I've never heard her use before, not even with the basketball players. The sound of it makes me feel colder than ever. I've never heard her swear before, either. "That dumb blond act might work with everyone else you know, but it's never worked with me. I know exactly what you are, and believe me, the four-letter word I'd use to describe you is not dumb." Her eyes flick over me disparagingly. "At least until recently it wasn't."

Is she ever right. I can't believe I'd fallen for that phone call. Still, Sarah's tears *had* been real . . . just not for the reason she'd said they were.

"You might as well know," Rachel says calmly. "I know all about last night."

I try pretending like I don't know what she's talking about, even though I do.

"Last night? Rachel, I—"

"Last night," she says pleasantly. "Your little jaunt to the Hamptons. Don't try to deny it. I was there. I saw you."

"You . . . you were there?"

I'm at a total loss as to how to proceed. Every nerve in my body is screaming, *Turn around and run!*

But somehow I'm rooted to the spot, my fingers clenched around my backpack strap. I keep thinking about Sarah. What if I run? What will Rachel do to poor Sarah?

"Of course I was," Rachel says, her voice dripping with scorn. "You think I don't keep an eye on my property? Why do you think I held on to my Jetta? Nobody needs a car in this city . . . unless they're going to be following people to the Hamptons."

God. I'd forgotten all about her stupid car, which she parks in a garage on the West Side Highway.

I say, keeping my voice low-pitched so Rachel can't hear how badly it's shaking, "Okay. So I was there. So I know about you and Chris. So what? Rachel, I'm on your side. I totally understand where you're coming from. I've been dicked over by guys before, too. Why don't we talk about this—"

Rachel is shaking her head. Her expression is incredulous, as if I, not she, am the one cracking up.

"There'll be no *talking* about this," she says, with a bark of laughter. "The time for *talking* is over. And let's get one thing straight here, Heather." Rachel uncrosses her arms, her right hand going to a lump I hadn't noticed before beneath her cardigan.

"I am the director," she goes on. "*I* am the one in charge. I decide whether or not we're going to *talk* about it, because I am the one who schedules the meeting. Like I scheduled the meetings for Elizabeth and Roberta. Like I'll schedule yet another meeting for Amber, later. Like I've scheduled this meeting, now, between you and me. I am the one in charge. Do you want to know what qualifies me to be in charge, Heather?"

I nod mutely, my eyes on the lump under her sweater. A gun, I think. A gun definitely qualifies Rachel to be in charge.

But it isn't a gun at all. When Rachel draws it out, all I see is a black plastic thing that fits snugly in her hand. There are two evil-looking metal pieces sticking out of the top, giving it an appearance not unlike the head of a cockroach. I have no idea what it is until Rachel flicks a switch with her thumb, and suddenly a thin blue electric line buzzes between the twin metal prongs.

Then I know, even before she says it.

"Heather, meet the Thunder Gun." Rachel speaks proudly, like some of the parents had on the first day of check-in, when they'd been introducing their kid to me. "A second of contact with the one hundred and twenty thousand volts the head of the Thunder Gun delivers can cause confusion, weakness, disorientation, and loss of balance and muscle control for several minutes. And the wonderful thing is, if blasted through clothing, the Thunder Gun leaves only a very small burn mark upon the skin. It's a fabulously effective repellent weapon, and you can order it from any number of catalogs here in the U.S. Why, mine only cost forty-nine ninety-five, nine-volt battery not included. Of course, it's not legal to own one here in New York City, but then, who cares?"

I stare at the crackling blue fire strip.

So this is how she'd done it. No chloroform, no bashing over the head with a baseball bat. She'd simply shown up at Beth's door, and then later, at Bobby's, stunned them, then shoved their limp bodies down the elevator shaft. What could be simpler?

And Detective Canavan had said killers were dumb. Rachel isn't dumb. What kind of doofus would have the savvy to pull off this kind of crime? Because so many young people kill themselves doing stupid stunts like elevator surfing, no one would ever think that the girls had actually been murdered, not when there was no hint of suspiciousness to their deaths.

No one except a freak like me.

No, Rachel isn't dumb.

And she isn't crazy, either. She'd thought up the perfect way to get rid of her romantic rivals. No one would have suspected a thing if it hadn't been for me and my big mouth.

If it hadn't been for me and my big mouth, Sarah and I wouldn't be about to become Rachel's third and fourth victims.

"But this isn't the only thing that qualifies me to be in charge around here, you know," Rachel assures me, casually gesturing with the stun gun to emphasize her point. "I have a bachelor's degree in chemical engineering. Did you know that, Heather?"

I shake my head. Maybe one of the RAs will key in to the office to pick up his mail. Yeah. Or maybe Cooper will have gotten that message I'd left on his cell phone. . . .

"It's amazing what one can do with a bachelor's in chemical engineering. One can, for instance, learn to build small incendiary devices—so simple, yet so effective. Do you know what an incendiary device is, Heather? No, I would imagine that you don't. After all, you were far too busy twitching your ass at the local mall to finish high school, weren't you? Let me see if you know this one. What do you get when you stand a bunch of blonds next to each other, shoulder to shoulder?"

I look at Sarah. She's still sobbing, but she's trying to do it quietly, so Rachel won't slap her again.

I shake my head.

Rachel laughs humorlessly and says, "A wind tunnel, Heather! A wind tunnel!"

"Oh, wow, Rachel," I say, amending my previous thought. She's definitely crazy. Nuts, even. "That's really funny. But you know what? I have to go now. Cooper's waiting by the guard's desk. If I'm gone too long, he's bound to come back here, looking for me."

"He can look all he wants," Rachel says with a shrug. "He doesn't have a key. And we aren't going to let him in. We're *working*, Heather. We have a lot of important work to do."

"Well, you know what, Rachel?" I say. "If we don't open the door, Cooper'll just have Pete call one of the RAs to let him in—"

"But the RAs don't have keys to the office anymore. I had the lock changed." Rachel's cheeks have twin spots of color in them now, and her eyes sparkle every bit as brightly as the thin volt of electricity that leaps from the prongs of the weapon clenched in her hand.

"That's right," she says happily. "I had the lock changed yesterday, while you were in the hospital, and I'm the only one with a key." Then she turns those too-bright eyes on me and says, "You understand, don't you, Heather? I mean, this isn't a career for you. This is just a job. Assistant director to Fischer Hall. It's just a rest stop between gigs, isn't it? A steady paycheck until you get the guts to go on the road again after your little dispute with your record company. That's all this position is to you. Not like me. Higher education is my life. My life, Heather. Or at least it was. Until—"

She stops speaking suddenly, her gaze, which had become a little unfocused, fastening on me like a vise. "Until him," she says, simply.

I want to sit down. My knees shake every time I glance at the weapon in Rachel's hand.

But I don't dare. Seated, I'm an even easier target. No, somehow I have to distract her from whatever it is she intends to do to Sarah and me—and I have a pretty good idea what that is.

"Him, Rachel?" I ask, trying to sound friendly, like we're just chatting over cups of coffee in the cafeteria, something we'd actually done, once or twice, before the killing had begun. "You mean Christopher, don't you?"

She laughs bitterly, and that laugh makes me more afraid than anything so far, even the stun gun.

"Christopher," she says, rolling the word on her tongue like it's a piece of chocolate—something Rachel never allowed herself to enjoy. Too fattening. "Yes. Chris. You wouldn't understand about Christopher, Heather. You see, I love him. You've never loved anyone before, Heather, except yourself, so you can't know what it's like. No, you can't know what it's like to feel that all your happiness in life is dependent on one single individual, and then—and then to have that individual turn around and reject you—"

The look she gives me could have frozen a hot buttered bagel. I think about mentioning that I know *exactly* what she's talking about . . . that this is how I'd felt about Jordan, who is at this very moment probably playing Mad Libs with Tania Trace in his hospital bed.

But somehow I don't think she'd listen.

"No, you wouldn't understand that," Rachel says. "You've always had everything you've ever wanted, haven't you, Heather? Handed to you on a silver platter. Some of us have had to work for what we want, you know. Take me, for example. You think I always looked this good?" Rachel runs a hand up and down her lean, hard, thousand-crunches-a-day abs. "Hell, no. I used to be fat. A real lard ass. Kind of like you are now, actually. A size twelve." She laughs. "I drowned my sorrows in candy bars, never worked out, like you. Do you know I never got asked out—never, not once, until I turned thirty? While you were strutting around like a little slut for Cartwright Records, I had my nose buried in my books, studying as hard as I could, because I knew no one was going to swoop down and offer *me* a recording contract. I knew if I wanted out of my hellhole of a life, I was going to have to use my head."

I glance at Sarah. She's looking out the window, desperately hoping, I can tell, that someone will walk by and notice what's going on inside.

But it's raining so hard, no one is on the street. And the few people who are out hurry past with their heads tucked beneath umbrellas.

"It was the same with *him*," Rachel says. "I wanted him, so I did what I had to in order to get him. I knew I wasn't his type. I figured that out after he . . . left me. Which is when I knew. I knew I had to make myself over to *be* his type. You wouldn't understand that, of course. You and Sarah, you think men should want you because of your *personality*, don't you? But men couldn't care less about your personality. Believe me. If you hadn't let yourself go the way you did, Heather, you'd still have Jordan Cartwright, you know. All that fuss about wanting to sing your own songs. My God, you think he *cared* about that? Men don't care about smarts.

After all, what's the difference between a blond and a mosquito?"

I shake my head. "Honest to God, Rachel, I don't—"

"A blond keeps on sucking, even after you slap her." Rachel throws back her head and laughs some more.

Oh yeah. I'm a dead woman. No doubt about it.

When's it gonna be my turn
To fly without my
Wings getting burned?

When's it gonna be my turn
For people to stop shakin' their heads
saying "She'll never learn?"

When's it gonna be my turn
To be called smart and strong
And not stupid and wrong?

When's it gonna be my turn
To look at you and hear
You say
It's your turn
It's your turn
It's your turn

Heather Wells, "My Turn"

30

She's crazy. I mean, only a lunatic would stand there, telling me dumb blond jokes, while threatening me with a stun gun.

I've dealt with lunatics before. I worked in the music industry all those years. Nine out of every ten people I'd met back then had probably been clinically insane, including my own mother.

Can I talk Rachel out of trying to kill me?

Well, I can try.

"Seems to me," I say carefully, "that the person you ought to be angry with is Christopher Allington. He's the one who did you wrong, Rachel. He's the one who betrayed you. How come you've never tried to toast him?"

"Because he's my future husband, Heather." Rachel glares at me. "God, don't you get it? I know you think men are disposable. I mean, things didn't work out with Jordan, so you've just moved on to his brother. But I, unlike you, believe in true love. Which is what Christopher and I have. I just need to get rid of a few distractions, and then he'll come around."

"Rachel," I say, appealing to whatever is left that might still be normal inside her. "Those distractions. They're *human beings*."

"Well, it's not my fault the poor things were so heartbroken when Christopher dumped them that they did something as reckless as attempt to elevator surf. I tried my best to counsel them. You, too, Heather. Although no one will be very surprised to see you've chosen to take your own life. You don't have that much to live for anymore, after all."

Her thought process is so skewed that I can't quite follow it. But now that she's made it clear that I'm her next victim, I'm doing some pretty fast talking, let me tell you.

"But, Rachel, it will never work. I already went to the cops—"

"And did they believe you?" Rachel asks calmly. "When they find your broken, bleeding body, they'll know you just did the whole thing to get attention—planted that bomb, then killed yourself when you realized you'd been discovered. And it won't even be so hard to understand, since your life's been in such a downward spiral lately. Jordan getting engaged to that other girl. His brother—well, his brother just doesn't seem interested, does he, Heather? And you and I both know how much you're in love with him. It's written all over your face every time he walks into the room."

Is that true? Does everyone know I love Cooper? Does *Cooper* know I love Cooper? God, how embarrassing.

Wait a minute. What am I listening to this lunatic for, anyway?

"Fine, Rachel," I say, playing along because it seems like the only way out. "Fine. Kill me. But what about Sarah? I mean, what's poor Sarah ever done to you? Why don't you let Sarah go."

"Sarah?" Rachel glances at her graduate assistant as if she's only just remembered she's in the room. "Oh, right. Sarah. You know, I think Sarah's going to just . . . disappear."

Sarah lets out a frightened hiccup, but a stony look from Rachel silences her.

"Yes," Rachel say. "I think Sarah is going to go home for a few weeks to recover from the horror of your death, Heather. Only she's not going to make it. She's going to disappear somewhere along the way. Hey. It happens."

"Oh no, Rachel, please," Sarah chokes. "Please don't make me disappear. Please—"

"Shut up," Rachel screams. She raises a hand to hit Sarah again, but freezes when the phone on my desk rings, jangling so loudly that Rachel jumps, and the blue streak of lightning between the blades of the gun sways dangerously close to me. I leap back, falling against the door, and spin around to grasp the knob.

In a split second, Rachel is on me, a spindly arm going around my neck, choking me. She's surprisingly strong for such a slight woman. But even so, I could have shaken her off . . .

. . . could have if it hadn't been for the sputtering stun gun, which she shoves beneath my nose, hissing, "Don't try it. Don't even think about it. I'll blast you, Heather, I swear it. And then I'll kill you both."

I freeze, breathing hard. Rachel is plastered to my back like a cape. The phone keeps on ringing, three times, four. I can tell by the ring that it's an on-campus call. I whisper, my voice rough with fear, "Rachel, that's probably the reception desk calling. You know I told Cooper to wait outside for me. He's at the guard's station."

"In that case," Rachel says, releasing her stranglehold on my neck but keeping the stun gun within inches of my throat, "we'll be on our way. I'll deal with you"—she flings a warning look in Sarah's direction—"later."

Then she opens the office door and, glancing furtively left and right, shoves me out into the empty hallway . . .

. . . but not far enough that she isn't within blasting range. She directs me to the elevators across from our office door— the elevators that were, unfortunately for me, unscathed by yesterday's explosion in the service shaft—and pounds on the up button. I pray that the doors will open and the entire basketball team will emerge and tackle Rachel for me.

But no such luck. The cab has been sitting empty on the first floor, and when the doors slide apart, there's no one inside.

"Get in," Rachel orders, and I do as she says. Rachel follows, then inserts her pass key and presses twenty.

We're going to the penthouse. And there won't be any other stops along the way.

"Girls like you, Heather," Rachel says, not looking at me. "I've been dealing with girls like you my whole life. The pretty ones are all alike. You go through life thinking everybody owes you something. You get the record contracts and the promotions and the cute guys, while people like me? We're the ones who do all the work. Do you know that Pansy is the first award I've received in my field?"

I glare at her. This woman is going to kill me. I don't see any reason to be polite to her anymore.

"Yeah," I say. "And you got it for cleaning up after your own murders. That stuff in those girls' files—about Elizabeth's mom wanting her sign-in privileges revoked, and Mrs. Pace not liking Lakeisha—that stuff never even happened, did it? Those women never called you. You made all that stuff up, as a way to justify your meetings with those girls. What did you talk about when you were meeting with them, anyway? What kind of twisted, sick stuff were you terrorizing them with?"

"Heather." Rachel looks at me critically. "You'll never understand, will you? I've worked hard all my life for what I have. I never got anything easily, like you. Not anything, men, jobs, friends. What I do get, I keep. Like Christopher, for instance. And this job. Do you have any idea how hard it was to get myself a position at this school, in the same *building* as him? So you understand why you have to die. You're jeopardizing too much for me. If you hadn't started snooping around, I'd have let you live. We made a nice team, you and I, I always thought. I mean, when I stand next to you, I look extra thin. That's a real bonus in an assistant."

The elevator pings, and the doors slide open. We're on the twentieth floor, in the hallway outside the president's penthouse. I know the minute we step onto the gray carpeting that the motion detector will be set off downstairs at the guard's desk. Would Pete glance at the monitor and see Rachel and her stun gun?

Please look, Pete. I try to use Vulcan mind control on Pete, even though he's twenty floors down. *Look, Pete, look. Look, Pete, look . . .*

Rachel pushes me out into the hallway.

"Come on," she says, pulling out the building's master key. "I bet you always wanted to see where the president lives. Well, now's your chance. Too bad you won't live long enough to enjoy it."

Rachel unlocks the front door to the Allingtons' apartment and steers me into the foyer. Tiled in black and white, this is where Mrs. Allington had stood and accused me of chasing after her son like a harlot. The foyer opens into a spacious living room, walled on two sides by French doors leading out onto the penthouse terrace. Like the Villa d'Allington, the predominant decorating theme appears to be black leather, and lots of it. Martha Stewart, Mrs. Allington apparently is not. Well, I kind of already guessed that.

"Nice, isn't it?" Rachel says conversationally. "Except for those hideous birds."

Just off the foyer, in that six-foot-high wicker cage, the cockatoos whistle and dance, eyeing us suspiciously. Rachel aims the stun gun at them and laughs as they shriek at the sight of the leaping blue flame.

"Idiot birds," she says. Then she grabs hold of my arm and starts pulling me toward a set of French doors. "Come on," she says. "It's time for your big finale. I figure a star like you would make a really dramatic exit. So you're not going the elevator surfing route. You're going to plunge off the roof of Fischer Hall . . . kind of like that turtle, in that movie your psychotic friend in the cafeteria is always talking about. Only you, unfortunately, won't be saved by a rope shot from inside your shell."

Before I have a chance to react, a door on the far side of the living room is thrown open, and Mrs. Allington, in a pink jogging suit, stares at us.

"What the hell," she demands, "are you two doing here?"

Rachel smiles pleasantly. "Don't mind us, Eleanor," she sings. "We'll be out of your way in no time."

"How did you get in here?" Mrs. Allington begins striding toward us, looking furious. "Get out, this instant, before I call the police."

"I wish we could, Eleanor," Rachel says, to the woman who, in a different world, might have been her mother-in-law. "But we're here on official residence hall business."

"I don't give a damn why you're here." Mrs. Allington has reached a wall phone. Now she's lifting up the receiver. "Don't you know who my husband is?"

"Look out, Mrs. Allington," I yell.

But it's too late. Like a striking cobra, Rachel lashes out with the stun gun.

Mrs. Allington stiffens, her eyes going wide, like someone who'd just gotten some very bad news . . . maybe about her son's LSAT scores, or something.

Then she seems to fling herself over the back of one of the leather couches, twitching until she lies in a heap on the parquet floor, her eyes still wide open, her jaw slack and shiny with saliva.

"Oh my God," I cry. Because it is, without a doubt, the most horrible thing I've ever seen . . . worse even than what I'd seen Tania Trace doing to my then boyfriend. "Rachel, you killed her!"

"She's not dead," Rachel says, the disgust in her voice obvious. "When she comes to, she'll have no idea what hit her. She won't remember her last name, let alone me. But that won't be unusual, for her. Come on," she says, and grabs my arm again.

Now that I've seen firsthand what that gun could do, I'm in no hurry to experience it. I realize I'd been stupid not to try to get away from Rachel downstairs. Sure, she might have zapped me, then hauled me into the elevator. But I'd have been dead weight, and it would have been difficult for her. This way, it's too easy for her, and more difficult for me. The only place I have to go is down.

This thought is enough to cause me to make a break for it.

I yank my arm from Rachel's grasp and run. I don't know why, but I head for the door through which Mrs. Allington had come. I can't run fast, being so stiff from what had happened in the elevator that day before, and all. But I know I've surprised her when Rachel lets out a furious scream. Surprising her feels good, because it means she doesn't have the upper hand anymore.

I have only fleeting glimpses of the rooms I tear through. A dining room that looks as if it hadn't seen any diners in a long time, the long mahogany table highly polished, seating for twelve, a sideboard with fake fruit on it. Fake! Then a kitchen, spotlessly clean, blue and white tiles. A kind of den, again with French doors on two sides, and a wide-screen TV in front of another leather couch, this one in avocado green. On the TV is a Debbie Reynolds movie. *Tammy and the Bachelor*, I think. On the couch is a basket of yarn and a bottle of Absolut. Mrs. Allington doesn't mess around with her leisure time.

I bang through the only door in the den that doesn't lead to the terrace and find myself in a bedroom, a dark bedroom, all the curtains pulled shut over the French doors. The bed is king-sized and unmade, the gray silk sheets in a tangle at one end. Another wide-screen TV, this one tuned to a talk show, the sound off. There're a pair of black briefs on the floor. Chris's room? But Chris lives in the law school dorm. Which can only mean the Allingtons sleep in separate rooms. Scandal!

There are no more doors, except one to President Allington's bathroom. I'm trapped.

I can hear Rachel coming, slamming doors and screaming like a banshee. I look frantically around the room for a weapon, and come up empty-handed. Because of the track lighting in the mirrored ceiling—I'll think about that one later—there isn't even a lamp I can unplug and swing at her head. I think of sliding under the bed, hiding behind a set of those damask curtains, but I know she'll find me. Can I talk my way out of this? I've talked my way out of worse jams than this. I can't quite think of any right now, but I'm almost sure I have.

Rachel comes careening into the room, stumbling over the threshold and blinking as her eyes adjust to the sudden darkness. I stand on the opposite side of the room, behind the massive bed, trying not to be distracted by my reflection on the ceiling.

"Look, Rachel," I pant, talking low and fast. "You don't have to kill me. Or Sarah, either. I swear we won't tell anyone about this. It'll just be our secret, between us girls. I totally understand where you're coming from. I've had guys jerk me around, too. I mean, Chris definitely isn't worth going to jail for—"

"I won't be going to jail, Heather," Rachel says. "I'll be organizing your memorial service. And my wedding. I'll be sure to play all of your greatest hits at both. That is, if there's more than one. Weren't you kind of a one-hit wonder, anyway? Such a shame. I wonder if anyone will even show up at your funeral. After all, you're already a has-been at—how old are you, anyway? Twenty-five? Twenty-six? Just an ex-pop star who's let herself go."

"Twenty-eight," I say. "And fine. Kill me. But not Sarah. Come on, Rachel. She's just a kid."

"Aw." Rachel smiles and shakes her head at me. "Isn't that sweet? You begging for Sarah's life like that. When in real life, I know how much she annoys you. See, that's the problem with girls like you, Heather. You're too *nice*. You have no killer instinct. When the going gets tough, you cave. You're born with all the advantages, and you just throw them away.

You let your body go, your man slip away, your career go down the toilet. Jesus, you even let your own *mother* rob you blind. And yet you're still so . . . *nice* about it. I mean, you and Jordan? Still friends. You can't stand Sarah, and here you are, pleading with me not to kill her. I bet you still send your mom Mother's Day cards, don't you?"

I gulp. And nod.

Well, what else am I going to say?

"See," Rachel says. "Now that's just sad. Because nice girls, they always finish last. I'll actually be doing the world a favor by killing you. It's natural selection, really. One less blond to watch go to waste."

With that, Rachel comes at me, diving across the bed, stun gun first.

I whirl around and throw back the curtains. I unlatch the first set of French doors I reach and hurl myself out onto the terrace.

Wake up, look around
Everybody's got their feet
On the ground
No way I'll do the same
I'm over you,
No one to blame

Get out, out of my life
I'm not your mother
Won't be your wife
Go on, go out that door
Don't you mess
with me no more
It's all over
Just leave it be
I'm over you
Get away from me

Heather Wells, "Get Out"

It's still raining—harder than ever, actually. The sky is a leaden gray all around me.

I've never realized it before, but Fischer Hall is the tallest building on the west side of the park, and the penthouse terrace affords spectacular views of Manhattan on four sides, of the Empire State Building to the north, just visible through the mist, the fog-shrouded void where the World Trade Center had once stood to the south, the sodden East and West Villages.

An excellent place, I realize, to shoot a scene from a movie. *Teenage Mutant Ninja Turtles*, perhaps.

Except that this is no movie. This is real life. *My* life. For however much longer it lasts.

The wind up on the twentieth floor is strong, and drizzle spits in my face. I have a hard time figuring out just where I'm headed, since everywhere I look, I see only geranium planters precariously perched on low stone balustrades over which I can picture my body very easily tumbling.

Not knowing where else to go, I duck my head and start running around the sides of the Allingtons' apartment, to the opposite side of the terrace. With no sign of Rachel following, I have a minute to pause and open my backpack, still hanging from its strap across my shoulders, and fumble inside it for that canister of pepper spray I could swear was still in it. I have no idea if the thing will still work, but at this point, anything that will keep me from meeting the volts from that stun gun is worth a try.

I find it. I release the safety catch when a deafening crash occurs just behind me, and in a shower of splintering wood and flying glass, Rachel leaps through a set of French doors—like Cujo, or a teenage mutant ninja turtle—not even bothering to unlatch them first. She hits me with the full force of her body, and we both go down onto the wet flagstones.

I land solidly on my sore shoulder, effectively knocking all the breath from my chest. But I try to keep rolling, over shards of wood and glass, to get away from her.

She's on her feet before I am, and coming toward me at full charge. Through it all, she's managed to hang on to the Thunder Gun.

But I still clutch the pepper spray, hidden in my fist. When she bends over me, her dark hair already becoming plastered to her face by the rain, her lips are curled back in a snarl not unlike Lucy's when she's riled by a tennis ball or a Victoria's Secret catalog.

"You're so weak," Rachel sneers at me, and she waves the stun gun under my nose. "How can you tell a brunette?"

I try to maneuver myself into a position from which I can spray her directly in the face. I don't want the wind whipping the stuff back at me.

"I don't know what you're talking about," I wheeze, still breathless from the impact of my fall. God. I can't believe I once bought this woman *flowers*.

And okay, they were only from the deli. But still.

"You know how you can tell a brunette?" Rachel grins, her face just inches from mine. "Turn a blond upside down!"

As she lunges to blast 120,000 volts into my right hip, I lift my hand and launch a stream of pepper spray into her face. Rachel shrieks and backs up, throwing an arm up to protect her face . . .

Only the nozzle won't push all the way down. So instead of a jet of chemical poison hitting her in the eye, the stuff just foams down the side of the canister, soaking into my stitches and burning me badly enough to make me go, "Ow!"

Rachel, realizing she hasn't been hit after all, starts to laugh.

"Oh God," she brays. "Could you *be* more pathetic, Heather?"

But this time, when she lunges at me, I've rolled to my feet, and I'm ready for her.

"Rachel," I say, as she comes at me. "There's something I've been wanting to tell you for a long time. Size twelve"— wrapping my stinging fingers around the hard canister, I slam my fist as hard as I can into Rachel's face—"is not *fat*."

My knuckles explode in pain. Rachel screams and staggers back, both her hands going to her nose, from which an astonishing amount of blood is spurting.

"My nose!" she shrieks. "You broke my nose! You fucking bitch!"

I'm barely able to stand, my shoulder is throbbing so badly, my hands feeling as if they're on fire from the pepper spray. I have shards of glass stuck to my back, the knuckles on my right hand are numb, and blood is coming from a cut somewhere in the vicinity of my forehead: I'm blinking both rainwater and my own blood from my eyes. All I want to do is go inside and lie down for a while and maybe watch the Food Network, or something.

But I can't. Because I have my psycho boss to deal with.

She's standing there, holding her nose with one hand, and the stun gun in the other, when I tackle her, flinging my arms around her narrow waist and bringing her down like a hundred and twenty pounds of Manolo Blahniks. She falls, writhing in my grasp, while I desperately try to snatch the stun gun from her hands.

And all the time, she's sobbing. Not with fear, like she should have been—because, make no mistake about it, I have every intention of killing her—but with anger, her dark eyes glittering with such intense hatred of me that I wonder how I missed seeing it there before.

"Nice girls finish last, huh?" I say, as I kick her as hard as I can in the knee. "How's this, then? Is this *nice* enough for you?"

Except that it's like I'm kicking one of those crash test dummies. Rachel seems impervious to pain . . . unless it's something to do with her face. Her precious nose, for example.

And she's strong—so much stronger than I am, despite my killing rage, and my advantage in height and weight. I can't budge the gun from her hands. I've read about people who, in moments of desperation, develop the strength of someone twice their size—mothers who lift cars off their injured infants, mounted cops who pull their beloved horses out of sinkholes, that kind of thing. Rachel has the strength of a man . . . a man who sees his life disintegrating before him.

And she's not going to give up until someone's dead.

And I'm starting to get a very bad feeling that that someone is going to be me.

It's all I can do to keep my hands fastened over hers on the grip of the stun gun. My fingers are slick with rain and blood, and sore from the stitches and the pepper foam. It's hard to hold on. Rachel has managed to climb to her feet in spite of my attempt to kick her legs out from under her, and now the two of us struggle in the pouring rain for mastery of the weapon. The force of our struggle has sent us staggering dangerously close to the terrace wall.

Somehow, Rachel manages to twist herself so that it's *my* back that's pressed up against a overflowing geranium planter not unlike the one that nearly killed Jordan. My face toward the sky, I can't see with all the rain streaming down. I close my eyes and concentrate on the nearly impossible task of keeping Rachel's arms high above me, not letting those buzzing prongs anywhere near my body. I feel the planter wobble, and then I feel it give, and though I don't open my eyes, I hear the enormous crash it makes seconds later as it hits the sidewalk below.

The most frightening part, however, is the length of time that elapses between the moment the planter careens off the terrace and the sound of the impact as it strikes the earth. I count to nearly ten.

Ten seconds of freefall. Ten seconds to contemplate death.

My arms are weakening. I know I'm crying, because the salt from my tears stings the cuts on my face.

And above me, Rachel laughs, sensing my weakening.

"See," she's saying. "I told you, Heather. You're too nice to win. Too weak. Not in good enough shape. Because size twelve *is* fat. Oh, I know what you're going to say. It's the size of the average American woman. But guess what? The average American woman is fat, Heather."

"Oh my God." I spit rainwater and blood from my mouth. "Rachel, you're sick. There's something really wrong with you! Let me get you some help—"

"What have you got to live for, anyway?" Rachel asks, as if she hasn't heard me. Because she probably hasn't. "Your music career's in the toilet. Your boyfriend dumped you. Your own mother stabbed you in the back. You should have died yesterday, in the elevator. And you should have died the day before, only my aim was off. Just give it up, Heather. Nice girls never win—"

On the word *win*, Rachel begins slowly bending my arms. I can't fight her superior strength much longer. I'm weeping openly now, struggling against her, trying not to listen to her singsong voice as it coos, "Think about it. Your death'll make MTV News. Maybe not the *Times*, but the *Post* for sure. Who knows? They might even do an *E! True Hollywood Story* about you . . . one-hit wonders who didn't live to see thirty . . ."

I open my eyes and glare at her, unable to speak, since every bit of strength I have is concentrated on keeping her from electrocuting me.

And it's when I feel the tremble in my arms, the shaking of muscles weakened from overuse, that I hear Rachel's triumphant laugh, and her final taunt.

"Heather," she calls gleefully, her voice sounding far away, though she's still looming above me. "How many blonds does it take to screw in a light bulb?"

And then her head explodes in front of me.

Seriously. One minute it's there, laughing in my face, and the next it's gone, whipped back by the force of an object that strikes it so hard, blood sprays from the wound and blinds me. The stun gun goes dead in her hands, and her body falls away from me, landing with a sickening thud on the wet flagstones.

I cling to the terrace wall, wiping my face with the backs of my hands—the only uninjured parts of my body—and sobbing. The only sound is the hiss of the rain and someone's ragged breathing.

It takes me a while to realize that the breathing isn't my own. When I'm finally able to see, I look up, and see Rachel laying at my feet, blood pouring out of an indentation on the side of her head and tingeing the rain puddles all around her pink.

And standing before me, a bloodied bottle of Absolut in her hand, is Mrs. Allington, her pink jogging suit drenched, her chest heaving, her eyes filled with contempt as she stares down at Rachel's prone body.

Mrs. Allington shakes her head.

"*I'm* a size twelve," she says.

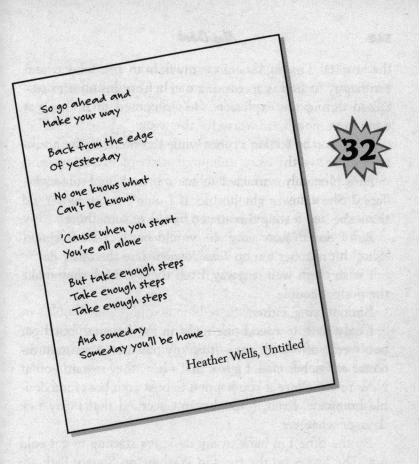

So go ahead and
Make your way

Back from the edge
Of yesterday

No one knows what
Can't be known

'Cause when you start
You're all alone

But take enough steps
Take enough steps
Take enough steps

And someday
Someday you'll be home

Heather Wells, Untitled

I only end up spending one night in the hospital—on account of all my stitches tearing open and the multiple contusions and glass shards embedded in me.

And even that is one night too many, if you ask me. Do you know what their idea of dessert is in the hospital? Yeah, that'd be Jell-O. With fruit in it. Not even mini marshmallows. Everyone knows Jell-O is a *salad*, not dessert.

Plus they don't even have bathtubs in the hospital. If you want to get clean, it's a shower or sponge bath only.

Whatever. I try to use my time there wisely. My time in

the hospital, I mean. I sneak off my floor to visit Julio, whom I'm happy to find is recovering nicely from his injuries sustained during the explosion. He's supposed to be back at work next month, no worse for the wear.

I also stop by Jordan's room while I'm there. In the hospital, I mean.

He's plenty embarrassed to see me, and his bride-to-be, Tania? She's downright hostile. If I didn't know better, I'd think she was feeling threatened by me or something.

But I don't know why she would be. Her latest single, "Slut," hit number ten on *Total Request Live* the other day.

I wish them well, anyway. I tell them I think they make the perfect couple.

I'm not lying, either.

I only have to spend one night in the hospital, but I get two weeks off—with pay—from my position as assistant director at Fischer Hall. I guess that's how they reward you at New York College if you happen to bust your boss for a double homicide. Even if you haven't accrued that many sick days, or whatever.

By the time I'm back to my desk, it's starting to get cold out. The leaves on the trees in Washington Square Park are changing, turning shades of red and gold that pale in comparison with the colors the freshmen in Fischer Hall have dyed their hair in preparation for Parents' Day.

Seriously. It's like working in a clown college, or something.

Things at Fischer Hall have changed in other ways as well since I've been gone. For one thing, with Rachel in jail awaiting trial, I'm getting a new boss. I don't know who yet. They're still interviewing people.

But Dr. Jessup is giving me first pick.

I'm thinking it might be nice to work for a man for a

change. Don't get me wrong, female bosses are great and all. But I could do with a break from all that estrogen in the office.

Sarah agrees. She and all the student workers are a lot nicer to me now that, you know, I risked my life in order to catch the person who was killing their fellow residents. I hardly ever hear about Justine anymore. Except for the other day, when Tina turned to me and said, "You know, Justine used to never wear jeans to work like you do. She told me it was because she could never find any small enough to fit her. I sort of always hated her for that."

Even Gavin is finally listening to me, and has completely given up elevator surfing. He's taken up exploring the city's sewers instead.

I figure he'll be giving that up soon enough, too, though. I mean, the smell isn't exactly making him the most popular guy on his floor.

Oh, and the Allingtons moved. Just to the building next door—the one Donatello or whichever teenage mutant ninja turtle it was jumped onto in the movie. But still, it's far enough away that Mrs. Allington feels that she and the birds will be more comfortable . . . especially since they're now living in a building that they don't have to share with seven hundred undergraduates and a residence hall staff.

Those undergraduates weren't sorry to see the Allingtons go, but the same can't be said about their son. Chris's turned into something of a celebrity himself, using the notoriety he gained from Rachel's obsession with him—which made all the headlines—as leverage for his plan to open his own nightclub in SoHo. Law school, apparently, had been his father's dream for him, and now that offers for his story have come pouring in from the Lifetime Channel and *Playboy*, Chris has broken free from the filial yoke and is pursuing his own devices.

I'm betting those devices will get him arrested fairly soon.

The Fischer Hall residents, student government, and staff came up with what we consider a fitting tribute to Elizabeth Kellogg and Roberta Pace: We planted two trees—twin dogwoods—in a pretty section of the park, with a plaque under them that reads *In Memory Of* and lists their names, the dates of their births and deaths, and the words *They Will Be Missed*. Millions of people will see it—both the plaque and the trees, which the guys from the horticulture department tell me will flower in the spring—just as hundreds of students will benefit from the scholarship, also started by us, in Beth's and Bobby's names.

I'm excited to see the trees in full bloom. It's about the only thing I have to look forward to these days, since I already found out—at last—what Cooper thinks about me.

Not that he knows I know. He probably has no idea I remember. It was when he came bursting out onto the penthouse terrace, just seconds after Mrs. Allington knocked Rachel senseless with her Absolut bottle. He'd gotten the message I'd left on his cell, and had come rushing over to the hall with Detective Canavan, only to learn from Pete—who'd seen Rachel and me going into the penthouse on his monitor—that not only was Rachel alive, but that the two of us had apparently gone upstairs to pay a call on Mrs. Allington (the film quality on the security monitor wasn't fine enough for Pete to see that Rachel was actually holding a stun gun to my throat at the time, something we're working on correcting, campus-wide).

While Detective Canavan dealt with the unconscious Rachel and wobbly Mrs. Allington, Cooper knelt beside me in the rain, asking if I was all right.

I remember blinking up at him, wondering if what I was seeing was just some weird hallucination, like the one of

Rachel getting her head bashed in. I'd been pretty sure, at the time, that I was dying, on account of the sting of the pepper spray in my stitches, and the glass shards piercing my back, and my sore shoulder and stuff.

Which might be why I kept saying—the way I remember it—over and over, "Promise you'll take care of Lucy. When I'm dead, promise you'll take care of Lucy."

Cooper had taken his leather jacket off—the one with my bloodstains all over it—and draped it over me. It was still warm from his body. I remember that. And that it smelled like him.

"Of course I will," Cooper had said to me. "But you're not going to die. Look, I know you're hurting. But the paramedics are their way. You're going to be fine, I promise."

"No, I'm not," I'd said. Because I'd been sure I was going to die. Later, the paramedic told me I was in shock, on account of the pain and the cold and the rain and all.

But I'd had no way of knowing that at the time.

"I'm going to be dead at twenty-eight," I'd informed what I'd taken to be a hallucination of Cooper. "A one-hit wonder. That's all I am. Make sure that's what they put on my head-stone. *Here lies a one-hit wonder.*"

"Heather," Cooper had said. He'd been smiling. I'm sure of that. That he'd been smiling. "You're not going to die. And you're not a one-hit wonder."

"Oh, right." I'd started laughing. Then I'd started to cry. And I hadn't been able to stop.

It turns out this is a pretty common symptom of shock, too. But again, I hadn't known that at the time.

"Rachel was right," I remember saying, bitterly. "She's right! I had it all, and I blew it. I'm the biggest loser in the world."

That's when Cooper forced me to sit up, took me into his

arms, and said, very firmly, "Heather, you're not a loser. You're one of the bravest people I've ever met. Anyone else, if they'd been through what you have, what with your mother and my brother and your career and all of that, they'd have given up. But you kept going. You started over. I've always admired the way, no matter what happens, you just keep going."

I'm sorry to say that at this point, I responded, "You mean like that little pink rabbit with the drum?"

I like to think that was the shock, too.

Cooper played along. He'd said, "Exactly like that little pink rabbit with the drum. Heather, you're not a loser. And you're not going to die. You're a nice girl, and you're going to be just fine."

"But . . ." To my shock-clouded brain, this assertion sounded troubling, given my earlier conversation with the woman who'd been trying to kill me. "Nice girls finish last."

"I happen to like nice girls," Cooper had said.

And then he kissed me.

Just once. And on the forehead. The way, you know, your ex-boyfriend's big brother would kiss you if, say, you'd been attacked by a homicidal maniac and were suffering from shock and he didn't think you'd remember it anyway.

But I did. And I do.

He thinks I'm brave. No, wait: He thinks I'm one of the bravest people he's ever met.

And he likes me. Because he happens to like nice girls.

Look, I know it's not much. But you know what?

It's enough. For now.

Oh, and one last thing:

I never did go back to that store and buy those size 8 jeans. There's nothing wrong with being a size 12, for one thing.

And for another, I've been too busy. I passed my six months' probation. I start my freshman year at New York College in January. My first class?

Intro to criminal justice.

Well, you have to start somewhere, right?